MUSIC BOX

'They took those people — women, children
. . . They lined them up at the riverbank —'
    'That's why I come America, Anni.'
    'It makes me ashamed to be . . . Hungarian,
Papa,' she said, voicing what she'd been feeling since she'd opened the notebooks earlier
in the day and discovered that you didn't have
to search far to find Dante's Inferno.
    'You no Hungarian, Anni,' he said, putting
his arm around her. 'You American, Anni. *We*
American. We get away . . . all of that.'
    So he'd told her all these years. But he'd
also told her that nationality wasn't something you could shed, like an unwanted piece
of clothing. Hadn't he brought her up to
believe that in her soul, she was a Hungarian
as well as an American, whose rights were
protected by the Constitution?
    Now, though she hated herself for it, she
couldn't help but wonder whether the sweet,
safe promise of democracy had lulled him
into believing that the past was merely a bad
dream. What dark memories and horrors had
her father put behind him when he'd fled to
America? And did she really want such a
question answered?

Music Box

Deborah Chiel

**Based on the screenplay by
Joe Esterhas**

CORONET BOOKS
Hodder and Stoughton

British Library C.I.P.

Chiel, Deborah
  Music box.
  I. Title
  813.54 [F]

ISBN 0 340 53019 7

Printed and bound in Great Britain for Hodder and Stoughton Paperbacks, a division of Hodder and Stoughton Ltd., Mill Road, Dunton Green, Sevenoaks, Kent TN13 2YA. (Editorial Office: 47 Bedford Square, London WC1B 3DP) by Cox & Wyman Ltd., Reading, Berks.

For George Coleman

PROLOGUE

The little girl's cheeks were bright with fever, and her pale blond hair, normally carefully combed and braided, was plastered across her sweat-soaked forehead. She tossed and turned on her bed, taking short, raspy breaths and occasionally whimpering in her sleep.

Outside, a howling wind beat against the snow-covered window, rattling the glass with the full force of the storm coming in off Lake Michigan. But the bedroom was warm and snug, dark except for the dim light from the lamp on her dresser.

The little girl's father had pulled the rocker closer to her bed. From time to time, he reached over and gently stroked her arm. His hand, callused and chapped from years of manual labor, contrasted sharply with the child's baby-soft skin. Even more incongruous was the pink, spindly legged stuffed lamb, christened "Lambie-pie" by the little girl, that lay cuddled in the man's lap. It was her favorite toy, and normally she couldn't sleep without it curled next to her, under her arm. But tonight, as she'd squirmed in her sleep, the lamb had ended up on the floor, and the man had bent down to retrieve it.

He peered through the darkness to check his watch, which read three-twenty. The doctor had told him to give her a teaspoon of the medicine every four hours, and she was about due for another dose. But he was reluctant to wake her; she'd slept so poorly during the early part of the evening. Still, if anything were to happen to her . . . He'd rather cut off his hand than lose this beautiful, beloved child.

As if to make the decision for him, the girl's eyelids fluttered open. "Mama, Mama," she moaned hoarsely.

"Hush, Anni, it's okay," the man whispered. "Papa here, Anni." He reached over and pulled the covers up around her shoulders.

She shook her head weakly. "I want my mama." She began to cry, so piteously that her father could hardly hold back his own tears. He thought, *Poor little baby, of course you want your mama. You miss her, baby, don't you? So do I.*

"Come, Anni," he whispered. "I give you some medicine, you feel better. Ya, good girl."

He was due at the mill in two hours, and he hadn't slept a wink all night, but he'd already decided he would stay home that day. He couldn't leave his Anni, not when she was so sick.

She had dropped off for a few moments, but now she stirred again. "Papa," she said. "I'm thirsty."

He touched her forehead with his palm and was relieved to find that she felt cooler now. Perhaps the fever was breaking.

The little girl took a few sips of water and lay down again. "My throat hurts me so much, Papa. Will it go away by tomorrow so I can build a snowman with Karchy?"

"Shh, we see in morning. Look, here the Lambie. Now go to sleep, Anni. I hold your hand 'til you wake up."

The little girl sighed and snuggled up closer to him.

2

"Tell me a story, Papa. You know the one . . . about the little girl in Budapest."

"Okay, but first you close eyes," he said softly. And then he began, "Long time ago in Budapest is castle by beautiful Danube River where live mama, papa, and little girl. Name little girl was . . ." He waited for her to finish the sentence, but she was already fast asleep.

CHAPTER
1

The lively swell of violins and enticing aromas of the St. Elizabeth's Hungarian Festival spilled through the open windows of the church, beckoning to latecomers. The festival, held annually in the basement recreation hall, was one of the fall highlights for Chicago's sizable Hungarian community. It drew not only the neighborhood loyalists who still showed up for Mass on Sundays but also the younger generation and former parishioners who'd deserted the working-class West Side for the more upscale Chicago suburbs.

The event was their big chance to come home and catch up with relatives and old friends, to gossip about who was getting married, who was having babies, who was cheating on their husbands or wives. And it was a chance for everyone—young and old—to indulge themselves in the deliciously fattening Hungarian delicacies specially prepared for the occasion by the cream of the neighborhood cooks and bakers. This was one night to forget about diets. The competition among the ladies was good natured but intense. You didn't dare buy from one vendor and ignore the next.

The food booths that lined the walls were festooned with green and white streamers, Hungary's national colors. But they could have been covered in olive-gray and still pulled in the customers, because the foods were irresistible: spicy *kolbasz* salami; the muffinlike *pogacsa*, stuffed with meat and cheese; crackling strips of *szalona*; feathery light *palacsinta*, filled with chocolate, apricot, or prune *lekvar* and dusted with confectioners' sugar.

To add color and give the room atmosphere, the decoration committee had put up huge, grainy black-and-white posters of famous Budapest landmarks—Castle Hill, the Parliament building, the ruins of Aquincum, the Citadella. And in the centermost place of honor was a picture of Budapest's nineteenth-century monument to Hungarian prosperity, the Chain Bridge, its huge sweeping steel girders curving majestically above the Danube and the fierce stone-carved lions guarding the bases on either side of the river.

The first wave of customers had loaded up their plates and found seats at the tables along the walls. Between mouthfuls, they tapped their feet to the exuberant sounds of the Magyars, a semiprofessional band that was widely considered to be the best of its kind in the entire Chicago area.

The Magyars was a family act—two brothers, a cousin, and a nephew, all of them decked out in brightly brocaded costumes that were supposed to conjure up images of gypsies and Old Country carnivals. Fortunately, the Magyars' music was more authentic than their outfits, because this crowd loved to dance. So when the Magyars struck up the opening bars of a *csardas*, the audience applauded and stamped its feet to show approval.

"Come on, Papa, they're playing our song," Ann Talbot sang out, grabbing her father's arm and extricating him from his circle of cronies.

"Ai, find someone younger," Mike Laszlo scoffed. But

he smiled with pleasure and allowed his daughter to lead him onto the floor.

They made a handsome couple: Mike, pushing seventy, but still fit and brawny from all the hard years he'd put in at the Gary steel mills; Ann, looking younger than her thirty-three years and dressed for the occasion in the delicately embroidered red-and-white outfit that her mother had brought with her from Hungary. Even a casual observer could see the family resemblance. Both were fair complexioned, and Ann had inherited Mike's wide brow, his light brown eyes, handsome features, and the determined set of his mouth.

She'd also inherited his love of dancing, though she was as graceful as he was awkward. Now, as they performed the intricate folk steps they'd danced together at so many other festivals and celebrations, their mutual enjoyment was obvious. As far as Mike was concerned, his daughter was the prettiest, most wonderful girl in the room, and he didn't mind letting the world know that he adored her. As the music slowed, he grabbed his daughter in a tight bear hug and grinned.

"I twenty years old, I marry you right now!" he declared with a twinkle in his eye.

Ann threw her arms around his neck and laughed. "I'd be too old for you."

She tried not to wince as Mike missed a step and landed on her toes. But her father caught her grimace. "I step on your feet," he said contritely.

"You did not!" she lied with a broad, unconvincing smile.

Ann Talbot would have stopped at nothing short of perjury to keep from hurting her father, who had singlehandedly raised her and her older brother, Karchy, after the death of their mother. With the help of a neighborhood lady whom he'd paid to do the light cleaning and laundry and to cook them dinner five nights a week, he'd nursed his two children through illnesses, held them when bad

6

dreams woke them up at night, got them up for church on Sundays, and made sure they did their homework and didn't run with the wrong crowd.

He'd given them enough love for two parents. He'd worried about them when they got to high school and started going out on dates and staying out late. He'd waited up for them plenty of nights, wondering, were they okay? Were they someplace they shouldn't be? Would they come home safe and in one piece? And he'd watched both of them get their high-school diplomas.

Karchy, who was older than Ann by six years, was more of an athlete than a student. Conceived and born in the poverty and squalor of a postwar Austrian refugee camp, Karchy was a scrawny, scrappy kid who looked like the runt of the litter for many months after the Laszlos arrived in Chicago in 1952. He'd filled out enough so that by high school he was playing varsity football. But he was still a scrapper, and though he spoke without the trace of an accent, he'd never quite lost his old country air.

Karchy had his father's bearish physique and cheerful, uncomplicated personality. Mike had pushed his son to get interested in something besides sports, but Karchy would just shrug his shoulders and point at his sister. "Leave it to Ann to make the grades. She's the brains in the family. I got the beauty."

In fact, though Karchy was good-looking enough that he had his pick of the girls in high school, Ann was the *real* beauty—so pretty that sometimes, when Mike would see her from a distance, running halfway down the block to meet him after work, or up on stage performing in a school play or singing in the choir, he could hardly hold back the tears of pride. To think that this delicate-faced child with the golden smile and the bright eyes that shone with intelligence was really his little Anni!

She was Mike's little fairy princess, whose wavy blond hair, happy smile, and engaging personality had made her the darling of the neighborhood. How he and Ilona had

7

given birth to this All-American girl, Mike had never figured out. And so smart, too. She'd earned straight As from first grade on, and by the time she was in junior high, her teachers were telling Mike that he'd better be saving his pennies to send his daughter to college.

College? A Laszlo? Mike had laughed aloud. But he knew the teachers were right about Ann. Because as sweet and good-natured as she was, he also saw in her the same stubbornness and steely determination that had helped him survive in the refugee camp and bring his family over to America. Once she put her mind to something, there was no stopping her. And now, here she was, a lawyer.

As the music picked up speed, Ann stamped her feet and twirled her skirt, then clapped her hands once, twice, three times. She'd been dancing the *csardas* since she was a small girl, and the steps came naturally. Dancing with Papa and Karchy was one of the reasons she kept her calendar free every year for the St. Elizabeth's festival—not to mention the excuse to indulge in the rich, spicy food she didn't otherwise permit herself.

Now she smiled as she watched her big brother come charging across the room to claim his turn. It was a Laszlo family joke that from the moment Ann had learned to walk, she'd tagged along behind him, so relentlessly that his friends had nicknamed her "the shadow." She'd almost burst with pride when he made the high-school football team, and she'd cheered him on at every home game he'd ever played. Though she'd shouted and argued with him (and her father) for days about the war in Vietnam, when Karchy had enlisted and been sent to Saigon, she'd written him three times a week, without fail.

She'd stuck by him after he came home, too, especially during those first months before he went back to work at the mill. All he'd wanted to do was watch TV, a joint in one hand, a beer can in the other. That, or take drives to the lake, where he'd stare moodily at the waves, chain-smoking one cigarette after another.

8

She'd never admitted to anyone, least of all Papa, how frightened she'd been then for Karchy. Her formerly cheerful, easygoing brother had seemed possessed by powerful and mysterious demons. And though she'd stopped believing in God, she'd spent more than a few Sundays in church, praying that Karchy would forget about whatever it was he'd seen in Vietnam and get back to his normal self. For as different as their lives might be, Karchy—and Papa, too, of course—was her family, her shield against all that was bad in the world. She depended on and adored them both.

The feeling was mutual. When people asked Karchy why he hadn't yet settled down with one woman, his stock reply was "Because I still haven't found a girl who's as pretty and smart as my baby sister."

Whether it had been her prayers or, more likely, the healing power of time, Karchy had eventually emerged from his depression and straightened himself out. He'd stopped smoking dope, though he still sometimes drank too much beer, as evidenced by the belly that hung over the top of his pants. Judging from his deeply flushed cheeks, tonight was one of those times.

"Hey, I wanna dance with Annie," he yelled above the din, punching Mike's arm.

His father grinned with contentment. Hungarian food, music, and the company of his family. What could be better? "Broke her foot," he told Karchy.

"You broke your foot?" Karchy faked a look of concern. He got down on his knees and grabbed Ann's leg, pretending to examine it.

"Karchy!" scolded Ann, her face red with embarrassment.

Karchy roared with laughter. He loved teasing his little sister. Even though she was a dynamite criminal lawyer with one of the best trial records in Cook County, he could still get the better of her. "What? I ain't seen your foot before?'' he hooted. "I seen everything else, too. I'm your brother, remember?''

"How could I forget?'' Ann hissed, pulling him to his feet. She threw a glance at her father that said, *Tell him to behave himself.*

Mike shook his head fondly, enjoying Karchy's antics. Saluting his kids, he announced, "I'm gonna go eat some *szalona.*''

Predictably, Ann called after him, "It's not healthy for you, Papa!''

Just as predictably, Mike ignored her and headed for the *szalona* stand, where Johnny Szalay was flipping strips of bacon as if he'd been born with a spatula in one hand. Johnny was an old friend with whom Mike had shared many pitchers of beer and lots of good memories, so naturally he owed Johnny his patronage. But respect was a different matter altogether. "Aw, you don't know how to make the *szalona.* You don't put enough the grease,'' Mike razzed him.

Now, if there was one thing Johnny never skimped on, it was grease. The more lard the better, was his motto. "Come on, Mike, try one.''

Mike reached for his wallet, then changed his mind as he spotted his eleven-year-old grandson standing alone at the edge of the floor. Mikey was dressed in his usual T-shirt and baggy pants. But over the shirt he was wearing an embroidered Hungarian vest, and his long thin arms dangled at his sides as if he didn't know what to do with them.

"Okay, Mikey, we gonna go dance!'' Mike shouted at his namesake, but Mikey backed away, his brown eyes widening with panic. "I can't dance, Grandpa!'' he protested loudly.

"Come on, come on, we dance!'' Mike insisted. He grabbed Mikey's arm and dragged him into the middle of the dance floor. Then he pointed to Ann and Karchy,

10

whirling in time to the frenzied rhythms of the *csardas*, and he stamped his feet to the beat of the music.

Mikey giggled and glanced around, checking to see whether anyone were watching them. Grandpa Mike was so different from his other grandpa. Sometimes Mikey wondered what the two men thought of each other or what they talked about when they were together. Of course now, after the divorce, they almost never saw each other anymore. Mikey often wondered whether they were glad or sad about that.

"Come on, like I show you," Mike urged, demonstrating as he spoke. "Move the feet, move the hip, move the ass—"

"Grandpa!" Mikey interrupted him, his face beet-red with embarrassment. He stared down at the floor, wishing he could be instantly transported out of the auditorium and into his bedroom, so he could play his new Nintendo game without anyone bothering him. He'd told his mom a zillion times that he didn't want to go to the Hungarian festivals anymore, because he was an American—like his dad and Grandpa Harry.

Yes, she would say patiently. Of course you're an American. But so am I, and Uncle Karchy, and Grandpa Mike, too, even though he talks with an accent. I want you to be proud of your American side *and* your Hungarian heritage, too. Understand?

Yes, he'd say, nodding his head. Mostly he was agreeing with her because he didn't want her to be mad at him. Being Hungarian was okay, especially the food part, and Grandpa Mike was the greatest. But he hated when they started talking Hungarian. "Munchkin talk," the kids at his school called it. Uncle Karchy had taught him some Hungarian swear words, and that was pretty cool, but mostly he couldn't understand a thing they were saying. And he sure couldn't do these dances, no matter how many times Grandpa showed him the steps. Didn't Grandpa *care* how dumb he looked?

11

Mikey guessed not, because Grandpa was laughing his head off and saying, "You gotta move!"

The way he was shaking his hips reminded Mikey of an Egyptian belly dancer he'd seen once on television. He wondered if that's who Grandpa was trying to imitate. Mikey smiled. The more he thought of Grandpa as a fat belly dancer dressed in veils, the better he liked the joke. A tiny giggle burbled up to the surface. Mikey tried to hold it back, but then he felt another giggle escaping, which grew into a full-blown chuckle, so that pretty soon he was belly-laughing so hard that tears were coming down his cheeks.

"Yah, that's it!" Mike shouted, stomping his feet and clapping his hands as the musicians crescendoed to a frenzied finish.

Mikey joined in the applause. He had to admit it: Grandpa Mike was one cool guy.

Ann occasionally suffered pangs of guilt about the fact that she wasn't giving her son any religious training. But since she herself didn't walk into church more than once or twice a year, she'd be a hypocrite to insist that Mikey attend Sunday school. Years earlier, during her pregnancy, she and her ex-husband had had long, serious discussions about how they wanted to bring up their unborn child. She was a lapsed Catholic, David an equally unenthusiastic Methodist. Both of them thought that ethics and values counted for much more than religiosity.

Newlywed and madly in love, they'd felt sure they could rise above their differences. They'd shared so many interests, not the least of which was that they were both lawyers. For David, the law was a family affair: His father was the founding partner of one of Chicago's most prestigious firms. He, however, wanted no part of corporate law. Like Ann, he was headed for the public-defender's office, where he could get solid trial experience and put his idealism to good use.

From the moment they'd met in their first year of law school, they'd spent hours together, drinking coffee and arguing legal theory. They'd been friends and study partners first, lovers later. When they decided to get married, neither David's father nor Mike was particularly happy about the match, which made them both all the more determined to prove their parents wrong.

Ann was sure that as far as Harry Talbot was concerned, her Chicago birth certificate in no way abrogated her ethnicity. But for all his stuffed-shirt WASPish ways, he had a strong streak of mischief, and she suspected that he rather enjoyed telling people he had a Hungarian daughter-in-law. He was genuinely fond of her, and she of him.

Eventually the fathers had achieved an uneasy truce for those few, infrequent occasions when the families were forced to converge. The true coming together had occurred, of course, after Mikey was born. He was the only grandchild on either side, and to their credit, neither Mike nor Harry had wanted to miss any of his growing up. Oddly enough, Harry sometimes reminded her of her own father.

Though for different reasons, they were both fiercely patriotic, devout believers in the American dream. And much more important as far as Ann was concerned, each in his own way was a terrific, devoted grandfather. So the cultural boundaries were crossed: Thanksgiving was celebrated American-style at Harry's; Christmas Eve dinner was held at Mike's.

They'd eaten their last holiday meal together three years ago, when Ann and David's marriage had unraveled to the point that they could no longer fool themselves into believing there was anything left to save. Today, divorced two years and supposedly moving ahead with their separate lives, they were still friends. Sort of. Occasionally one would slip and let loose a sharp, hurtful jab, a piercing, poignant reminder of those lacerating verbal blows they'd so often inflicted upon each other in the waning months of their marriage.

Ann supposed that meant they still had some good feelings left for each other. Too bad they couldn't do a better job of letting those feelings come through. On the other hand, maybe they took potshots because they'd never let themselves confront the depth of their disappointment over their joint failure.

They'd started out as everyone's definition of a great couple: attractive, bright, fun, obviously destined to be successful. So where had they gone wrong? That was the question that still haunted her in the middle of the night when she couldn't sleep. Not that it really made any difference at this point, except that Ann hated to leave loose ends untied. And *In re Talbot vs. Talbot* was definitely still in her file of unresolved matters. It was as if they'd argued themselves into a corner from which there was no escape, though what the argument was about she would have been hard pressed to say.

None of the easy explanations fit—not sex, money, or another lover. No, the Talbots had been done in by something far more complicated and intangible, something that had to do with diverging values and sensibilities. What was important to her had become increasingly unimportant to him. What he admired she had begun to reject. But rather than respecting their differences, as they'd been able to do in the past, they'd come to actively dislike each other for them. So that ultimately their terrible, wrenching fights had nothing to do with what side of town they'd come from, or which religion they'd been brought up in, or whether they were WASP or Hungarian.

And yes, she wanted Mikey to be proud of his Hungarian heritage, but she wasn't about to send him off to Mass every Sunday while she read the paper and drank coffee.

It was Karchy who'd come up with a compromise that pleased everyone. If Mikey wanted to go to church with Pop, that was the kid's business. But how about they all

14

make sure to come by Mike's house afterwards for breakfast?

Thus a Laszlo family tradition had been created—or, more correctly, revived. As kids they'd always congregated in the kitchen on Sundays to read the funny papers while Papa fried them bacon and eggs. Little had changed since then: same red-brick house, same sunny kitchen with the painted wooden cupboards, formica-topped table, and the wallpaper Karchy and Ann had picked out together after Karchy's return from Vietnam. Except that now Ann worried about the amount of cholesterol Mike was eating and what it was doing to his heart.

This Sunday was no exception. "You can't eat this stuff, Papa," she scolded as she watched him and Karchy grill thick slabs of bacon on the stove.

Her warnings fell on deaf ears. Mike winked at his grandson, as if to say, *There she goes again.* Mikey, who enjoyed ganging up with "the boys" against his mother, winked back.

"I don't want healthy, I want greasy!" Mike chortled, waving a strip of bacon at her. A glob of fat dripped down the side and landed with an angry sizzle on the open flame of the element. Ann wrinkled her nose in disgust, though actually the bacon smelled delicious.

"It's Hungarian food, Annie," teased Karchy. "What's the matter? Don't you like Hungarian food no more?"

They read from the same script, word for word, week after week. Next he or Papa would make some crack about how she was always dieting and trying to stay skinny instead of turning into one of the fat Hungarian women from down the block.

Karchy reached for a piece of thick-sliced rye to sop up the bacon drippings. "She don't eat nothin' but that frozen stuff now, Pop. Lean cooseene," he said, deliberately mispronouncing the word. "That stuff don't even help you fart, Pop. That's what happens out in the suburbs, Pop. They don't even fart out there."

15

Ann threw Karchy a dirty look. He'd teased her mercilessly all through childhood, and he saw no reason to stop now just because they were adults. His gibes were how he showed his love.

"What?" He grinned. "I'm just tellin' the truth, that's all. You used to fart like hell when we was kids."

Mikey burst out laughing, beside himself with the pleasure of hearing a grownup use the word *fart* three times in the space of two minutes. Ann's shoulders were shaking with suppressed giggles, and then she, too, broke down and joined in the laughter. "Karchy," she said, trying for sternness, "if you don't stop right now—"

"What? What'd I say?" he demanded, all hurt innocence.

How would she ever teach her son any manners with his uncle and grandfather putting on a show for him?

Mike was still chuckling as he deftly flipped the bacon strips onto bread slices.

"Can I have one, Grandpa?" Mikey asked eagerly, glancing at his mother out of the corner of his eye. Not that she'd ever said no, he couldn't have a bacon sandwich. But Mikey was never sure when his mom was going to be really strict and when she was just sort of kidding around.

"Hell, ya, you gonna have some," Mike said, shoving a plate in his direction. "Healthy body make healthy spirit, right, Mikey?"

"Right, Grandpa!" Mikey flashed him a grin and took a huge bite of the grease-soaked bread.

"It's disgusting," Ann commented with a forgiving smile.

"It's great!" Mikey enthused. "Can I have another one?"

Mike nodded, then announced, "I gonna go get us some wine." He was back a moment later with a bottle of cold red wine and a bottle of seltzer to make a "froccs": two parts wine to one part soda water.

"Can I have some wine?" Mikey pleaded.

"No," Ann told him, knowing full well it didn't much matter what she said.

Sure enough, Mike said, "Hell, ya. You gonna get wine."

"Papa . . ." Ann began.

"Healthy body makes a healthy spirit!" chorused her son and her father in unison.

Hell, why did she even bother? She shrugged her shoulders to signal her surrender and joined in their laughter. She supposed the best she could do was watch that Papa made Mikey's drink good and weak. Beyond that, all she could do was sit back and enjoy the pleasure her men took in one another's company. And consider how fortunate she was to be blessed with such a wonderful family.

CHAPTER

2

On any given day the corridors of the Municipal Court-house in Daley Center were crowded with the usual mix of pimps and worn-out hookers; well-dressed drug dealers who could have passed for stock traders visiting from the Merc; bail bondsmen and sour-faced cops; assistant D.A.s and defense attorneys. Ann had been walking these hall-ways almost from the moment she'd graduated from law school, and she was well acquainted with the principals.

Not for her the quiet, ordered calm of the law firms that catered to corporations or to decorous wealthy clients whose estates needed tending. The hubbub of criminal law was what called to her: the thrust and parry of the cross-examination, the task of winning the jury's confidence, the minute examination of the law to find the chink in her opponent's armor. She'd put in her time at the public-defender's office—a rigorous apprenticeship that had erased whatever vestiges of shyness she might have harbored. There she'd made a name for herself as a compassionate, adroit attorney who could think on her feet and get the jury to see things her way.

Of course, everyone knew that the P.D.'s office was just

a way station. It was a training ground where lawyers could show off their stuff until they got tapped by one of the law firms that represented the hard-to-defend clients—the ones who needed extra-special expertise. So Ann wasn't surprised when Mack Jones, with whom she'd often sparred across the courtroom aisle, invited her to dinner, ordered an expensive bottle of wine, and proceeded, between the salad and dessert, to explore the possibility of her coming to work for him.

Ann had always admired the way Mack fought his court battles. Over dinner, she'd discovered that she also liked his candor. "Look here," he'd said bluntly, "I've been watching you in court for quite some time now. You've got fire and ambition, a quick mind, and a sharp tongue. And you can see the other side, even when you don't want to admit it. I can tell from the look in your eyes. I think you're a damn fine lawyer, which is ninety-five percent of the reason I want to hire you."

He'd paused to take a sip of wine, then continued: "But it sure as hell doesn't hurt that your maiden name is Laszlo. Or that you speak a bit of Hungarian. I'm a black man, and I already have a Jewish partner. The idea of rounding out the balance with a woman of your considerable talents who can also help bring in the ethnic vote appeals to me quite a bit. Does that offend you?"

She'd carefully considered his question, then shook her head, no. Mack Jones was too dedicated an attorney to hire someone he didn't respect professionally. Her gut instinct had told her they'd make a good mix.

Five years later, she was a partner, and the firm of Jones, Lehman & Talbot had more business than it could handle. She liked some of her clients better than others. The drug dealers bugged her the most: smart-ass bastards who dressed like yuppie investment bankers and carried thousands of dollars of cash in their Mark Cross leather briefcases. When she thought too much about them selling drugs that ended up in the hands of kids like Mikey, she

19

could almost hate herself for arguing their side of the story. What kept her going was the belief she shared with her partners that everyone was entitled to fair representation.

Even a son-of-a-bitch like Doug Griffin, who'd been collared by a couple of narcs for dealing coke. If Ann was sure of anything, it was that Doug was small potatoes. But he acted like he was big time, and he'd been flashing bedroom eyes at her from the moment Sandy Lehman had made the introductions a few moments earlier on the way to his bail hearing.

Griffin had gotten cocky and stepped in deep shit, which was why the whole team—all three partners, plus their private investigator, Georgine Wheeler—had convened at the courthouse this morning. But Griffin hadn't yet figured out that the next few years of his life depended on some pretty fancy legal maneuvering. From his unschooled point of view, his case was open and shut. He'd already said as much to Sandy. Now he was repeating his rap for Mack and Ann's benefit.

"He began the *Miranda*, but then the other agent, the one with the ponytail, he said, 'Cuff him,' and the first one never finished the *Miranda*."

"Bingo!" Sandy interjected. A good-looking man in his midforties, he was dressed as usual this morning in one of the custom-tailored three-piece suits that he wore whenever he had to appear in court. Ann had never met a man as obsessed with his appearance as Sandy. He loved to eat, but he rarely walked away from the table without announcing that he was planning to lose fifteen pounds, starting tomorrow. Once he'd even confided in her that he spent a not inconsiderable sum of money each month on a lotion that was supposed to prevent him from losing more of his dark, curly hair.

He'd provided Ann with a hefty shoulder to cry on when she was going through the worst of her divorce blues, but he'd had the grace to understand that even though she'd ended up in his bed after one very late night at the office,

20

what she wanted from him was friendship, not sex. He also happened to be a crackerjack lawyer with an admirable understanding of the criminal law codes.

Today, however, Ann thought he was being overly optimistic. Since when had they begun to believe that the Chicago cops always told the truth in court about whether or not they'd followed proper procedure? An alleged drug dealer claimed he hadn't been read his rights. Who was the jury going to believe? The men in blue or a guy who was accused of selling coke, crack, and Lord knew what else?

"They won't cop to it," she said, playing devil's advocate, a tactic that often worked to their advantage. Mack or Sandy would rise to her challenge with a stronger argument on their client's behalf.

Mack was feeling more sanguine about what they had going. "You twist their nuts, they yell ouch. The jury'll hear it," he said succinctly.

Of course, a lot depended on witnesses, alibis, and corroboration, which was where Georgine came in. Universally known as George, she was a warm and outgoing black woman who preferred African prints and turbans to suits and was not averse to throwing her weight around if she felt that circumstances demanded it.

George had known Mack, who was ten years her senior, from when she was a kid growing up in the projects, and he was one of the older boys who kept the bad guys in line. She'd come knocking on his door, asking for a job, as soon as she graduated from high school, and she'd been working for him ever since. Mack had asked her one time how she'd gotten to be so good at what she did. "I'm just plain naturally nosy, is all," she'd replied.

But George was much more than a private investigator. She doled out moral support or tongue-lashings, as she saw fit; kept them laughing through the tough times; brought them homemade chicken soup redolent with cloves of fresh garlic when they were sick. The firm couldn't have managed without her.

She'd already done some of her homework on Doug Griffin. "Two witnesses," she reported. "One's a hype, the other's solid gold."

Ann immediately felt more hopeful. "We dirty the hype, rub some off on the gold," she said. This was the fun part: adding up what you had to work with, figuring out the strategy. Sandy often told her she'd make a great poker player, the way she liked to line up her cards and never showing her hand until it was absolutely necessary. And always with a perfectly straight face.

Griffin caught a whiff of her excitement. "Just exactly how are you going to do that?" he wanted to know.

"She'll do it," Sandy said confidently.

Ann ignored Griffin's question. Better for their working relationship if he figured out from the get-go that just because she would be arguing his case in court didn't entitle him to engage her in conversation. She'd tell him what he needed to know. Period. Early in her career she'd learned the fine art of representing defendants who made her want to puke. Turning her back to him, she asked George, "What about that Band E we've got tomorrow morning?"

George shook her head. "They don't want to deal."

"They'll deal," Ann said with a smile. She checked her watch. If the bail hearing began on time, she could be back in the office by ten-fifteen, read the Band E file, and do up her notes for the next day's meeting. After that she'd get started on the housing-discrimination case that had come in late yesterday.

Her new client, Robin Mueller, owned a pet-supply shop on Sheridan Road that catered in large part to the rich young couples who lived in the neighborhood. Too busy or not yet ready to have children, they lavished their love on their pedigreed dogs and cats, and they spent lots of money at the Animal Emporium.

Now Robin and the woman she lived with wanted to

buy a two-bedroom co-op a couple of blocks away from her store. She'd negotiated with the sellers and arrived at a price, which she was willing to pay in cash. The hitch was that the co-op board had rejected her application. They weren't required to give her any explanation, but Robin was sure they'd figured out she was a lesbian.

Probably they felt safe because most rejected candidates were reluctant to make waves. But Robin, a soft-spoken, pretty woman in her midthirties, was angry enough that she was ready to fight. "I *know* some of those board members," she'd told Ann with tears in her eyes. "They don't mind having a dyke take care of their precious dogs and cats, but I guess I'm not good enough to live next door to them."

Bastards! Ann had thought, listening to Robin. She couldn't wait to get started. This was precisely the kind of case she and George could sink their teeth into and come away feeling they'd accomplished something worthwhile.

Engrossed in her mental planning, she missed noticing that Griffin was checking her out with obvious growing interest. He liked this lady lawyer—pretty, good body. Tough as nails on the outside, but he bet that in bed she was smooth as velvet. His kind of chick. He wondered whether there were a husband or a boyfriend in the picture; somehow he thought not. Maybe if made his moves right, the two of them could get something going.

His voice oozing honey, he said, "You must be a very foxy woman," and he casually put his arm around her.

Ann jerked away, as if he'd come at her with a hot iron. "Remember who you are, scumbag!" she snapped.

Looking for male sympathy, Griffin rolled his eyes at Mack and Sandy. But neither of them was about to be enlisted as an ally. Sandy pretended to be engrossed in his notes. Mack conspicuously turned his head to greet one of his colleagues. Griffin got the point and kept his mouth shut as they covered the rest of the distance to the courtroom. Ann Talbot didn't know what she was missing. He had plenty of women nipping at his heels. Who needed this snotty broad anyway? Just as long as she did her job the way she was supposed to, so that he stayed out of jail.

Ann, meanwhile, had far more important matters on her mind than Doug Griffin. He was nothing more to her than a pesky fly to be swatted away with the back of her hand if he had the temerity to cross her path. Of much greater concern to her at this moment was conferring with George about how to handle the discrimination case. Clearly there was some digging to be done here—and nobody did this kind of work better than George.

Their discussion was interrupted, however, by her father's friend, John Szalay, who worked as a Municipal Court security guard when he wasn't frying bacon. "Annie!" he called, frantically waving his hand to get her attention.

She waved back and kept walking. But instead of letting her go, John grabbed her arm and said, "Your secretary's been trying to reach you. Call your dad."

Normally not prone to panic, Ann heard the urgency in his voice and wondered whether he knew more than he was telling her. She hated to abandon her colleagues. But it was extremely unlike Papa to track her down at work. Something must be terribly wrong.

Mack had overheard John's message. Now he gave her a gentle push and said, "Go! We've got you covered here."

"Great. See you later," she called over her shoulder and rushed off to find a phone. Her high heels clicked a staccato pattern of worry and tension on the terrazzo floor. Fragmented images of possible catastrophe flashed through her head. Mikey? No, couldn't be that; the school would have called. Maybe Papa was sick . . . a stroke . . . a heart attack . . . How many times had she begged him to take better care of himself? Or maybe there'd been an accident at the mill and Karchy was hurt.

As she fumbled in her purse for her wallet and groped with trembling fingers for a quarter, she was gripped by a

24

strong premonition of disaster. For a crazy moment she blanked out and couldn't remember her father's phone number—the very same one he'd had ever since she was a little girl. *Have to calm down*, she told herself. She was being ridiculous. She forced herself to take a deep breath, her mind cleared, and she quickly punched the numbers. *Please, God*, she prayed silently. *Please let it be all right.*

The phone rang once, twice. Nervously drumming her nails against the glass of the phone booth, she whispered into the receiver, *Please, Papa, answer the damn phone.* A moment later—it felt like hours—Mike finally picked up. The sound of his voice at the other end did nothing to reassure her. And all he would say was, ''Come quickly, Anni.''

CHAPTER

The three things of which Michael Laszlo was proudest were his children, his American passport, and the house he and Ilona had bought in 1955, the same year Ann was born. Growing up, Ann loved to hear her father's story about the day he'd walked into his lawyer's office and signed the papers that had made him a homeowner. "Imagine, Anni," he would always say, "we come only three years before, hardly a penny in pockets. You see—in America, *anything* is possible!"

The two-story red-brick bungalow house was small— snug, was how the real-estate agent had described it. For a long time, until Mike had built on an extra room in the back, the children had shared a room. There was only one bathroom, of course, so getting everyone washed and out in the morning was usually pretty hairy. But the rest of the modest houses on the quiet, tree-lined block were equally well kept up, and most were owned by other recently arrived immigrants whose children were about the same ages as Karchy and Ann.

In the winter, when the cold winds swept off the lake and the snow seemed to fall more days than not, the families mostly visited with one another indoors. But come summer-time, with its gift of daylight that lasted well past nine o'clock, everyone regrouped outdoors. Every free moment they had, whenever they could break away from whatever chores their parents had set them, the kids would spill out into the yards and onto the sidewalks, to pick up where they'd left off the previous October when the cold weather had brought an end to their long hours of outdoor play.

They'd break up into groups according to age: The bigger boys played softball in the middle of the street, grudgingly allowing the occasional car to pass. Cheering them on from the sidelines were their actual and would-be girlfriends, who carefully did their nails and giggled over which boy was a good kisser and who tried to go all the way.

The little kids, when they weren't soaring on the swings or flying down the slide at the schoolyard playground at the end of the block, organized endless games of Red Rover, tag, and hide-and-seek that had them breathlessly pursuing one another until their mothers called them in to eat supper or to go to bed. And the fathers watered the lawns and weeded the gardens and kept silent vigil over them all.

Not that there was anything to fear in this safest and most secure of neighborhoods, where every face was familiar and front doors were always left unlocked. They were one great extended family. They prayed at the same church, shopped at the same three or four stores, consulted the same doctor when they were sick, the same lawyer when they were, infrequently, in trouble.

After work, when the supper dishes were done and dusk was beginning to fall, they'd bring out icy bottles of beer or soda pop and settle down to trade gossip and friendly insults up and down the street. The women bragged about their children and shook their heads over the shocking rise in the price of chicken and pork, while their husbands argued about politics and whether the Cubs could win the pennant.

One year, when they were older and earning money,

Karchy and Ann had chipped in and bought Mike a hammock to set up between two trees in the backyard. Mike had dutifully strung up the hammock every summer, but he never really took to it. Eventually Ann realized that he was happiest sitting on the concrete steps in front of the house, surveying his domain—his tiny but immaculate lawn and his well-tended flowerbeds.

He liked to brag that he had the greenest grass on the block, the prettiest flowers; that nobody had tomatoes or cukes as sweet and tasty as the ones he planted every spring in the vegetable garden in back of the house. When his children teased him about his green thumb, Mike would remind them that he'd been a farmer back in Hungary. The love of the land was in their blood, too, even if they didn't have the good sense to feel it.

Times had changed, of course, and now there were plenty of kids whose names he didn't know, whose parents' homes he'd never visited. Some of those kids were black, but that was okay with Mike; their families were God-fearing, church-going people who painted their houses and mowed their lawns and appreciated the value of a dollar, same as he did. He didn't care what color his neighbors were. He still enjoyed sitting outside when the weather was fine, keeping track of what was going on, keeping an eye on the kids playing ball or jumping rope to make sure they didn't go running out into the street.

Today, however, the children were all in school and the street was deserted. A chill winter wind had pedestrians clutching at their hats and scarves as they hurried to their destinations. Thick clouds scudded overhead, holding a strong promise of snow. But with the temperature hovering at thirty-five, the weather forecasters were predicting nothing more serious than a heavy downpour by nightfall. Still, anyone with a bit of sense was staying indoors on this gray, end-of-January morning.

Thelma Holmes, who'd bought the Zawicki house, was spending the day catching up with her cleaning and laundry. Beef stew for dinner, she decided, when she opened the door to pick up her mail. Something thick and hearty. Maybe she'd bring a bowl over to Mr. Laszlo. Wondering whether he was home, she glanced across the street and was astonished to see someone huddled on the steps of his porch. In fact it looked like Mr. Laszlo, sitting out there in the cold without so much as a sweater.

She wondered what on earth possessed the man. Should she walk across and ask him if he was all right? It would be the neighborly thing to do. But something about the way he was sitting, like a wounded animal drawn inward to protect himself from further hurt, warned her off.

Shaking her head, Thelma started back inside. He was a nice man and he had no business sitting there half undressed as if it were the middle of July. She took one last look over her shoulder and was relieved to see a car turning the corner at the end of the block. It was that dirty white Volvo that belonged to Mr. Laszlo's daughter, the one he called Anni.

Good, she thought. His daughter will see to the trouble, if there was any. Then, her conscience clear, Thelma went back inside to start on her stew.

Ann had followed the same route from downtown to her old neighborhood so many hundreds of times that she could almost have driven the roads blindfolded. As it was, she made this trip on automatic pilot, traveling as fast as was safely and legally possible and cursing aloud every red light and stop sign along the way.

Her father hadn't said much—just enough for her to determine that no one was dead or in the hospital. His normally strong, gruff voice had been reduced to a barely audible mumble, but the message had nevertheless come through loud and clear: He needed to see her as soon as possible.

She turned left past the grade school where she'd learned to read and write. The red-brick building looked scruffy and tired compared to the newer and better equipped elementary school that Mikey attended. But she still had fond memories of Miss Fisher, her first-grade teacher; of winning the class spelling bee three years in a row; of playing the lead role in the sixth-grade production of *Carousel*; of the playground where she'd jumped rope for more hours than she could count.

And best of all, she could recall that hot, dark summer night when she was thirteen and Bobby Mazrik had spun her around on the merry-go-round until she was dizzy. Then he'd pulled her into the shadows and kissed her—*on the lips*—for so long she thought she was going to faint. Now Bobby was married, the father of three kids, and selling boats near Rainbow Beach. He was balding and so quiet you could hardly get more than a sentence out of him, and still Ann felt a thrill when she thought about that moment years ago.

Some of her friends, the kids she'd grown up with, looked down on the old neighborhood. They'd persuaded their parents to sell and move out to the suburbs, where it was cleaner and safer. Though she'd made the same move herself, because she wanted Mikey to go to the best school possible, she still loved coming home to her block.

Here were her roots, her childhood. Her dolls and toys were packed away in a trunk in the cellar. Every award she'd ever won in high school was proudly displayed in her bedroom, and her prom dresses, cleaned and stored in plastic bags, hung in her closet. The rooms were decorated with the same furniture they'd had since she was twelve, and on the walls were the same pictures—photographs of Karchy and herself, cheap landscape scenes that reminded Papa of Hungary. She wouldn't have dreamed of trying to get Papa to leave. She'd be wasting her breath. He loved his home as if he'd built it himself, with his own hands, from the foundation up.

It wasn't hard for her to understand how he felt. Though Papa didn't talk much about his life in Hungary, she knew he'd been a farmer who'd had to scrabble to make a meager living from his few acres. Then, when the Communists had taken over at the end of the war, he'd lost even that. He'd been dispossessed of his land, his livelihood, eventually his country. The house, modest as it was, and the surrounding patch of yard—they *belonged* to him. Nobody could ever take that from Mike Laszlo.

Sometimes when Papa was looking especially tired and worn, Ann would reluctantly look ahead to that distant time when he'd no longer be able to take care of himself. She hated even to think of it: putting the house up for sale, figuring out what to do with all the possessions they'd collected over the years, making room for the strangers who would be coming in with their own furniture and family traditions.

That day was far in the future, however. At the moment, she had to worry about the present. And if the sight that greeted her as she pulled up was any indication, she had plenty to worry about.

"Papa, are you crazy?" she shouted, getting out of the car and hurrying up the sidewalk. Mike was wearing nothing more than a cotton T-shirt to protect him against the raw dampness.

"Papa, you're going to catch pneumonia!" she scolded. "What are you doing?"

Mike stared dazedly at her. He was holding several pages, stapled together, that flapped in the wind. "They say I . . . kill people," he muttered. "I . . . torture—"

"What?" He wasn't making sense. Could he have suffered a stroke? Why was he behaving so strangely? Very gently she said, "What are you talking about, Papa? C'mon, let's go inside."

She wasn't sure he'd heard, because he neither moved nor spoke. "Papa?" she repeated, her voice trembling slightly.

His eyes reminded her of Mikey's reaction when she and David had told him they were getting divorced—the look

31

of someone who feels betrayed and cannot begin to express the hurt and anger.

But who on earth would want to betray Mike Laszlo? Those papers . . .

"Give them to me," she said.

Silently he handed them over.

"United States Department of Justice" declared the heading across the top. "Office of Special Investigations." Beneath that, in bold, black lettering, were the words "ORDER TO DEPORT: Michael J. Laszlo."

Ann scanned the lines, reading but hardly taking in their import. She flipped to the next page and the page after that. Then she went back to the beginning and started again, reading more carefully this time, automatically deciphering the complicated legal language that Washington seemed to do better than anyone else. Here was a document that threatened to destroy an innocent man's life, and the bureaucrats still couldn't manage to put it in plain English.

Nevertheless, the most important facts jumped out at her. The United States was accusing Papa of unimaginably vile war crimes, of deeds so heinous that he was no longer welcome in his adopted country. He was to be stripped of his citizenship and sent back to Hungary, to be dealt with there by a government he bitterly and vociferously opposed. He was, in effect, being sentenced to die.

Of course, this was all a terrible mistake—one that, fortunately, she was trained to deal with. But in the meantime, the more immediate problem was to get Papa inside, where it was warm. She put out her hand and he stood up, obedient as a small child seeking to be comforted by his mother. She'd never seen him look so defeated as he did now, shuffling into the house with the gait of an old man.

Those bastards! she thought, letting the door slam behind her. *Building up a case without bothering to check whether or not they had the right man.*

Mike lowered himself heavily into his favorite chair, below the crucifix that he and Ilona had hung the first day they moved in. One of Ann's oldest memories: Mike sunk into the chair, watching television, while she and Karchy did their homework on the kitchen table. The fabric on the arms was worn away, and Ann had wanted to pay to have the piece reupholstered in a pattern of his choosing. But Mike had waved away her offer and draped a plaid blanket over the ragged patches. He was an old man; he didn't need new and fancy. She should save her money for the kid.

She went into the kitchen and boiled water for tea, made a cup for herself, and laced Papa's heavily with honey and lemon. Then she came back into the living room and smiled as she handed him his favorite mug. The rest of the mail lay scattered on the carpet where he must have dropped it when he opened the envelope from the government.

"I don't know nothin' about . . ." He took a long swallow of tea and cleared his throat. "I work in the mill, I raise kids, this my country. Now they say . . . Anni, they want to take citizenship away. They can no do that. I here thirty-six year, I . . ." His voice trailed off.

"They must have you mixed up with another Michael J. Laszlo," she said, after she'd finished studying the charges listed against him. She put the papers aside and reached for her mug. "There are a lot of Michael J. Laszlos in the world, Papa."

That wasn't good enough. "How can they mix up?" he demanded.

Ann had seen it happen dozens of times before. The government got so enthusiastic about the merits of its case that it overlooked certain key inconsistencies that put the lie to its accusations. Or it presented witnesses whose testimony shrieked of coercion. Or evidence that had been collected in a slipshod manner.

Wasn't this precisely the reason she believed so strongly that everyone was entitled to fair representation? Sure, you got stuck once in a while with a creep or two, like that druggie entrepreneur this morning. But if law firms like hers didn't exist, or if she chose her clients by the color

33

of their collar or the size of their bank accounts, then only the rich and powerful would have their moment in court. Which would mean that a decent, loving man like her father could lose everything he'd worked for because of some bungled paperwork.

Ann leaned forward and patted her father's arm affectionately. "This *other* Michael Laszlo must have lied when he got his citizenship. He's accused of war crimes—"

"I was farmer!" Mike yelled. He sprang out of the chair and began pounding his fist into the palm of his hand. "What I know war crime? I don't do nothin' *like that*. I no like *that*!"

"Papa, it's *not* you," she reminded him, worried for his heart. His face was beet-red and he was breathing in short, panting bursts.

Ann knew what he must be thinking. She'd heard him often enough, carrying on about "filthy Communists, all their stupid talk of workers' paradise. Some paradise," he'd scoff, "with KGB spy behind every door, waiting to hear one bad word so they can send you for life to labor camp in Siberia. Communist mean no food. No land. No freedom. No nothin'."

Ann stood up, took both his hands in hers, and stared into the brown eyes that were the same shade as her own. Had she ever loved her father more? What hadn't he done for her all these years? She could never repay him for the love and warmth he'd given her. Such a gruff, rough man, but he'd rarely shown her and Karchy anything but his most tender self.

"They made a mistake. We'll clear it up," she assured him, silently begging him to put his faith and trust in her. "Don't worry."

The deportation order called for Mike to appear at the Federal Building for a hearing on the following Monday, but Ann didn't want his weekend spoiled with this mess hanging over him. So by dint of considerable string-pulling and calling in of favors, she was able to have his appointment rescheduled for Friday. That left him to endure only two days of tension, which he managed to get through with a minimum of cursing and bellowing.

He was alternately angry and morose. The latter worried her more. It was so unlike Papa to brood; now even Mikey could hardly get him to smile. As often as she promised him she'd straighten out the whole business in five minutes flat, he didn't seem convinced that his name would be cleared. Karchy finally had to tell her to leave him alone and let him sulk. She'd be feeling plenty pissed too, he said, if somebody were to come along and call her a Nazi.

A *Nazi*. Until Karchy spoke the word aloud, Ann hadn't actually considered the deeper implications of the charges against Michael J. Laszlo, whoever that other man might be. Karchy was absolutely right. There was no point in trying to talk Papa out of his black mood. He'd cheer up quickly enough as soon as the hearing was behind him and his faith in American justice had been restored.

Trust Karchy to understand. Although she was the one with the college education—not to mention that she was the supposedly more sensitive daughter—Karchy often surprised her with his sharp intuition, especially about their father. Maybe that was because of what he and Papa had gone through together in Europe. While she could only imagine the hardship and poverty of their day-to-day life in the refugee camp, Karchy had actually lived through it.

Though he'd been all of three when the Laszlos had finally left the camp, he always insisted that he had memories of those days. "When it was just the three of us," he'd tease her to make her cry. As a little girl, she was tortured by the fact that the family had existed for a time without her. Even worse was knowing that Karchy could actually remember their mother singing and telling him folktales about the witches and goblins who lived in the Hungarian countryside. Whereas Ann's memories of her mother were all secondhand, distilled from photographs and the stories she'd been told by her father or brother.

So perhaps Karchy shared a special bond with Mike, or perhaps he took after Ilona, who had been, by all accounts, an unusually gentle and compassionate human being. Ann had reached the stage in life when she could allow Karchy that. Because, face it, everyone always said she was her father's daughter: energetic, outgoing, ambitious, a real go-getter.

Easygoing Karchy, on the other hand, was content (or so he said) to work at the mill, hang out with his pals, go bowling, play softball, or catch a movie in his spare time. He preferred to leave the fast-tracking to his sister. Occasionally, as now, he'd feel it necessary to remind her to slow down and take a moment to consider the human, emotional side of the issue. If Karchy were any indication, their mother must have been a remarkable lady.

But Papa was pretty damn special himself. Ann felt grateful that she'd chosen a profession that so well equipped her to extricate him from this horrible case of mistaken identity. He looked so awkward and ill at ease, seated next to her in one of the waiting rooms on the thirty-seventh floor of the Federal Building. Partly it was the suit. She'd told him to wear it in order to make a good impression on the government attorneys, but he looked like a greenhorn, right off the boat.

The jacket had just fit him ten years ago, and these days the middle button was fighting a losing battle with his midsection. The shirt looked so tight around the collar, she wondered how he could breathe. As for the pants . . . Ann wondered whether she should have insisted that he invest in a new pair. But she knew her father would never have agreed.

He simply wasn't a man who would ever look comfortable in a suit. He rarely wore one, not even to church.

"You look nice, Papa," she lied, brushing some lint off his shoulder. He looked like an old man today, so gray and tired. She guessed he hadn't slept well—and how could he? His own beloved government was calling him a criminal and threatening to throw him out of the country. *His* country.

She'd warned him to be quiet and let her do the talking. "Papa, I speak their language," she'd said, and he'd promised to keep his mouth shut. She only hoped he could keep that promise.

"Mrs. Talbot?"

The receptionist at the front desk poked her head in the door of the waiting room and gestured for them to follow her down a long, carpeted corridor. Although Ann hadn't been up here before, the atmosphere felt familiar. She thought, *They should hang a sign on the door: Caution! Lawyers at work.*

They passed one desk after another at which young and not-so-young women sat, dutifully clicking the keys of their computers. A lot of Ann's friends from high school had taken jobs as secretaries after graduation. But for her father's unwavering belief that she was too smart to settle for anything but the best, she easily could have joined their ranks.

Across from each desk, the doors closed or partly ajar, were the lawyers' offices. She didn't have to peek inside to know that most were occupied by men in three-piece suits. The federal judicial system was still stuck in the past, and only a handful of women attorneys had succeeded in breaching its defenses. These federal government jobs were considered plum positions, excellent steppingstones to top-drawer firms at top-level salaries. The lawyers behind those doors were sharp, aggressive, and, not infrequently, more than a little cocky. After all, they had the power of Washington and the American people on their side.

So what? She was one hell of a lawyer, and a challenging opponent always roused the tiger in her. Not that Papa's case would ever come to that. She glanced at him sideways as the receptionist pointed them to a room at the end of the hall. His face was impassive, but when she squeezed his hand, his palm was soaked with sweat.

They walked into what was obviously a conference room, though it was missing the usual solidly built, highly polished table. What the room didn't lack, however, was a stunning panorama through the wall-length, floor-to-ceiling windows. Downtown Chicago lay spread out before them like a boardgame. To the east, the sun was glinting off Lake Michigan, which stretched as far as Ann could see. But she gave only a moment to the view before she put out her hand to the man who stood waiting for them.

"I'm Ann Talbot," she introduced herself.

"I'm Joe Dinofrio. Hello."

He had a nice, firm handshake and a pleasant, self-assured manner. Ann guessed that he was about her age and that he was getting ready to move on to private practice. Maybe he was even figuring to go out in a blaze of glory called the U.S. versus Michael J. Laszlo.

"This is my father," she said, matching his low-key tone.

"Mike Laszlo," Mike spoke up. He reached out to shake the other man's hand and caught Dinofrio's momentary hesitation.

Ann saw it, too, and took a deep, angry breath to compose herself. Her heart ached for the insult to her father. She was determined, though, to keep her emotions firmly in check. If she didn't set the example, how could she expect Papa to do likewise?

Dinofrio was surprised by the family connection between Laszlo and this attractive woman who was very far from his image of Hungarian immigrant stock. But all he said was, "Are you here as Mr. Laszlo's attorney, Mrs. Talbot?"

Ann shook her head. "No. I thought we could clear this up—"

Just at that moment, they were joined by another man, a little older than Dinofrio, carrying a thick file under his arm. He had the kind of looks that under other circumstances Ann might have found attractive: unruly dark hair, sharp brown eyes peering at her from behind horn-rimmed glasses, a slim build that radiated nervous energy. He was less polished than Dinofrio. Ann noticed that the paisley tie didn't quite match the stripe of his suit.

"This is Jack Burke. He's from the Office of Special Investigations. I'll be helping Jack prosecute the case," said Dinofrio. "Mrs. Talbot, Mr. Laszlo."

Burke glanced at each of them in turn. Something in his eyes warned Ann that *this* was the guy to watch out for. She'd seen that expression before: the look of a man who was hungry to prove his case and win, willing to fight dirty if that's what it took.

Having been on the receiving end of such battles a couple of times, Ann had made it her business to think about what drove such a man. She'd come to realize that the hunger to see justice done was often fed by a darker emotion than the high-minded beliefs bandied about in the courtroom. What motivated Jack Burke? she wondered.

Again Mike put out his hand, but Burke simply stared at him, not even bothering with a pretense of politeness.

"Look," Ann said, trying hard to mask her fury at the slight. "This is a mistake. You've got the wrong Michael J. Laszlo."

"Like hell we do," Burke replied flatly.

Ann could feel Mike bristling beside her. She put a restraining hand on his arm and asked, "I beg your pardon?"

"We don't have the wrong man," he said, carefully enunciating each word, as if he were speaking to a deaf person.

Jack Burke had often wondered how he'd react when he finally met up with Michael Laszlo, whose personal history had by now become almost as familiar to him as his own. For over a year, he'd become increasingly intimate with the man. He'd spent countless hours poring over stacks of documents: dozens of photographs; yellowing state papers emblazoned with the official Nazi seal; witnesses' transcripts, painstakingly translated into English.

Their collective testimony was so heart-rending that some days he thought he'd go mad if he read another word. He'd lost weight because he was often too sick to his stomach to eat. At night he was frequently shocked awake by vivid nightmares peopled by Laszlo's victims, screaming, "You must help us! Find him!"

Although he'd tried to maintain his objectivity as an investigator, he'd nevertheless developed feelings about Laszlo. How could he have done otherwise, given the cumulative weight of the evidence against him? To call him a cold-blooded sadist was an understatement. Laszlo appeared to have been wholly devoid of mercy or remorse.

Like a bloodhound intent on his prey, Jack had sniffed out Laszlo's trail from Budapest to Chicago. And he'd discovered, to his astonishment, that the Nazi murderer had transformed himself into a model citizen: an exemplary father; a regular church-goer; well regarded at work. The only blot on his record was that he'd been arrested for demonstrating against the Hungarian National Folkdancers.

In law school, Jack had been exhorted to ask the right questions in order to arrive at a clear-headed understanding of the law. Alone in his tiny office in Washington, he'd been haunted by one overwhelming question, which probably not even Laszlo himself could answer: Why? Why had he chosen to systematically humiliate and brutalize other human beings? And there was another, no less important, question: How had he lived with himself and his conscience all these years?

So here was Laszlo, looking much older and more worn than the man in the pictures, but Jack could still have picked him out in a crowd. For so long he'd studied those features: the heavily lidded eyes; the jowly cheeks; the high, wide forehead. The woman—Laszlo's daughter, poor soul—had inherited her father's forehead and strong cheekbones. Had she also inherited his capacity to brutalize? Or did such characteristics, like certain genetic defects, skip a generation?

The pressure had been building in Mike like a simmering volcano. "I don't do none of this!" he burst out. "This not me! I good citizen in old country. I farmer. I citizen. I good American."

"If you're a good American, Mr. Laszlo, then this country's in deep shit!" Jack shot back.

Ann was beginning to feel as if she were up against a lynch mob. These two creeps had already tried and convicted Papa. Now they were just looking around for a tall enough tree so they could hang him. Well, screw that! Since when had the United States of America become a police state?

"What the hell is this?" she blazed. "You don't speak to him this way! He has rights! I won't allow *anyone* to speak to him this way!"

"I know why you do this to me!" Mike bellowed, poking Jack in the chest.

"Please, Papa," Ann said, trying to pull him away from Burke.

He stared at her blankly for a moment. Then he stepped back and growled, "The Communists do it to me, Anna. They get back at me—"

"Because of what happened with the dancers?" Jack snorted contemptuously.

"I go on TV, talk to newspaper—"

"That's what I expected you to say." Jack waved his hand dismissively.

"I'm not interested in what you expected anyone to say!" Ann snapped, stepping forward to stand between Burke and her father. "You're charging a man with something he would have done—"

"*Allegedly* would have done," Dinofrio broke in smoothly.

"I don't need any legal pointers from you, either." She glared at him an instant, then redirected herself at Burke. "He's been here for thirty-six years. Why wasn't he charged earlier?"

"We're not charging him with anything. This isn't a criminal proceeding," Jack said impatiently. This woman was supposed to be a lawyer? Apparently she'd totally misinterpreted the intent of the affidavit.

"He did nothing!" Ann declared, her voice rising indignantly. "You want legal pointers? I'll give you one: In this country, he's innocent until proven guilty!"

Jack grabbed his file folder and brandished it at her. "The witness reports were locked away in the basement of the United Nations until last year. That's why we didn't charge him earlier!"

"How very convenient for you," she said coldly.

"No. How very convenient for *him*."

She could see this exchange was getting them nowhere. For whatever sick reasons, Burke was out for blood. And Dinofrio was obviously happy to ride along for the hunt and feast on the carcass. She'd heard of such situations, where overly zealous prosecutors bent the rules to build their cases. Documents could be doctored, testimony distorted. A vaguely veiled threat, subtle intimidation, not-so-subtle outright bribery—all time-honored ways to provide the sacrificial "guilty party" who could be held accountable for a crime he or she never committed.

So they had witnesses. According to her father and his friends, anyone who wanted a bigger apartment or a better job was happy to be a witness, especially against an old man in America whose life meant nothing to them. The Communists could find plenty of witnesses with no problem.

"Come on, Papa," she said, taking his arm. "Let's go."

But Mike wasn't about to slink out like a beaten animal. He pulled away and moved in on Jack Burke. "All bullshit! The Communists make all up! You America, you my government, my America, you help them do this to me? I don't hurt nobody. I work in the steel mill. I raise boy and girl. My boy American soldier, he fight in Vietnam. My girl, she American lawyer. But you listen to the Communists!"

Jack forced himself to hold his ground in the face of

42

Laszlo's verbal assault. After all the data he'd absorbed, the man held no surprises for him. No doubt he knew a hell of a lot more about Laszlo than his American lawyer-daughter did. That thought provoked a wry smile, which he barely concealed.

"You! You laugh at me? You son-a-bitch!" Mike clenched his fist, ready to swing. "You do this to me?"

"Papa, don't!" Ann cried out in Hungarian. She blinked back tears of frustration. This kind of ugly confrontation was exactly what she had hoped to avoid. "Come *on*, Papa," she said, tugging at his upraised arm.

With one hand firmly grasping him by the elbow, she nodded a curt good-bye to the men and started for the door.

But they weren't finished yet. They had still more bad news for her.

"The Hungarian government has already filed for extradition," Dinofrio said. He could have been reading the time or the weather, for all the emotion he showed.

Mike whirled around. "What? What that mean?"

"It means," Jack answered, savoring the moment, "that if your citizenship is taken away, you'll be sent back to Hungary for trial."

"You send me back to the Communists? You send me back to die?" Mike's body sagged, as if he'd just taken a blow to his gut. He stared bleakly at Jack, who glared back at him, untouched by Mike's distress. Mishka Laszlo, as he'd been known in Hungary, had been notoriously short on pity. Jack preferred to save his compassion for those poor souls—living and dead—who'd had the misfortune to pass Laszlo's way.

"That's why you demonstrated and got yourself arrested five years ago, isn't it?" Jack taunted him. "To give yourself an alibi in case this ever blew up in your face."

Desperate to escape Jack Burke's venom, Ann tugged at her father's arm. "No one's going to take your citizenship away, Papa," she said sharply.

Mike stumbled as he left the conference room, but Ann

grabbed him before he fell. He kept silent the whole length of the hallway. As soon as he and Ann were alone, safely inside the elevator, he said, "What we gonna do?"

Ann had been asking herself the same question, as well as why they wouldn't believe her that Papa wasn't the man they wanted. She'd told him not to worry, and he'd trusted her. It was a simple mistake, she'd said, one easily fixed. But now she saw she'd been wrong. These men *wanted* to believe Mike Laszlo was a criminal. They didn't want to listen, only to talk about what they'd read about him. Didn't they understand that papers could be forged?

"I don't know," she replied, still sifting through the various options. "We'll get you a good lawyer. We'll get you the *best* lawyer."

"*You* gonna be my lawyer."

She was touched by his confidence in her, but it was a terrible idea. "I don't know anything about naturalization. We've got to find the best immigration lawyer. I'm a *criminal* lawyer, Papa," she explained.

"They say I criminal. They say I criminal against humanity, Anni," he said, lowering his voice. He shook his head and folded his arms across his chest, as if to say, You'd better do this job for your papa.

He didn't have to say a word for Ann to read his mind: Those guys in their fancy suits could go to hell and kiss his ass. Because with her help, he was staying right here, in the US of A.

CHAPTER

4

The Holy Cross Cemetery was located just outside the city limits, a pleasant enough drive from the West Side churches whose deceased members were laid to rest there. It stretched out for several neat, tastefully landscaped acres. For the most part the markers were simple, unpretentious gravestones, though an occasional angel or statue of the Blessed Virgin Mary broke up the uniformity of the rows. Here the ethnic groups that had stayed separate in life came together in death: The names on the stones represented all the dispossessed states of eastern Europe—Hungary, Poland, Rumania, Albania, Lithuania, the Ukraine.

Ann and Karchy knew their way around Holy Cross as well as many of the priests who officiated there. Since childhood, they'd been coming with Mike to visit Ilona's grave four or five times a year: on her birthday, on the anniversary of her death, on Easter, Christmas, and Mother's Day. Ilona had loved flowers, so they always brought her an abundant bouquet, which Mike took his time choosing.

One Mother's Day when Ann was fifteen and starting to

assert herself, she'd told her father that she wasn't in the mood to ruin her Sunday by hanging around the grave of someone she'd never even known. Mike had slapped her so fast and hard she'd almost fallen to the floor; it was hard to say who was more shocked by his reaction. She'd locked herself in her room and cried until her eyes were swollen. In the end, Mike and Karchy had gone off without her, but she got little satisfaction from her victory. Elusive though she was in death, Ilona was a presence in Ann's day-to-day life, and those few minutes of silent communication nourished their connection.

Now that Mike was retired, he'd fallen into the habit of making the trip out to Holy Cross every week or so, to make sure the grass was cut and the plot well tended. Sometimes Ann fretted that he went too often, that he was dwelling too much on the past. But the visits seemed to give him pleasure, and besides, she'd learned her lesson at fifteen that some issues were sacrosanct.

So when he suggested, as they were leaving the Federal Building, that they drive out to the cemetery, she said, of course. She understood perfectly. In moments of crisis, some people sought comfort in church; Papa needed to be with Ilona.

He said hardly a word all the way there, except to remind her to stop at the flower store, where, as usual, he spent a long time picking the freshest and most colorful bouquet. Ann was glad for the silence. The subject occupying both their thoughts felt too hot to touch just yet.

She walked a step or two behind Papa as he trudged up the hill to Ilona's grave. When had his step gotten so slow? she wondered. She'd always thought of Papa as a big, powerful man, but suddenly he seemed smaller, more compact.

He carefully placed the flowers on the ground and bowed his head, as if in prayer. Ann shivered and rubbed her hands for warmth. The sun was still strong overhead, but the ground underfoot was icy from last night's light snow.

46

Though she was wearing a wool suit, she hadn't dressed to be outdoors. Her raincoat and high heels gave her scant protection against the cold.

Finally, after several long minutes, he turned to her and said, "First time you kiss boy, he touch you, I no know what to say. We come here. Words easier here. Your mama help me. What I know about to raise a girl?" He smiled sadly to himself. "You remember, tubusom?"

Ann nodded. "I remember." She'd made the mistake of telling Karchy, and he'd run to Papa with the news. She hadn't spoken to Karchy for a week afterwards.

Her father seemed lost in his thoughts. A gusty wind was beginning to blow, but Ann didn't dare disturb his reverie.

"We were in refugee camp, after war," he said at last, speaking so quietly she had to strain to hear. "Austria. I meet your mama there. We have Karchy. It was bad. Dirty. No food. They come around to camps, Hungarian Communist official from Budapest, look for anti-Communist. They know you anti-Communist, they put your name on list. They send you back to Hungary, say you war criminal, hang you from tree. *Repatriation*, they call it."

She already knew most of what he was telling her. She'd pieced it together from bits and snatches of conversation, mostly between Papa and his pals. And she'd used her imagination to fill in the blanks.

"We got to come out, get away. At the camp, no food. Everybody know America got quota for farmer. If you say you farmer, you come to America quick. I say I farmer. We come here quick."

"You weren't a farmer?" A prickle of fear stung the back of her neck.

"Ya. I farmer." He shrugged. "When I boy."

"What were you?" she asked in a voice full of trepidation.

Mike looked at her with eyes that begged for understanding. "I policeman. I gendarme. I *csendor*."

She sucked in her breath, not trusting herself to speak.

"You no look at me like that, Anna," Mike said. His tone was between an order and a plea.

He bent down and fidgeted with the flowers, arranging and rearranging them as he spoke. "I no do nothing bad. Crazy Nazis—Hungarian Nazis, Arrow Cross—take over, I gendarme. I say to them, I wanna be clerk in office, no hurt nobody. I got nothin' against Jew and gypsies. That what I do. I clerk in office and play music. Don't hurt nobody."

More than she'd ever wanted anything else in the world, she wanted to believe him. His explanation made perfect sense. He'd been desperate to make a decent life for his family. He had a wife and baby who were starving. In America there was plenty to eat and plenty of opportunity to make money if you were willing to work hard. And Papa was willing.

But no one was standing at the gateway to the Promised Land, waiting to greet him with open arms. So he'd told a lie. He'd erased his past, which would have kept him from leaving Europe, possibly forever, and recreated himself as a farmer. She could understand that. Wouldn't she have done the same herself under similar circumstances?

"Anni," Mike said, reaching out to her as if grasping for a lifeline. "You see the legal paper, what they say I done. You think I do that, tubusom?"

"No," she whispered, groping for the truth and finding it. She threw herself into his arms and hugged him tightly. "No, Papa, I don't."

Ann couldn't let her father go home alone, not after what he'd been through this day. But he hated to be coddled, and whenever she showed him any extra attention or concern, he turned into a surly bear. So, using her son as an excuse, she pressed Mike to join them for an early dinner. What with all the anxious conversations between Ann and Karchy, Mikey had figured out that something was up, though he didn't know exactly what. He'd feel a lot better, Ann told her father, if he saw for himself that Grandpa was fine and just the same as always.

Mike could hardly say no to such a request. Besides, he'd been too preoccupied the last couple of days to do any grocery shopping, and suddenly he was starving. "Chicken paprikash?" he asked hopefully. "With *krumpli*?"

Ann would have served him caviar and champagne if that's what he wanted. Whatever it took to pick up his spirits.

Her house in the lakefront suburb of Wilmette had never looked so warm and welcoming as it did this afternoon. She'd loved the place from the first minute she and David had stepped through the doorway, accompanied by a too talkative realtor who didn't have the good sense to keep her mouth shut and let the place sell itself. It had everything Ann was looking for: large rooms, lots of sun, an eat-in kitchen with space enough for the family to cook together, and a generous backyard, in which they could put up a swing set and sandbox for Mikey.

The neighborhood had felt right, too. The schools were excellent, and there were lots of other young couples who were also just starting families, so Mikey (and whoever else might come along) wouldn't have to go far to find friends.

Over the years, they'd furnished their home slowly and carefully. Many of the pieces—the round oak dining-room table, the pine breakfront, the slat-backed rocking chair in the bedroom—they'd bought at antique stores they happened to pass on drives through the Michigan countryside.

David was less enamored of old things than Ann. But then, his history was all around him: The Talbots had lived in Illinois and Wisconsin for over 150 years, and three generations of his mother's relatives were buried next to her. Whereas for Ann, save for some distantly related cousins in New York whom she'd never even met, she,

Karchy, and Papa constituted the entire American branch of the Laszlo family tree.

When they'd split up, David had suggested she keep the house and furniture. He could afford to be so generous: He'd just been named a partner at his father's law firm and would soon be earning a quarter of a million dollars a year. She suspected, but wisely refrained from saying so, that he relished the idea of starting over, from scratch.

Later she'd heard via Mikey that his dad was moving into an "awesome" high-rise apartment with a great view. His dad, Mikey excitedly reported, had bought stereo speakers that were six feet high, and his girlfriend (gulp!) was helping him pick out lots of other stuff. Neat, huh? Mikey had said, searching her face to make sure she wasn't angry at his enthusiasm. Really neat, she'd assured him, mentally shaking her head at David's need for excess in creating his personal pleasure palace in the sky.

Each to his or her own, she'd reminded herself. Meanwhile, she'd had the marvelous fortune to be left with these familiar surroundings. Much better for Mikey, who still had his same house, friends, and school. And, unfortunately, the same routines, such as playing video games when he should have been doing his homework.

She unlocked the front door and called, "Mikey?"

No response—but she could hear the telltale singsonging blips of Nintendo, Mikey's latest passion. Time was when he used to help her with dinner, play with his collection of model cars and airplanes, even read a book once in a while. Now it was all she could do to tear him away from the tiny animated stick figures zigzagging madly across the TV screen.

"All he does is play that damn game," she muttered.

"He boy. Boy gotta play," Mike said placatingly.

His attempt to soothe only made her angrier.

Papa had raised Karchy and herself according to strict rules and expectations. He'd been a firm proponent of old-fashioned discipline—until he became a grandfather. Suddenly all his beliefs had gone flying out the window, to be replaced by one simple rule: He boy. Boy gotta p'ay.

No wonder Mikey idolized his Grandpa Mike.

The door to Mikey's room was partly ajar. Ann pushed it the rest of the way open and got ready to remind Mikey that they had an agreement about when and for how long he was allowed to play Nintendo. But she bit back the lecture when she saw her ex-husband seated on the floor next to their son.

Some days she thought Mikey looked just like a Laszlo. Other days she could see only the Talbot in him: David's full lips that so easily turned pouty; his huge, doe-soft eyes; the straight brown hair that seemed always to be falling over his forehead, no matter how often it was cut; the protruding ears, a Talbot family characteristic. Today, Mikey looked pure Talbot.

"Hi, Mom," he mumbled, still intent on the game. A second later he tore his eyes away from the screen and noticed Mike. "Hi, Grandpa!" he shouted, jumping up to hug him.

David stood up slowly and brushed off his pin-striped trousers. He'd taken off his jacket—a concession to the game—but he was still wearing his vest, and his yellow rep tie was perfectly knotted.

"I didn't know you were coming over," Ann said. She wasn't pleased to find him here, and she wanted to make sure he knew it.

"I took the afternoon off." He nodded at Mike. "Hello, Mishka. We saw you on TV."

Mike didn't understand. He thought maybe David was making a joke, something to do with the video game. He hadn't been on TV for a long time, not since they'd showed him demonstrating against the dancers in front of the Dance and Arts Center.

"Yeah, we saw you on TV, Grandpa," Mikey chimed in.

Still confused, Mike turned to Ann, who was equally

confused. But as the explanation dawned on her what they were talking about, her face reflected so much pain and rage that Mike, too, suddenly understood.

"We talk later. All fake!" he said defiantly. He glared at David, as if daring him to contradict. Not wanting to upset the child, he said, "You wanna make the popcorn, Mikey? Lotta salt. Your mama always hide salt from Grandpa, but we put lotta salt, garlic, paprika. Okay, Mikey?"

Mikey looked sideways at his mother to gauge her reaction. His mom was weird. Sometimes she was real uptight, especially about homework and junk. And other times, especially when Grandpa was around, she let him have fun and do neat stuff.

He held his breath, wondering which way she'd go, worried that she might feel she had to act strict in front of Dad. Was he going to have to beg her, or would she just be cool and say okay? He concentrated on sending her an ESP message: YES, YES, YES.

Ann smiled and nodded at Mikey, whose big brown eyes seemed to be beaming her the message that his life's happiness depended on making popcorn with his grandfather.

"Yeah!" said Mikey, punching the air with his fist.

Mike clapped him on the back and chuckled mischievously. "Come on, we go find salt!"

Left alone, Ann and David struggled to move onto neutral ground. She always found it odd that a tightrope of tension existed between herself and this man whom she'd once thought she knew so well. They'd shared so many wonderful moments of love, affection, laughter, great sex. Hours of stimulating conversation. The birth of their son. Now he seemed almost like a stranger. She could hardly remember what it felt like to make love to him.

Nor could she trust him anymore to say the right thing when she most needed emotional support. Like right now, contemplating the fact that Burke and Dinofrio had seen fit to go public with their ridiculous, baseless allegations about Papa.

We're not charging him with anything. This isn't a criminal proceeding, Burke had said.

So instead of taking their case to court, they'd brought it to the media. A clever public-relations ploy. Long-lost Nazis always got big play from the TV and newspaper reporters. For good reason: How unnerving to discover the monster in one's midst, his true character camouflaged behind a mask of normalcy.

Her father, however, was *not* a monster. Of that she was certain.

Nevertheless, she felt sickened and dirtied by the accusations, unfounded though they were. Her father's picture had been broadcast into hundreds of thousands of homes all over the Chicago area. No matter that he was innocent. He'd been made to *seem* guilty. And that's what people would remember about Michael J. Laszlo, long after the charges had been dropped, the deportation order dismissed.

The strain of the day was beginning to hit her. She wanted a hot bath, a glass of white wine, the warmth of her bed. Before she could have any of those things, however, she had to attend to business. The first order was to deal with David. She told herself to be pleasant, but the best she could do was barely civil.

"Did he do his homework?" she asked.

David made a sour face. "Give him a break, will you, Ann?"

Stung, she snapped, "You give him enough breaks."

It was true. David played the classic, overly indulgent part-time dad. He fed Mikey the worst kind of crap, took him to two and three movies a weekend, bought him the latest Nintendo games as soon as they hit the stores.

David grabbed his jacket. "I guess I'd better go." He smirked as he walked past her. "Hey," he said, "I didn't know I'd married into Dr. Mengele's family."

With that sentence, he'd succeeded in ripping apart the last tenuous strands of affection and good will that had bound her to him.

"Okay, I'm sorry," he backtracked, regretting his lapse of good taste. "I didn't mean it."

Ann heard him calling good-bye to Mikey and her father, and still she didn't move to go after him. After such flippant cruelty, she couldn't even imagine how to speak to him.

She glanced around Mikey's room, which she and David had painted together one weekend long ago, in another lifetime. She remembered that they'd put up a picture of the cow jumping over the moon and a Maurice Sendak poster.

Now the walls were covered with big-boy posters: the Chicago Bears, Rambo, Indiana Jones, and "Save the Whales" (her contribution). Mikey's bookcase was a jumble of books, video tapes, shoeboxes in which were stored his baseball-card collection, an enormous conch shell David had brought back from the Bahamas, and what was left of his dinosaur and model-airplane collections. T-shirts, dirty socks, and jeans were jumbled up next to the closet.

Usually the disorder annoyed her. Today it gave her solace. Here, within these four walls of her home, were normalcy and reality. Outside and beyond was the madness. Having found her calm, she hurried after David and caught up with him as he was getting into his car.

"He didn't do it," she said.

"I didn't ask you, did I? That's the one question lawyers never ask, right?" he said evenly.

Ann had always used David as a sounding board. Old habits died hard, she realized, as she heard herself telling him, "He wants me to represent him."

David shook his head. "If it were *my* dad, if it were Harry, I wouldn't represent him. What if he *did* do it?"

He could see from her expression that she wasn't satisfied with his response. So what else was new? She'd stopped liking his answers a long time ago. And he'd finally stopped feeling bad that he couldn't please her anymore.

He wanted to say, *Grow up, Ann. Take a walk in the real world.* Instead, to make up for his earlier, tactless remark, he said, "He'd still be your dad. You'd still love him. Blood is thicker than spilled blood—that's the bottom line."

She was appalled by his assumptions. "What happened to you, David?"

As usual, the reproach in her voice infuriated him, made him feel less than he was. Somewhere along the line she'd gotten so bloody high-minded. Or perhaps she'd always been like that, and he'd simply outgrown her relentless sense of integrity. In either case, he was damn sick and tired of her tiresome lectures about morality.

"Maybe I grew up," he said sourly.

"Did you? That sounded like something Harry would say, not you."

"Hey, I'm not taking my father on as a client. You are, right? Right!"

Needing to have the last word, he answered his own question. The sound of his slamming car door rang out like a shot.

Clutching her elbows for warmth, Ann glared at the car as it sped off into the deepening late-afternoon dusk. *Asshole.* At least he'd gotten one thing straight: She was going to be representing Mike.

Had there ever been any doubt about that?

CHAPTER

George's motto was, Expect the worst, and you'll never be disappointed. Ann generally disagreed with such negative thinking. But this evening, she could see the wisdom of her friend's philosophy. Expecting the worst after a disastrous day, she was pleasantly surprised when the evening took a turn for the better.

Papa and Mikey had decided to take charge of dinner. So they informed her after she tracked them down in the kitchen, whispering conspiratorially over a bowl of popcorn. She'd only get in their way, so they kindly suggested she disappear while they created their Hungarian gourmet masterpiece.

Ann knew she'd pay at the other end when she'd be left with a sinkful of pots and pans to wash up. But they both looked so sweet and determined, she could hardly squelch their enthusiasm. Besides, the prospect of a couple of hours of peace and quiet was far too tempting to resist. So she went off to her room, checked in with the office to make sure no crises were brewing, then settled into the tub for a long, soothing bath.

Dinner was delicious—chicken paprikas, done to moist,

golden brown perfection, and Mike's favorite diced potatoes drenched in paprika and garlic and smothered in onions. He'd learned to cook after Ilona's death from the neighborhood ladies, who'd showed him how to make the most basic of the Hungarian dishes he loved.

Over the years he'd expanded his repertoire, learning along with Ann when she was old enough to be trusted in the kitchen. These days he seldom bothered to make the effort, but when he was in the right mood, he could still put together a meal worth waiting for.

By the time they had called her in to eat, the dining-room table was already set, and Mikey stood by his chair, beaming with excitement. Ann opened a bottle of wine to drink with dinner and poured Mikey half a glass, which he was always permitted at family celebrations. For some reason, tonight seemed to qualify as a special evening, one she knew she'd long remember, though she wasn't sure what they were celebrating. Togetherness, perhaps. Family solidarity. Their love for one another. Papa's faith in her ability to exonerate him. Her belief in his innocence.

All three got slightly tipsy, and Papa began talking about the old days, when Ann and Karchy were little. Ann sat back and watched Mikey listen with wide-eyed, rapt attention. He seemed never to tire of hearing these family stories, especially when the joke was on his mother.

"More, Grandpa, tell me more." Mikey kept egging him on. And Mike managed to dredge up yet another tale of how Karchy had outwitted his sister. After all he'd been through today, it was good to see Papa so animated. Trust Mikey to bring out the best in him. She felt blessed by this moment—blessed to have such a father and such a son.

They ate chocolate ice cream for dessert. Then it was time for Ann to tackle the dishes and for Mikey, finally, to do his homework. Mike was staying over, as he often did when he came for dinner. He settled himself in front of the TV in the family room with a promise to come in and kiss Mikey goodnight when he was ready. As usual, he dozed off in his chair but roused himself in time to shuffle into the boy's bedroom after Ann had turned out Mikey's light.

"You sleepin'?" he whispered.

Mikey made room for his grandpa on the bed and propped himself up on one elbow. "No."

"You say you prayer?"

"Yeah," Mikey lied. He didn't really pray anymore—not unless he counted crossing his fingers and making a wish when he really wanted something. But his mom had explained that even though she and his dad didn't believe you had to say formal prayers to God, Grandpa did. So if Mikey wanted to tell what Mom called a "white lie," in order not to upset Grandpa, that was okay with her.

"Good," said Mike. "I say always prayer. Say the prayer, do the pushup. Maybe it do good, maybe no. You gotta pass, run, try everything for the touchdown."

Mikey smiled in the darkness. He loved when Grandpa talked man to man like this and gave him advice, like he was the coach of a football team. Like the Chicago Bears. *Yeah!*

"You do you pushup?"

"No."

"C'mon, c'mon," Mike said, pulling back Mikey's covers. "We do the pushup."

"Right *now*?"

"Ya, ya, come on, right now," Mike said, rolling up the sleeves of his dress shirt. "Healthy body makes healthy spirit."

Mikey was laughing as he climbed out of bed. Pushups were Grandpa's favorite exercise. He'd showed Mikey how to do them a million times. And every time he said the same thing: Healthy body makes healthy spirit. But the pushups were hard to do. You had to concentrate on not moving your hands and bending your arms just the right way. Mikey figured he could keep his body healthy by playing basketball and football.

"Put foot all way down, like I show you," urged Mike, checking Mikey's form.

Mikey craned his neck and imitated Mike as best he could. His mom was always telling Uncle Karchy that Grandpa wasn't as young as he used to be. But for an old guy, he sure was strong. Mikey kind of wished Grandpa would get tired and stop doing the pushups so that he could stop, too. Of course, it was fun to exercise with Grandpa, but it was more fun to snuggle up next to him in bed and tell jokes.

The bedroom was dark, except for the light that shone in from the hallway. Standing just outside, Ann heard her father counting out the beat, setting the pace for himself and Mikey. The shadow from the half-open door fell across their faces, obscuring their features. But she could make out Mikey's thin, short arms and legs, struggling to keep up with Papa's stockier, more muscular body.

Smiling at the sight, she wondered whether she should step in and say, Enough, time to go to bed. No, let them have the extra few minutes with each other. It would do them both good.

"Faster. Faster. Good! Mikey gettin' big, gettin' strong. Faster!" Papa was saying.

She shook her head as she walked into her bedroom. The man was a regular drill sergeant. She'd been spared the calisthenics, probably because she was a girl. When had he given up trying to get Karchy to do them?

Mikey collapsed on the floor as soon as he reached number ten, but Mike kept on going until he'd counted out twenty-five. He grinned triumphantly at his admiring grandson.

"God, you're strong, Grandpa," Mikey marveled.

"Gettin' weaker every day." Mike was panting to catch his breath.

Mikey hooted at the joke. "No, you're not!" he protested. Not his grandpa!

Mike pretended to groan as he moved closer to Mikey. "Hey," he said, still huffing for air, "you wanna talk about the TV?"

"Yeah, okay." Mikey shrugged, as if it didn't much matter to him.

Mike wasn't buying that for an instant. He peered through the darkness at his grandson's face, trying to get a clue to what he was really feeling and thinking. "It no me they talkin' about," he said slowly, groping for the right words. "They make mistake. It no me. I don't do nothin' wrong. Don't kill nobody. That no you grandpa."

Mikey plucked nervously at a piece of loose skin on his upper lip. "I know, Grandpa." He nodded without looking up, wishing Grandpa would change the subject. He didn't want to talk about this dumb Nazi stuff. Of course it was a *mistake*. He had the best grandfather in the whole world, and nobody had to tell him that Grandpa was innocent. He already *knew* that.

His grandfather seemed to read his thoughts, because the next thing he said to Mikey was, "Naw, hell, you don't know nothin' yet. I'm gonna prove. I *gotta* prove. *Then* you know."

Now he had the boy's attention. Mikey was staring at him wide eyed and open mouthed, with the same look he got when he was concentrating hard on one of his video games.

"Somebody say you somethin' about you grandpa," Mike went on, "you say, 'Fuck you, jump in the lake'—"

"I can say *that*? The *F*-word?" Mikey could hardly believe his ears. His mom hated when he cursed, and the *F*-word was the most forbidden of all curses. But now Grandpa was actually giving him permission to use it.

"Ya." Mike lowered his voice. "You no tell Mama, though. *Secret*, okay?"

Mikey considered the question seriously. This was no

small secret to keep from his mother. But wasn't it almost the same as telling Grandpa a white lie about prayers? It was keeping quiet about something so as not to upset a person you really loved. He was getting good at that. Sometimes his dad said stuff about his mom that Mikey didn't repeat when he got home because he knew it would only get her mad.

So he decided, okay, he could have this secret with Grandpa, and he nodded his agreement.

Mike smiled and raised his hand to do a high-five, lightly smacking his callused palm against Mikey's much smaller one. He was getting to be such a big boy. Smart, too, like his mother.

Mikey yawned and blinked his eyes, which were suddenly feeling very heavy, as if they might shut down on him any minute. Already almost asleep, he leaned his head against his grandfather's shoulder and momentarily fell out. Then, like a puppy waking up for a quick stretch, he shook himself awake.

"Grandpa? Love you," he mumbled sleepily, and he reached out for a hug.

Ann had been trying to read. But their conversation, which she couldn't help but overhear, had distracted her. Mikey was so much like her. He always needed time to turn a question over in his mind before he could say yes. Papa had told her that Mama had been the same way, that she'd taken her time saying yes when he'd proposed. Now, as Mike walked past her room, Ann quietly called, "Papa?"

He stopped in her doorway and waved goodnight.

"I'll represent you, Papa," she said.

"Good, tubusom."

"Just 'good,' that's all?"

"Ya, good," he repeated. What more was there to say?

Ann sat up and studied his worn, weary face. Did he understand what lay ahead of them? She thought not. She dreaded it, but what choice did they have? Who better than his own flesh and blood could protect him in court, make sure he was allowed to stay in America, where he belonged? He would be fighting a life and death battle, against fanatics whose reasons for hating him weren't even personal, which made them all the more dangerous.

"I'm going to have to know everything about you, Papa. I have to know everything they might know," she explained. "I want you to stay with us for a while. We can work better here."

Mike stared at her quizzically. "I got my own house."

She shook her head and brushed away the hair that fell over her eyes. "It's going to be a lot of work, Papa. It's not going to be easy."

He smiled tiredly, and suddenly he looked so fragile and vulnerable that Ann felt their roles had been reversed. She had become the parent-protector, he the frightened child. Swiftly she got out of bed and went to him, putting her arms out to hug and comfort him.

"It'll be okay, Papa," she promised, holding him tightly.

"No, Anni," he said, staring bleakly into the future. "I live too long. It never gonna be okay again."

The next several days were madness. Ann's home phone didn't stop ringing. Half the newspaper reporters in the greater Chicago metropolitan area seemed to be covering the story, not to mention the television and radio stations. And all of them needed "just a few minutes of your time, Ms. Talbot, to ask you just a couple of questions about your father."

But when she started getting crank calls and obscene hate messages, she decided the hell with it and unplugged her answering machine. Mikey didn't need to hear that kind of crap. For that matter, neither did she. What she needed was peace and quiet to organize her case, but peace and quiet were in short supply, even at work, as soon as the media had figured out she was the Talbot in the firm's name.

Reporters lay in wait for her like sharks sniffing out freshly spilled blood, their notebooks and mikes at the ready. Her curt "no comment" did nothing to discourage them. Apparently they assumed that if they were persistent enough, she'd change her mind and answer their questions.

Fat chance of that, she thought gloomily as she turned into the parking lot next to her building on Dearborn Street. She'd learned long ago in the public-defender's office that journalists were a greedy lot, not easily sated. No matter what choice morsels she might offer them, they'd only hunger for more. Better to keep quiet and hope that they'd lose interest.

She glanced out the windshield, on the lookout for a couple of national tabloid stringers who had taken to lurking in front of her office. No one seemed to be hiding in the bushes. Maybe they'd finally given up.

Grabbing her briefcase, she slid out of the car, locked the door, and walked briskly toward her building. A shrill, raucous whistle suddenly split the air. Ann kept moving without so much as a glance in the whistler's direction.

"What a honey!" yelled her admirer.

Was the press stooping to a new low in vulgarity? *Screw you*, she silently cursed him.

"Hey, stuck-up!" called a familiar-sounding voice. "Don't you even talk to your own brother?"

Laughing at her paranoia, Ann turned and smiled at Karchy. She must be in bad shape if she hadn't recognized his distinctive wolf call. "What are you doing here?" she asked, giving him a hug and a kiss. "Why didn't you come in?"

"Because I'm not dressed for goin' in, that's why." He pointed to his parka, grungy overalls, and workboots, then handed her a sheet of paper. "I got this list of names you wanted from the mill."

She glanced at the list of people who'd said they'd be

willing to vouch for Papa's good character. Most of them had met Papa just after he'd arrived in Chicago. Some of them might even have known him in Hungary. Their testimony ought to count for something . . . she hoped.

Karchy was disappointed by her reaction. He'd collared a lot of Mike's old buddies, and every one of them had promised to do whatever he could. So how come she was looking like she still wasn't sure this would do the trick? Nervous, he demanded, "You gonna get him outta this, Annie, ain't ya? This ain't him."

"Yes, sure." She nodded, wondering whether she could share her fears with Karchy.

"You better. This was a bar fight and he needed me, I'd slice some nuts. He busted his gut in that fuckin' mill—thirty years he did it. He didn't do it for himself, Annie."

"I know that," Ann reminded him, exasperated.

Sometimes Karchy could be a bully. "You know that, huh?" Then he relented. "I know you know that."

He glanced at his watch. His shift started in forty-five minutes, and if he didn't get going he'd be late. But all the bad press was making him half crazy. He wished it were he, not Annie, slugging it out with the other side. They were fools and cowards who knew *nothing*! Probably had holes in their pants where their balls should be.

Annie meant well, but she was a girl, sweet and polite. And this fight needed a man's words. "You know how to slice some nuts, Annie? That's what I want to know." To illustrate his point, he grabbed at his crotch.

Ann grimaced and stuck her hands in her coat pockets. It had turned sharply colder, not the kind of weather to be standing around outside. She wanted to be in her office, her fingers wrapped around a cup of hot coffee, far away from Karchy and this ridiculous conversation. "Why are you always so . . . crude?"

"You know any way of slicin' nuts without it bein' crude? You better get crude, Annie. You better get real crude."

He nodded grimly, and suddenly she'd had about as much of his advice as she could take for one morning. Okay, so he meant well, but he was making her feel as if this mess were *her* fault. That maybe she hadn't done enough to make the charges go away. Another minute and they'd be sparring with each other, like they were kids again, and that sure wasn't going to help Papa's case. But he ought to realize he wasn't the only one in the Laszlo family with streetsmarts.

She leaned up, kissed him quickly on the cheek, and before he could say another word, she marched off toward her office. Poor Karchy. She knew his anger with her was born of his sense of frustration and helplessness. Still, his criticism hurt. He was her big brother, and he could still get to her better than anyone else.

Bad enough she had to fight the government and all the nameless hatemongers. But Karchy, too?

Two cups of coffee later, Ann still couldn't concentrate enough to get any solid work done. She kept finding herself staring out the window, fervently wishing she could get her hands on the *real* Michael J. Laszlo, whoever he might be. Now, there were a pair of nuts that deserved to be sliced—for the crimes the government said he'd committed in Hungary *and* for the havoc he'd wreaked in her father's life.

She stood up with a restless sigh and prowled about her office, stopping to gaze absentmindedly at her diplomas, laminated and framed on the wall. University of Michigan, B.A. University of Chicago, LL.D. Tough schools. Impressive credentials. She'd worked damn hard to earn those initials after her name.

You didn't find very many first-generation Hungarian kids at the University of Chicago Law School. How many mill workers could afford to send their kids to private colleges? Of course, she'd chipped in as much as she could save from her summer and after-school jobs, but still her education had cost Papa plenty. Not that he'd ever once complained.

It had never occurred to her to wonder why he'd so willingly scrimped and saved, when he could as easily have tried to marry her off to one of the boys from the neighborhood or left her to struggle on her own if she wanted to go to college. Lots of her friends' fathers had done just that. But Papa had unstintingly given her every opportunity to prove she could be whatever she wanted in life. Such generosity spoke volumes about a man's character. She only hoped she could speak as eloquently on his behalf.

The back of her neck ached, as it always did when she hadn't made the time to drop by the gym. What with all the pressure she was feeling to tie up the loose ends on her pending cases so that she could focus on Papa's, she hadn't allowed herself the luxury of a run or a swim. But it was more than lack of exercise that accounted for her tension this morning.

She'd spent a good part of the previous night wide awake and staring into the darkness of her bedroom, attempting to plot her course for the next few weeks ahead. First and foremost, of course, was putting together the best possible defense for Papa. But there were other considerations as well. Her partners, for example. Both Mack and Sandy had offered to do whatever they could to help.

But was it fair to involve them and the firm in what was really her family's business? She thought not. Such a small firm as theirs couldn't afford the false stigma of "Nazi sympathizer."

When she marched into Mack's office before lunch and said as much to her partners, they shook their heads in disbelief.

"I don't get it. This is *your* office. This is *our* firm. We're partners," Sandy reminded her.

"I don't want you to lose clients because I'm working out of here on this case," Ann said, spelling it out for him again. "Come on, Sandy, just let me do you a favor, okay?"

Sandy stared at her as if she had begun babbling in tongues. "No! Where the hell are you going to work?"

"I can work out of my ex-father-in-law's office," she said. Not that she'd exactly asked him yet, but she was quite sure he'd agree. Harry was perverse enough to get a kick out of saying yes to just such a request.

Sandy rolled his eyes incredulously and turned to Mack, who simply shrugged his shoulders, as if to say, don't look at me.

"I love it," Sandy hooted. "Harry Talbot, the *distinguished* Harry Talbot. He was in the O.S.S. during the war, you know. Then the O.S.S. becomes the C.I.A., and they set up their first spy apparatus in Europe by putting a bunch of Gestapo guys on the payroll. Word is that Harry used to sip his bourbon with Klaus Barbie."

Ann glared at Sandy. He was a great guy, but he had the most irritating habit of setting himself up as an expert on subjects he knew not a goddamn thing about. Who the hell did he think he was, telling her about David's father? "The word I heard is that Harry sipped his bourbon with senators, congressmen—I heard he even sipped bourbon in the White House now and then. I never heard anything about Klaus Barbie."

"I said," Sandy reminded her with a smirk, "he was 'the *distinguished* Harry Talbot,' didn't I?"

Mack leaned back in his chair and listened to her go at it with Sandy. He'd thought all along that Ann was making a big mistake in defending her dad. But, figuring it was none of his business, he'd kept his mouth shut. Now he realized he had to say his piece, because she looked like she could be stepping into big trouble, and nobody else was yelling at her to watch out.

Motioning to Sandy to be quiet, he said, "You do *yourself* a favor, Annie. Get somebody else to represent your father. Get that guy in Cleveland—he handled that

Demjook guy, Demjoke, whatever the sucker's name was."

Ann played nervously with the file folders on his desk, straightening them into neat piles. "He wants *me* to represent him."

"Aw, man." He waved his hand dismissively. "What do you know about what happened forty years ago in some goddamn part of the world you never even been to? What the fuck does anybody know about their parents?" he asked rhetorically, warming to his subject. "Have you ever thought about how he makes love? What his fantasies are?"

"I know," she retorted. She appreciated his concern, but it was misplaced. "*I know him.* He raised me, Mackie. My mom died when I was two. . . . He was my mom and my dad and my best friend, always. We never had any secrets between us. *Never.*"

Mack saw the look in Ann's eyes and realized he could keep talking from now until forever and she'd still do things her way—she was that stubborn. But he figured he owed her one more try, so he gave her the benefit of his accumulated wisdom, for whatever it was worth. "Nobody knows. Nobody. You know nothing. The more we love them, the less we know about their lives."

She glared at him, knowing there was some truth to his statement but not wanting to hear it.

"I still don't understand why you can't work out of here," Sandy interjected.

Mack could see he'd gotten exactly nowhere with Ann. Trying to lighten the atmosphere, he joked, "Maybe she's afraid somebody gonna be goin' through her drawers."

"Nobody can get into those drawers. It's her goddamn Catholic upbringing. It's more repressive than AIDS." Sandy chuckled at his own wit, and Mack joined in.

"Very funny, Sandy." Ann wrinkled her nose in disgust. She loved her partners, but some days their humor was more junior high school than Mikey's.

They were still laughing and exchanging ribald looks when George poked her head in the office. She gave the men a look that said, Not one more word out of you two or you're dead meat, then turned to Ann. "He tellin' those princess jokes again? We goin' to lunch or ain't we?"

"We're going right now, George," said Ann, grateful for the interruption. She started out of the office without another word to her colleagues, but Mack called her back.

"Annie?"

She was about to tell him, Please, no more jokes. But he was already there. "It ain't funny, Annie," he said sympathetically. "It's Uncle Sam's big truck, comin' down full bore."

CHAPTER
6

Another night disturbed by dreams that raised more questions than she could answer. Ann woke up before the alarm rang, feeling gritty eyed and exhausted, and turned on the TV to catch the weather. The world outside her windows looked dark and discouraging. The forecast wasn't much more hopeful. Cold and windy. Possibility of snow flurries. Altogether an inhospitable, uninviting day—a day to snuggle in bed with a good book, a cup of coffee, and a box of chocolates.

Whoa, where did that fantasy come from? she asked herself as she stepped into the welcoming comfort of a hot shower. Maybe she should have thought longer about relocating her base of operations. In theory, it had seemed like a great idea to say yes to Harry Talbot's offer of space. This morning, as the reality hit her, she realized how much she would miss the warmth and familiarity of her own office—not to mention the support of her colleagues.

Still, as Harry had so astutely pointed out to her, whereas Jones, Lehman & Talbot depended on word of mouth and therefore had to be concerned with its reputation, Talbot & Talbot was protected by its size and stature as one of Chicago's top corporate law firms. Ann might not like their brand of law or the people they represented, but she'd be well served by Harry Talbot's willingness—some would say eagerness—to take on any opponent. And given that she was going up against the United States government, she'd be lucky to have him in her corner.

That didn't make her eager, however, to get herself set up in his shop. So it wasn't until early that evening that she finally made her way over to the nineteenth floor of the building on LaSalle Street where Talbot & Talbot was headquartered.

At Talbot & Talbot, no expense had been spared to create an ambience that exuded power and money. The name of the game was impress the prospective client, and Harry Talbot had given his designer carte blanche. David had bragged to Ann about the cost of the artwork hanging in the public areas and conference rooms. The furniture, mostly English and French antiques, was also worth a small fortune. The overall effect was that of a very exclusive private men's club, where members spoke in hushed tones about matters of the greatest import while servants hovered discreetly in the background, waiting to do their bidding.

The receptionist was elegantly dressed in pearls and a blue silk dress, and when she told Ann to go ahead back, her accent was English upper class. Ann shook her head amusedly as she admired the paintings in the hall that led to Harry Talbot's corner suite. Had they specially imported the woman for the job, or had she been provided by the interior designer, along with the thick carpeting and expensive wallpaper?

She still couldn't understand how David had opted to work in such an environment. How could he live with himself, defending big corporations, rather than real people, with real problems? It was her considered opinion that this level of luxury came with a heavy price tag, but far from feeling stifled by all the trappings, David claimed to be thriving.

The better question was, why did she care? Her close friends had pointed out to her that by clinging to the past she was keeping herself from moving forward. Let go of him, they'd urged her. He wasn't hers to wonder about anymore.

Good advice, Ann supposed. Easier to give than to follow. Because the question remained: How had David evolved into someone other than he'd been? Unless he'd always been that person and she hadn't seen it. But the same question arose: Why did she care?

Because he was my husband, she thought with a weary sigh. Because I want people to be who they appear to be. Because I hate unsolved puzzles.

The subject of her musings was at that moment standing in front of his father's well-stocked private bar, mixing a pitcher of martinis. Although normally a wine and beer man, when David drank with Harry, he showed his solidarity by opting for martinis, Harry's drink of choice.

He heard Ann's sigh even before she appeared in the doorway. It was a sound he recognized easily, having heard it often over the lifetime of their marriage—particularly at the end, when she seemed to have had a never-ending supply of reasons to be exasperated with him.

This was his turf, however, he reminded himself. He was the home team, she was the visitor. For once she wasn't going to make him feel as if he'd crossed over to the enemy lines. In fact, he was quite enjoying the irony of the situation: Miss Holier than Thou coming to pray at the temple of the infidels. And all because of Mishka, who'd made no secret of his feelings that his daughter could do better than marry a Talbot. Funny how these things turned out.

Was he bitter? He supposed so—a little, anyway. His ex-wife was beautiful, smart, and sexy, and he still had dreams about making love to her. But some part of him hated her for not accepting the man he'd become, the man he was comfortable being. Other people—*lots* of other people—thought highly of him, both personally and professionally. Only Ann seemed unable to make peace with the direction his life had taken.

Still, he agreed with his father's decision to offer her the use of Talbot & Talbot's resources, if only for Mikey's sake. Hell of a crazy thing if his own son were branded the grandson of a Nazi. The kid didn't deserve that label, and it behooved the Talbots to throw their support behind Ann so she could beat the charges. Because whether or not Mishka was guilty—and David would have bet money he wasn't—if anyone could win this battle, it was Ann.

He almost told her so when she appeared in the doorway, looking as tired and grim as he'd ever seen her. But the core of anger between them was still too deep and raw, and he'd learned from bitter experience the need to protect himself from her sharp tongue. So when she threw out a casual "Hi, David," all he did was wave a bottle of gin in her direction.

"I was just going to call you," he said as she wearily plopped herself down on Harry's sofa. "There's a laser display at the museum this weekend. I thought I'd take Mikey. You two have any plans?"

The weekend? She could hardly think past tomorrow. "No, that's fine," she agreed, knowing Mikey would be delighted to have extra time with his dad.

David gave the martinis one last brisk stir. "You want a silver bullet?"

Knowing she still had hours of work ahead of her, she nevertheless nodded yes. She rarely drank martinis; their peculiar appeal had always eluded her. But years back, when she first began visiting the Talbot home, she'd forced herself to acquire a tolerance for them. Martinis were what David's father traditionally served before dinner—unless there was reason to celebrate, in which case he uncorked a bottle of champagne.

73

Thinking she'd fit in better if she followed their customs, she'd learned to swallow the dry, slightly bitter mixture without puckering her lips. The taste was sharp and unyielding, much like the person David had become. Much like Harry Talbot, for that matter, for all of his exquisite good manners and affability.

David had once described his father as the kind of man who could smile and shake your hand, then stab you in the back when your guard was down. Certainly Harry had never been less than courteous to her, but she always kept one eye out for his knife.

Harry was an intimidating presence whose steel-trap mind and stinging way with words had earned him a national reputation as an attorney who fought to win. Surprisingly, he got on well enough with her own father. Over the years they'd established an easy camaraderie that had outlasted her divorce. Ann had never understood what, besides Mikey, they found in common to talk about, and seeing them together always made her think of the odd couple: the peasant and the aristocrat. Mike, so rumpled and weatherbeaten; Harry, the very picture of sartorial grace and elegance in his custom-made Savile Row suits.

Now, as he appeared in the doorway, he reminded her as always of a character out of a Louis Auchincloss novel— the venerable senior law partner. Though already in his midseventies, Harry showed no interest in retiring or even slowing down. He still stood tall and erect, and only his full head of white hair hinted at his true age.

"Hello, Harry," she said, getting up and offering her cheek to be kissed.

A hint of Harry's cologne wafted toward her. "We've finally gotten you to join us, have we?" Harry said smugly, nodding a greeting to his son. "After all those years of your ethnic airs about working up here—here you are."

He strode over to the bar and glanced disdainfully at David's drink. "How can you make a decent martini without sweet vermouth?'' he demanded of his son. ''Sometimes the apple really does fall far from the tree.''

David rolled his eyes at Ann as Harry made a great show of mixing a fresh pitcher of drinks. This was a longstanding argument between father and son, and normally Ann would have responded with some appropriately sympathetic gesture. But this evening she didn't have the patience to play the game.

''We've got our judge, Sam Silver,'' she announced, eager to hear Harry's reaction. Whatever her disagreements with his personal or business philosophy, she valued Harry's legal acumen, especially when it came to courtroom politics. After fifty years of practicing law in Chicago, he could rattle off the names and prejudices of the local justices like a kid quoting baseball statistics.

What he had to say now, however, wasn't encouraging. ''You would've had a much better chance with jurors,'' he informed her. ''You could've unleashed your entire black bag of courtroom theatrics. And the notion of a daughter defending her father would have struck some people as heartrending. It's not going to strike Sam Silver as heartrending, that's for sure.''

''Sam Silver? Are you kidding me?'' David threw in his two cents.

Ann ignored him and turned her attention to Harry. ''All I know about him is that he's fair.''

Harry eyed Ann speculatively. It took guts to do what she was doing, and he admired her loyalty. But Ann was made of strong stuff. She was a good girl and a hell of a terrific lawyer.

She could be attractive, too, if she'd do a little something with her hair and makeup and buy herself some decent clothes. She used to be a lot prettier and looser. Since the divorce she'd gotten so dowdy and serious.

''Sure Sam's fair,'' Harry agreed, sipping his drink. ''There's none better on the federal bench.''

Ann stared unseeing at the music box in front of her,

one of Harry's favorites from his collection. It was ornately carved in an early American motif and festooned across the top with prancing racehorses. Finally, she looked up and said, "I don't care that he's Jewish. I care that he's fair."

"Sure, I care that he's fair. And in this case I care that he's Jewish," Harry calmly replied, marveling at her naivete.

"He'll probably bend over backwards, though. He'll have to," David put in.

Harry ignored his son and addressed himself to Ann. "You think you can claim bias and have his verdict put aside? Maybe. But it's risky."

She blinked in surprise. "I wasn't thinking that at all," she admitted. Nor was it her style of practicing law. She intended to win her case on merit, not legal trickery.

"You don't have a prayer, you know that, don't you?" Harry asked, walking over and putting his hand on her shoulder. "You know what the Holocaust really is? It's the world's sacred cow. These people, the Holocaust survivors, they've got haloes around their heads. They're secular saints, that's what they are. You'd be better off grilling Mother Theresa."

He knew these were harsh words, but she needed a strong dose of reality. Evidently all they were serving in her neck of the woods were fantasies and fairy tales about the power of truth and justice. But truth could be interpreted—or misinterpreted—any number of which ways. Unfortunately, that was one lesson that couldn't be taught in law school. Sometimes you had to learn it the hard way. And sometimes, if you were smart enough to keep your ears and eyes open, you figured it out without getting kicked in the butt.

Ann was staring resolutely at the music box, and the tight set of her lips told him she hadn't much liked his lecture. No doubt she was angry that he'd been so blunt. People didn't appreciate candor because they were frightened by it. They wanted their facts to look and sound pretty—like his music boxes. But these little horses, for all their elaborate detail, would never go anywhere but in circles. And when he pressed the switch to turn on the music, as he did now, the sound was tinny, not true.

"How's my grandson?"

"Fine," she said curtly, wishing she'd never come to Harry with her problem. Her father's case was not about the Holocaust or survivors. It was about bureaucratic errors and mistaken identities—and the far-reaching hand of a foreign government intent on ruining the life of a former citizen.

"Fine? That's all you ever say about him. Is he playing with himself yet? You find any dirty pictures in his wallet?" Harry chuckled.

Dirty pictures? Mikey was eleven years old. "I don't look in his wallet," she retorted.

"Well, look," Harry suggested, shrugging into his overcoat. He headed for the door, clapping David on the back as he passed him. "By the way," he said casually, "Mishka didn't do it, did he?"

He was gone before she had a chance to open her mouth.

Two large cartons filled with manila files were waiting for Ann in the mostly bare office that was to be her temporary headquarters at Talbot & Talbot. Some eager-to-oblige secretary had apparently undertaken the task of unpacking the boxes, then stopped midway through, no doubt daunted by the task. A stack of yellow legal pads, two packages of pens, and a cupful of sharpened pencils had also been left for her. A phone, a lamp, and a large wastepaper basket completed the decor.

The previous occupant—most likely a young associate who'd probably seen the sun rise through the window more times than he or she cared to count—had left behind a couple of posters and, on the back of the door, a dartboard. Ann couldn't help but wonder if a picture of Harry

Talbot had graced the very center of the board. He was famous for treating his associates like skinheaded Marine recruits at boot camp. The men and women who made partner at Talbot & Talbot had earned their stripes the hard way. The vibes in the room spoke of many late hours and much mental anguish.

A veritable mountain of government documents was stacked atop the desk, awaiting Ann's perusal. She pulled up her chair and glanced at one pile of folders, stamped with "United States Government—Office of Special Investigations." Another folder read "United States Department of Justice. *The United States vs. Michael J. Laszlo.*"

Where to begin? she wondered, feeling overwhelmed by the sheer volume of material. An impressive amount of work must have gone into researching and compiling all this data. Too bad the sum total of it had pointed the government investigators in the altogether wrong direction. Now, thanks to their stupidity, she was left with the job of sifting through these horror stories, all of which supposedly featured her father in the starring role. And for this she paid a not inconsiderable amount of taxes every April?

The pale late-afternoon light was fading fast as she switched on the desk lamp. Might as well get on with it, she told herself. Find the clues that had misled the government, then track them herself until they led to the man who *really* was guilty of perpetrating these crimes.

Pen in hand, she flipped open the first folder and began to read the case against Michael J. Laszlo. By the third page, feeling slightly light-headed, she had to sit back and take several deep breaths before she could continue. She turned and stared out the window, seeing neither the gray dusk nor the lights from the windows across the way.

The initial affidavit, the one Papa himself had received, had used phrases like "crimes against humanity" and "unconscionable acts of violence and sadism." Ugly as the words were, they were abstract concepts that she'd pushed away, certain they had nothing to do with Papa or anyone else she knew.

Now she was discovering what was actually meant by such phrases. The notebooks were filled with the sworn statements of victims and eyewitnesses who were unsparing in their descriptions of brutality the likes of which she'd never even imagined. Why had no one warned her? Why hadn't anyone said, take care, this is strong stuff you're coming up against?

She forced herself to keep going through the notebooks, to continue making notes. *For Papa*, she told herself.

"Holocaust survivors," Harry called the men and women who had offered these soul-searing testimonies. But what did she actually know of the Holocaust, beyond what she'd learned in school about Hitler and his plan to exterminate the Jews? The Nazis were a terrible, sick aberration; genocide and concentration camps were too horrible to contemplate and were better left forgotten.

Except that these survivors couldn't forget. Even now, more than forty-five years later, they professed to recall in excruciating detail every grotesque humiliation, every act of sadism and murder. Reading their depositions, Ann felt as if she were peering over the brink, staring into the jaws of hell. Because certainly the incidents they were describing could not have taken place in the world as she knew it. People simply didn't treat other people with such flagrant disregard of humanity. Only monsters could be capable of committing such acts.

Papa was no monster. He was a loving, kind man. The worst that could be said of him was that he had a temper that occasionally got the better of him, and sometimes he could be crude and less than tactful. The same was true, however, of Harry Talbot, but that didn't make either of them Nazi collaborators, saluting "Heil Hitler" and torturing Jews.

Nevertheless, the voices of these elderly men and women were too compelling to ignore. Losing track of time and place, she immersed herself in their memories. And emerged, much later, hurting and crying for their pain. It made sense that after so many years, they still hungered for retribution. Such evil shouldn't go unpunished.

Nobody was served, however, by punishing the wrong man. *That only compounds the evil*, she wrote in large letters. *The innocent man becomes the victims' victim.*

The structure of Papa's defense was beginning to take shape.

Taking a sip of tepid coffee, she turned to the next page and glanced at what looked to be a copy of some sort of identification card. The picture on the card was blurred and fuzzy, but she could nevertheless make out the face of a handsome young man, resolutely staring into the eye of the camera.

She examined the page more carefully, slowly puzzling out the Hungarian words, saying them aloud to make sure she was reading them properly. Then she took an even closer look, and her case came crashing down around her.

Happy hour was in full swing at the Pewter Mug, the friendly, no-frills watering hole favored by the downtown legal crowd and financial types. Assistant D.A.s, public defenders, and buttoned-up law-firm associates stood two and three deep next to traders and investment bankers at the free hors d'oeuvres table, helping themselves to the Swedish meatballs and spicy chicken wings, which, in a pinch, could pass for dinner.

Pitchers of icy-cold beer and dangerous margaritas were the specialties of the house, and the bar at the front of the room was doing standing-room-only business. Most of the wooden booths were taken as well, but Ann managed to grab one all the way in the back. She sank gratefully into the dark corner and ordered a glass of wine.

Late as it was, she couldn't go home just yet. She couldn't face either Papa or Mikey, not with this acrid taste of anguish in her mouth and her eyes aching from unshed tears. She was staring morosely into her glass, engrossed in her thoughts, when suddenly Jack Burke was standing over her.

"Can I buy you a drink?" he asked, waiting to be invited to sit down.

"No," she said curtly, hoping he'd disappear into whatever hole he'd come from.

Jack pretended hurt surprise. "What? Not even 'No, thank you'? Just 'No'?"

"I said no," she repeated, furious at him for not respecting her privacy.

"I see. You got my package." He sat down across from her and held up two fingers, signaling the waitress. "I'll buy you another drink. You look like you need it."

Even if she'd been dying of thirst in the desert, Jack Burke was the last person on earth she'd want to buy her a drink. He had all but flat out admitted that he intended to destroy her father and ruin her family's happiness and honor. And now he had the goddamn nerve to sit there smirking, as if he expected her to thank him for the privilege of his company.

But since he'd forced his presence upon her, she supposed she should take advantage of the moment. Summoning whatever energy was left in her, she said, as calmly as she could, "You've got the wrong man."

Jack raised a skeptical eyebrow. "That's the perfect camouflage, isn't it? You raise some good, all-American kids, you avoid even any shadow of suspicion. *You're* his best alibi."

She was about to tell him he was full of shit when the waitress appeared with their drinks. Ann stared at hers, wanting it badly, but not wanting to take any favors from Burke.

He saw her reluctance and felt some sympathy for her. Whatever sins her father had committed, she was innocent. Those files must have made for devastating reading. He bet she could use a strong shoulder to cry on. Under other circumstances, he wouldn't have minded lending her his.

On the other hand, she was still claiming that Daddy was innocent. How much would it take before she stopped lying to herself and faced up to the truth? Deciding to give her a push in that direction, he pointed to her glass and urged, "Come on, drink it. It's not every day you find out that Papa's a monster."

Ann suddenly understood how anger could drive people to kill. He was taunting her. He was *enjoying* her pain. The man was sick. Maybe that was why he spent his life hunting down other sickos. He was looking for kindred spirits. She, however, had no such sick need. She threw down some money for her drinks, gathered up her coat and bag, and got up to leave.

Jack had other ideas. He wanted to talk to her—here, outside the courtroom, on neutral ground. He'd asked some of his Chicago lawyer friends about her, and everyone had said the same things: She was smart and honest and a formidable opponent. Jack wanted her on his side; he wanted her to see that she couldn't support her father's lies. Because to do so would make her guilty of the same deception.

Hoping to persuade her to stay, even for five more minutes, he reached across the table. She flinched as if his fingers were contaminated with deadly poison. "Maybe violence runs in the family," he lashed out.

"Fuck you!" she spat.

"I don't think so," Jack retorted, regretting his earlier sympathy. "You'd want to be on top all the time, wouldn't you?"

Pushed to the limit of her self-control, Ann swung at him with every ounce of energy she had left in her. But Burke was faster. He grabbed her arm and held it tightly. "When you see him tonight, think about that trick he did with the wires. You remember that part, don't you?" he sneered, his eyes glittering with hatred.

Ann gasped for breath, fighting not to break down. That would come later, when she was alone. Now all she wanted was to get away from his venom. She tore herself free of his grasp and hurried out of the room without another backward look. The next time they faced each other, in the courtroom, she'd be better prepared to fight back.

Once safely inside her car, however, Ann let go and cried. Tears streamed down her cheeks until she could taste the salt on her lips. She wept for the Holocaust victims whose stories she'd read today and would never forget. She wept for her father and for what Jack Burke was saying about him. And she shed a few tears for herself, as well, because though she wasn't usually given to self-pity, tonight she felt very sorry for herself.

She was exhausted and lonely and desperately in need of someone she could trust—and she couldn't think of a single person with whom she could share her burden. Certainly not Papa. Not Karchy, either, who would tell her she'd lost her mind if she even so much as hinted that maybe . . . just maybe . . . Papa was guilty.

No! It was impossible! Burke was playing mind tricks on her. Like any sharp lawyer, he'd picked up on her vulnerability and tossed his barbs at her as if they were so many poison darts. Shame on her for leaving herself undefended. She had to be stronger, more resolute, if she were going to win this battle. He'd shown himself to be a formidable opponent—armed and dangerous.

She could be dangerous, too, especially when she was protecting her own. Because whether Papa was guilty or innocent—and at the moment, she wasn't sure which way she would have voted—he was her father *and* her client. She wasn't about to let Jack Burke or anyone else ruin his life.

Or her life, for that matter. Pulling into her driveway, she checked her face in the rear-view mirror and saw a disaster staring back at her. But even worse than how she looked was how she felt—as if someone had punched her in the gut and knocked the wind out of her. And her instinct told her that things were only going to get worse.

As she unlocked the front door, the familiar sounds and aromas of home reached out to her like a warm, caressing blanket that she longed to grab hold of and cling to. But she couldn't permit herself that comfort until she'd confronted her father with what she'd learned today.

She needed answers from him to some very hard questions she'd been pondering all afternoon. She dreaded what lay ahead of her, dreaded the look on his face when she asked him, did he? was he? But she had no choice. Not if she wanted properly to represent him. Not if she wanted to live with herself and her conscience.

She went looking for Mikey and found him and his friend, Pete, sprawled on the floor of the family room, absorbed in Nintendo. In the few moments it took before he realized she was standing there, she watched him, her fierce video warrior.

He was growing so quickly that the jeans they'd bought in November were already too short. Any minute now and he'd be an adolescent. Then what would become of him? Would he lose his sweetness and begin to snarl at her because she was the enemy adult? When she looked at Mikey, she had no regrets whatsoever about having been married to David. If they could produce such a child—so sweet and steadfast and bright—then there must have been some rightness in their union.

With a grunt of satisfaction, Mikey plugged back into the real world and tore his gaze away from the TV screen. All wide-eyed innocence, he flashed his most charming smile at her. She saw right through his strategy of trying to deflect the inevitable scolding because he'd broken their rule about no videos before dinner. Tonight, however, she was too upset to care.

''Where's Grandpa?'' she asked him.

Mikey examined his mom more closely and realized

something was wrong. Her eyes were red and swollen, and there was black stuff under her eyes and on her cheeks. Plus she had a funny expression on her face, like she was about to cry but was trying very hard not to.

"He's in the kitchen," Mikey said nervously. Why wasn't she lecturing him about the Nintendo? It scared him when things didn't happen the way they were supposed to, because that's what had happened before his parents got divorced. They'd been so busy screaming at each other that they'd stopped yelling at him to pick up his toys or go to bed on time.

"I better go, Mikey," Pete announced.

Mikey waited for his mother to invite Pete to stay for dinner, but she just turned and headed off in the direction of the kitchen. Boy, he thought. If he ever forgot to say good-bye to one of *her* guests, she got good and mad at him for being rude. Now here she was, walking away without a single word to Pete.

Oh yeah, he decided, his hands prickling with tension. Something bad was definitely about to happen. He was pretty sure it had to do with the lies people were telling about Grandpa. He wished his mom would let him go talk to the judge. Because he'd get up in court and explain that he had the best grandfather in the whole world—and those Communists in Hungary who hated Grandpa could go to hell!

Mike loved cooking pork chops. He'd season them with plenty of paprika, garlic salt, pepper, and onions, roast them on the stove for an hour, and baste them when he thought of it with whatever wine or beer came to hand. His recipe was simple, delicious, and never failed—unless the chops got overcooked and tough, as they had this evening because Ann was late getting home. He'd twice already turned off the water for the noodles, and he'd even cut up the cucumbers for the salad—usually Ann's job.

Now, he impatiently stirred what was left of the sauce under the chops.

Reaching for more wine to salvage the chops, he caught sight of Ann in the doorway. All of the pent-up frustration of a worried father spilled out at her. "Where the hell you been?" he exploded. "I burn the pork chop. Lookit—"

Mike interrupted himself midsentence and stared curiously at his daughter, who looked pale and sick, as if she'd seen a ghost.

"Whatsamatter?" he demanded.

Ann shook her head, but he knew better than to believe her. She'd always held in her feelings, forcing him to guess when she was sick or frightened. Karchy spilled his guts like an old woman wanting to talk about her troubles. But Ann would keep her problems to herself, until he'd have to beg her to tell him what was wrong. Then all she'd say was what she said now.

"Nothing."

For Mikey's sake she sat down to dinner, though she had no appetite. Still she managed to swallow a few mouthfuls, just to reassure her son, who threw worried glances at her all through the meal. She forgot sometimes how sensitive he was to her moods. Had she been that tuned in to her father? Perhaps to his anger, which had erupted only infrequently. Otherwise, she'd taken for granted that Papa was there to depend on, and whatever he might have been feeling—loneliness, regret, disappointment—had been no concern of hers.

Now, however, the hidden, secret parts of his soul were very much her concern, and the confrontation that awaited them hung over her like a thunderstorm waiting to break. In the meantime, she performed all the dinner rituals on automatic pilot. She passed around the noodles, reminded Mikey not to talk with his mouth full, pretended to listen as he kept up a rapid-fire flow of conversation about the upcoming basketball tryouts at school.

Her heart ached to see how thrilled he was to have another man in the house again. He was so full of excitement as he explained to Mike his chances of getting picked for the first team. Poor kid. He'd already been through so much when she and David were breaking up. The last thing he needed was more turmoil in his life. As a parent, she was supposed to protect him from pain. Lately, she seemed to be falling down pretty badly on the job. Logic told her she wasn't responsible, but her guilt pushed her to give him an extra scoop of ice cream before she sent him off to do his homework.

Her gloominess was contagious. Mike avoided her for the rest of the evening, and Mikey was in bed and half asleep when she went in to kiss him goodnight. She envied his ability to fall out the instant his head hit the pillow. Tired as she was, she was too keyed up to sleep. So she opened a bottle of wine, grabbed a sweater, and snuggled into the couch on the glass-enclosed back porch.

It hadn't been cheap to winterize the porch, but the money had been well spent. Tonight, an almost full moon lit up the night sky. Gazing out at the snow-covered lawn and the lake beyond, she remembered what she liked about winter. On such nights, you could almost forget the cold and ice and think instead about coming back with rosy cheeks and tingling hands from an afternoon of skating or sledding, to curl up in front of a blazing fire and drink hot chocolate or mulled cider.

Not that she had much opportunity anymore for winter sports, but the image was cozy and comforting. The wine helped, too, warming her insides and numbing the edges of her confusion. She sipped it slowly, savoring the slightly spicy taste on her tongue, promising herself she'd stop before she got drunk.

"Anni?"

Mike's bulky body appeared in the shadows next to her. Shifting her legs, she made room for him on the couch. But instead of sitting, he moved closer to the window, appearing to study the landscape. His back still to her, he said quietly, "I go home tomorrow."

She wasn't surprised by his suggestion. She'd considered it herself. But she shook her head. "You can't. It's not safe."

Mike shrugged and turned to face her. "Just gonna pack clothes, bring here. Gotta meet George, give her stuff."

He heard her suck in her breath as he sat down next to her. He studied her face, but the shadows hid her expression. When she didn't speak, he reminded her, "I always tell something the matter, even when you no tell me."

"How would you feel if we had a Jewish judge?" she asked, dry-mouthed with nervousness.

Mike took his time answering. "You think it good idea? Funny idea, that sure."

"He's very fair. He's a good judge."

He felt her testing him. So. He'd understood that she would have to eventually, and he forgave her for not trusting him. "If you think, it okay."

Ann pushed herself away from the couch and stood up. She needed distance now, to ask the hard questions. Now it was her turn to hide her face, so he couldn't see how scared she was of what he might say. "Why didn't we ever have any Jewish friends?"

"How we gonna meet?" Mike hooted. "Our friends, we see at church on West Side. Jews live other side. At mill I got Jew friends."

She examined his statement, a geologist studying the layers of a rock formation. What lay on the surface told only half the story. "Why didn't you ever invite them to come over?" she asked him.

"They no invite *me* come over," Mike pointed out to her with easy logic. "Mill friends, your friends at mill, at bar after work, that's all."

Yes, that made sense. She had friends . . . other lawyers . . . whom she'd often gone to lunch and dinner with yet had never invited home. Of course, that had nothing to do with their religion. She couldn't have said whether they were Jewish, Catholic, or Protestant.

"University, you date the Jewish boys?" Mike asked.

She shook her head. "No."

"How come?"

"I don't know," she said slowly.

Mike leaned forward. "I tell you no date Jewish boy?"

"No."

"Then how come? You date lotta other boys."

She thought back to her college years, to the many nights she and her dorm mates had stayed awake until dawn, talking about boys, sex, politics, religion. They'd covered the spectrum of theologic belief; there'd even been one girl who called herself a Buddhist. But the men she'd gone out with? She couldn't remember one who was Jewish. Coincidence? Or had she deliberately avoided them, thanks to some implicit message from Mike?

"Tell me," she said, "about the Special Section, Papa."

"Special Section?"

"Yes, Papa," Ann prompted him, not daring to look at his face. "In the gendarmes there was a Special Section."

"Ya." Mike studied his sturdy workers' hands. "Nobody know too much about it. How many there are. Who is in." He stood up slowly and came to stand alongside her. "They Jew killers," he explained. "Close to SS, *Einsatzkommando*. I got nothin' do with them. I clerk in office."

Ann looked at him. "They have a photostat of a Special Section I.D. card with your signature and picture on it."

Mike made a low, growling sound in his throat. "It no possible!" He turned his head, ashamed for her to see him crying. "I no got nothin' do with them," he protested hoarsely. "How they can have I.D. card? It no possible!"

His anguish felt so genuine that she relented. "They don't have the I.D. card," she said, touching his arm. "They have a photostat of it."

89

"Photostat?"

She nodded, searching his face for the truth.

"Where they get this?" Mike asked suspiciously.

"The Hungarian government turned it over to them."

"Why they no give real card—why photostat—if they got the real?"

This was precisely what Ann had been puzzling over. "I don't know," she admitted.

"I know!" Mike announced. "Fake! They put my gendarme picture, my writing, to fake card." He smiled triumphantly at the clarity of his logic.

If only the matter could be so easily dismissed. The files, however, contained page after page of damning evidence. "They've got witnesses, Papa, who identify you," she said quietly, hating herself for having to tell him. "Killing people . . . shooting . . ."

"Bullshit! Communist say to them, better for you if you identify." He glared at his daughter, daring her to contradict him.

She wasn't about to call him a liar, however, not when she wanted desperately to believe him. Tired of playing devil's advocate, she asked, "Weren't there any records? There had to be some records about your assignment as a clerk."

"They gonna tell you they no got . . . lost in bombs. American drop bomb in war. I American, and I no can prove nothin' 'cause American drop bomb. Funny, ha?" He smiled ruefully.

Her only response was a strangled half sob.

"You upset."

"Yes," she whispered, finally giving in, wishing she were little again, so Papa could take her in his arms and promise that everything would be all right.

"You upset at *me*, Anni, or you upset at the case?" he asked gently, cupping her chin in his palm.

"It makes me sick, Papa," she declared, her voice thick

with emotion. "They took those people—women, children . . . They lined them up at the riverbank—"

"That's why I come America, Anni."

"It makes me ashamed to be . . . Hungarian, Papa," she said, voicing what she'd been feeling since she'd opened the notebooks earlier in the day and discovered that you didn't have to search far to find Dante's Inferno.

"You no Hungarian, Anni," he said, putting his arm around her. "You American, Anni. *We* American. We get away . . . all of that."

So he'd told her all these years. But he'd also told her that nationality wasn't something you could shed, like an unwanted piece of clothing. Hadn't he brought her up to believe that in her soul, she was a Hungarian as well as an American, whose rights were protected by the Constitution?

Now, though she hated herself for it, she couldn't help but wonder whether the sweet, safe promise of democracy had lulled him into believing that the past was merely a bad dream. What dark memories and horrors had her father put behind him when he'd fled to America? And did she really want such a question answered?

CHAPTER
7

"Ninety-four bottles of beer on the wall, ninety-four bottles of beer . . ." Mike sang loudly and wildly off key. Next to him in the front seat of his beat-up Chevy, Mikey beat his hand against the dashboard and jumped in to finish the verse.

Grandfather and grandson, both sporting Bears caps pulled down low over their foreheads, grinned at each other with the ease of two life-long comrades in arms. Whatever difficulties might lay ahead, for the moment, speeding along the Eisenhower Expressway, they were as carefree as two truant schoolboys, off on a lark.

Mikey flashed Mike an ear-to-ear grin. He loved visiting his mom's old neighborhood and poking around in his grandfather's house. Please, Grandpa, he'd begged. Can I come, too? I want to see George, and besides, you might need protection. Protection from whom? Mike had snorted with a smile that meant, Hurry up, get in the car.

The afternoon sun shone brilliantly in the cloudless blue winter sky, giving the illusion of warmth that was dispelled as soon as you stepped outside. But inside the Chevy, with the heater on high, they were warm and snug.

Turning onto his street, however, Mike discovered that some people had chosen *not* to be indoors on this cold winter day.

A scraggly group of picketers had gathered in front of his house, and as he got closer, he saw that they were carrying signs. Through the closed car windows, he could hear their muffled chant: "Laszlo is a murderer! Killer! Nazi! Send him back to Hungary!"

Mike slowed the car to a crawl and looked over at Mikey, whose eyes were as wide as saucers. "Maybe we oughta forget it," he suggested. "Go home."

Mikey clenched his fists in his lap, hating the ugly creeps who were marching back and forth along the sidewalk, insulting his grandfather. The picketers didn't scare him. He wanted to punch in their faces and scream bad names at them, so they'd know they better get the hell out of the West Side, where they didn't belong. "I'm not scared, Grandpa," he said grimly, tugging at his Bears cap.

"Me either," Mike agreed, wanting to set a good example for his brave little soldier of a grandson. A good officer, however, knew when to protect his troops, and he couldn't afford to take any chances with Mikey in the car. So instead of parking in front of the house as he normally would have done, he looked right and left. Then he made a quick U-turn in the middle of the street and headed around the corner to park in the back alley that ran behind his house.

Another car was already waiting there. Pulling up, Mike recognized George, who waved and quickly came over to join them.

"I gotta sneak in my own house like robber," Mike grumbled, taking the extra precaution of locking his car doors.

"It's white folks like you who ruin a nice integrated neighborhood." George laughed and said with a wink, "Hi, Mikey."

"Hi, George." Mikey smiled, happy to see George, whom he'd known all his life. She'd bought him his first teddy bear and showed him how to blow soap bubbles. She was one of his favorite people, because unlike most adults, she never talked down to him or made him feel stupid.

"Okay, Gypsy." Mike grinned. "You piss on the poor man. Everybody piss on the poor man. Gypsy, too."

All three of them joined in the laughter as they covered the short distance to the house. Their boots crunched loudly in the hard-packed, ice-covered snow that had fallen the previous day. Otherwise, the only sound were the barely discernible voices of the picketers, carried on the wind.

Mike fumbled with the key to the back door. Then he followed George and Mikey inside and bent to kick off his galoshes, happy to be in his own home again. When he picked his head up, Mikey was standing in front of the window in the living room, pulling the curtain back a couple of inches to get a better look at the marchers.

"Mikey!" he said, more sharply than he'd intended. "Don't go near the window."

"I'm not afraid, Grandpa," Mikey replied, caught up in his fantasy of throwing some punches and maybe bloodying a few noses.

The protesters must have been on the alert for signs of life, because the slight movement at the window immediately caught their attention. At once, they brandished their signs and intensified their shouts of "Killer! Killer! Nazi! Killer!"

Mikey squinted to read the slogans. He could make out some of them: "War Criminal Go Home!" "Nazi Killer!" "Six Million Died!" The rest he couldn't decipher. Six million *what* died? he wondered. Maybe his mother would know. He'd have to ask her when she got home from work.

From watching old movies, he knew that Nazis were scary men in uniforms who stuck out their arms every five minutes and, in thick German accents, barked, "Heil Hitler!" For sure, his grandfather wasn't a Nazi. These people outside on the sidewalk must be nuts. They couldn't even tell the difference between a German and a Hungarian accent.

George had gone off to the kitchen to boil some water for coffee. Now she appeared in the living room carrying a plateful of cookies and pastries she'd picked up at a nearby Hungarian bakery.

Mike smiled his appreciation. The cookies were Mikey's favorites. "I gonna get stuff you want—" he began.

Suddenly, an explosive *CRASH*! as a large rock hurtled through the window. A shower of shattered glass jumped out at him.

"Son-the-bitch!" Mike thundered. He jerked Mikey away from the window and pushed him into the corner, well out of harm's way. "You okay?" he demanded.

Mikey stared open mouthed at the rock, which had just missed his head by inches. He blinked back tears and nodded to let his grandfather know he wasn't a scared little baby. Had the rock been aimed at him or Grandpa? Either way, this was war—like in the books he'd read about the Wild West. The Indians were attacking, and the cowboys had to defend themselves and their homes.

Mike was on the same wavelength. With a stern glance at Mikey that said, stay put, he hurried to the front foyer closet and dug out Karchy's old baseball bat. Gripping it tightly in both hands, he held it up above his head and smiled grimly at Mikey and George.

George had her arms around Mikey, who was trembling like a scared animal. No wonder—what did he know about protests and rock throwing and people getting dragged away by cops?

"Stay cool," she warned Mike.

Mike hesitated a moment, then moved closer to the window and peered out at the protesters. Their mood seemed to have changed. Now, rather than parading neatly back and forth on the sidewalk, they were milling about noisily, taunting Mike to come out and talk to them.

"Talk?" he muttered. "I show them how I talk. With a baseball bat over their stupid heads I talk to them." He dangled the bat in front of him, swinging it gently and testing its heft. He could almost taste the pleasure of breaking some heads. . . . Self-defense, it would be. They'd thrown the first rock. He was only protecting his family and home.

While Mike was checking out the demonstrators, George was watching him. She didn't like what she saw. Alarm bells were ringing in her head, signaling trouble. Mike ought to have more sense than to wave that bat around in front of the window. That's how riots started. Those people out there only wanted to stir up a ruckus. They didn't want to *hurt* anyone.

Time to call for reinforcements. Ann should know that it was getting to look like high noon at the O.K. Corral outside her dad's place. Probably she ought to call the cops, too, just in case there was a showdown. "Where's your phone?" she asked.

"Kitchen," Mike grunted, not taking his eyes off the protesters.

George motioned to Mikey to come with her, but he stubbornly shook his head, *uh-uh*. If there was going to be action, he wanted to be in on it. He crept over to stand next to his grandfather, feeling safe as long as he was by his side.

In all Mikey's eleven years, nothing quite this exciting had ever happened to him. He couldn't wait until tomorrow to tell the kids at school. "And then my grandpa clobbered them. He was *awesome*." Maybe they'd even get their pictures in the paper or on TV. He looked again, hoping to spot some cameramen.

The group of protesters seemed to be getting larger and advancing steadily nearer. Those who'd been there all afternoon were cold and restless. The more militant among them weren't content to follow their original plan of a peaceful demonstration. The Nazi murderer Laszlo was right there, not a hundred feet away from them, barricaded inside his warm house. The hell with peaceful demonstration! Why not confront him and watch him squirm as he tried to lie his way out of the truth?

Someone thought he saw a flash of metal through the window. Instantly a rumor began to circulate through the group: He's got a gun. A couple of guns! The guy's an expert marksman. He personally shot thousands of Jews. Gunned them down in cold blood! Let's show this bastard he can't threaten us. He's got to pay for his crimes!

The sun was beginning to set, casting long, ominous shadows across the front lawn. The neighbors, returning from work, cast worried glances at the demonstrators and hurried into their houses. Almost everyone on the block was sympathetic to Mike. But nobody wanted trouble, and the crowd looked hostile and unruly.

The boldest of the demonstrators had dared invade Mike's yard, coming close enough that he could see their features. Anonymous faces, distorted now in masks of hatred and bitterness, scowled at him in the dimming light. Most were young, college-age kids. Several raised their fists and gestured to the others behind them: Forward! But no one seemed ready to take up the challenge. Still, Mike tightened his hold on the bat and cursed them bitterly under his breath.

Suddenly, from the back of the house, came a dull thud, followed by a series of ear-splitting crashes—metal ripping into metal.

"Oh, shit!" George exclaimed. She ran to the kitchen window with Mike and Mikey only a few steps behind her.

"Grandpa . . ." Mikey stared in horrified fascination at the furious mob that was venting its frustration by trashing Mike's trusty old Chevy.

Some of the rioters were swinging their wooden signs

against the car windows, shouting in triumph as they succeeded in shattering the windows and windshields. Others had come equipped with hammers and tire jacks, which they swung with abandon against the roof and sides of the car. Still others were making do with rocks they'd found in the alley to leave notice of their presence.

"Grandpa, what are they doing?" Mikey whispered, his voice rising in a frightened sob.

"You got insurance, don't you?" asked George.

Mike nodded wordlessly, sickened by this wanton destruction.

"Then you gonna make some money," she said drily. "I never been in no white riot before."

Mikey felt as if he were watching a movie about grownups who'd gone crazy or out of control and started doing things that normally weren't acceptable. If this *had* been a movie, he probably would have enjoyed the sight of them smashing the car, as if it were some old piece of junk that didn't belong to anyone.

However, the Chevy did belong to someone—namely, his grandfather. And Mikey had taken more rides in that car than he could ever remember. In fact, it was probably safe to say that he'd spent some of his best moments in the Chevy's front seat. So that as these—these *hooligans*, Grandpa had called them—continued to hack away at the Chevy, it was as if they were hacking off one of his own arms or legs.

Watching them willfully destroy a very important, special piece of his childhood, Mikey felt a murderous fire burning in his soul. He ached to lash out at these terrible people, to hurt them as viciously as they were hurting him and, worse yet, his grandfather. He didn't have to look at his grandfather's face to feel his suffering. At that moment, they were connected as surely as if they were Siamese twins who shared one heart.

In his confusion, he groped through his mental vocabulary to find the proper words that might bring a shred of comfort to his grandpa. But nothing in his short life, not even the pain of his parents' divorce, had prepared him for such an occasion. So there he stood, his face scrunched up to squelch the tears he refused to let flow, a small but powerful time bomb waiting to explode.

All he lacked was the match to set off the fuse, and that came a second later, with the unmistakable sound of more glass shattering in the living-room window. Mikey flinched. Then, as if to make up for having shown his fear, he whirled around and raced for the front door.

"Mikey!" screamed Mike, and he took off after him.

But Mikey had the advantage of youth. He had the door unlocked and flung open before Mike ever had a chance to stop him.

"Leave him alone!" Mikey yelled.

His adrenaline was pumping quarts of courage through his veins. Suddenly he wasn't the least bit afraid anymore. He was David, facing Goliath, armed with only his slingshot. He was Daniel in the lion's den. He could have slayed the dragon, could have singlehandedly conquered an entire army—all because he knew his cause was just and right.

"Leave him alone! He didn't do nothin'! Leave him alone!" His shrill voice pierced the early evening air, shocking the crowd into silence.

The picketers strained to get a better look at the young boy, standing like a stalwart sentinel on Mike Laszlo's porch, defending the old man's honor. You couldn't help but be impressed by his conviction or be touched by his sadly misguided intentions. A couple of the demonstrators let fall the snowballs they were getting ready to hurl at the window. The kid had taken the fun out of their impromptu target practice.

Indeed, the crowd might possibly have begun to disperse then. It was almost dark, and even the hardiest of the protesters were feeling the bite of the wind against their cheeks. They'd made their point. From here on in, Laszlo would realize he was a marked man, just as he'd once stalked and marked his victims. They could go home, get warm, eat their dinners. Put the Nazi out of their minds . . . until tomorrow, anyway.

They were about ready to break ranks—those closest to the street had already turned to go—when the front door was flung open again. This time the hateful monster himself emerged, a baseball bat in one hand. The implied threat of a weapon, rather than frightening the protesters, stirred their blood and reinvigorated their senses.

Forget about going home! A frenzied roar surged forward to greet Mike. He draped a protective arm around Mikey and lifted the bat skyward, as if daring the picketers to advance any further.

More provocation, too tempting to be ignored by the hotheads in the group who shouted their indignation and let loose a volley of rocks aimed directly at Mike. The barrage was badly aimed—few of the rocks even came close to the porch—but Mike was beyond making a distinction between accuracy and intent. He'd had it with these vermin who had trespassed on his private property and were menacing his grandson.

"Get outta here!" he bellowed. "Get the hell outta here!"

For his trouble, he was answered with another blast of rocks and stones. These landed nearer to their mark; several flew right past Mikey, who shrank further into the shelter of his grandfather's arms and began to cry. Suddenly, he'd had enough of being the brave little soldier. He was cold and scared. He wanted the protesters to disappear and leave his grandpa alone. Most of all, he wanted his mother.

As if by magic, in answer to Mikey's prayers, Ann's Volvo careened to a stop in front of the house. She was out of the car in a flash and running toward the house, spurred by the piteous tableau on the porch: Papa holding a baseball bat high up his head, like Moses holding the tablets of the Ten Commandments; Mikey, coatless and sobbing as he clung to his grandfather.

Not caring whose feet she trampled on, Ann pushed her way through the mob, calling, "Mikey, Mikey! I'm here, honey, don't worry!" Moments later she was on her knees, hugging him tightly in her arms, her tears mixing with his. She'd been frantic with worry ever since she'd gotten George's message: They're picketing your dad's house. Crowd looks angry.

Somebody—one of the neighbors, probably—must have called the police, because suddenly patrol cars were screeching down the street, blue lights whirring and sirens blaring. Nightsticks and bullhorns at the ready, the cops poured out of their cars and barked orders at the crowd to disperse. Pandemonium erupted. This was supposed to be a *peaceful* demonstration, and no one wanted to mess with Chicago's finest.

Over his mother's shoulder, Mikey tearfully watched the police herding the protesters out of his grandpa's yard and away from the house. "It's okay, Mikey. It's all over now," his mother kept telling him. He wanted desperately to believe her. But when he caught sight of the terrible look on his grandfather's face, he knew his mother was wrong. Things were neither okay, nor done with—and it was all the fault of these horrible, gross people who had insulted not just Grandpa but Mikey's entire family.

Surprising Ann with his strength, he suddenly wrenched himself out of her grasp and darted to the top step of the porch. "I hate them! I hate them!" he shrieked. "You Jews! You dirty Jews!"

A second later, Ann reached out and slapped him hard across the face. Mikey gaped at her, wild eyed as a ferocious dog ready to turn on its owner. She slapped him again with the full force of her palm, leaving behind the dull red imprint on his cheek.

Stunned beyond speech (it had been years since his mother had so much as spanked him), Mikey burst into tears and dashed past her into the house. Ann didn't have the energy to go after him. The tears flowing heedlessly down her cheeks, she slumped against the porch railing and stared at her hand, still tingling from the impact of the blow.

She thought, *I had to do that. He was hysterical. But you didn't have to hit him twice,* pointed out an accusing inner voice. *That was* your *hysteria.*

By now more patrol cars had arrived. There seemed to be almost as many uniformed officers as protesters. Upraised nightsticks were silhouetted against the sky. People were scattering in every direction, trying to save their skulls.

From one end of the block to the other, houses were lit up like jack-o'-lanterns. The neighbors were clustered at their windows and in their open doorways, wondering what all the excitement was about. A fire? A family fight? A break-in, perhaps. No, came the message, telegraphed up and down the street by the people who lived nearest to Mike. It was those damn lousy Commies, out to get Laszlo. But don't worry. The cops got it all under control.

Ann stared with amazement at the melee that had broken out in—of all places—her father's front yard. Thank goodness it was winter, so that at least his precious flowers weren't getting trampled. Then, catching herself in the absurdity of that thought when so much more than flowers were at stake, she went inside to check on her father and make peace with her son.

The rioters had left their mark. Shards of glass were scattered all over the floor of the living room, and the wind was blowing snowflakes through the two shattered windowpanes. George stood by the window, hugging her arms across her chest to keep warm. This was one for the books, she thought. White people turning against other whites. Go figure it!

But the ruckus was more than an interesting sociological phenomenon. Because these particular white folks, about whom George happened to care deeply, were feeling considerable pain at the moment. Mikey was huddled against the far wall, shaking with sobs. Sensing that he needed his mother, she'd given up trying to comfort him. Mike, too, seemed on the verge of tears. Her heart ached for them and for Ann, who looked equally distraught when she walked into the room.

George greeted her friend with a sorrowful shake of her turbaned head and a warm hug. She'd never seen Ann look so pale and ashen, as if the blood had been drained out of her.

Mike spoke first, breaking the silence. "Why they do this to me?" he whispered hoarsely. "It was no me! You know it no me!"

"*They* don't know!" Ann reminded him, impatient with his naivete. She turned to Mikey and pried his hands away from his face. Poor little kid, he looked like a beaten animal, licking his wounds in the corner. What he wanted—expected—from her were forgiving kisses and an apology. Perhaps she shouldn't have hit him. That wasn't her style of mothering, and they both knew it.

But she couldn't under any circumstances countenance the venom that had come spilling out of his mouth. So what she said was "You don't ever say anything like that again, you hear me?"

His bottom lip quivered so pathetically that she almost relented. But he had to understand that ugly name-calling solved nothing. Hatred and prejudice only bred more bigotry. How had she failed to convey that to him? Had she not learned the lesson well enough herself?

Grabbing his hand, sweaty and wet with tears, she repeated, "You hear me?"

Mike saw what she was doing and jumped in to help her. "Your mama right, Mikey," he said somberly. "These people, they think I bad man. They throw rocks at wrong man. But they right to throw."

He knelt in front of the boy and went on. "They no bad

people out there, Mikey. They good people. You understand, Mikey?''

Ann wondered whether her father really believed what he was saying. She wasn't sure she herself agreed with him about the protesters' right to throw rocks. Peaceful demonstration? Yes, certainly she could go along with that. She'd been among the first to applaud and defend Papa's right to demonstrate against the Hungarian ballet company.

Violence, however, was another matter altogether. She couldn't imagine lifting a hand to strike another human being. . . . Except Mikey. The sound of her hand smacking against his cheek echoed through her mind. Perhaps, after all, her beliefs weren't very different from Papa's. Perhaps he was simply less of a hypocrite.

Mikey nodded gravely as his grandfather explained. ''We come this country, everybody call us name. Greenhorn . . . dirty greenhorn. D.P. Dirty D.P. We people. No dirty, Mikey. Jews people, too. Like us.''

''I'm sorry, Grandpa,'' Mikey said, thoroughly ashamed that he'd messed up so badly. He didn't *really* think Jews were dirty. He didn't even know why he'd said what he had. But somehow the words had come flying out of his mouth—and then it was too late to take them back. Now his mom was mad at him, and Grandpa and George probably thought he was a jerk, too.

What if the protesters told the judge that Mike Laszlo's grandson had called them dirty Jews? What if they used that as further proof that Grandpa was a Nazi? Had he gotten his grandfather into even worse trouble than he already was?

He hadn't felt this miserable since the day his parents had announced that they were splitting up—because of him, he'd been sure of it. If he was never bad, always did his homework, went to bed when he was supposed to, cleaned up his room, maybe they wouldn't fight as much. Then they could stay married. Eventually his mother had convinced him that the divorce had absolutely nothing to do with him. But this time, if Grandpa got kicked out of America, he *would* be partly to blame.

Ann saw the angry, telltale scowl on her son's face and reached out to gather him up in her arms. Poor baby. His face always betrayed him.

Satisfied that a truce had been negotiated between daughter and son, Mike came over to join George at the window. A few diehards were still standing their ground. They were surrounded by a cordon of police, who'd herded them off Mike's property and onto the far side of the sidewalk. Their chant, muted but audible, floated in through the broken window.

"Nazi! Killer! Nazi! Killer! Nazi! Killer!"

Mike glanced at Ann, trying to calm Mikey as she dried the tears off his flushed cheeks. "It my fault," he said softly, thinking out loud. "I no should bring boy."

Ann shook her head. It wasn't his fault or anyone else's. Besides, they'd all learned some painful but important lessons here this afternoon. She suspected they'd be learning many more before they were through confronting the past. "I'm glad you brought him," she told Mike, trying to smile. "After all, you did right."

But Mike gave no sign of having heard her. He sighed deeply and stared off into the middle distance, his face as impenetrable as stone. And outside, still the chant continued: "Nazi! Killer! Nazi! Killer!"

CHAPTER
8

Harry Talbot refused to think of his chauffeur-driven Mercedes limousine as a luxury or a needless affectation. He was an extremely busy man: He served on numerous civic and corporate boards, had his full load of clients, and still handled much of the administrative decision-making at the firm—no small feat for a man who was well into his seventies (though he didn't like to make too much of his age).

Time was money. Since he had a dearth of the former and plenty of the latter, it only made sense that he be driven back and forth to work every day. Let others fume and fret while they got stuck in traffic for hours. Harry read the newspapers, reviewed cases, made calls from his cellular phone. His BMW was strictly for tooling around on weekends, when he drove to the club to play golf or took his family to dinner or the theater.

The chauffeur lived in an apartment above the garage. He'd been with the Talbots for years. Teddy was like part of the family, sometimes performing double duty as cook, when the regular cook had a day off. His pot roasts were tender and juicy, his turkeys outstanding.

So David had explained to Ann shortly after their first

date, when they'd been caught up in the throes of getting to know each other and falling in love. Years after the fact, Ann could only imagine what she'd thought about meeting, much less making love with, someone who considered a chauffeur commonplace. Perhaps that should have been the tip-off to her—that beneath the student-radical outerwear he was trying on for size, David was more comfortably dressed in the pin-stripes, suspenders, and wing-tip shoes that were the corporate lawyer's standard issue.

Over the years, Ann had often ridden in the limo's spacious back seat, but she'd never gotten used to the idea of giving orders to the nattily uniformed driver. She was even less comfortable now that Teddy was well into his late sixties and could hardly stand up straight some days on account of his rheumatism.

Nobody, however, was asking her, she reminded herself, as she stood by the curb, watching the Mercedes glide into the reserved parking spot in front of Harry's building. Still, it pained her to see Teddy wince as he climbed out of the car, then pull open the back door and give Harry a hand to help him out. Did the man enjoy his work? She hoped that that, rather than finances or misplaced loyalty, accounted for why he hadn't yet retired.

Harry looked pleased to see her waiting for him. He handed her a copy of the *Tribune*, folded to the front page, and said, smiling broadly, "You must be elated this morning."

Elated was hardly the word. Sick to her stomach was more like it, she thought, gawking at the two-column photograph of her father, baseball bat high above his head and one arm around Mikey, facing the crowd. "ACCUSED NAZI DEFENDS HIS FAMILY" screamed the headline above the photo.

Of course. She should have realized that the newspapers would play up the demonstration. But between taking care of Mikey and making arrangements with Karchy to get Papa's windows fixed and his car towed to the garage, she'd been too busy to worry about media coverage. She hadn't even bothered to turn on the television last night. Had the local news covered the story as well?

Harry was chuckling as they walked through the ornate marble-ceilinged lobby toward the elevators. Good old Mishka. He must have put on quite a show last night. "An old man in a Bears cap with his arm around his grandson, being threatened by a screaming mob. Your jury will love that, though I think he should be shot for taking Mikey over there."

"What jury?" Ann demanded, jabbing the elevator button. Harry's reaction to the newspaper coverage annoyed her. This was her family—*his* grandson—whose picture was splashed across the page. What was obviously a big joke to him smelled like serious trouble to her. The Laszlos hadn't asked to become celebrities, and she didn't like the publicity that went along with their new status. "I won't have a jury," she reminded him.

An elevator door opened and they stepped inside. Harry pushed the button for their floor, waited until the car began to rise, then said, "Of course you will. You won't have any jurors, but the world will be your jury. Even paragons of virtue like Sam Silver are human beings. I did some checking on your prosecutor."

Momentarily surprised by his unexpected segue, she spoke more sharply than usual. "I didn't ask you to do that."

Harry was impervious to her tone. One of the secrets of his success was that he didn't wait to be asked. Whenever possible, he took the initiative, followed his instincts, and pursued whatever avenue looked green and promising.

Ann was his *ex*-daughter-in-law, but Mikey was still very much his grandson and he carried the name of Talbot. Harry wasn't about to allow 150 years of American family heritage to go down the toilet because Ann was too proud to ask for help. *No* lawyer he'd ever met was too good to need an occasional push in the right direction.

He therefore chose to ignore her comment and went on as if she hadn't interrupted: "He was a federal prosecutor in Philadelphia . . . a good one. He never lost a case. Four years ago he walked away and went to California. Did Legal Aid work, if you can believe that. Nine months ago, he walked into Justice in Washington and volunteered for Special Investigations. I can make some calls to Philadelphia and see what happened there."

"I can handle my own cases, Harry," she snapped, furious at him for interfering. "I don't need any help."

For a smart girl, she was playing it very dumb. Ann's reaction was worse than misguided; it was just plain dangerous. "From what I hear," he informed her, "with this particular case you're going to need all the help you can get."

She glared at him, torn between curiosity and anger. "What does that mean? Hear from who?"

Just then, the elevator hit their floor and the door slid open. Ever the gentleman, Harry stepped aside to let Ann pass, then followed her into his firm's reception area. "Whom," he said. "Hear from *whom*. Hell, I thought you knew the English language."

What she didn't know was how many more heart-rending descriptions of Nazi horrors she could handle. Not that she had much choice. Whatever leads there were to be found, no one was going to hand them to her in the form of a neatly typed and bound legal brief. It was up to her to go digging, to probe among the affidavits and law books like a scientist searching for a cure for a fatal illness.

She spent the day holed up in her office, with the door shut to discourage visitors, reading and taking notes. A short break for lunch—a sandwich and coffee at her desk—and then she went back to work, stopping only to check on Mikey and to tell her father not to hold dinner for her.

Yes, she'd remember to eat, she promised him. Most likely she'd order in a sandwich.

By late afternoon, she'd put down the eyewitness accounts and turned instead to the case-law books, hoping to find guidance in legal precedent. Normally, this sort of painstaking research was the province of promising young associates. Now, however, with Mike's future hanging in the balance, she didn't dare trust the legwork to anyone but herself—and George.

The woman was one in a million. Ann had valued her friendship since the day they'd met. George was smart, stubborn, tireless; a sturdy shoulder to cry on, a terrific single-mother role model. The color of a person's skin was irrelevant to George; once you proved to her satisfaction that you were a decent, caring human being, she was there for you, no questions asked. Ann couldn't imagine how she would have managed without her.

Someone had to go nosing around in the dark corners of Mike's life. Someone had to talk to his friends, track down his enemies, trace his habits. Ann didn't have the time, the inclination, most of all the expertise that George could bring to the assignment.

Much of what George routinely did was dirty work—asking suggestive questions, dropping hints, pursuing rumors that were usually better left unrepeated. Some investigators had an unfortunate way of never getting clean of the filth. George was able to shake the muck off her hands and walk away smelling like roses.

Unlike many of her colleagues, unless her mark was a real lowlife, she didn't enjoy ferreting out anyone's nasty secrets. She would walk in humming, drop her report on the desk, and happily announce, "He's clean. Pure as Ivory Snow." It was Ann's most fervent wish that George would be humming about Mike.

She was slumped over a law book, exhausted and overdosed on coffee, when George showed up much later that night. She came bearing gifts of a sort—an armful of books recommended for Ann by Sandy Lehman, which she unceremoniously dropped on Ann's desk. Unbuttoning her coat, she took note of the greasy crumpled paper bags (lunch *and* dinner), the stack of styrofoam coffee cups, the cans of diet soda, the bottles of aspirin and Maalox. Not a pretty sight, no, ma'am. Ann was going to get herself sick with this case if she didn't take care—and then where would they all be?

"Don't you got a boy at home to take care of?" she asked, pointing an accusing finger. George knew full well that the boy was doing just fine with his grandpa. But if Ann wouldn't worry about her own health, maybe she'd go on home for Mikey's sake.

"I've got a case to win," Ann said, her voice rising with excitement. "Listen, George. It happened before, in Detroit. They put a man on trial, prepared this elaborate case, brought a bunch of witnesses over here. A man named Narik, accused of war crimes in Lithuania. *And they had the wrong man!* The witnesses were all mistaken! They simply had the wrong man. The judge found him innocent." She smiled tiredly and pushed her hair away from her face. "So. Tell me about my dad, George."

George plopped herself down and pulled her notebook out of her bag, though there wasn't much to report. Thank God the man was straight as an arrow. "He goes to church, to the cemetery, to the corner bar, the bowling alley. He buys strudel at the bakery. He plays checkers in the park—never loses, from what I hear."

Ann marveled at the touching ordinariness of her father's life. "I couldn't ever beat him either," she admitted.

"He makes a few bets on the Cubs and Bears games," George went on, glancing at her notes.

"Wait 'til I tell Karchy!" Ann laughed. "He's always after Karchy about betting."

She stood up and bent her head from side to side, trying to stretch her tired neck muscles. The endless hours of concentration had taken their toll; her back ached, and she had a pounding headache. But the Narik case had given her hope, and so far George didn't seem to have turned up any damning evidence.

George scanned the next page and asked, "Do you know an Irma Kiss?"

"Who?" The name was vaguely familiar, but Ann couldn't put a face to it.

"Irma Kiss. Mrs. Irma Kiss. She's a widow, lives three blocks from him—"

"Mrs. *Kish*," Ann corrected her. "It's *Kish* in Hungarian. Yes, I know Mrs. Kish. She makes doughnuts at the church."

"Well, that ain't all she makes." George smirked. "Maybe it's Kish, but he's *kissin'* her."

"What!" Ann stared at her friend in open-mouthed amazement, as if she'd just been told that Santa Claus and his team of reindeer had landed on the roof.

"Off and on, for about ten years now." George nodded. "Three, four times a month."

"I don't believe it!" Ann exclaimed, struggling to imagine Papa with . . . Mrs. Kish! Of all people! She was a plump, gray-haired lady who often appeared on Papa's porch at suppertime, carrying a casserole dish of sausages or stuffed cabbage, and she never seemed to take off her apron. Did she wear it to bed, too? But she had to be at least fifty-five, maybe even older . . . maybe even as old as Papa. . . . She stopped short as the realization flashed through her mind that had her mother lived, Ilona today would probably look much like Mrs. Kish.

But Papa, that sly devil! Ann giggled. He'd never so much as let on. "Oh my God, I don't believe it!" she exclaimed, the giggles growing into full-blown gales of laughter at the unlikely thought of her father in the throes of passion with St. Elizabeth's preeminent doughnut baker. *Mrs. Kish!* Every time she remembered George saying "That ain't all she makes," she was hit anew by a tidal wave of hilarity that she couldn't have held back if she'd tried. The mirth came bubbling out in great whoops and guffaws that had more to do with the accumulated tension of the last several days than with the fact of her father sleeping with . . . *Mrs. Kish!* She gestured helplessly, *I'm sorry*, and sank down in her chair, wiping the tears from her eyes.

George, meanwhile, was calmly regarding Ann with the detachment of a psychiatrist clinically observing a slightly deranged patient. She didn't know the particular lady in question, but Mike had always struck her as a normal, healthy male with normal, healthy male appetites that needed satisfying. George wasn't the least bit surprised he was helping himself to some sweet dessert. *Good* for him.

What was the big joke? she wondered. It was sure going right over her head, though she was glad to see Ann laughing. Lord knew the girl could use a couple of yuks. Finally, however, she decided, enough was enough. "You gonna listen to me, or you gonna keep giggling at me like a teenager?" she demanded.

Ann was gasping to catch her breath. Yes, she nodded. She would listen.

"He doesn't spend a lot of money, but outside his savings account, he doesn't have anything to spend," George informed her. "He doesn't even have any credit cards. He doesn't believe in them."

"I wish I didn't." Ann snickered. "Mrs. Kish!"

George ignored the interruption. "He spent a little more for a while a couple of years ago, but then he learned to stick to ten-dollar bets. Who's Tibor Zoldan?"

Ann shrugged and glanced at the pile of books George had brought her. The volume on top was titled *The Holocaust in Hungary*. She put it aside and looked at the next one: *Scroll of Agony*. The one below that was called *The Final Solution*.

"I don't know. Probably one of his friends from Hungary," she said, continuing to sort through the books. The titles, weighty and intimidating, demanded her attention.

"Mike wrote Zoldan a check for two thousand dollars three years ago," George explained. "That's the biggest check he's ever written. This group he belongs to, the Attila Circle? It's just a bunch of old guys who get the picket signs out whenever some dimwit Communist diplomat makes the mistake of coming here. They don't do it a lot lately, though, 'cause they're all gettin' too old to hold up the signs."

The two women smiled at each other. No news was good news. The less George could find on Mike—and Ann was sure she'd searched high and low—the easier it would be to go into that courtroom and win this case.

"Honest to God, darlin', there ain't no devil here to advocate." George chuckled.

Ann made a circle of her thumb and forefinger. A-okay, kiddo. That was fine with her. Deciding she could call it quits for the night, she idly flipped through another one of the books, a collection of poems and artwork by children in Nazi death camps. Many of the drawings were of houses in front of which tiny stick-figure children were playing ball and jumprope. Others portrayed flowers and meadows, trees with birds perched on the leafy branches. One young artist had written underneath her sketch, "I never saw another butterfly."

There were photographs of some of the children, most of whom hadn't survived the camps. Someone, perhaps the photographer, must have told them to smile. Their lips were tautly stretched into a brave imitation of happiness. Their gaunt, sad-eyed faces looked wise beyond their years, as if the suffering and horror they'd witnessed had destroyed their innocence. They stared longingly into the future that would never be theirs, silently pleading that they not be forgotten.

One skinny-limbed little boy stood out from the rest, because his smile seemed, not a death's-head mockery, but genuine and spontaneous. He looked so full of mischief and fun that you could almost imagine that his photo had been included by mistake among these other pictures.

Ann could hardly tear her eyes away from the picture. She read the caption: "Shmulik Bernshtayn, eleven years old. Died February 4, 1944."

Sentenced to death before he ever had a chance to explore the world beyond the barbed wire of the concentration camp. And why? Because Hitler and his impassioned supporters had needed a scapegoat to bear the brunt of their madness. They'd found six million scapegoats among the Jews, including Shmulik Bernshtayn, by virtue of his having been born a Jew, in the wrong country, in the wrong decade.

Eleven years old. Exactly the same age as Mikey.

The following morning Ann was lured awake by a bright splash of sunshine across her pillow and the tantalizing aroma of coffee and French toast. She lay still for a moment, getting her bearings, then remembered it was Saturday. That accounted for the quiet murmurings drifting her way from the kitchen. Papa and Mikey must have gotten up early to cook breakfast before Mikey went off with his father.

Shaking herself to consciousness, she glanced at the clock-radio on her bed table. Ten o'clock! That got her standing upright in a hurry. How could she have slept so late? Why hadn't anyone knocked on her door? She should have been up hours ago. The day was almost half gone, and David would be here any minute to pick up Mikey.

She threw on a robe, splashed some water on her face, and ran her fingers through her hair, rushing to see Mikey before he left. They'd hardly had a chance to talk since the other night, and this morning, it felt especially important that she give him a hug and a kiss good-bye. The memory of that other dead child had haunted her sleep and troubled her dreams. Physical contact with her son was what she needed to shake off the depression she'd carried home with her from the office.

She almost missed him. He already had his coat on and was heading out the door when Ann came hurrying into the kitchen.

"Good-bye, Grandpa," he said, not bothering to acknowledge his mother.

Mike, outfitted in one of Ann's aprons, was busy clearing away the dirty plates, sticky with syrup and jam. As usual, when Mike was in charge of the cooking, the counters were covered with used mixing bowls and spilled ingredients, and the sink was spilling over with dirty dishes.

"You watch yourself, okay? Have a good time," he instructed the boy. He tugged at the zipper on Mikey's parka and gave him a hug, then pointed him in Ann's direction.

"Bye, Mom," Mikey dutifully mumbled, eager to make his escape before she started grilling him about homework and tests. She never had time anymore to ask him about the *important* stuff, like the basketball tryouts. All she wanted to know about was *school*. Yuck!

Luckily, Grandpa was home when Mikey had come running in with the news that he'd made the team. Now he couldn't wait to tell his dad and Grandpa Harry. As for Mom—forget it. She still hadn't apologized for slapping him.

Ann let him get as far as the front door. Then she quietly reminded him, "I didn't get a hug."

But apparently she would have to do without today. Mikey gave no sign of having heard her. He only had eyes for Harry's Mercedes, parked at the curb, with Teddy patiently waiting to help him into the back seat. She sighed as she watched the car pull away. Time and again, she'd suggested to David that he use his own car, not the limo, for his weekend outings with Mikey. It was only one of many childrearing issues about which they disagreed.

Determined to shake off her gloom, she wandered off

116

to the kitchen to pour herself a cup of coffee. Then she tracked Mike down in the family room, where he sat staring disconsolately at the darkened television set.

"What the hell I gonna do now?" he asked, sounding like a sulky kid whose best friend has left town. "Saturday, Mikey and me watch the cartoons. I gonna watch cartoons anyway." He pressed the power button on the remote control and ran through the channels until he found what he was searching for—a Roadrunner cartoon.

She perched on the arm of the couch and sipped her coffee, savoring this moment of quiet. "I didn't know you made bets," she said.

Mike kept his gaze on the Roadrunner, who, true to his name, was whipping back and forth across the screen. A moment or two later, he looked at Ann and grinned sheepishly. "Don't tell Karchy, though."

She laughed, willing to be his accomplice. "We're going to do some work this weekend."

"I don't wanna do no work," he said grumpily. "I wanna watch cartoons."

He behaved like a petulant child sometimes, she thought exasperatedly. Shit, she'd sure as hell much rather put her feet up and relax than spend the day grilling him. Her temper rising, she wondered, did he think she was putting in these ridiculously long hours for her health? It was *his* citizenship, not to mention *his* skin, they were fighting to save.

But lashing out at him would accomplish nothing, and hadn't he taken enough abuse lately? Suddenly ashamed of herself for not being more patient and understanding, she took a deep breath and counted to ten. It worked. Instantly she felt calmer. "Where did I put my tape recorder?" she wondered aloud and went to find her briefcase.

Mike grunted his irritation and turned up the volume, hoping Ann would get the hint and leave him in peace.

"Hey, Papa," she called from the hallway, "who's Tibor Zoldan?"

Mike grimaced and slouched into the depths of the couch as Ann walked back into the room. Finally he said, "Zoldan friend from refugee camp. Then he go back to old country. Then he come from old country out here. Give him some money, get start. Then he get himself killed, car accident. Then I no get money back."

So the money hadn't gone to pay a gambling debt. The revelation stunned and touched her. Here was Papa, who all his life had skimped and saved and denied himself so much. Yet in an act of friendship, he'd lent a man money—and for Papa, two thousand dollars was *serious* money. And then the man had died, and Papa would never be repaid, but he'd never said one word to her about his loss.

Had he confided in Karchy? Probably not, or Karchy might have come to her with the story. Which was reason enough for Papa to have kept it to himself. The three of them had traditionally taken one another's privacy for granted. Certainly she'd learned the hard way to guard her secrets. Apparently, so had Papa.

So, to work.

She positioned the tape recorder on the coffee table, squarely in front of Papa. "Are you ready?"

"Anni. I don't wanna do this, Anni," he pleaded. "I spend whole life tryin' forget what I see. Now I gotta remember?"

"We have to, Papa," she said, fussing with the machine to avoid catching his eye. Her heart ached for him, but to excuse him now would be misplaced compassion. The government's prosecutor wouldn't hesitate to ask even the most personal questions. She couldn't anticipate them until she knew all the answers.

But where to begin? Might as well plunge right in, she decided. Get the worst over with first. "How's Mrs. Kish?" she blurted out.

"Who?"

She cleared her throat nervously, hoping she wouldn't lose it and get the giggles. "Mrs. Kish, Papa. Irma."

"Irma?" he demanded hotly. His cheeks the color of beets, he leaned forward and turned off the tape recorder. "Jesus Christ, Anni! Damn lawyers, they find out everything!" he said indignantly.

Ann dug her nails into her hands, bit the inside of her cheeks, thought sad thoughts . . . anything to keep from laughing. *It's not funny*, she scolded herself. Papa was understandably mortified by the idea of talking to her about what he did in bed. But then she made the huge mistake of sneaking a peek at Mike, whose hang-dog expression was all the confirmation she needed about Mrs. Kish, and she was sputtering with laughter.

Mike smiled grudgingly to let her know that he, too, could see the humor in the situation, and then he couldn't resist her infectious chuckles.

"Why didn't you ever marry her, Papa?" Ann asked, when they'd both calmed down and caught their breath.

"I could never marry nobody after your mama," he said simply.

She patted his hand affectionately, loving him for his loyalty, and turned the tape recorder back on.

"How about you, Anni?" he asked.

She cocked her head, not understanding. "What about me, Papa?"

"You meet nobody since you got the divorce?"

Off went the tape recorder. She was taken aback by his bluntness. It was so unlike him to pry into her social life. But then, this was altogether a highly unlikely conversation. She didn't usually inquire about his women—not that it had ever occurred to her that he was sexually involved with any. "Sure I've met some men, Papa."

"You ever go meet them like I go meet Mrs. Kish?"

"No," she admitted.

"How come no?"

"You didn't raise me like that, Papa," she replied. Of

course, the truth was much more complicated, but this wasn't an area she particularly wanted to get into with her father. Her lack of a sex life was a sore spot.

She'd tried to convince herself that she must not be meeting the right men, since none of them turned her on. But recently she'd begun to think that perhaps *she* was the one with the problem. Probably she worked too hard, and what with worrying about Mikey, not to mention Mike and Karchy . . . When this was all over and done with, maybe she'd buy some new clothes and get a different, younger-looking haircut.

"Maybe I make a big mistake, huh?" Mike joked uncomfortably.

"No," she said softly. "No, you didn't make a mistake, Papa."

At that instant, she wanted nothing more than to tell her father how much she loved him. She wished he could say out loud how much his happiness meant to her. But she couldn't easily make such pronouncements, especially not to her father, even now as she felt his love reaching out to her.

Her thoughts drifted back to her childhood, to all the wonderful moments they'd shared. Papa had never once failed her when she'd needed him. He'd made her laugh, answered her questions, held her hand so she'd always felt safe. She prayed she could adequately repay him.

"You gonna ask questions?" Mike prompted her, grinning self-consciously as he turned the tape recorder back on.

"Yes," she said. Better to get on with it. "Papa, how did you join the gendarmes?"

Mike nodded. "We live in village. We poor, very poor. No go school. I like *csendor*, pay good money, got a nice uniform, a feather on the hat."

Ann rocked back and forth in the chair, listening carefully. She smiled encouragement. Yes. Yes, this was exactly what she wanted to hear.

CHAPTER
9

Ann spent hours with Mike, quizzing him about his past—family, jobs, friends, political and religious associations, hobbies, vices, likes, dislikes; name it, she asked it. By the end of their last session, her head was swimming with information. She felt sure there was no aspect of his life she hadn't explored with him; no nook or cranny that she hadn't investigated.

If there were any holes or weak links in his story, she had to be the one to find them, so that the prosecuting attorney wouldn't. She forced herself to deal with him as tough and unsparingly as she would any hostile witness and put him through as tough a catechism as any she'd ever faced in religious class. And time after time, Mike passed with flying colors.

The silver lining in the cloud was that she got to know him as few daughters ever got to know their fathers. Ironically, she felt grateful for the opportunity, though the circumstances were certainly not of her choosing.

And then she decided it was time to play hardball. Whatever rumors Harry Talbot had heard from his friends in high places (and certainly he had plenty of them), he wasn't sharing any of the details. His only advice to her was to go for the jugular. She took him seriously and plotted her moves with the aplomb of a military tactician. Step number one was to hold a press conference the day before the trial was due to begin. When she worried aloud to David that no one would show up, he laughed and said that that was the least of her problems.

His prediction of a standing-room-only turnout was right on the money. The local as well as national media showed up in full force. Every bureau chief in town—from the *New York Times* to *USA Today* to the *National Enquirer*—sent a representative. *U.S. vs. Laszlo* was the kind of sensational case that sold papers and played well on television. It had all the right buzzwords: Nazis, Holocaust victims, blue-collar son, yuppie daughter. Not to mention a dizzying number of too-good-to-be-true angles: Laszlo was being represented by his *daughter*? Who used to be married to old man Talbot's son? Fabulous! And now she's working out of Talbot's office instead of her own firm, where she's usually taking care of the underdogs? Interesting . . . very interesting.

Not half as interesting, however, as the reason why Ann had summoned them to the Talbot conference room on this dreary morning. Mindful of Harry's comment that the world would be watching and judging, she'd dressed for the occasion in her most demurely alluring pink-on-black pin-striped suit. She was primed and ready to talk sweetly and smile for the cameras, but the real story centered around the envelopes that had been neatly stacked on top of the long walnut conference table in front of her.

The envelopes, many of them simply addressed to Michael Laszlo, Chicago, U.S.A., had begun to arrive a couple of days after word of the case had been leaked to the press. It was Mike who came up with the solution for how to dispose of them, a decision Harry had hailed as a brilliant public-relations gesture. Ann had winced at his cynicism. Now, gazing at the crowd of scoop-hungry journalists and photographers, she realized the wisdom of his perspective.

She also appreciated the support that both he and David were showing her by attending the press conference. Their presence, Harry's particularly, sent a signal that only the most novice reporter could possibly miss. Harry Talbot was one of Chicago's best-known, most highly regarded citizens. He was practically an official civic treasure. If he stood behind Mike Laszlo and his daughter, then you had to think twice as to who here was telling the truth. Easy enough to point a finger at some guy with a foreign accent, but where was the proof, goddamnit?

Generations of butterflies were getting born in Ann's stomach as she took her place at the head of the table. Though she'd faced many a tough judge and jury, today she felt unaccountably nervous about the outcome of her performance. And this was only act one, she reminded herself, clapping her hands to quiet the room.

It took a few minutes before the buzz of chatter had died down. Finally, the reporters were done trading gossip, and they took out their pencils and notebooks. The TV cameras were turned on her, ready to roll. Satisfied that she had everyone's attention, Ann held up a handful of the envelopes, displaying the postmarks: Austria, Hungary, Uruguay, Argentina, Australia . . .

"They're from all over the world," she declared. "Most of them are scurrilously pro-Nazi. We've received $26,432 in contributions so far, most of it in small denominations." Gratified by the expressions of consternation across the room, she paused to let the figure sink in. "My father has decided to contribute the money—and whatever future monies we receive—to the Simon Weisenthal Foundation for the identification and capture of war criminals."

That was the sum total of her announcement—short and simple, just as she'd planned it. In the momentary silence that followed as the reporters scribbled down her remarks, she smiled graciously for the cameras and nervously waited for the inevitable questions.

What she got instead was a spontaneous round of enthusiastic applause that brought tears of relief to her eyes. If she could win over this roomful of cynics, she and Papa had a damn good chance of winning in the courtroom.

Her next step was to establish contact with the enemy. She called Jack Burke and invited him to have dinner with her. Understandably, he sounded wary but curious. "Nothing up my sleeve," she'd quipped. And if he believed that, she'd offer him shares in the Brooklyn Bridge.

He'd hemmed and hawed and finally agreed to join her. But he'd hooted at her choice of restaurant. The Hungarian Rendezvous? She had to be kidding. Not at all, she'd protested. The Rendezvous served the best roast duck in town, the sweet dessert *palascintas* were sublime, the service was better than respectable, and you didn't have to shout to be heard above the din.

Okay, so she wasn't being altogether honest. The Rendezvous was home territory, the scene of every Laszlo celebration from the time Ann was old enough to sit at the table and feed herself. The owner and staff, most of whom were related to one another, doted on Ann and treated her like part of the family. She definitely had the home-court advantage there, but the food really was excellent. Besides, Ann quite liked the idea of Burke getting up to argue his case tomorrow with a bellyful of rich, spicy Hungarian cuisine. Nobody ever said life was fair.

For the second time that day, she'd chosen her outfit carefully, exchanging the pin-striped suit for a red wool dress that showed off her figure and just bordered on seductive. She'd taken extra time with her hair, brushing it until it fell into soft, shiny waves around her face, and she applied more than her usual quick dab of blush and lipstick. At the last minute, she'd put on her long strand of pearls—an engagement present from David.

As she waited for Burke to arrive at the restaurant, she studied her reflection in the mirror above the bar. She was almost shocked to discover a very pretty, familiar-looking face staring back at her. Amazing what soft lights and a few extra minutes getting dressed could do for a girl. Lifting her glass of wine, she silently toasted her mirror image and considered how out of touch she was with that part of herself.

Somehow she'd turned into a woman who didn't care about how she looked or dressed, who didn't have time to worry about feeling soft and sexy. Too many other, more important things to do was her standard excuse. But it was hard to feel or think sexy when she hadn't had a date in months. The only men she ever went out to dinner with were her partners or, very occasionally, David. She could just imagine their reactions if she showed up all decked out, with extra makeup and pearls.

So why had she made the effort for Jack Burke? Partly for strategic reasons—distract the enemy with her womanly wiles. Such thinking jeopardized her status as a card-carrying feminist, but she'd learned through bitter experience that there were any number of ways to win a difficult case. Sometimes you simply did what you had to do.

Sometimes you got all dressed up because a man gave you a certain . . . buzz in the pit of your stomach. And even if you basically despised that man, who, for his own peculiar reasons, was bent on ripping apart your life, you needed to give him a glimpse of what he might have had with you. If you'd met, as the saying went, under different circumstances.

However, the circumstances that stood between herself and Jack Burke couldn't have been more unfortunate. What a shame. He really was extremely attractive, she sighed, catching a glimpse of him in the foyer. "Hi!" she called to get his attention.

Jack almost didn't recognize the woman waving at him from the bar. The Ann Talbot he was expecting to see was uptight, purse-lipped, and angry. Tonight she was looking positively *radiant*. True, she'd scored points this morning with her grandstand announcement about the Weisenthal Foundation. Surely that couldn't account for the glow on her cheeks and the welcoming smile.

She even *smelled* nice, he noticed as they shook hands. What the hell was going on? "You wanna take another swing at me, is that why you called?" he said, only half joking.

"Look, I'm sorry," Ann apologized. She didn't blame the guy for being suspicious. "But I've always had a working relationship with the other side."

"So the night before we go to court you decide to work on your working relationship." He shook his head. "I don't believe it for a minute. What do you really want?"

She smiled. "The chicken paprikas."

That got a smile out of him. She was quick and funny. He liked funny women. You didn't often find them. But this one brought some baggage along with her—a father whose idea of a good time was raping Jewish girls. And come tomorrow morning, they'd be fighting it out in court. However, that was tomorrow morning, and in the meantime, a man had to eat. And maybe he'd misjudged Ann Talbot. Okay, he'd give her a second chance. He had nothing to lose.

Gabor, the maître d', kissed the back of Ann's hand and chatted with her in Hungarian as he showed them to their table. The language was impenetrable—totally unrelated to any Jack was familiar with. Whatever they were laughing about, he hoped he wasn't the punchline of the joke.

At least Ann Talbot had good taste in restaurants. The tables were far enough apart that though the place was full, you didn't feel crowded. A band of violinists, dressed in brightly colored shirts and scarves tied around their heads, roamed the room, playing lively gypsy melodies at a level that didn't rule out conversation. Jack studied the menu and wine list, which offered mostly Hungarian labels, none of which he'd heard of. Finally he decided to let Ann make some suggestions, since she was obviously a regular here.

The flickering candlelight played gently across her face as she gave the waiter their orders—goulash soup with dumplings for two, then chicken paprikas for her, the roast duck for him. Suddenly he had the feeling that this evening's dinner was going to be a whole lot more pleasant and productive than their two previous meetings.

Come to think of it, he *had* been kind of rough on her that night at the Pewter Mug. No wonder she'd tried to throw a punch at him. And how could he not have noticed before how pretty she was?

They made small talk—about the Chicago winter weather and the Bears—until the soup arrived. Ann was starving and she ate with gusto, again to Jack's surprise. He hadn't figured her as having such a hearty appetite. By the time the waiter brought their entrees, along with bowls of roasted potatoes and cucumber salad, he was very much looking forward to finding out who Ann Talbot was, besides being the daughter of a Nazi murderer.

Apparently, she felt likewise. "So tell me about yourself," she said, spearing a potato. "How'd you end up working for the government?"

A fair but boring question, one he'd answered so often he could sum up the answer in a couple of quick sentences. "My dad was on the force, but I knew I didn't want to be a cop," he explained. "I got my degree, went to work for the county as an assistant D.A., and after a while Uncle Sugar came after me."

A moment of awkward silence, as each contemplated the reality of what had brought them together at this table. Jack quickly changed the subject. "So how did a Laszlo marry a Talbot?" he inquired.

Ann shrugged, momentarily taken aback by such a bluntly personal question. Burke certainly couldn't be faulted for shyness. However, she supposed her former marriage was something of an oddity. Most people didn't have the courage—or was it naivete?—to make such cross-cultural leaps.

"We met in school. Some differences aren't that important on hayrides and gin jugs," she said lightly.

She had to be putting him on. "*You* went on a gin jug?" He raised a skeptical eyebrow. "I can't see you on a gin jug."

"I went on a lot of gin jugs," she told him, trying not to sound defensive. What did he take her for? A tight-assed prissy bitch who'd camped out in the library? "I went on a lot of hayrides, too."

"So, what happened?" he teased. He hadn't missed the hint of irritation in her voice, and he understood that he had hit a nerve.

"On the gin jugs and hayrides, you mean?"

"Yes." He paused, realizing he'd overstepped a boundary that was probably better left uncrossed, then back-tracked reluctantly. "No."

"I don't know," she said quickly, alternately annoyed and flattered by his interest. Nevertheless, alarm bells were buzzing in her brain. This was thin ice she was skating on. The fact that she was even tempted to discuss her failed marriage with Jack Burke was proof positive that she'd gone too far with her fiction of a friendly pretrial get-together. He was the enemy. She couldn't afford to forget that, not even for a moment.

Jack considered the rich-looking red wine, took another long sip, and savored the intensity of its full-bodied flavor. "I'll bet you do know," he challenged her, and he wondered, *Am I drunk*?

Why else would he be pushing her to open up to him, hurling darts at her personal life in the hope of scoring a bull's-eye? Because it was kind of fun to see her squirm. She obviously didn't like talking about herself any more than he did. He knew about secrets, about feelings you kept well buried because you couldn't face them. But what secrets could she be hiding behind the veil of those big brown eyes that were staring at him with such intensity?

Ann wasn't surprised by his response. Though she rarely revealed much about herself, she'd discovered long ago that people often assumed they knew her better than they did. The truth was that her public persona was a mask she put on to create a quick and easy connection between herself and others. She *appeared* to be getting close to them, and yet she really gave away very little. David was one of the few who'd managed to break through her reserve. But David was different. David was a Talbot.

Remembering with a sharp pang how good it had once been between them, she rested her chin atop her folded hands and contemplated the middle distance, as if the answers lay somewhere out there. "Maybe I wanted to become too American," she murmured, "and then I realized I was trying to become too American. Maybe the man I married wasn't the same man who became my husband."

Their eyes locked, and goddamn it if he didn't want to reach out and hold her hand. He *must* be drunk. Or crazy. Or else Ann Talbot was taking lessons in seduction from the Sirens. Because like the sailors of ancient times, he was perilously close to being lured into rocky waters by the sound of her voice. Something strange and wholly unexpected was happening to him tonight, something frightening—and exciting.

Ann was only dimly aware of the effect she was having on Jack. Her mind had gone veering off in the direction of the David she'd once known, territory she'd visited often and kept coming back to, despite the aridity of the terrain. Such excursions were usually fruitless, yielding few new insights or information. So she reined in her wistful thoughts of the past and what might have been and abruptly returned to the present.

"See," she said flippantly, breaking the spell. "I told you I didn't know."

Jack sighed, whether with relief or regret, he wasn't

certain. He drained his wine glass, then refilled both glasses. "What is this stuff?" he asked, determined to keep the conversation light. "It's good."

"It's Bull's Blood. It sneaks up on you. Then it clobbers you. It's a Hungarian trait."

He smiled and saluted her with his glass.

Ann took a deep breath, summoning up courage for the bomb she was about to drop on Burke. Like a poker player with a good hand, she'd known from the moment the information had arrived on her desk, compliments of George, that she'd be a fool not to play her cards. And if she'd had any doubts, Harry Talbot had disabused her of them in no uncertain terms. When she'd gone to Mack for a second opinion, he'd agreed with Harry for once. But the unanimous vote didn't make her next move any easier, especially now that she'd broken bread with the enemy and found a decent human being beneath the wolf's clothing. Tomorrow, however, when he walked into court, he'd be set to pounce with every weapon in his arsenal. The time had come to show Jack Burke that she was also armed and dangerous.

She leaned forward and said, very quietly, "I'm sorry about that case."

She spoke so softly he wasn't sure he'd heard her right. *That* case? Puzzled by the sudden turn the conversation had taken, he shook his head. "What case?"

Ann's eyes never wavered from his face. Her voice was velvet but edged with steel. "That racketeering case you decided not to prosecute in Philadelphia. That pension-fund official."

As the words sunk in and he realized how she'd set him up, his face visibly paled. He never would have believed she had it in her—which showed what a schmuck he was, still after so many years of knocking around and taking more than his fair share of kicks. *Damn!*

"You're really something, you know," he rasped. "You're as ruthless and deceptive as your old man."

Her hands were shaking beneath the tablecloth, but her

perfectly composed face betrayed no emotion. Ruthless? Damn right she was ruthless! She was fighting for Mike's life, and that didn't come cheap. She was hereby putting Jack Burke on notice that she would stop at nothing to clear her father's name.

"I hear they squeezed you from the top," she went on in the same calm tone. "I hear you couldn't live with letting them do that to you. You must've felt very guilty. You must've had principles."

He glared at her, too angry to speak. Was this her idea of fun? Had she rehearsed her speech before a live audience of Papa Mike and his Nazi friends so that they could give her pointers on how to squeeze the last drop of blood out of him? Or did this kind of sick stunt come naturally to her?

Well, maybe he was the biggest sucker she'd ever faced across a table. But she'd just proved beyond a shadow of a doubt that the rotten apple didn't fall too far from the tree.

"I didn't mean to upset you," she said gently.

"Yeah, but you did." He stood up and threw forty bucks on the table to cover his share. This was one woman to whom he didn't want to owe a penny. "You find the soft flesh and you twist the knife. Isn't that the way the game is played? You shove the other side off-balance."

She wanted to cry out that she had no choice, didn't he see that? She had to save Papa's life, or else what did her life matter? As for playing the game, she was a beginner— but a fast learner. And she wasn't yet through with him.

Forcing back the sob she felt rising in her gut, she let him have it with both barrels blazing. "Didn't Legal Aid work ease your guilt? What if going after war criminals doesn't do it either? What are you going to do then, Jack? Get yourself born again? Find Jesus?"

Her rancorous sarcasm acted like a pail of cold water across his face, galvanizing him to respond. "Do you really think you need a self-serving reason to prosecute a war criminal?" he spat. "How about what they did? Isn't that good enough for you?"

Ann's smile faded as he turned and strode away from the table, eager to put distance between them. She leaned back in her chair, shaking from the effort of the last few minutes.

It would have been easy to hate herself for what she'd just done. But it was easier to hate what Jack Burke was trying to do. She at least had the excuse of self-defense, because in defending her father she was just as surely defending herself. What excuse did Burke have for trying to atone his sins by libeling an innocent man?

The day got off to a bad start. Ann was feeling tired and out of sorts, probably because of last evening's confrontation with Burke. Mike, usually Mr. Nerves of Steel, was looking so pale and shaken that Ann wasn't sure he'd make it to the courtroom. To top it all off, Mikey wouldn't stop complaining about being sent off to school as if this were a perfectly ordinary day.

Didn't Grandpa need *him* in the courtroom? he whined over his bowl of Cheerios. This just happened to be his family, too, he reminded his mother, in case she'd forgotten. And how did she expect him to concentrate on dumb old arithmetic and social studies when all day he'd be thinking and worrying about the trial? Didn't she believe a kid could learn something from actual real-life experience?

After the third "No, you're not coming and that's final!" Ann threw up her hands and stomped off to her bedroom to get dressed. David had offered to take care of Mikey this week so she could devote all her time to the trial. Now, as she pulled her most conservative suit out of the closet, she found herself wishing she'd said yes to him.

Her fingers were shaking so badly she could hardly manage the buttons on her ivory silk blouse. This was too much for her to handle alone. She had to look over her notes one last time before court was in session, try to keep Papa from falling apart, plus cope with Mikey, who'd turned into a cranky five year old. Instead of responding to him as if he were a sensate human being, what she ought to do was smack his bottom and throw him in his room until the schoolbus arrived.

She picked up her brush, quickly fluffed her hair into place, and was brought up short by the cool voice of reason, proclaiming, *He's just a little boy.* Okay, so maybe she wasn't being fair. He was getting so big that sometimes she forgot he was only eleven. Poor baby. All hell was breaking loose around him, and she didn't even have the time to help him make sense of what was going on.

So now she could add *bad mother* to the list of all her other failings.

The full-length mirror on the back of the closet door told her that she was the very image of a serious, sedate defense attorney. The pearl earrings were a nice touch, but something more was needed. She rummaged in her jewelry box. The long strand of pearls? Too stylish. A simple gold chain? Too blah. Her fingers closed around her cross, a gift from Papa when she'd turned eighteen.

It was a beautiful piece of delicately wrought gold, one of the few possessions Mama had brought with her from Hungary. Ann cherished it for its sentimental value, but she felt too uncomfortable with the symbolism to wear it often. She held it up against her blouse to get the effect and thought, *I look like a nun.* She could see the headlines now: "Accused Nazi Killer Defended by Nun." The cross went back in her jewelry box.

She was gathering up her papers when the doorbell rang. Now what? A reporter, looking for a personal angle on the story? Or maybe Mrs. Kish, come to give Papa a good-luck kiss? Or perhaps it was Jack Burke, dropping by to say he'd realized he'd made a terrible mistake, that he'd stumbled on the wrong Michael Laszlo, and please, could they call the whole thing off? She hurried to get the door before Mikey did and steeled herself to greet whoever was lurking on the other side with a firm *Go away, we don't want any.*

But her frown, forbidding enough to discourage the Grim

Reaper himself, immediately turned into a warm, heartfelt smile at the sight of George, stamping her feet to clean the snow off her boots. She was desperate for a cup of hot coffee, she declared with an impish grin. And she just happened to be in the neighborhood, so she thought she'd drop by.

Of course, since George lived way the hell on the other side of town, they both knew that was bullshit. But how typical of her to guess that Ann might welcome the moral support, even if she was too proud to ask for it. Also typical was the way she brushed off Ann's thanks with a shrug and a look that said, c'mon, what are friends for? Then she inspected Ann's outfit, nodded her approval, and went off to the kitchen for that cup of coffee.

A second later the schoolbus turned the corner and Mikey stopped complaining long enough to give Ann a hug before he took off at a sprint. And then it was time for them to leave for the courthouse. George insisted on driving, so Ann slid in next to her, and Mike huddled in the back seat.

He was too nervous to say more than a word or two the whole trip into town. Until this morning, his anger had sustained him. Now, with the specter of the courtroom ordeal hovering over him, he felt smothered by a blanket of dread that he couldn't seem to throw off. Hope had deserted him. Hunching his shoulders, he gazed blindly out the car window, oblivious to the efforts of Ann and George to cheer him up.

"Smile, Papa. I want them to see you smile," Ann urged as they neared the Federal Court Building. She knew he must be dying inside, but she couldn't let him get out of the car looking like a prisoner on his way to the gallows.

"How can I smile?" Mike wailed plaintively. "I scared I gonna pee my pants."

Her heart ached for him. But she knew that if he stepped out of the car and into the glare of the waiting cameras looking like a scared rabbit, he'd be judged guilty before he even walked into the courtroom. She had to stop thinking of him as her father and start treating him as she would any client. So instead of giving him sympathy, she began issuing brisk instructions. "Talk to George a lot. Smile at George a lot. I want them to see you being very friendly with George."

"I'm not Jewish," George jokingly stated the obvious as she pulled up in front of the courthouse.

"You're the next-best thing," Ann said drily, fumbling with her seatbelt.

George threw her a look of mock indignation, then braked sharply. "Oh my Lord!" she muttered.

Ann silently echoed her shock. She'd been warned to expect a heavy press turnout, but what awaited them was nothing short of a full-fledged media circus. It seemed as if every reporter in town—and at least as many from out of town—had decided to cover the story. Was Papa's trial the only newsworthy event of the day?

Like a pack of hungry bloodhounds, the reporters descended on them, yelling questions and thrusting microphones under their noses. Lightbulbs flashed crazily, and only some agile maneuvering by the police, who were also out in force, saved them from being totally surrounded by the crush of journalists.

By unspoken agreement, the two women positioned themselves on either side of Mike and elbowed their way through the narrow path that the cops had cleared for them. Mike moaned and instinctively lowered his head as they steered him past the two opposing camps of protesters that had also massed to greet him.

The atmosphere was electric with tension as the protesters, separated by rows of cops from the antiriot division, screamed and flaunted their placards. "Nazi Killer!" "Never Forget!" "Avenge Holocaust Victims!" read the slogans on one side of the plaza. A few hundred feet away an even larger crew had gathered, holding up signs that declared "Mike Laszlo Is Innocent!" "Justice for *All* Americans!" "Stop the Commie Conspiracy!"

The clamor of the crowd hit them like a wall of sound as the two factions caught sight of Mike. A wedge of anti-Laszlo picketers surged forward. One young man, his eyes glittering with hatred, let fly a gob of saliva, just missing his mark. Several others began fighting with the cops to reach Mike. "Give him to us! He's a murderer!" they yelled as they were hustled away in handcuffs.

A cordon of police moved in and hurriedly escorted Mike and the women up the steps. They were moving so quickly that as Mike crossed the threshold, he stumbled and just missed falling flat on his face. His curses were drowned out by the deafening roar that went up as they disappeared into the courthouse.

Inside, the hubbub was only slightly less overwhelming. The normally half-empty corridor was today packed with people gawking at Ann and her father. Security was tight. In addition to extra police, guards were stationed next to the metal detector, checking bags and purses before anyone was allowed entry into the courtroom.

Another contingent of journalists, identified by their plastic press badges, jostled for space in the crowded hall. Some stood posing for their cameras, doing live setups in Spanish, French, and German. When Mike passed by them, the cameras quickly panned his way.

As if on cue, he raised his head in their direction. Ann held her breath, then sighed with relief. She could see that his earlier fear had dissipated, and now he was ready to give these people the show they were so obviously craving.

If they were expecting a coward who didn't have the guts to look his accusers in the eye and deny his guilt, they had underestimated him. He was a fighter, and he had nothing to be ashamed of, nothing to hide. Now he was about to announce that to the whole world.

Take a good look, she silently commanded his audience. *Does this look like the face of a murderer?*

CHAPTER
10

Karchy had already arrived and was anxiously pacing the front of the courtroom, gaping at the spectators' section. So many people . . . why would so many people care about Pop's case? Didn't they have anything better to do with their time than spend the day staring at him and listening to the lawyers argue?

Could be they were just curious to see a trial, as he had been before he'd gone to see Annie argue a case. This courtroom was a lot bigger and more impressive than the one he'd visited. Must have cost plenty to build, all that steel and glass. Maybe some of the steel had even come from his mill.

He ran his hand across the gleaming wood surface of the table in front of him and thought, *Someone takes good care of this furniture. Keeps the place polished and looking good.* That was as it should be. This was the U.S. Government courthouse. U.S. Government property. There was the American flag, up at the front, next to where the judge would sit. Judge Silver. A good, fair judge, according to Annie, even if he was Jewish.

Karchy saw his family walk through the door and waved

to get their attention. Ann took one look at him and wished she'd given him instructions about what to wear. As usual, Karchy had dressed down—jeans, sneakers, a windbreaker. Why hadn't it occurred to him even to put on a tie? And did he have to look so rumpled, as if he'd just rolled out of bed?

As he hurried forward to join them at the defense table, she sighed with exasperation. But she bit her tongue to keep from remarking on his attire. Lately Karchy had been dropping hints about feeling like the odd man out, what with Papa staying at her place and all. So she wasn't sure whether or not he was teasing when he said, "Hey, Pop, can I sit up here?" Then he winked to show he was only kidding, trying to get Mike to relax.

"Papa!" Ann whispered, poking Mike in the ribs. "Papa, give Karchy a hug."

"What the hell for?" he demanded.

Ann brushed an invisible piece of lint off his jacket and faked a smile. "Give him a hug, Papa. Smile." Didn't he get it? For the reporters. For the cameras. For all the people who were watching Mike Laszlo with his family and judging their every move.

Finally Mike did get it. He enveloped Karchy in a hearty bearhug and set his face in a smile that merited an Academy Award for most convincing performance.

He glanced at Ann, who gave a tiny nod of approval and muttered, "Talk to George, Papa."

Karchy glared at his sister. Where did she get off, treating Pop like a circus monkey who had to do tricks for the audience? What would he have to do next, climb up to the top of the flagpole and clap his hands for peanuts? Ann's tone of voice made Karchy think twice about arguing with her. But he couldn't understand why Pop didn't speak up, instead of shrugging his shoulders helplessly.

"Lotta people here, Gypsy," Mike said finally.

The words sounded stupid, even to Ann, but George had often played this game in the courtroom. Get the defendant to chill out. Make him look like he didn't have a care in the world because he was Mr. Innocent himself. Which Mike was, at least as far as she could tell. And she wasn't often wrong. So she grinned and said, "Listen here, Mike: You think the Bears got a chance this year?"

"Hell no," Mike replied mournfully, warming to his favorite subject.

Ann, meanwhile, had sent Karchy back to his seat and was now taking a quick survey of the room. Both Harry and David were there; they must have come early, because they were right up in front. Mack and Sandy were a couple of rows behind them. Who was minding the store? she wondered, grateful that they'd both cleared their calendars to be with her today. She didn't recognize anyone else— except, of course, at the prosecution table just across the aisle, Joe Dinofrio and, next to him, a grave-faced Jack Burke.

She was about to cross the aisle to speak to Dinofrio, when the court clerk appeared at the front of the courtroom and declared, "The United States of America versus Michael J. Laszlo, the Honorable Samuel T. Silver presiding."

Ann inhaled sharply. No matter how many trials she argued, she always experienced the same brief flicker of tension as the clerk made his announcement that court was in session. Like a panicky student moments before an important exam, she'd suddenly be flooded with doubts: Had she prepared well enough? Was her opening argument good enough? Did she have all her facts in order? Was there anything she'd forgotten?

The panic inevitably subsided as soon as the judge began his or her opening remarks. She'd once asked Mack if he'd ever experienced such anxiety attacks. Nothing to worry about, he'd assured her. She'd get over them. But she hadn't yet, and today the anxiety was compounded by Papa's palpable tension as Judge Silver strode into the room.

A dignified, gray-haired man, Sam Silver had an undeniable presence about him that bespoke judicial authority. Though he'd been appointed to the federal bench by a Republican administration, Silver had many close friends among the Democratic party leaders. More important, he had a reputation for not bringing politics into the courtroom and was generally considered to be tough but even-handed. Even with accused Nazis? Ann wondered.

The judge took his seat and gazed out at the standing-room-only throng. "I will tolerate no outbursts, disturbances, or interruptions," he stated in a tone that immediately established his control over those assembled in the room. The crowd instantly quieted. "If any of you have problems with your headsets, please bring your problems to the clerk's attention." That dispensed with, he nodded at the prosecutors. "You may make your opening statement, Mr. Burke."

Jack had slept poorly after the ugly scene in the restaurant with Ann Talbot. Finally, at five o'clock, he'd surrendered to insomnia and wearily peeled himself out of bed to go over his notes and rehearse his remarks. Now the adrenaline was flowing, and a surge of energy shot through him like a bolt of lightning.

All the weeks and months of painstaking, gut-wrenching investigation that had led to this day of reckoning! He'd never stopped to analyze what had fueled his passion to unmask Michael Laszlo. Perhaps his opposing counsel had guessed correctly that he was doing penance for knuckling under in the pension case. But who gave a damn about motives when the cause was undeniably right and just?

Now the final act was about to commence, and he was looking forward to bringing down the curtain on Laszlo's gruesome charade as right-minded citizen and devoted father. Too bad about the daughter, but she should have thought twice before fucking with him. When Papa Laszlo had been wiping her nose and reading her fairy tales, he'd

140

been brawling with the neighborhood toughs. He could show her a thing or two about fighting dirty.

Rule number one was to wipe her out, pretend she didn't even exist in this courtroom. He didn't even glance at her as he approached the bench and stood sideways so he could address the judge as well as the spectators. Clasping his hands behind his back in a pose he'd copied from the family minister, he said, "Thank you, Your Honor," and he began speaking in a low, steady voice.

"The issue in this case is simple. The evidence will show that Michael J. Laszlo lied on his application for American citizenship and was granted that citizenship under false pretenses. His citizenship, consequently, must be taken away."

Jack could sense the audience hanging on his words in the hushed courtroom as he launched into the meat of his argument. "Michael J. Laszlo lied to hide the fact that in the latter months of 1944 and the early months of 1945, he was a member of an SS-organized Hungarian death squad—the Arrow Cross, called the Special Section, a unit of the Hungarian gendarmes. He committed crimes so heinous that the mind boggles in trying to comprehend them."

He took a step or two toward the defense table and gestured at Mike, who sat stone-faced and rigid as a statue. "We are not speaking here of the banality of evil, of an anonymous bureaucrat sitting in an office giving orders, or a gendarme executing orders. We are speaking of a man who committed these heinous crimes with his own hands. We are speaking of *evil incarnate*."

Jack bowed his head a moment, as if in horror-stricken contemplation of the image, then concluded, "Thank you, Your Honor."

He knew, without being told, that he'd just delivered one of the finest arguments of his career—born of an absolute, unwavering belief in the rightness of his cause. The silence that followed him back to the prosecution table was as eloquent as a standing ovation.

"Ms. Talbot." Judge Silver invited Ann forward.

Ann squeezed Mike's hand under the table, and George, seated to her left, gave her a discreet thumbs-up. Her previous misgivings fell away as she rose and plunged right into the cold, murky depths of the case.

"Your Honor, the issue here is not whether my father lied on his application for American citizenship. That is a smoke screen. Yes," she declared unwaveringly, "my father *did* lie."

A chorus of stunned gasps followed her admission. Then pandemonium erupted in the courtroom, and Ann's next few words were lost in the chorus of whistles and boos. Karchy jumped up, protesting loudly. Was she nuts? Where did she come off, calling Pop a liar? What the hell . . . Only Harry's restraining arm kept him from bolting from his seat.

A couple of reporters sprinted for the exits as Judge Silver glared over the tops of his bifocals and banged his gavel. It took only a few seconds for order to be restored, so that Ann could pick up the thread of her argument.

"My father lied," she announced, speaking slowly to emphasize every word, "because he did not want to be repatriated by a Communist government that either executed or sent to Siberian work camps all those who opposed it. My father never stopped being opposed to the Communists. Yes, he was a gendarme," she paused, as if daring the audience to react again. "But he was *not* a member of the Special Section. He was a clerk in an office. He requested that assignment at a risk to himself because he could not tolerate the brutalities he witnessed his fellow gendarmes commit. My father is, simply, an innocent man, unjustly accused."

A half smile lit up her face as she turned toward Mike, encouraging all those present to see him as she did. "He has lived in the United States for almost forty years, a

142

model citizen who raised two children by himself and worked in the steel mill. He is a man who is being punished by proxy—by a Communist government for an action he committed against the representatives of that government five years ago. This was that action.''

Earlier, she'd arranged for a videocassette machine to be brought into the room. Now, at her signal, the lights went dim. The videotape began to roll, with Ann providing the narration.

''At an appearance here of the Hungarian National Folkdancers, a group financed and organized by the Hungarian Communist government, my father pelted the dancers with four bags of human excrement. The performance was halted. The tour was canceled. My father was arrested; the charges were eventually dismissed.''

Protected by the darkness, Mike smirked at the shot of himself, five years younger and a few pounds thinner. He and his pals had done a good job that day. He'd never regretted it for a moment, not even after the cops had thrown them all in jail for disturbing the peace. His kids had yelled at him plenty after they'd bailed him out. But he didn't care. He did what he had to, and the hell with it.

Others in the courtroom were already familiar with the incident. Some of the spectators, who had themselves participated in it, grinned with smug satisfaction. Mack nodded approvingly: Good girl, planting the image in Judge Silver's mind of Mike as fearless fighter of Communists.

''His action caused an international furor,'' Ann continued. ''The Hungarian Communist government lodged an official protest with the State Department objecting both to his action and the dismissal of the charges. His action was a protest against the repressive policies of the Hungarian Communist government, policies that resulted in the deaths of 15,000 people during the Hungarian revolution of 1956. Since then, my father has been a strong anti-Communist activist.''

The tape ended with a shot of Mike among a group of demonstrators in front of the Hungarian Consulate, on the anniversary of the November day in 1956 when Russian troops had rolled into Budapest. He looked grim and determined as he held up his sign, which proclaimed "Hungary for the Hungarians."

Ann blinked as her eyes readjusted to the light. Then she turned toward Judge Silver and quietly declared, "My father is not an evil man. My father is a good man, the kind of man who is willing to put himself at risk against injustice. I know that. And before this trial is over, I will prove it to you, too."

The hell you will, thought Jack, wishing he'd known about the tape ahead of time.

"Thank you, Your Honor," Ann concluded, and she returned to her seat.

The judge looked at Jack. "You may call your first witness, Mr. Burke."

Though it was hardly necessary, because he'd long since memorized the names, Jack consulted his sheet. The hell with the goddamn tape, he decided. Ann Talbot didn't have a prayer of a chance against the show he was about to put on.

James Nathanson was the kind of witness lawyers loved to call to the stand, especially at a jury trial, because his warmth and well-spoken manner immediately inspired listeners to trust him. A pleasant-faced man in his midsixties, Nathanson had testified at countless trials and wasn't easily rattled. Jack had decided to call him first, in order to immediately establish the government's credibility.

After he'd been sworn in, Jack suggested to Nathanson that he explain the nature of his work to the court. "I am employed by the United States Department of Justice," Nathan replied, looking up at the judge. "In the Immigration and Naturalization Service, at the forensic-document laboratory in Bethesda, Maryland. I am a senior forensic-document examiner."

"Approximately how many questioned documents have you examined and rendered reports on, Mr. Nathanson?" asked Jack, beginning to take him through his carefully rehearsed testimony.

"Well over a hundred thousand."

"Your Honor," Jack interrupted him, "at this time I offer James Nathanson as an expert witness in the area of questioned documents."

"He may testify as an expert," Judge Silver approved.

By now a screen had been set up in front of the empty jury box, and the lights went dim again. A slide came up on the screen of two separate identification cards. On it each card had a full-face photograph of a man, shown from the neck up, beneath which was inscribed a date and signature. The photos were strikingly similar—and strikingly familiar to anyone who knew Mike Laszlo.

"What is the date of the Special Section identification card?" Jack asked, using a wooden pointer to indicate the card on the left.

"November 1, 1944," Nathanson replied, ignoring the murmurs of shock that swept through the courtroom.

Jack pointed to the second card on the screen. "What is the date of the immigration card issued upon arrival to the United States—the so-called green card?"

"February 12, 1952."

"What is your conclusion concerning the two documents?" Jack asked, moving away from the screen to ensure that the judge had a clear, unobstructed view.

"My conclusion is that the photographs are of the same man, and the signatures are of the same man: Michael J. Laszlo."

Mike exhaled sharply and muttered something under his breath that Ann, who was concentrating on Nathanson's testimony, didn't hear. She motioned him to keep quiet. Thus far, she could have written Burke's script herself, but she needed to stay alert in case he came up with any surprises.

145

"Did you conduct an examination as to the authenticity of Government Exhibit One, the Special Section identification card?" Jack continued.

Ann was on her feet in a flash. This was precisely what she'd been waiting for. "Objection, Your Honor! Government Exhibit One is *not* a Special Section identification card. It is a *photostat* of a Special Section identification card."

The judge raised a skeptical eyebrow. Counsel for the defense was splitting hairs, and they both knew it. But she was also technically correct, and he couldn't very well overrule on the grounds that she was being too picky about Burke's choice of words. Very well, he nodded. "Sustained."

Jack, however, had prepared Nathanson for this possibility. "I conducted a full-phase examination of the photostat I was provided to determine whether there had been an alteration in any form," he explained in his calm, measured way.

"What methodology did you use?"

"I studied the document under a low-power stereoscopic microscope to determine background tone. In addition, I did a photo study using different filters, different types of film, different lighting conditions, looking for alterations."

"And what is your conclusion?"

"There is no alteration of any kind. The exhibit is authentic."

Authentic.

Nathanson's expert conclusion echoed through the hushed room.

Jack thanked his witness with an approving smile. Returning to his seat, he addressed himself directly to Ann for the first time since they'd entered the courtroom: "Your witness."

"Mr. Nathanson," Ann began, walking right up to the

witness box, "when you say you did a photo study . . . you mean you did a photo study of a *photostat*, don't you?"

"Yes," he conceded.

She was on sure ground now, leading him down a winding, complicated path that required a quick, logical mind to keep up with her. "Did the fact that Government Exhibit Number One is a photostat of a document, and not the document itself, hinder you in any way?"

He shook his head. "I felt I was not restricted by the photostat."

"Would you have felt more confident in your conclusions if you were dealing not with a photostat but with the identification card itself?" she asked.

Mack and Sandy exchanged knowing glances. An old trick of Ann's: asking a question to hammer home a point, not because she actually expected the witness to admit that yes, he would have preferred working with the original rather than the photostat.

"I feel just as confident in my conclusions without it," Nathanson said unequivocally.

"Mr. Nathanson," she pressed, "in analyzing a *photostat* to authenticate the document itself, is it possible to consider the *texture* of the document itself?"

The audience was getting restless. They'd come expecting fireworks and high drama, not a tedious exchange about the validity of original documents versus photocopies.

"The photostat, examined microscopically, would show any alterations in the paper," Nathanson asserted.

"Can you authenticate the *age* of the paper itself, the document itself, with a photostat of it?" she asked, watching the judge out of the corner of her eye.

Nathanson hesitated for the first time since he'd taken the stand. "Indirectly, yes."

"Indirectly."

"Yes," he reiterated, sounding more sure of himself again. "Using the stereoscopic equipment."

She pounced on the opening he'd left her. "But the only

way to authenticate it *directly* is by having the document itself.''

Another hesitation, then a reluctant ''Yes.''

''Mr. Nathanson, the conclusions that you reached here today are not conclusive, are they?'' Ann prompted him, barely disguising the triumph in her voice.

''I don't know what you mean.'' Nathanson cast an apologetic glance at Jack and Dinofrio, both of whom were looking thoroughly disgusted.

''A fingerprint, for example, matched against another fingerprint . . . The conclusions you have reached as a result of your tests are not on an equal level with fingerprints, are they?''

''In my opinion, they are,'' he said, finally rattled.

''Your *opinion*.'' She echoed him, adding the unflattering emphasis.

Sandy punched his knee with excitement. She'd done her homework—and then some. He peered across the rows, trying to get Harry Talbot's reaction to Ann's performance, but there were too many heads in the way. No matter. Annie Oakley had both guns loaded and blazing.

''Yes,'' he snapped, thoroughly annoyed at having been bested by this young woman. As she retreated toward the defense table, he breathed an almost audible sigh of relief. He'd be glad to be dismissed so he could get back to his hotel and have lunch.

His relief was premature, however. She appeared to have remembered another question, because she suddenly turned back to him and asked, ''Mr. Nathanson, are you Jewish?''

George chuckled silently at her audacity. The rest of the onlookers, Mike included, couldn't contain their astonishment at such a bold, out-of-left-field query. Even Judge Silver's stern demeanor couldn't prevent the stir of excitement that buzzed through the room.

David rolled his eyes at Ann's egregious breach of good taste. His father, on the other hand, was smiling in admiration as he calculated what it would take to get her on his litigation team. At the rate she was going, by the time she was done with this trial, she'd be able to name her price. And she'd be well worth it, too.

Jack immediately leapt to his feet. "Objection, Your Honor! Mr. Nathanson's religion is not relevant here!" he protested.

"It relates to the witness's objectivity, Your Honor," Ann retorted just as quickly. "He just said he was offering his opinion!"

"He offered conclusions based on thirty years of experience in the Department of Justice—directing it for ten years and having examined thousands of documents," Jack countered vehemently, outraged by her thinly cloaked anti-Semitism. He was stunned that she would sink so low. Surely Judge Silver, of all people, could see right through her pathetic rationalizations.

To his shock, the judge responded in Ann's favor. "Overruled. You may answer the question," he instructed the witness.

"I am Unitarian, but I am part Jewish, on my father's side," Nathanson reluctantly admitted, as if he concurred with Jack's opinion that the information was irrelevant.

"No further questions, Your Honor," Ann said, a glint of triumph in her eyes.

"We will adjourn until tomorrow morning," the judge announced with a sharp rap of his gavel. His robes trailing behind, he quickly disappeared through the side door that led to his private chambers.

As soon as he was gone, the reporters were out the door and racing to call their papers or stations. The other spectators, less driven to leave in a hurry, exchanged gossip and impressions as they gathered up their belongings. The more curious among them strained to catch a glimpse of the defense attorney with her father. Those who knew the family or were familiar with the case recognized Karchy hurrying toward the defense table.

The consensus among the courtroom pundits was that Ann Talbot had won this first round handily. Their decision was supported by Jack Burke's glum expression as he remained seated at his table, conferring with his colleague. The day, which had started off so well for them, had ended on an unexpectedly sour note. Jack was still smarting from Ann's last zinger.

"First witness, and that's her bottom line: Are you Jewish?" he grumbled to Dinofrio, who shrugged philosophically. Win some, lose some. Sure, easy enough for Dinofrio to be cool. He was only along for the ride.

Meanwhile, there across the aisle, Ann and Mike were smiling like two cats who'd just swallowed the proverbial bowl of cream. Jack's stomach knotted with anger—or maybe it was indigestion from last night's overly rich dinner. All in all, these Hungarians were turning out be a major pain in more than one area of his anatomy.

Contrary to what Jack might have expected, Ann wasn't holding any celebrations after court. Sure she had come out ahead this afternoon. She'd had a couple of lucky breaks, especially when Silver had overruled on the question of religion. However, tomorrow was another day, another round of witnesses—and it was those witnesses who were preoccupying her on the drive back to Wilmette.

Nathanson had been relatively easy to nail. But she'd have to watch her step in cross-examining the people Burke had brought over from Hungary. They were survivors, elderly, some of them not well. Their written statements alone had been enough to make her weep. She could only imagine how powerfully moving it would be to see and hear them talk about their experiences. If she tried to nail them with the same sharp knife she'd used on Nathanson, Burke could win his case right there.

Mulling over her options, Ann was oblivious to the discussion swirling around her in the car. She seemed to be the only one whose mind was still on the case. Mike, who'd loosened his tie the instant they were out of the courtroom, sat next to Karchy in the back seat, arguing about the union election at the steel mill. George, who had her own strong opinions on the subject, kept turning around and throwing in her two cents.

They were only a couple of miles from home when a lightbulb went off in Ann's head and she tuned back into the conversation. "George," she said quietly, interrupting her friend in midsentence, "I want you to find out where the witnesses from Hungary are staying. I want to know who they see. I want to know what they talk about."

George snorted. "How'm I gonna find that out?" She was the best private eye in the city, but she wasn't a damn psychic.

"You've got your ways, don't you, George?" Ann said persuasively, not doubting for a second that George could handle this assignment. She could almost do it herself, if she had the time. But she didn't, and George was the expert spy, even if she occasionally needed some coaxing to undertake the particularly nasty assignments.

"They're gonna be talkin' Hon-garian," George pointed out, deliberately mispronouncing the word—a good sign. If George could joke about a job, that meant she'd already begun to figure out how and where she would find the information.

"I can understand Hungarian," Ann reminded her with a sly smile.

George still had her misgivings. This was real dirty Deep Throat stuff they were talking about. If anyone else were asking, she'd have turned him down faster than you could say boo. But Ann was family, and her daddy's future—his life—was on the line. She didn't see that she really had much choice in the matter.

That question having been settled, a mischievous grin played across her lips as she contemplated the logistics. Difficult . . . challenging . . . but by no means impossible. Might even have some fun with this one.

Karchy was also amused by the image of poor George, struggling to make heads or tails of a Hungarian phone call. His sister was one smart cookie, he thought admiringly. For a moment there during the trial, he'd been pissed off at her, but she knew what she was doing, all right. He chuckled, remembering how she'd twisted Nathanson like a pretzel.

"Karchy!" Mike said abruptly. "You wear suit tomorrow. You sit next to me, too, like Anni. Both my kids."

"It's at the dry cleaner's, Pop," Karchy informed him, surprised that his father was suddenly taking an interest in his wardrobe.

"Get it, Karchy," Ann chimed in, glad that Mike had brought up the subject. And now that he mentioned it, he was right about Karchy sitting with them. But not, she shuddered, while he was wearing that awful windbreaker. She'd overheard Harry congratulate Mike for having such a classy, intelligent daughter. It spoke well of him, Harry had said. Made a good impression on the judge. But she wondered what kind of impression Karchy had made on the judge—or if the judge even knew that Mike had a son he was proud of.

Karchy scowled. Just like the bad old days, when Pop and Annie would gang up on him—about staying in school, cutting down on his drinking. . . . Name it, they'd nagged him about it. He'd always been torn between enjoying the extra concern and attention and resenting his younger sister's interference. However, since it was easier to say yes than argue with them, he growled, "Okay, I'll get it," and he glared out the window at the rapidly deepening dusk.

A few minutes later they were home, and there was Mikey, shooting baskets in the snow-covered driveway, his unzipped parka flapping in the wind. Ann waved as she was getting out of the car and thought, *What's wrong with this picture?* Then it hit her: At this hour, especially when she wasn't home to supervise, he was usually deep into a vicious game of Nintendo with one of his friends.

"Hi, Grandpa. Hi, Mom," he called cheerfully, hurrying over to greet them. "Hey, George," he waved. "Uncle Karchy, you staying for dinner?"

Ann bent to kiss him. "O my God!" she exclaimed, bending down to get a closer look at his face. His left eye was badly bruised and swollen, and it was fast becoming rainbow colored.

"It'll be okay," Mikey said quickly, turning away. His big worry was that Grandpa might think he was a wimp or a sissy because he'd taken a punch. It hadn't been a fair fight—two against one. But he'd managed to throw a couple of punches himself, and one of the guys had walked away with a bloody nose. "It doesn't hurt—really it doesn't," he lied bravely.

"Come on, let's put something on it," Ann said gently, barely holding back her tears.

"It was just a fight, Mom, that's all," Mikey assured her, ever sensitive to her emotions. He wished they could just drop the whole thing. "Hey, Grandpa," he said brightly, "you wanna play Nintendo?"

Ann could see that her father wasn't interested in playing any games, Nintendo or otherwise. He was glowering with such pain and murderous rage that she could *feel* how badly he wanted to lash out and smash some heads. She understood from her gut, because she, too, was feeling that rage. How *dared* they touch her son?

It was as if Mike were reacting for both of them when his fury suddenly spilled over and he slammed his fist against the car.

"Goddamn 'em to hell!" he exploded. "Son-the-bitches! Goddamn 'em to fuckin' hell!"

They had pizza for dinner, which they ate quickly and for the most part silently. Mikey, who was usually good for three or four slices, gave up after two and asked to be excused to his room. Despite his protestations, Ann knew he had to be hurting; his eye was twice its normal size and shut tight. She ached for him, but she knew he'd only feel worse if she babied him. So she gave him two aspirins, set him up on his bed with an ice pack, and promised to come talk to him in a little while.

Karchy and George left soon afterward, and Mike, who couldn't stop yawning, went off to read his Hungarian newspaper. Left alone to do the dishes, Ann was grateful for the solitude, calmed by the mundane task of loading dishes into the dishwasher. Scrape, rinse, stack . . . so simple. You didn't have to waste a moment's thought. If only more of life could be reduced to such fundamental rituals.

She sighed as she twisted the tie on the bulging trash-bag. Normally, Mikey was responsible for taking out the garbage, but tonight he had more than earned his dispensation. Flicking on the porch light, she pushed open the back door and stepped outside, to be greeted by a blast of frigid night air. She crammed the trashbag into the metal garbage can, slammed shut the lid, and hurried back into the house.

The darkness felt particularly inhospitable this evening. As a child she'd been fed a steady diet of folk tales featuring demons and witches who came in the night to snatch their human victims. She hadn't been scared then, but tonight she couldn't wait to get back inside, safe from the evil spirits that seemed to be lurking in the bushes.

A moment later, the door locked and bolted, she could laugh at her fears. Next, she'd be seeing ghosts and carrying a rabbit's foot for good luck. Still, she reminded herself soberly, there *were* people out there—*real* people, not demons or spirits—who truly believed that Papa was evil and needed to be punished. Mikey had taken the first blow. She was determined that it be the last her family suffered.

Turning off the lights, she went upstairs to check on

him. He was lying on his bed, staring off into space, the ice pack covering his eye.

"How is it?" she asked, sitting down next to him on the bed.

He shrugged—no big deal—and got straight to the topic that interested him much more. "Can I go to the trial?" he wanted to know, pushing for the sympathy vote.

Ann stroked his head. Her stubborn baby. "You've got school—"

"I know all about that stuff anyway," he interrupted, correctly guessing that missing school was not the real issue. "Grandpa told me all about it."

Strange. Mike had never told her a word about the Holocaust, nor Karchy either, as far as she knew. "What did he tell you?" she asked, curious to hear what he'd said to Mikey.

Mikey nervously bit his lip. "It's a secret, just between him and me."

"You can tell me, can't you?" she coaxed, smiling to herself. Those two had more secrets between them than the C.I.A.

He hesitated, making up his mind whether his mother could be trusted. His grandfather had sworn him to secrecy, but he was persuaded by her cool hand stroking his throbbing forehead. "He said it was all a big exaggeration—the Holocaust and stuff. It's all made up."

The words, uttered so innocently, so casually, stunned her. Desperately she cast about for an explanation. Perhaps Mikey had misheard Papa . . . because of his accent. Sometimes she had trouble herself understanding him. "He said that?" she asked, hoping Mikey didn't hear the tremor in her voice.

Mikey knew right away that he'd made a very big mistake. He sat up and clutched at her arm. "You're not gonna say anything, are you?"

He looked so forlorn that she almost said, don't worry, of course not. But then she decided, no, he'd already heard

155

too many lies. She couldn't compound her father's sin by telling another untruth. So she kept silent, kissed the top of his head, and went to find her father, who was already in his room, doing his pushups. He was breathing heavily and counting aloud, as he flexed his elbows and lowered his chest to the floor.

"How could you say that?" she demanded angrily, her voice very high and thin.

He looked up at her, then let his body collapse to the floor. "What I say?" he asked.

"To Mikey, about the Holocaust." She spat out the words.

"I don't say nothin' to him," he said, slowly getting up and brushing off his hands.

Her eyes filled with tears, and her heart was pounding so wildly she thought she might faint with rage. "Don't lie to me, Papa!"

"I no lie to you. I say nothing." He gestured angrily with his hands, as if to wipe out her accusation.

"Yes, you did," she insisted through clenched teeth. "He told me!"

They glared at each other—she, pale and trembling; he, red faced with the effort of controlling his temper and his tongue.

"He didn't, Mom," came Mikey's voice. "It was Grandpa Talbot."

He stood in the doorway, his left eye a swollen, multi-hued badge of courage. Stifling a sob, he stole a quick peek at his grandfather, then looked back at his mother to see whether she believed him. *Please*, he implored her. *Don't ruin everything between me and Grandpa.*

All she said was "Go to bed, Mikey."

"You said you wouldn't say anything," he reproached her tearfully. *And if Grandpa stops loving me, that'll be almost as bad as you and Daddy getting divorced.* Then he turned and stomped out of the room, a betrayed, pathetic waif clutching his ice pack.

"You think I lie to you, tubusom?" Mike said, his voice hoarse with emotion.

She didn't know what to think. She desperately wanted to believe him; she wanted to believe Mikey. Except that then she also had to believe that it was Harry who had fed that terrible misinformation to Mikey. And why would he ever have told Mikey such stories? Unless he thought they were true . . . which he couldn't possibly. Could he?

Then suddenly she was flooded with a wave of shame so thick she thought she would choke on it. What kind of a terrible daughter was she, so quick to accuse her father over her ex-father-in-law? What made one more credible than the other? A closet full of expensive suits? A limo? A name that instantly opened doors? Or had she, too, bought the government's line, without even knowing it?

"You think I lie, Anni?" Mike repeated, knowing that the rest of his life depended on her answer.

"No, Papa," she said, reaching out to be encircled by his arms. "I'm sorry, Papa. I'm so sorry."

CHAPTER
11

The scene in the courtroom on the second day of the trial was much the same, except for Karchy's presence next to Mike at the defense table. Jack glanced at him squirming uncomfortably in his suit, and immediately recognized him from the pictures he'd looked at of the Laszlos. So they'd trotted out the entire family for Judge Silver's benefit . . . except for the grandson. Probably they were holding the boy in reserve in case they felt desperate enough for a kiddie act.

Jack smiled smugly as the clerk announced that court was in session, and the judge took his seat. He had a little surprise of his own this fine morning, and he couldn't wait to lay it on the counsel for the defense.

He didn't have long to wait. Judge Silver liked to get started promptly. "You may call your next witness, Mr. Burke," he said.

Jack stood up. "May we see you in chambers, Your Honor?"

The judge looked momentarily surprised, then nodded. "You may."

Mike tugged at Ann's sleeve. "What's goin' on, Anni?" he whispered nervously.

"I don't know," she told him, trying to hide her concern. She signaled to Karchy and George to keep Mike calm, then quickly followed Jack and Judge Silver to the latter's office behind the courtroom.

"I have some good news, Your Honor," Jack announced as soon as they were all seated. "The Hungarian government has turned over the Special Section I.D. card itself to the Justice Department labs in Washington."

He shot a glance at Ann. To his pleasure, she was looking every bit as stunned as he'd hoped.

"Well, maybe that will clarify everything," Judge Silver remarked. "Do you have a problem with that, Ms. Talbot?"

"No, Your Honor," she began, furious that this development had caught her so empty handed. How perfectly convenient for Burke . . . *too* perfectly convenient. And how nice for him that Silver was eating it up with a spoon. Well, screw clarification. This "good news" smelled as rotten as yesterday's fish, and she wasn't going to pretend she wasn't offended by the stench. "Yes, Your Honor, I do have a problem," she edited herself, turning to address Jack directly. "As soon as I score some points on one of your witnesses, they throw something into the pot from Budapest. Are *you* prosecuting this case, or are they?"

"Come on," he said contemptuously, enjoying her obvious distress. The trap was set. Now he couldn't wait to spring it. "We've been working for months through the embassies to get the card itself. You've been carrying on so much about the photostat you should be jumping for joy."

Zing! He sat back and watched her try to wiggle her way out of that one. It was hopeless, and she knew it.

"I'll let your forensic-documents man examine it first," the judge decided. "Will a week be sufficient?"

She surrendered gracefully. She had no other option. "Thank you, Your Honor."

The judge glanced at Jack. "I have no objection to that," Jack said cheerfully, feeling as if he'd just settled the score for the Bull's Blood. And this was only the beginning of the end of Ann's case.

They resumed their places in the courtroom and picked up where they'd left off. "We call Istvan Boday, Your Honor," Jack declared.

Boday was a frail, elderly man who looked as if he could have been blown over by the least puff of wind. He was dressed in a suit a couple of sizes too big for him; it might have been borrowed, or perhaps it had fit him once, long ago, when he was younger and fuller. Stooped over his cane, he stopped to rest every few seconds as he slowly shuffled up the aisle, looking neither to the right or to the left.

Ann watched her father glance at Boday when he passed the defense table. She could detect not even a glimmer of recognition in Mike's expression.

Finally, Boday made it to the witness box, and the clerk stepped forward. "Do you swear to tell the truth, the whole truth, and nothing but the truth, so help you God?" he recited, holding up a Bible for Boday to take the oath.

"Ya, I do," Boday replied in a barely audible voice, his hand shaking as he placed it atop the Bible.

Judge Silver leaned over and asked, "Mr. Boday, do you speak English?"

"Little."

"We can use the headsets if you'd like to speak Hungarian," the judge offered in a kindly tone.

"I try English," Boday said, shaking his head.

Jack walked up very close to the box so that Boday would have no trouble hearing him. He'd come to admire the man in the short time they'd spent together going over Boday's testimony. Though he was physically thin and weak, he had an inner strength that had been forged in the

160

fires of hell. And he'd been waiting for this moment for almost half his life.

"Where do you reside, Mr. Boday?" Jack smiled encouragingly.

"Budapesht, Hungary," Boday replied, giving the name of the capital its Hungarian pronunciation.

Jack moved quickly to the heart of the testimony. "In December of 1944, Mr. Boday, where did you reside?"

"In Budapesht ghetto," said Boday, fixing his watery blue eyes on some unseen point in the middle distance. "Our family . . . we must go to the ghetto. It order."

"Mr. Boday, can you describe to us the events of December 14, 1944?" Jack asked gently.

Boday nodded, but when he opened his mouth, nothing came out. He cleared his throat and began speaking very slowly. "Night. Seven o'clock. One room we in. My mother, father, my brother. My wife, Clara. My boy."

"How old was your boy?"

"He seven year old." Boday shifted his body, trying to get comfortable. "They come . . ."

"Who came, Mr. Boday?"

"Special Section. They come in, machine gun, uniform. Black. All black." He faltered momentarily, then took a deep breath and resumed his story. "On arm, how you say? Insignia. Cross. Arrow Cross."

"Did you know about the Special Section before?" Jack went on, probing Boday's memory as delicately as a brain surgeon.

"Ya. We see. Ghetto no permit inside soldier. Special Section go everywhere."

"How many of them were there, Mr. Boday?"

"Four. Two leader. One, have scar on face. Other, big boss. *Mishka.*"

"His name was Mishka?" Jack raised his voice. He wanted to be sure the entire courtroom heard.

"Ya." Boday nodded. "They call to him Mishka."

"What does *Mishka* mean in Hungarian?" Jack asked, walking a few steps toward the defense table.

"Mike. Name for Mike."

"What did they do, Mr. Boday?"

"Mishka," Boday said, his voice cracking slightly, "he do most talk. He say, 'You got jewel, diamond. All you Jews got gold. You give.' My father say, 'We got nothing.' "

"What happened then, Mr. Boday?" Jack asked very gently.

The old man shuddered, remembering. "Mishka . . . he take my wife, my Clara. He say, 'Open mouth, pig.' She scared, cry. He take her mouth, open mouth with hand. He look at teeth. He laugh. He say, 'Plenty gold.' "

An undercurrent of shock ran through the courtroom.

"What did he mean?" Jack prompted.

"They take, steal, everything. Jewel, painting, furniture, teeth. Everything," Boday continued his recitation.

"What happened then?"

"They take us from ghetto. Very cold. Snow. We march in street. My mother fall. One of them, not Mishka, he beat her on head with rifle. We keep march. We no see Mama again. She stay in street."

"Where did they march you?"

"They march us to the Duna, riverbank, Danube. By bridge, Lanchid. To field. Many people there, Jews. Mishka laugh, we march. He say, 'All you get bath. Water cold, kill fleas.' "

"What happened on the Danube riverbank, Mr. Boday?"

"They tell us, stand close, front each other. Three and two. My father, me, my boy. My brother, my Clara," Boday replied, still staring off into the distance, as if he were watching the scene being replayed in front of him. "We stand close. They take wire, they wrap wire around us, two group. Very tight. We can no move."

The silence in the room was absolute. Nobody moved

or even seemed to breathe. With trembling fingers, Boday picked up his glass and took a few sips of water, spilling a few drops on the wooden counter of the witness box. "They move us to edge of bank of river. Mishka say, 'Sorry, we no got enough the bullet.' "

Again he broke off and inhaled deeply. Another drink of water, then he went on: "He take pistol. He go behind my Clara. He say, 'One for you, pig.' He shoot. He come behind us. He put pistol to my father head. He shoot. Then they push us in Duna."

Someone in the audience sighed noisily. Others were sobbing as they searched in their pockets and purses for tissues to muffle their crying.

"He shot your father in the head and dumped all three of you in the river?"

"Ya," Boday said wearily, turning his gaze back to Jack. "He push from edge. We wire together. We can no move. Duna very cold. They think we all die."

"How did you survive, Mr. Boday?"

Boday shrugged his shoulders forlornly. "I don't know. I feel I dead. Can no move. We got sweep to bank. I get hand out, take wire off. Father dead. Boy dead. I no see Clara and brother. They dead, too."

"Mr. Boday," Jack asked, "is that the man who shot your father and your wife and dumped you in the river?"

He pointed to the photograph of Mike from his ostensible Special Section I.D. card, which was being displayed on the screen to Boday's left.

Boday slowly turned his head and stared at the photo. "Ya, that is Mishka," he agreed without a moment's hesitation.

"Is there any doubt in your mind that it's the same man, Mr. Boday?" Jack pressed him, praying that Boday would repeat the answer he'd given in his sworn statement.

The old man straightened up in his chair and spoke with absolute certainty. "I see him forty-four year, every night I close eyes. *It is Mishka.*"

Jack nodded his thanks. A job well done. "No further questions, Your Honor. Your witness."

Ann stood up slowly to begin her cross-examination. Though she'd already read through Boday's testimony three or four times, hearing him tell it today in person had been extremely painful. And with good reason, she told herself, approaching the witness box. It was a harrowing story, and she had no intention of trying to cast doubt on its authenticity. On the other hand, she couldn't allow Boday to leave the stand without questioning his memory of the man who'd killed his family.

Mike's hand, when she squeezed it for encouragement, was cold and wet with perspiration. Beads of sweat dotted his forehead as well. She'd tried to warn him about what he'd hear in court. She'd even tried to get him to read some of the stories, Boday's included. And this was just the beginning.

Approaching the witness box, she almost lost heart. Boday looked so old and fragile, like a rare porcelain figure that had to be handled with the greatest care. By his own description, he'd already been through the tortures of the damned. How could she in any way add to his pain? What kind of a person did that make her?

She played nervously with the opal ring, her birthstone, which she'd taken to wearing again since her divorce. Another present from Papa—and Karchy—when she'd graduated second in her high-school class. Papa had chosen the ring himself. He'd been so proud of her.

What kind of a person was she? The kind who would do whatever she could to save her father's life.

That thought propelled her forward to face Istvan Boday. "Would you like to take a short recess before we begin, Mr. Boday?" she offered gently, as much for her sake as his.

He shook his head, no, and scrutinized her as if trying to find in her face a resemblance to the man he'd been asked to identify from the Special Section photograph.

"Mr. Boday," she began, rubbing her ring, "how did you identify my father as the man who did this to your family?"

"They come to me six month ago, show me photograph," he replied flatly, trying not to show his contempt for his tormentor's daughter.

She tried to stifle her excitement. "They brought you his photograph and you said that was the man?"

Jack saw immediately where she was headed and jumped to his feet. "Objection, Your Honor! The witness is misspeaking himself," he asserted, determined that Ann not succeed with her ploy.

"He's coaching the witness, Your Honor!" Ann shot back, equally resolved to win this point.

"Mr. Burke, I'm overruling your objection," Judge Silver announced, "but I will ask you, Ms. Talbot, to phrase your questions more carefully in the future. Please continue, Mr. Boday."

"They show me many photographs, of many people," Boday said testily, disturbed by the heated exchange between the two lawyers.

"Who showed you the photographs, Mr. Boday?" asked Ann, choosing her words carefully.

"Four of them come." He paused, getting it clear in his mind. "Mr. Burke, man from American Embassy, man from Hungarian Interior Ministry, and translator."

"What did they tell you?" she said quietly.

Boday pursed his lips thoughtfully, recalling how the men had crowded into his tiny one-room flat to talk to him. There hadn't even been room enough for all of them to sit. "Mr. Burke, he say he investigate war criminal. He find in United Nations my affidavit what happen. He say they think they have man."

"And then they showed you some photographs?"

"Ya." Boday nodded. That's exactly how it had been.

"How many photographs were there, Mr. Boday?" Ann wanted to know.

"Many," he replied, wondering what it mattered, why she cared about the number. What was important were the facts—her father was a murderer. That man . . . sitting just across from him. Even with his head averted, Boday could feel Mishka staring at him as if he were a ghost come to haunt his dreams. And so he was . . . for by murdering his family, Mishka had robbed him, too, of his life. He'd spent all these years in a twilight existence, filled with shadowy memories of what might have been. If not for that man. . . .

"Mr. Boday?" Ann repeated herself. "How many? Ten, twenty, a hundred?"

Irritated by her heckling, he flung numbers at her. "Twelve . . . fifteen."

"Which was it? Twelve or fifteen?" she persisted.

"Objection, Your Honor!" called Jack. "She's badgering the witness."

Judge Silver didn't have to think twice before responding. "Sustained," he declared, casting a concerned look at the witness.

But Boday was stronger than he looked—and he'd come prepared for the worst. "I no remember," he stubbornly informed Ann.

"You don't remember," she repeated, crossing her arms and seemingly deep in thought. Then she asked, "Mr. Boday, how were the photographs displayed to you?"

He cocked his head, confused by the unfamiliar English word. "*Display?* I no understand."

"Shown to you, Mr. Boday," Ann translated with a fleeting smile. For a moment, he'd reminded her of Papa, whose command of the language was unpredictable. How many thousands of times had she had to translate words and expressions for him?

"They put on table," Boday told her.

"And of these twelve or fifteen photographs, where was my father's picture on the table?"

"I don't remember exactly." What he did remember

166

was that they'd spread the pictures out on his table, large enough only for two people to sit. The lightbulb above had happened to burn out that morning, so someone—the translator?—had dragged the lamp from the corner.

They'd hovered over his shoulders, urging him not to rush when he'd pointed right away to Mishka's picture. Take his time, be sure, they'd told him. He was sure. He could never forget that face. But where among all the pictures had been her father's? Such a question. She must be crazy, he decided, like her father.

"You don't remember that, either?" Ann persisted, not unkindly. "Well, was it among the others? Was it placed separately? Was it on top?" Her tone suggested that she was trying to be as helpful as possible.

"No, it among them. One of the many," he said disdainfully.

"Were the photographs all the same size, Mr. Boday?"

"Ya."

"Were the men in the photographs shown you the same age?" Out of the corner of her eye, she caught a glimpse of Harry, beaming his approval.

"Ya," he spat. "Every one young—like Mishka."

Jack smiled. Laszlo had ripped out his guts, but he sure hadn't killed the guy's spirit. Piss and vinegar. You couldn't ask more of a witness.

Ann walked right up to the witness box, close enough that she could see the hatred glinting in his eyes. "How long did it take you to recognize the photograph, Mr. Boday?"

He shrugged. He supposed he could remember if he tried hard enough, but it was a stupid question, not worth his energy.

"You said you'd dreamed about him every night for forty-four years. You said you couldn't forget," Ann pressed him. "So *how long did it take you*?"

Daughter of a murderer, he thought. Once, he and Clara had had dreams of their son becoming a lawyer. Difficult,

167

but not impossible, for a Jew in Hungary. Until the Nazis had come to power. The Nazis and Mishka had made it impossible for their son ever to become anything besides a painful, cherished memory. "I don't remember exactly," he said, carefully pronouncing each word as he would with a deaf person.

"You don't remember that, either?" Ann reiterated, her voice dripping with incredulity. "Can you give us your best estimate, Mr. Boday?"

"About five seconds," he rasped, tightening his grip on his cane until his knuckles went white.

She felt as if she'd been ambushed. The onlookers sensed it, too. Depending on where their loyalties lay, they responded with muffled applause or boos. Judge Silver rapped his gavel, demanding order, and the reactions quickly subsided. Not so Ann's anger—with herself, as well as with Boday—which drove her to strike back quickly, unthinkingly.

"Are you a member of the Communist party in Hungary, Mr. Boday?" she demanded, sure that she'd found his Achilles heel.

Jack was immediately on his feet, shouting, "Objection, Your Honor! Irrelevant and immaterial!"

"It relates to his credibility as an objective witness," Ann retorted heatedly. "Your Honor—"

Boday didn't wait for the judge to decide which of them was right. It had been a long trip from Hungary, and he hadn't slept well the last two nights in the hotel. The bed was too hard, the room too warm, the city streets below his window too noisy with raucous horns and sirens.

He was an old man, and he'd had his fill of being harassed by this young woman who spoke so sweetly that you almost missed the dagger in her hand. She knew, though she pretended not to, that her father was a Nazi bastard murderer, who deserved nothing less than to be shoved up against a wall and shot. Now he wanted to be well away from her and Mishka and all these stupid questions, such as was he a member of the party.

"No," he said, his voice thick with scorn. "I no like Communists. They know I no like them. What they can do to me? I old man, no have family. *Nobody* can no hurt me no more."

They stared at each other as if they were the only two left in the room. A half-formed thought flashed through Ann's mind but disappeared before it was fully conceived. Something else she wanted to ask him . . . But it wouldn't come, so she merely said, "No further questions."

"We will have a one-hour lunch recess," Judge Silver announced. It had been a long, difficult testimony for all concerned. What he needed now was some nourishment and an hour alone with a Mozart concerto playing in the background.

At least one person in the courtroom was pleased with the outcome, however. With weary satisfaction, Jack contemplated the sight of an obviously worried Ann trying to pacify her dispirited father and brother. "She walked right into it," he told Dinofrio, stepping forward to help Boday out of the room. "Right smack into it."

"Georgine Wheeler, please," Ann said, holding the phone in one hand, a pen in the other. Perched on the edge of the table, she tapped her foot impatiently while the person at the other end of the line went to find George. While she waited she wrote quick, almost undecipherable notes to herself—questions for George, questions for Papa, instructions for Mikey's babysitter about what to make for dinner.

A cup of take-out coffee sat cooling in front of her, and the air was rich with the odor of garlic—garlic pickles and spicy garlic salami, Karchy's idea of a well-balanced, fortifying lunch. He was the only one of the three of them who had an appetite this noon. She was too tense to think about food, and Mike sat hunched over on his chair, staring off into space.

Karchy, however, true to his philosophy of "Ya still gotta eat," was devouring his salami on rye with great gusto. "This is good salami," he announced to no one in particular. "Hey, Pop." He held up a waxpaper-wrapped package. "You want a salami sandwich? I got an extra."

Mike glanced dully at his son, shook his head, and retreated back behind his wall of silence.

"Hello, Mishka," said Harry, walking into the room and extending his hand. "How you holding up?"

"Okay, Harry." Mike attempted a smile but winced at the "Mishka." Harry had used the nickname for years, but suddenly the sound of it grated in his ears.

Ann acknowledged Harry with a wave, but her mind was elsewhere. She had a bad feeling about this morning, and the afternoon's witness would probably offer more of the same gut-wrenching testimony. How could they possibly win against such stories? How much more could Judge Silver listen to without turning against her father?

"Come on, George," she muttered urgently into the phone, wishing they'd arranged to check in with each other. Where *was* she with the information Ann needed? She couldn't take another session like the one she'd just blown.

A muffled voice came on the line, talking to someone in the background. "Georgine Wheeler!" Ann barked into the receiver, trying to get the speaker's attention. Was anybody *there*?

Karchy had picked up on Ann's tension, and now he began to vent his bitterness about what he'd been forced to listen to. "I don't understand what the hell's goin' on here," he complained loudly to Harry. "I mean, Jesus! They put some old fogey on, bring him out of the retirement home, he says all this *shit*! . . . I mean, Jesus Christ! This guy couldn't even get a driver's license in this country. No shit, he couldn't even get a goddamn driver's license!''

Feeling better for having expressed himself, he remembered his manners and said, "Hey, Harry, you want a salami sandwich?''

"Are you kidding?" Harry's patrician nostrils flared. Karchy should know better than to eat that poison. Salami was for people who were too ignorant or arrogant to understand that cholesterol was a killer. Harry attributed his longevity and health to his healthful, low-fat diet, a topic about which he could go on for hours.

Educating Karchy, however, could wait for a more opportune moment. There were more pressing matters to be dealt with now—first and foremost, Mike's very obvious distress. "The trouble is," he opined vigorously, launching into yet another of his favorite subjects, "these clowns in Washington today are so full of shit and glasnost and building Hilton hotels over there . . . This would never have gotten into a courtroom in the fifties!''

Mike nodded his head automatically, leaving Harry to wonder whether the man had heard a word of what he'd just said. It certainly wasn't like Mishka to sit there, silent as a dummy, instead of coming back with one of his marvelously antiliberal (in the worst, ACLU-sense of the word) comments. But who could blame him, after what he'd just been subjected to?

Ann was feeling no such constraints. She'd been itching to give Harry a generous piece of her mind. Covering the phone with her hand, she lashed out at him, "How could you say that to Mikey?''

"What did I say to him?" Harry asked, taken by surprise.

"About the Holocaust," she snapped.

"I don't know *what* you're talking about," Harry replied, all innocence. "Mikey and I don't discuss politics.''

Ann glanced uncertainly from Harry to her father. One of them had to be lying to her, but . . .

Her speculation was interrupted as George flew into the room, beaming with excitement.

"I've been trying to find you," Ann said quickly, beckoning her into a corner for privacy. The look on George's face told her what she needed to know, but she wanted cold, hard facts—which George handed her in the form of a legal-sized page of names and numbers. The two of them huddled together, reviewing the information and formulating a strategy.

Watching them from across the room, Harry tapped a thoughtful finger against his pursed lips. There were paths to be pursued . . . people who could be consulted. . . . Better to wait, he cautioned himself. See how this thing plays itself out. Don't intrude unless you're called upon.

"I love salami," Karchy remarked, taking a big bite out of the second sandwich. "You like salami, Harry?" he asked, breaking Harry's train of thought. "Here, come on, I'm not gonna eat all of this. Take it!"

With the self-satisfied look of a man who's about to initiate a friend into the pleasures of the flesh, he all but forced the sandwich into Harry's hand. Harry grasped the offering between the tips of his fingers, showing as much enthusiasm as he might if he'd just been handed a steaming dog turd. The curl of his lips wasn't hard to read: *These people*, he seemed to be thinking. *They really are a different breed.*

Judit Hollo was a tiny, gnarled woman in her seventies, dressed completely in black—black dress that reached almost to her ankles, black sweater buttoned to her neck, black stockings, and lace-up shoes. Even the babushka she wore tied at the chin to cover her gray hair was black.

Ann's first thought upon seeing her was of Baba Yaga, the witch who had featured so prominently in the Slavic fairy tales of her childhood. But whereas Baba Yaga was usually a fearsome, man-eating creature, Judit Hollo seemed not only harmless but downright endearing in a grandmotherly sort of way. Indeed, she wasn't too far from the fantasy grandmother Ann had created for herself when she was no more than three or four and had first realized that not only was she motherless but grandparentless, as well.

The old lady's raisin-brown eyes twinkled in her wrinkled, weathered face as she settled into the witness box and tried on the headset she'd been provided with.

Judge Silver, who seemed particularly taken with the witness (*Perhaps he never knew his grandmother either,* thought Ann.), smiled as he leaned over to speak to her. "The questions will be translated to you, madam, and your answers will be translated to us," he explained. "Am I being translated to you now?"

Her wrinkles rearranged themselves in a smile, and she nodded.

"Good," said the judge. He adjusted his earphones and signaled Jack to begin.

"Where do you reside, Mrs. Hollo?" Jack asked.

"In Budapest, Hungary," she replied, her voice high and quavering.

"Mrs. Hollo," Jack went on, not wasting any time, "where were you on the afternoon of January 11, 1945?"

"I was at work. I worked at the dry-steam cleaners. I left work early that day because the bombings were especially heavy. My home was only about a half kilometer from the shop. I was walking down the Calvin Square. Many buildings were on fire. There was smoke everywhere. The air-raid sirens were on. I was at the Calvin Square when I saw them."

Her plain-spoken words managed to invoke a compelling sense of time and place that was conveyed even in translation. Ann, listening without the aid of earphones, was mesmerized by the drama of her recitation.

173

"Who did you see?" asked Jack, as involved as the other listeners, though he'd already heard her story.

"There were three men in black uniforms," she said, holding up three swollen-knuckled fingers. "I knew they were Special Section, Arrow Cross. They were talking to a woman and a child—a boy, about ten years old—looking at their papers. They were shouting. I was frightened. I ducked into a doorway."

"How far were you from them?"

"About four stores away."

"What happened then, Mrs. Hollo?"

"One of them said to her"—she lowered her eyes, as if ashamed to speak the words aloud—" 'You gypsy whore, what are you doing here?' "

"What did the woman say?"

"She said, 'No, I am not a gypsy.' They shouted at her. They said, 'So you are a Jew.' She said she was not. Then the one who did most of the talking said, 'You are not a Jew? Then tell your boy to say the Our Father.' "

Mrs. Hollo pointed to the glass of water in front of her, as if asking permission to drink it. Jack nodded, of course, and waited until she'd had her fill. Mrs. Hollo smiled her thanks at him. He was a nice man; he talked to her politely and asked her how she was feeling. She liked this Jack Burke. She liked that he wanted to put Mishka in jail, where he belonged.

"What happened then?" he asked quietly.

"She started to cry," Mrs. Hollo replied, the tears visible in her own eyes. "He yelled at the boy, 'Say the Our Father, Jew!' Then the boy started to cry, too."

"What happened then?" The simple, three-word question echoed again through the courtroom, like the mournful tolling of a bell.

Mrs. Hollo fiddled nervously with the knot of her babushka. "The one who did most of the talking, he said to the woman, 'Take off your clothes.' She started crying more. The others laughed. She couldn't speak. She was crying very hard.'' Mrs. Hollo gulped and looked around, as if pleading with the spectators to believe her.

They not only appeared to believe her, they were weeping with her.

''He . . . he took a revolver out,'' she went on tremulously, ''and put it to her head.'' It had snowed the day before. But that day was clear, and the sun was shining so brightly, glinting off the metal revolver. A beautiful day, if only she could have felt safe enough to enjoy it.

''What happened then?'' asked Jack, his voice almost a whisper.

''He shot her in the head. The boy . . . the boy threw himself atop her. He shot the boy in the head.'' She darted a glance at the defense table and nodded defiantly. ''One of them said, 'Come on, Mishka, let's get out of here.' They just walked away.''

Jack loudly cleared his throat before he continued. ''Mrs. Hollo, is that the man who shot that boy and his mother on the eleventh of January, 1945?''

He pointed to the screen displaying Mike's photo on the Special Section card. It took her only a couple of seconds to respond with a resolute nod of her head. ''That is the man,'' she declared unequivocally.

''Are you positive?'' Jack asked, walking over to stand next to the witness box, as if to get her view of the screen.

She sounded almost insulted by the question. ''He walked right by me when they left. He was so close, I could have reached out and touched him.'' She glanced again at the defense table, and this time her gaze lingered on Mike for a second or two before she averted her eyes.

Jack inclined his head toward her in thanks, then gestured to Ann. ''Your witness.'' *And let's see how far you get with this, lady,* he told her silently. He could feel Laszlo falling, falling into his hands; he could almost hear Judge Silver's pronouncement: *Guilty.*

Ann had listened to Mrs. Hollo's testimony with rapt attention; she'd been moved by her story. But in effect, all of it was irrelevant to the line of questioning with which she was about to proceed, and she felt astonishingly calm as she came forward to cross-examine the woman.

She leaned an elbow on the witness box and said, as if she were speaking one friend to another, "Mrs. Hollo, did you make a phone call to Budapest last night?"

Bewildered, the old woman turned for help to Jack, who was already on his feet and shouting, "Objection, Your Honor! That is irrelevant and immaterial. This woman is not on trial here!"

Mrs. Hollo nodded energetically as the translation came through her headphones.

"It relates to her state of mind, Your Honor," Ann quickly defended herself.

"Her state of mind is not at issue here!" Jack, in turn, appealed to the judge.

Judge Silver peered at Ann, as if appraising her motives. Her question *was* most unusual, but then, this was a most unusual situation. Thus far Ms. Talbot had impressed him as serious and professional. She didn't strike him as the kind of attorney who frivolously wasted the court's time with tangential detours. Very well, he decided. "I will allow it, but you'd better show me quickly how it relates."

Jack tried hard to hide his disappointment as the judge directed Mrs. Hollo to answer the question. She was a tricky one, Ann Talbot was. What was she getting at, anyway? What the hell did it matter whom that sweet little old lady called in Budapest? What she'd *seen* forty-four years ago was the issue they were concerned with in this courtroom.

"I called my son," Mrs. Hollo replied. She still couldn't get over how easy it had been to reach Attila from the phone in her hotel room. The connection had gone through one, two, three. Now if only it were that simple to call from Budapest to her sister in Kaposvar!

"What does your son do in Hungary, Mrs. Hollo?" asked Ann, poker faced.

Jack leapt to his feet again, furious that Ann had strayed so far afield. "Objection, Your Honor! Her son's private life has no bearing on—"

Judge Silver thought otherwise. "Overruled," he declared in no uncertain terms, leaving Jack to wonder about Jewish judges who bent over backwards to prove their objectivity.

Ann breathed a silent sigh of relief that the judge was giving her so much latitude, and she repeated her question. "What does your son do in Hungary, Mrs. Hollo?"

Mrs. Hollo was happy to tell the young woman about Attila. "He is deputy to the assistant agricultural minister," she said proudly. She could only wish that every mother should have such a son to take care of her.

The woman's tone of voice reminded Ann of how she herself sounded when she bragged about Mikey being elected vice-president of his class. Did all mothers feel that same way about their sons? "Tell me more about your son, Mrs. Hollo. Is he a Communist official?"

"This is red-baiting, Your Honor!" Jack protested. The woman was *obsessed* with Communism, as was her father. Or more likely she'd figured out, no doubt with Mishka's help, that screaming "Communist!" was a terrific diversionary tactic.

"Your Honor," Ann said, clasping her hands demurely as a nun, "this woman is here as an objective witness. I must be able to ask questions regarding her motivation."

"How the hell did you know she called anyone?" Jack shouted at her, suddenly becoming aware that Mrs. Hollo had been set up.

Judge Silver glared at Jack. There was to be no profanity in his courtroom! On the other hand, the prosecution had raised an excellent question—one that he wanted resolved to his satisfaction before they proceeded any further.

"Will you approach the bench, please." He beckoned to the two attorneys, who came to stand before him, a study in contrasts. Ann looked cool and collected next to Jack, who was red faced with anger over his opponent's latest foray.

"How did you know she called someone?" the judge asked Ann sternly.

"I didn't. I was fishing," she explained.

Convinced that she was flat-out lying, Jack lost his temper. "What the hell did you do? Wire her room?" he demanded.

Ann stiffened. "If Mr. Burke is accusing me of an illegal act, Your Honor, he should do it formally."

"Sure!" Jack exploded. "And allow you to turn this into a three-ring circus!"

The judge motioned him to be silent, then turned to Ann. "I'm going to allow you to continue this line of questioning, but I'm not going to allow it much longer if you don't reach your point."

"Thank you, Your Honor," she said, knowing better than to mention that she intended to make her point as soon as Jack kept quiet long enough to allow the witness to answer her questions.

"My objection stands for the record," Jack announced huffily.

"Your objection is overruled for the record," Judge Silver informed him; then he made it official by telling the court clerk, "The objection is overruled."

Ann walked back toward Mrs. Hollo and picked up where they'd left off. "Your son is a Communist official?"

"He is an official of the government," Mrs. Hollo corrected her.

"He is a member of the Communist party?" Ann persisted.

Mrs. Hollo shrugged. She supposed so. "The officials of the government are members of the Communist party."

"After you identified my father's photograph in Budapest," Ann continued, "did you speak to your son about it?"

"Yes."

"What did he say to you?"

"He told me I should tell the truth about what I saw."

Ann's voice boomed out suddenly: "And did he tell you that my father was once arrested for disrupting the American tour of the Hungarian National Folkdancers?"

"Objection!" Jack called, this time not even bothering to get out of his seat.

"Overruled," the judge shot back, engrossed in the back-and-forth between the two women.

"He did not tell me," Mrs. Hollo said indignantly. "I did not know it was the man I identified until the newspaper in Budapest printed it last week."

Jack groaned quietly and sank back in his chair. Dinofrio, beside him, looked equally disturbed.

"I see. But you're aware of it now," Ann remarked.

"Yes. But it doesn't have anything to do with my testimony," Mrs. Hollo argued, shaking an angry finger at Mishka's daughter, as if to say, *Shame, shame*.

"Doesn't it?" Ann said coolly. "No further questions, Your Honor."

"You may step down, madam," the judge told Mrs. Hollo, whose eyes followed Ann all the way back to the defense table. She opened her mouth as if she had something more to say, then changed her mind and obediently made her way out of the box.

Jack held his breath as the judge glanced at his watch. No breaks or recesses now, please. His upcoming witness would undoubtedly clear everyone's mind—particularly Judge Silver's—of Ann Talbot's shameless obfuscations. It would be his pleasure, once the trial was over, to tell her a thing or two about motives and easing one's guilt. At the rate she was going, she'd be lucky if Jack didn't report her to the Chicago Bar Association.

Then, to his relief, Judge Silver said, "You may call your next witness, Mr. Burke."

He stood up and straightened his tie. "We call Geza Vamos," Jack announced. He looked over at Mike, who was stifling a yawn. Was the guy getting bored with all this talk? He was, after all, a man of action, not words—although he'd never been tongue-tied when it came to telling his victims what he wanted from them. And just in case he'd forgotten, or hadn't heard enough today, Geza Vamos would be happy to remind him of the good old days, when Mishka got all the action he wanted.

CHAPTER
12

The first thing Ann noticed about Geza Vamos was that he couldn't seem to stop blinking as he nervously surveyed the courtroom. The second thing she realized was that his gaze managed to rest everywhere but on her father, who stared woodenly at the man, as he had at the previous two witnesses. If he'd ever seen them before in his life, he certainly gave no sign of it.

Not that Vamos had a particularly memorable face. He was a thin, slightly stooped man who appeared to be in his midsixties, with sunken cheeks and a nose that looked as if it had been broken a time or two. More remarkable were his hands: He had long, thin fingers that he brushed through his hair or across his forehead whenever he spoke.

Jack reminded himself to be careful with Vamos; the man was as jittery as a spooked cat. "Mr. Vamos," he began in a slow, careful tone, "where were you between December of 1944 and January of 1945?"

"In Budapesht, forced labor," Vamos replied, speaking in broken English.

"Where did you work, Mr. Vamos?" Jack asked, quickly establishing the facts.

"At bank of Duna, Danube River, Lanchid Interrogation Center," Vamos recited dutifully.

"What were your duties there?"

"Clean up." Vamos's fingers scratched at the stubble on his cheek.

"What was the Lanchid Interrogation Center?"

"Two building, warehouse; field lead to river."

Jack paused a moment, wanting the image to settle into the minds of his listeners. *Two building, warehouse; field lead to river.* Such a modest, commonplace setting, nestled on the shore of the Danube, beneath the Chain Bridge, one of Budapest's most famous, nineteenth-century landmarks. "What was it used for?"

"To interrogate Jews by Nyilas," Vamos replied, switching into Hungarian.

"Nyilas is the Arrow Cross?" the interpreter broke in.

Vamos nodded. "Yes. And Special Section."

"Did you meet a Special Section man there known as Mishka?" Jack went on.

"Ya." Vamos jiggled his knee. "Everybody know Mishka. Everybody afraid. Mishka worst there."

"Why was that?"

He grimaced. "Mishka enjoy."

"What did you see Mishka do at the interrogation center that you observed him enjoying?" Jack carefully phrased his question.

"Mishka liked kill Jews," Vamos said, speaking in a dull monotone. "But Mishka liked kill gypsy more than Jew. Mishka tell everybody, 'Gypsy come here, you give me.' He get . . . how you say this?" Frustrated that he didn't have the fluency in English, Vamos shook his head and went back to Hungarian. "He hated the gypsies so much. He'd say, 'Hey, Gypsy,' even to Jews."

Ann heard a sharp hiss of surprise from George and felt, rather than saw, George glance briefly at Mike, who sat stolid faced. Her heart skipped a beat—she knew what George must be thinking. *Hey, Gypsy,* Mike would say

182

affectionately, putting his arm around George. *Hey, Gypsy, you my girlfriend, ya?*

So what? It was just a catch-all word of endearment, she told herself, like referring to Hungarian musicians as gypsy bands. Coincidence. Nothing more. She forced her attention back to Vamos, who was responding to Jack's last question, which Ann had missed.

"Mishka like game," he was saying softly. "Inside, they ask, 'You have gold, diamond?' Jew not say anything. Mishka take outside, play game."

"What was this 'game' like?" Jack asked, drawing quote marks in the air to emphasize the irony of the word.

Vamos sucked in air and closed his eyes, remembering how he and his fellow laborers would scurry off to find something to clean in the dark corners furthest away from where Mishka played his games. Always the fear haunted them: What if Mishka ran out of gypsies or Jews and chose them next to play his game?

"He put bayonet in earth. He tell gypsy, 'You get on earth, you get exercise,' " Vamos replied, pulling at his chin.

"How do you mean?"

"Body over bayonet, arm and leg on earth, push up and down." Vamos sighed deeply at the memory.

Ann's heart was pounding so rapidly she thought she might faint. What Vamos was describing . . . NO! She pushed the image away and took deep breaths, trying to calm herself. Coincidence—that was all it was. Lots of people did—

"Pushups?" Jack said, sounding incredulous, echoing the word that was shrieking in Ann's head.

"Ya, ya." Vamos bobbed his head like a kewpie doll. "Mishka like pushup. He do pushup, too. No bayonet."

The pen slipped out of her hand, now dripping with perspiration. George gave her a quick, inquiring look. Mike, next to her, didn't move a muscle. She gripped the edge of the table, as if to steady herself. NO! NO! NO!

183

screamed her inner voice, wanting to silence the halting flow of Vamos's damning words.

"So," Jack summarized, feeling the palpable sense of shock and outrage in the courtroom, "he would have them do pushups over the bayonet—"

"Ya, ya," Vamos broke in, the English words tumbling out in his eagerness to get his audience to understand exactly how it had been. "Till fall. Then we throw in Duna. Clean up. I do cleanup."

Sighs and muffled moans rippled through the onlookers, more than a few of whom had lost family to the Nazis or were themselves survivors of the death camps. They knew better than anyone how apt a description was Vamos's matter-of-fact recitation.

Sandy Lehman buried his head in his hands. An occasional synagogue-goer who usually attended services only on Yom Kippur and Rosh Hashanah, he'd fidgeted through the rabbis' sermons about preserving and keeping sacred the memory of the Holocaust. Such high-flown oratory was easily brushed aside. Whereas what he was hearing now—had been hearing all day—made him sick with grief. Suddenly he was experiencing an unaccustomed emotion: He felt set apart because he was a Jew. It wasn't a feeling he liked very much at all.

Karchy, slumped in his chair next to Mike, belched quietly, emitting a strong scent of garlic. He was restless and—though he wouldn't have admitted it to his sister— he'd had his fill of listening to these horror stories.

He only half believed these people: How could they so clearly remember the exact words someone had spoken such a long time ago? Pop's memory was sometimes faulty these days, and he had a hell of a lot more on the ball than this Vamos character or the two who'd come before him. So who cared if the man they called Mishka did situps? He did situps. Pop did situps. Even little Mikey had started doing situps.

Karchy reached his arm over his father's chair and pulled

at Ann's sleeve. But she ignored him, so he gave up and tuned back in to Vamos's story.

"Did you ever have occasion to speak to Mishka?" Jack was asking him.

Vamos recoiled at the very thought. "No can speak," he protested. "We speak, Mishka hit with gun. No can look, how do I say . . ." He searched for the words and found them in Hungarian. "We were not permitted to look into his eyes. We cast our eyes down whenever we were around him."

Jack nodded and moved on. "Mr. Vamos, was there an ammunition shortage while you were at the interrogation center?"

"Ya."

"What effect did that shortage have on the center?"

"Big trouble," Vamos said, licking his lips nervously. "They no can shoot. No got bullet. They play game with bayonet." He gestured with his long fingers, trying to explain the game. "They take wire, wire people together; shoot one, dump all into Duna."

"Did you ever see the man known as Mishka do that?" Jack asked, strolling close enough to the defense table that he could see the pained look on Ann's face.

"Ya. Many times."

"How many times, Mr. Vamos?"

Vamos, who had been following Jack with his eyes as he paced the front of the room, flinched with fear when he suddenly discovered Mike Laszlo in his field of vision. Quickly averting his gaze, he stammered his response. "Tw . . . twenty, thirty . . . River red. Ice on side of river red. Bodies—how you say?—corpse on side of river blue. Duna blue. Blue Danube." He shuddered, recalling how the bodies would occasionally wash up onto the riverbank.

Jack took a few steps to the side, so as not to obstruct either the judge's or the witness's view of the screen, which by now seemed a permanent fixture in the courtroom. "Mr. Vamos," he said, deliberately pausing to heighten the already considerable tension in the room, "Mr. Vamos, is that the man you knew as Mishka at the Lanchid Interrogation Center?"

For the fourth time, Mike's photo from the Special Section card appeared on the screen.

"Ya," Vamos said quietly, without even glancing at the screen.

"Will you look at his picture, Mr. Vamos?" Jack asked politely, not surprised by the witness's resistance. Based on how the man had behaved at their earlier meeting, he'd half expected him to fall apart during testimony.

Vamos looked everywhere but the screen, then repeated himself. "Ya."

"Please, Mr. Vamos," Jack said again, this time more insistently, "can you look at his picture?"

Vamos shook his head, scratched his cheek, pulled at his hair. Finally, he forced himself to take a quick look at the photograph, then immediately looked away. "It is him," he said, trembling with the effort.

Jack nodded his thanks and turned to Ann. "Your witness."

Mack Jones, who must have watched his partner conduct hundreds of cross-examinations, could tell right away that something was up with Ann. Usually she was on her feet and walking toward the witness box so fast that she risked bumping into her opposing counsel. Now, though, she seemed to be moving in slow motion, so that it took her forever to walk to the front of the room. And instead of jumping right in with her first question, she stood quietly a few seconds, as if gathering her thoughts.

Mack nudged Sandy. Was he noticing it, too? Sandy nodded, confirming his impression. No, indeed, this wasn't at all like Ann—who, in fact, was struggling with a slew of conflicting emotions that were making her temporarily tongue-tied.

Then her lawyer's training got the upper hand and she

gently told Vamos, "I'm sorry to have to ask you these questions."

He smiled tentatively, revealing a row of yellowing, crooked teeth.

"Mr. Vamos," she said, sounding more confident, "do you know Istvan Boday?"

Vamos wrinkled his forehead, causing Dinofrio to whisper to Jack, "She's going up the wrong tree." Jack nodded, but he felt less sanguine than his colleague about the direction Ann was taking. She'd earned his grudging respect—not as a human being but as an agile manipulator of courtroom procedure.

"I know he witness," Vamos told her. "I read in Budapesht newspaper, he witness."

"Did you know him in Hungary?"

"No. I no meet."

"You never spoke to him in Hungary?" Ann reiterated.

"They tell us no speak to each other, no meet," Vamos explained, wondering whether Mishka had ever bragged to his daughter about the games he'd played during the war.

She blocked out all her doubts and pressed on. "Why is that, Mr. Vamos?"

"They no want us talk each other about case. What we say . . . clean." He shrugged. It was obvious.

"So, you never spoke to him in Hungary?" she said, hating herself.

"No. I no meet," he insisted.

"You never spoke to him on the plane over here?"

Jack had told him to watch out for Mishka's daughter, but Vamos couldn't help but wonder whether Mr. Burke were mistaken. She couldn't be very smart if he had to explain all this to her. "They have us come different plane."

"You never spoke to him in your hotel?" Ann continued.

"Different hotel," he said, jiggling his knee again.

"Mr. Vamos." She folded her arms and studied him reproachfully. "Do you lie often?"

The words were hardly out of her mouth before Jack was on his feet, proclaiming, "Objection, Your Honor! She's insulting—"

"Sustained," Judge Silver said.

"No," Vamos hastily defended himself. "I no lie!"

She came back at him just as quickly: "Then why don't you tell us about your meeting in your hotel room last night with Mr. Boday?"

"Your Honor!" Jack declared, feeling queasy, "this witness just said he's never met Mr. Boday!"

Ann ignored his interruption and kept hammering away at the witness. "You met with him in your hotel room last night, didn't you, Mr. Vamos?"

Vamos looked at the floor and feebly shook his head, just as Judge Silver, looking concerned, said, "Mrs. Talbot . . ."

Ann recklessly disregarded Judge Silver and pressed on. "Didn't you!"

"She's badgering this witness, Your Honor!" shouted a red-faced Jack, outraged by the judge's failure to call a halt to Ann, who was riding roughshod over his obviously confused witness.

But before Judge Silver had a chance to intervene, Vamos hung his head and acknowledged, "Ya. He come to my room."

"Jesus Christ!" Jack muttered, falling back into his chair. Dinofrio threw him a shocked look, and Jack shrugged. He sure as hell didn't know what this was all about. But one thing had become blindingly clear to him: Ann Talbot would stop at nothing to clear her father's name.

The courtroom was humming with startled whispers, and even the normally unflappable Judge Silver seemed to have been stunned by Vamos's admission. As the hubbub increased, however, he quickly recovered his aplomb and banged his gavel, demanding silence. Ann paced back and forth, waiting to continue questioning Vamos, whose head was still bent in shame, as if he expected to be punished for his lie.

When the room was quiet again, Judge Silver motioned Ann to continue. This was for Papa, she reminded herself, as she turned to the hapless Vamos. "So you were lying before when you told us you'd never spoken to him?" she declared pitilessly.

"Ya. I lie." He didn't dare look her in the eye.

"Do you lie *often*, Mr. Vamos?"

Jack closed his eyes and groaned softly, and even Harry shook his head in dismay at her scathing tone.

It took whatever strength was left in him for Vamos to lift his head and look directly at Ann. His eyes were jumping with fear as he struggled to make her see that sometimes you had to tell the truth as you saw it, to protect someone who'd meant no harm. In a voice that pleaded for understanding, he said, "Boday came to my room. He want to know about wife and brother. He don't never know what happen to wife and brother. He ask if—"

"Did you and Mr. Boday go over your stories, Mr. Vamos? Did you compare notes?" It didn't matter what he answered. It was enough to plant the suspicion in the judge's mind.

"Boday ask me if I remember," Vamos frantically explained. "He show me wife's picture."

Ann had accomplished the job she'd set out to do. "No further questions, Your Honor," she said quietly.

Watching her walk back to her seat next to Mishka, Vamos tasted bile in his mouth. He couldn't live with the burden of his failure. "Please," he begged the judge, "how you can do this? I come here, I tell truth."

"You may step down," Judge Silver said firmly. He felt for the man, but they'd already had enough drama today. He wanted no more scenes in his courtroom. Vamos threw him an entreating look and seemed about to object. But the habit of obedience was too deeply ingrained in him. One didn't argue with authority, neither in Hungary nor in America.

He stumbled from the witness box and began to make his way toward the back of the courtroom. Suddenly, as if pricked by some long-festering wound, he stopped just short of the defense table and found himself face to face with the man he'd identified as Mishka. For an instant their eyes locked. Then Vamos, quivering like a cornered deer, quickly lowered his gaze and stood absolutely still, too frightened to move.

"Go on, Mr. Vamos," Judge Silver gently encouraged him. "No one will hurt you here, Mr. Vamos."

For the few moments it took before Vamos recovered himself, Ann feared for him, he was shaking so badly. A part of her wanted to call out: Are you all right, Mr. Vamos? I'm sorry, Mr. Vamos. I know you're not really a liar. What frightened her even more was that his temporary paralysis was quite obviously the result of being in such close proximity to her father. This was no faked performance; she could almost feel the current of tension between them.

Finally, to her intense relief, Vamos nodded at the judge and, with eyes averted, scurried past them and left the room. After the door had swung shut behind him, Judge Silver cleared his throat and announced, "Considering the lateness of the hour, we will adjourn until tomorrow morning."

However, to his surprise and annoyance, Jack waved a dissenting hand. "Your Honor," he announced, "we have one more witness."

Ann quickly scanned the roster of witnesses. "I show no other witnesses, Your Honor," she called out, furious at having been caught unprepared.

"She's just arrived from Hungary and would like to return as soon as possible," Jack explained, which only further incensed her.

"Your Honor, I have to object," she insisted. "There is no mention of any other witness in my case file."

"We located the witness yesterday. She took the first plane from Budapest." Jack delivered his rejoinder with an oily smoothness that disgusted Ann and persuaded the judge.

"You may call your witness, Mr. Burke," he declared, readjusting his robes.

Ann frowned with concern as Jack said, "We call Eva Kalman, Your Honor."

She followed Eva Kalman's progress up the aisle and noted that though she seemed about the same age as the previous witnesses, she was very poised and wore a soft gray knit dress that emphasized her trim figure. Her blond hair was stylishly cut, her face was carefully made up, and her nails had been manicured with light pink polish. Who *was* she? Ann wondered, this surprise witness the prosecution had pulled out of a hat like a magician's rabbit.

Mike was wondering the same thing. "Who is she, Anna?" he whispered, as the woman was being sworn in and fitted with a translation headset.

"I don't know," she said, more worried than she cared to admit to him. She glanced inquiringly at George, who answered with a shrug of her shoulders that she was just as mystified as they were. But mystery or not, Ann would have to cross-examine Eva Kalman, so now, as Jack approached the witness, Ann picked up her pen and got ready to take notes.

"Mrs. Kalman," he began, "what is your occupation?"

"I am a psychiatrist specializing in rape trauma," she said, speaking Hungarian in an educated, upper-class accent.

"Are you a member of the Communist party in Hungary?" Jack asked, glancing briefly in Ann's direction.

"No," Mrs. Kalman replied, with the briefest smile.

"Do you have any family members who are members of the Communist party?"

"No."

"Have you spoken to any of the other witnesses in this case?" he continued, having learned his lesson.

"Your investigator came to see me yesterday morning," she reminded him. "I arrived today. I have spoken to no one."

"Mrs. Kalman," Jack said quietly, "can you describe to us the sequence of events that began on the sixteenth of December, 1944?"

Mrs. Kalman folded her hands in her lap and cleared her throat. Then she began to speak in a low, conversational tone that utterly belied the content of her story. "I was returning home from a piano lesson. It was early evening. A car stopped in the street. There were two men inside. They were wearing the uniforms of the Arrow Cross. They asked me for identification. I had left my purse at the piano lesson, so I had no papers."

She glanced at the audience, as if to ensure that they were paying attention. Then she went on: "One of the men—he had a long scar on the left side of his face—he said, 'Look how pretty this pig is, Mishka.' They said I was a Jew. I told them I was Roman Catholic."

Jack nodded gravely and said, "How old were you when this happened to you?"

"I was seventeen."

Ann tried to imagine Mrs. Kalman as a pretty, giggling seventeen year old, her head too full of boys and music and dancing to remember her papers. Probably it was cold that December night, and she couldn't wait to get home, where it was warm and comfortable and a fire was blazing in the stove. Her parents would have been waiting for her to have dinner, served in the chandeliered dining room by the maid; certainly, there would have been a maid and perhaps a cook, as well. Then, afterward, she would have gotten right down to her homework, or perhaps first she would have practiced awhile on the piano.

What could have gone through her head when the car pulled up next to her in the twilight and she'd seen the Arrow Cross uniforms? At seventeen, would she have understood what it meant when the men called her a Jew? Or would she have naively assumed that she was protected by her religion and her innocence?

"Please continue, Mrs. Kalman," Jack was saying.

Mrs. Kalman fiddled with the hair at the nape of her neck as she said, "They told me I was under arrest and put me in the car. They drove over the bridge, the Lanchid, and turned into the buildings on the riverbank. They were quite friendly, actually, in the car. They asked me about playing the piano. They took me into the building . . . into a little room."

She hesitated, pressed her lips tightly together, and took a deep breath. For a moment Jack worried that she had changed her mind and decided not to testify. She seemed to be searching within herself for the strength to go on. A vein in her neck beat a rapid pulse, attesting to what an effort this must be costing her. Finally, she began again. "There was nothing in the room but a mattress on the floor."

Another long pause. There wasn't a sound in the courtroom.

"They told me to stand against a wall," she said, her composure rapidly crumbling. "They told me to take my clothes off. I started to cry. . . . I told them I was a virgin. They laughed. Mishka said, 'We will teach you to play us like you play the piano.' "

She made a noise in her throat that was halfway between a sigh and a moan, and she looked at Jack with wet, stricken eyes. Then she said, "Mishka took out a revolver and he . . . forced it into my mouth. The other one tore my clothes. He lighted a cigarette. . . . He put the cigarette against my . . ."

Mrs. Kalman turned her head and stared out the window. A light snow was falling, just barely visible in the fading afternoon light. As if their heads were connected by a thread, Ann automatically followed her gaze and wondered whether the world looked different to you after such an experience.

"They took turns," Mrs. Kalman went on, her voice low and tight. "I passed out. There were others . . . men who came into the room . . . and left . . . and came back. I lost track of time. They burned me. Someone kept taking my picture. . . . The flash of the camera would awaken me."

She began to cry, the tears running down her cheeks in streaky, mascara-blackened tracks. Many in the courtroom were crying with her, including George, who sniffled and dabbed at her eyes with a tissue, and Ann, who'd long since stopped taking notes. Karchy was shaking his head and rubbing a fist against the palm of his other hand, and Mike had tears in his eyes.

"Then, I don't know how much later, it was Mishka again. 'Pig,' he said, 'you have learned to perform very well.' And he started again. Their spit . . . the semen . . . blood . . . They turned me into a toilet."

As her audience strained to hear her halting words, Judge Silver glanced at Jack, tacitly inquiring whether he wanted to break for a few minutes. Jack shook his head, no. Better to go on and let her get through it as quickly as possible. He didn't understand where she was finding the courage. Listening, he felt weak-kneed and nauseated. She was a strong woman. An exemplary woman.

She was sobbing as she choked out the words. "Mishka said, 'You are tired, pig. You need exercise.' The other was there. He laughed. They stood me up. They carried me outside. It was cold . . . it was so cold. On the ground, in the snow, there was a bayonet."

Jack urged a glass of water into her trembling hands; she nodded gratefully, took a few sips, and struggled to

194

catch her breath. Calmer now, she went on: "They told me to get down on my hands and feet over the bayonet. They told me to exercise. I heard them laugh. Mishka said, 'A healthy body makes a healthy spirit.' The bayonet was at my stomach. I pushed myself up once, and then I fell . . . onto the bayonet." Pausing to wipe away her tears, she concluded: "I remember nothing else. I was told that I was found on the bank of the river."

"Mrs. Kalman," Jack said very quietly, "is that the man known to you as Mishka?"

"Yes," she replied, her anguished sigh cutting through the silence in the courtroom. "That is the man."

Wondering whether she'd finally gotten the point about her father, Jack turned to Ann, who was staring fixedly at the floor. "Your witness," he said curtly.

Her tongue felt as if it were sticking to the roof of her mouth. She could hardly swallow, much less stand up and begin her cross-examination. Slowly, very slowly, as if she had lead weights attached to her limbs, she rose to her feet. She was conscious only of Mrs. Kalman's ashen, tear-streaked face, her father's labored breathing, the blood pounding in her ears. Nothing else existed for her at that moment.

"No questions." She choked out the words.

Jack's stunned disbelief was mirrored by Judge Silver and the rest of the onlookers. Jack recovered first. "The government rests," he said quickly, before she could change her mind.

The courtroom was in an uproar: Reporters hustled to get to the doors; Mike's supporters jeered and screamed their protests; his foes, mindful of Mrs. Kalman's fragility, broke out in subdued applause. Some of the onlookers—Harry, Sandy, and Mack, among them—began pushing their way forward through the swirling crowd, anxious to reach their friends.

And then, above the tumult and confusion, an anguished voice rang out through the room. "No!" Mike cried. "I not do this! *It is not me!*"

Shaking his fist like a scorned prophet, he stood weeping, shoulder to shoulder with Ann, who seemed oblivious to his pain. "I did not do this!" he wailed, shambling, bearlike, toward the witness stand.

Mrs. Kalman recoiled as he approached, crying, "I not do this to you! I no beast! I am father! I was husband! I loved my wife! . . . I no could do these things!"

He stopped just a few feet away from her and reached out a hand, as if in supplication. "Please, tell them!" he pleaded with her in Hungarian. "I did not do these things!"

Mrs. Kalman's lips curled with scorn as she scrutinized the blubbering old man. "Yes," she answered him in Hungarian. "Yes, you are the beast."

With every ounce of energy left in her, she let fly at Mike a thick glob of spittle that landed square on his cheek. For an instant he was too shocked to respond. Then he touched his hand to his face, and his fingers came away dripping with saliva. And then he crumpled in a heap to the floor.

The already noisy courtroom exploded with cacophonous, ear-splitting clamor as Karchy rushed forward and grabbed his father up in his arms. Shouting for someone to get a doctor, he loosened Mike's tie and felt for his pulse. Where the hell was Annie? he wondered. She ought to be right here, holding Pop's hand. He needed the both of them now.

Mesmerized by the sight of Papa cradled in Karchy's embrace, Ann stood frozen to the spot, too spent to move. Someone tapped her on the shoulder—Jack Burke, who knowingly eyed Karchy and Mike.

"Great timing," he cracked. "What do you wanna bet there's nothing wrong with him?"

She brushed him away as she would a pesky housefly and looked past her father to the witness stand. Mrs. Kalman was staring straight at her—and she was smiling with grim satisfaction.

As she paced the hospital emergency room, waiting for the doctor to finish examining her father, Ann was still thinking about Mrs. Kalman's smile. Though she'd stopped smoking five years ago and hadn't touched a cigarette since, she'd just bummed her fourth of the evening and was wishing she had a pack in her purse. Karchy had gone into the examining room with Papa, for which Ann was grateful. She was past talking, past answering his questions.

Wrapped up in her thoughts, she didn't even notice that her father's doctor had walked into the room until he was already in midsentence. "His blood pressure's sky high," the young resident reported. "He has a slight arrhythmia—not uncommon for his age. I don't see anything immediately life threatening. Look," he paused, as if embarrassed to bring up the subject but needing to make a point, "I know the pressure he's been under. I don't know how much more pressure his system can take."

Ann nodded dully. "Can I go in there?" she asked. Mike had been barely conscious in the ambulance on the way to the hospital, and she hadn't spoken to him since before he'd fainted. But in the time it had taken for the doctor to treat her father and make his diagnosis, Ann had come to a decision. Now she needed to look in Papa's eyes and see what she could find there.

He lay half undressed on a cot, and his skin was still gray and waxy. But at least he was awake and listening attentively to Karchy, who was in the middle of a story about one of the men down at the mill. Not wanting to startle him, she stood quietly in the doorway until he spotted her.

"I want to talk to Anni, Karchy," he said at once.

Karchy glanced from his father to his sister, opened his mouth, and seemed about to protest that he belonged there with them. But Pop's tone of voice was one he recognized from childhood, so he mumbled, "Yeah, sure," and he reluctantly left the room.

Mike had one arm hooked up to a monitoring machine, and he looked so frail and helpless that Ann almost reached over to stroke his forehead, as he used to do to her when she was little. She wished she could tell him, Don't worry, Papa, it'll be all right. She felt constrained, though, by Mrs. Kalman's smile—that, and her own uncertainty.

He seemed to intuit that if they were to make peace with each other, it was up to him to take the first step. "I know what you think, Anni," he said weakly. "They say things . . . it make it sound to you . . ."

His voice trailed off. Ann was still silent, and he knew he had to try again, before the gulf between them grew too wide to bridge. "I see your eyes, Anni," he told her. "You gotta answer question: My father . . . this beast?"

Finally, she took pity on him. "Papa, I know—"

"No! In your heart, Anni," he said, demanding more of her than she was yet ready to give him. "You gotta answer."

She tried to smile, failed, and settled for "Let's go home."

"I go my own home. I don't care what happen to me. I go my own house. I no hide no more." He glared at her, daring her to disagree.

They both knew he was making a mistake. And the worst of it was that Ann couldn't bring herself to argue with him.

Late at night, when Mikey was safely tucked in and she'd finished whatever work she'd carried home in her briefcase, Ann liked to walk down to the dock at the edge of her backyard and watch the stars shining on the lake. In the summers, before she and David had split up, he would usually join her, at least for a few minutes. She would dangle her legs over the side and feel the water splashing up against her bare feet, and she'd think about the turns her life had taken that had brought her to own a lakefront house.

In wintertime, David was less enthusiastic about stargazing down by the water, where the wind blew especially cold. She didn't mind. She was just as happy to bundle up and sit there by herself, until her cheeks began to burn from the cold and she knew it was time to go back inside.

She supposed she'd developed her affinity for the water because of having grown up in a city where you were never very far from a beach. The lake calmed her; it provided her with an ever-changing, sometimes turbulent canvas onto which she could project and examine her deepest feelings. Often, she would come away with a sense of clarity that otherwise eluded her. Tonight, however, her state of mind, like the sky overhead, remained dark and cloudy.

She was getting ready to go back inside when she heard footsteps behind her, and then George's voice reached out to her in the darkness. "Hello, darlin'."

"What do you think, George?" she said, after her friend had brushed away the powdery snow and settled down next to her.

"About what?" George asked rhetorically, pulling her scarf tighter around her neck. The cold weather drove her crazy. Any day now she'd be moving south, she kept threatening her colleagues. "I think," she said quietly, pulling a photograph out of the envelope she'd brought with her, "that I got me a devil to advocate."

In the darkness, Ann could barely make out the features of a balding man in his sixties.

"Tibor Zoldan," George told her. "That traffic accident wasn't just a traffic accident. He was run over by a hit-and-run driver on the West Side."

Ann didn't think she wanted to hear the rest of the story, but she didn't know how to say that to George, who took her silence for interest and kept talking. "For nine months, from the time Mike wrote this guy that two-thousand-dollar check three years ago, his monthly cash spending ran a thousand over what it had always run. It *stopped* running over the month this guy Zoldan got run over."

"I don't care," said Ann, staring out at the ice-flecked water. "I don't care what it sounds like. I don't care what it looks like. He's not a monster, George. I'm his daughter. . . . *I* know that better than anyone." She stood up and glanced sideways at George, whose eyes reflected her own pain. "I never thought *you'd* let me down." She lashed out at her friend, for lack of a better target.

"I'm never gonna let you down, darlin'," George quietly assured her. But Ann, already halfway down the dock, didn't even bother to wish her goodnight. She was angry at George and even angrier at herself. In a sense, though, George had done her a favor, coming to her with Tibor Zoldan's story. The answers weren't to be found out here in the night. Even the lake, with its unpredictable tides and crashing waves, could fool you into believing it was something other than it seemed.

But Papa . . . Papa was the constant in her life, and no matter what the mounting evidence made him *appear* to be, she knew, *better than anyone*, that he was a fine and loving person. She couldn't sleep tonight without telling him that to his face.

Checking her watch, she saw that it was already past ten. The drive to Berwyn would take at least half an hour. No matter, she decided, hurrying into the house and grabbing her keys and wallet. Papa never went to bed before midnight.

A mournful Dylan tape, the perfect counterpoint to her melancholic thoughts, accompanied her all the way to the West Side. She was weeping silently as she pulled up in front of his house. A light was burning in the living room, another one upstairs in his bedroom. Her heart was pounding as she parked the car and hurried up the sidewalk.

Through the thin white curtains, she could see the television flickering. Good, he was still up; unless he'd dozed off watching TV, as he often did. She banged on the door, not stopping to think that he might be frightened by an unexpected late-night visitor.

It took him a minute or two to walk over and peer cautiously through the glass panel. Then his look of suspicion gave way to bewilderment and concern as he recognized his daughter. He flung open the door, obviously prepared for more bad news.

Ann shook her head—no, don't worry—and quickly stepped out of the cold and into the warmth of the home in which her father had taught her so many lessons about what was important in life. Before he had a chance to speak, to ask her why she had tears in her eyes, she smiled and put her arms around him. She said simply, "I love you, Papa."

How could she ever feel otherwise?

CHAPTER
13

Harry Talbot's house in Kenilworth was worlds apart from anything Ann had ever known, growing up on the West Side. To begin with, it could be more accurately described as an English Tudor-style mansion—three stories and twenty-five rooms furnished with museum-quality antiques and original artwork. Many of the pieces had belonged to Harry's parents: The Talbots had been wealthy for a long time and the family believed that money invested in paintings and fine furniture was money well spent.

The house was kept up by a staff of six, including Teddy the chauffeur, a cook, a valet, and a housekeeper who'd been hired to supervise the rest of the servants after the death of Harry's wife, whom Ann had never met. The housekeeper was superbly efficient, meeting even Harry's impossibly high standards. His home was his castle, he liked to tell people, and he wanted it run as smoothly as he ran his law firm.

Ann's earliest visits to Kenilworth had been nerve-wracking ordeals. Meals in the formal dining room were especially fraught with potential dangers, as she strained to remember to put her linen napkin on her lap and which fork to use for which course. She'd almost worried herself into a fever when Mike and Karchy were invited to dinner to celebrate her engagement to David.

She'd coached them for hours about the niceties of social etiquette until they'd rebelled, accusing her of getting to be too refined and stuck-up for her own good. Of course, Karchy had showed up without a tie, and Mike had spilled red wine all over the ivory damask tablecloth. Miraculously, Harry and Mike found a common interest in anti-Communism, Karchy got points for having served in Vietnam, and the evening passed without any major disasters.

Since then Ann had spent enough time at the mansion that the opulence barely fazed her, and her father and brother could be depended on to hold up their ends when the two families came together there. That happened rarely now, because of the divorce—usually only on Mikey's birthday, which this year fell on the Sunday after "Black Friday," as Karchy had taken to calling that long, harrowing day in court.

They were all gathered in the dining room—Ann, Mike, Karchy, Harry, David, and Mikey, the guest of honor—singing "Happy Birthday" and waiting for Mikey to blow out the twelve candles (and one for good luck) on the double-layer chocolate-frosted cake the cook had baked that morning. Mikey's eye was still slightly puffy and red, but he was smiling, and he looked happier than he had in days. Ann knew that all the talk about the trial was affecting him more than he'd ever admit. But the cake, presents, and all the attention had transformed him into a carefree kid again, if only for the afternoon.

David gave his son an affectionate pat on the shoulder and urged, "Make a wish, Mikey."

As Mikey closed his eyes, his Grandpa Harry joked, "When *I* was twelve years old, I wished for the maid." But no one in the room had any doubt about the wish

Mikey was sending that day to the birthday-cake gods: *Make the judge say Grandpa is innocent.*

With one deep breath, he easily blew out all the candles and grinned as his family reacted with applause and good-natured laughter. He was old enough now to understand that his parents were *never* getting remarried, but when they were all together like this, Mom and Dad and everyone else, he couldn't help but cherish a teeny-weeny hope that maybe things would work out the way he wanted them to. That's what had happened in a movie called *The Parent Trap*, which he'd seen once on TV. So why not in real life?

One of the servants (it always cracked Mikey up that Grandpa Harry had people waiting on him at home) came forward, plucked the candles off the cake, and began to cut generous slices. In Mikey's opinion, Alice—the cook—made the *best* chocolate fudge cake, and his mouth watered as he waited for his piece.

His Grandpa Harry had other matters on his mind. "Well, young man," he teased, "do you want to miss the train?"

"What train, Grandpa?" Had Grandpa planned a surprise trip for him? Was he going to get to miss school? Couldn't they eat their cake first?

"The hell with the train, let's eat the cake," yelled Karchy, whose stomach was always ready to be filled. He winked at Mikey and Mikey gratefully winked back, knowing that sometimes Grandpa Harry forgot to pay attention to what anyone else wanted.

Harry looked from Karchy to his grandson to the plates waiting to be passed around, and a compromise was struck: The maid was instructed to bring a tray of cake and drinks into the recreation room, so that Harry wouldn't have to postpone the pleasure of presenting Mikey with his birthday present.

The whole family trooped down the hall after Harry, who made a big deal of insisting that Mikey close his eyes and be the first one in to the huge, wood-paneled rec room. Then, with a ceremonious flourish, Harry pushed open the doors and beamed with pride at his gift.

Mikey gasped with pleasure when he caught sight of the elaborate electric train set that had been laid out atop the billiard table in the middle of the room. There was every manner of railroad car, from locomotive to Pullman to caboose; tracks that twisted under bridges and looped over tunnels; flashing signals and platformed stations complete with place names.

"Is it really mine?" Mikey breathed, so awestruck by the beauty of the trains that he forgot to say thank you.

The look on his face was reward enough for Harry, who along with his valet had spent hours fiddling with the antique set. The end result was almost a work of art.

"Are you just going to stand there, or are you going to run her?" Harry asked gruffly, his arms enveloping Mikey in a warm birthday hug. Mikey wriggled free and hit the control panel; the train came alive with a shriek of whistles and clanging bells. As the wheels chugged and lights flashed, the rest of the grownups gathered around the table, oohing and aahing their delight.

"Hey, Mishka," Harry shouted above the noise, "come over here and help me teach this grandson of ours how to run a train. You people have a lot of experience with trains, don't you?" he joked.

Mike grinned good-naturedly as he walked around the table to join them.

As the maid began to circulate with the tray of refreshments, Ann and David watched their son being fussed over by his adoring grandfathers and uncle. "He's really growing up, isn't he?" Ann remarked, almost regretfully.

David nodded, then broached the subject on all of their minds: "Why don't you let him come to the trial? He keeps asking me about it."

"No," she said flatly, annoyed that she couldn't even have one afternoon's respite from the case.

"He hears about it from his friends," David argued. "He sees it on TV. He wants to know the truth, that's all."

"Dad told him the truth," she said, taking a piece of cake from the maid.

But that wasn't good enough for David, who'd given a lot of thought to the matter. "He wants to know it *himself*, Ann. He doesn't want anybody to *tell* him what it is. It's called growing up."

She stared at him, confused by the bitterness in his voice.

"Sooner or later, everybody has to do it." David's parting shot caught her with a mouth full of cake. He'd already left the room by the time she was ready to deliver her comeback.

It didn't go to waste, however, because a few minutes later Harry sat her down with a glass of champagne in one of the big leather club chairs and launched into the same topic. "You should let him go to the trial, you know," he informed her above the sound of Mikey's gleeful shrieks mingled with the noise of the trains. "He wants to go."

Ann was beginning to feel like the victim of a conspiracy. "He's too young," she retorted, irritated by his unwarranted interference. What Harry Talbot didn't know about raising children could fill a library.

"The hell he is!" Harry barked. Realizing she'd respond better to reason, he softened his tone. "It wouldn't hurt to have him there, especially after that woman's testimony."

"I'm not going to use him," Ann said, appalled by the suggestion.

"I'd look at it as letting him do something he wants to do," Harry explained, employing the same sort of logic that had worked magic for so many of his clients.

She shook her head. "I'm not that cynical."

"Of course you are," he shot back. "You're a lawyer, just like me."

She thought, *I hope* not *just like you.* "Did you really drink with Klaus Barbie, Harry?" she asked, reckless from the champagne.

"No." Harry smiled, following her train of thought. "I never met him. I drank with a lot of others like him, though."

She was taken aback by the image of Harry Talbot drinking Scotch with known Nazis, and the shock showed on her face.

Harry was more amused than insulted by her naivete. "What do you think happened after the war?" he asked, then answered his own question: "The Russians had been our allies. We weren't prepared to spy on them. The Nazis had the best anti-Communist spy apparatus in the world. We *needed* them."

She was more than shocked. She was appalled. "How could you sit down with . . . monsters?" She stumbled over the label that had so recently been applied to her father.

Harry calmly took a bite of cake and washed it down with a sip of champagne. "None of the men I knew were monsters. They were all salt-of-the-earth types like your old man."

His implication was crystal clear. But before she had a chance to rebut him, the maid interrupted with a message. "Telephone call for you, Mrs. Talbot."

Ann gave Harry a look that meant, I'll get back to you on this later, and she went to take the phone in Harry's study. It was her least favorite room in the house, dark and unrelievedly masculine. The bookcases were filled with his military memorabilia, a locked cabinet at the far end contained his gun collection, and autographed pictures of Harry and some of Washington's most conservative politicians hung on the wall above his desk.

But the study offered quiet and privacy, and this call was bound to be important. She'd given Harry's private

207

number to only a couple of people. With any luck, one or the other of them would have good news for her.

She was so absorbed in her conversation that she didn't notice Harry until after she'd said, "Thank you," and hung up. He'd clearly been eavesdropping, but she was too shaken up to care. "My forensics man says the I.D. card is authentic," she told him, dropping into a chair.

"Yes, I know." He lowered himself into his high-backed desk chair. "I still have friends in Washington with my kind of old-fashioned values," he said, in answer to her questioning look.

She drummed her fingernails on the edge of his desk, considering whether to bring him into this. "We're dead, Harry. This case is over; that woman on the stand, spitting at him . . ."

"Courtroom theatrics," he calmly declared. "You know all about courtroom theatrics. You're very good at them."

The compliment flew right by her. "Now this I.D. card." She fretted, rubbing her forehead as a sharp pain stabbed between her eyes. "I don't know how to fight it, Harry."

Harry picked up a sword-shaped silver letter opener and touched his finger to its tip, which was surprisingly sharp. "Do you need help, my dear? I thought you never needed any help. I thought you could handle your own cases."

"Yes, I need help, Harry," she declared, as if reciting a secret oath of initiation. She knew that he was savoring this moment, that he was taunting her because he was sure she'd crossed over to his side. Fine, she could let him have his small victory, if it meant there was still hope for Papa.

"Don't worry about it," he told her, flashing the same smug grin he'd worn when he'd presented Mikey with the trains. "That I.D. card doesn't mean a damn thing."

She eagerly clutched at the lifeline he was holding out to her. But his next remark seemed so wide of the mark that she was sure he was toying with her.

"Do you know anything about harlequins, my dear?"

The trial of *United States vs. Michael J. Laszlo* convened for the third day under much the same circumstances, except that even more journalists and photographers had converged on the courthouse, and Harry Talbot's years of trial wisdom had prevailed. When Ann and Mike stepped out of their car, they were accompanied by Mikey, looking scared and hanging on to their hands for dear life as the media descended on them.

Harry watched through the courtroom window as the three braved the gauntlet of protesters, pro and con, whose fervor only seemed to have increased over the weekend. When they'd disappeared through the door of the courthouse, he strolled to his front-row seat, smiling in anticipation. Thanks to his adroit top-level string-pulling, the day promised to be both lively and entertaining.

Jack was less amused when he picked out Ann's young son, seated next to his grandfather at the defense table. He should have known she would stoop that low—principles weren't her strong suit. She was probably desperate after the beating her side had taken on Friday, so sure, why not drag the kid into court and show him off like a pet monkey? He felt for the boy, who was bug-eyed with amazement at all the people who'd come to watch his grandpa get put away for life.

And now for the defense's feeble attempt to make themselves a case. Jack smirked as Judge Silver announced, "You may call your first witness, Ms. Talbot."

Ann stood up and fingered her mother's cross, which she'd decided to wear today, the symbolism notwithstanding. Heavy-handed, perhaps—but no more so than bringing Mikey with her, and not when she was points behind in a no-holds-barred fight. "We call Vladimir Kostov, Your Honor," she responded.

Jack was on his feet in a flash. "I have no such witness on my list, Your Honor."

"May we approach the bench, Your Honor?" Ann requested, aching to remind her opponent that he'd pulled precisely this same number on her the previous week. Common sense prevailed, however, and instead she politely informed Judge Silver, "Mr. Kostov is a reluctant witness, Your Honor. We served him a subpoena last night on the basis of information received two days ago."

"Who the hell is Vladimir Kostov?" Jack snapped.

Probably his weekend had been a hell of a lot better than hers, but ah, revenge was sweet. "He is a K.G.B. defector," she disclosed. "He serves as a consultant to the C.I.A. He is under federal protection."

"I don't believe this!" Jack blurted out, every bit as stunned as she'd hoped. "You subpoenaed a C.I.A. consultant in a case brought by the government? How the hell did you find him? What does he have to do with this case?"

"That will become apparent during his testimony, Your Honor." Ann addressed her response to the judge and had the pleasure of watching Jack throw up in his hands in disgust.

Judge Silver nodded his approval, having similarly granted permission to the prosecution the last time court had been in session. "You may call your witness," he instructed the defense counsel.

"We call Vladimir Kostov," declared the clerk, summoning to the stand a lean-faced middle-aged man with hard, cold eyes. Kostov was impeccably dressed in an expensive-looking French-cut suit, and designer cologne trailed behind him as he walked up the aisle.

"Do you swear to tell the truth, the whole truth, and nothing but the truth?" recited the clerk.

"I do," Kostov declared in heavily accented English.

"Mr. Kostov," Ann said, trying to think of Kostov as an ally rather than the enemy Russian Papa had always railed against, "when did you defect to the United States?"

"Two years ago," he replied, thinking what a charming young woman this lawyer was.

"And where did you reside previously?"

"In Moscow."

"And what was your occupation there?"

"I was lieutenant colonel, counterintelligence section, K.G.B.," he told her pridefully.

Ann noticed him preening and silently thanked him for it, knowing his arrogance would strengthen their argument. "While you were with the K.G.B., were you familiar with Operation Harlequin?" she asked, hacking the first chink in the government's case.

"Yes." Kostov nodded. "I was."

"What was Operation Harlequin, Mr. Kostov?"

He'd been asked the very same question hundreds of times during his C.I.A. debriefing. "It was program to assassinate character of those living in West considered enemies of socialist state by means of falsified documents," he recited, as if by rote.

"Jesus Christ!" Jack swore under his breath to Dinofrio.

Others in the courtroom reacted with equal surprise.

"How was it put into effect?" Ann continued, ignoring the undercurrent of shock.

"Scientists from Soviet Union and other socialist countries were put into special department in Moscow. It was their mission to scientifically devise ways to forge documents in such manner no amount of analysis would reveal it falsity."

"How many scientists were involved in this program?"

"Thirty-six." A carefully selected, elite group of men, the finest he'd ever had the privilege to work with.

Ann's voice sounded cool and composed, though in fact she'd been fascinated by the cleverness of the clandestine operation ever since Harry had described it to her. "Did they devise ways to forge documents that no amount of analysis would reveal to be false?"

"Yes," said Kostov, wondering whether she were married.

"Were forged documents used by the K.G.B. against anyone?"

"Yes. To my personal knowledge, they were used against television commentator in West Germany."

"What was the document that was forged in the case of the West German man?" she inquired, trying to suppress her excitement.

"It was an *Einsatzkommando* identification card. *Einsatzkommando* exterminate Jews and gypsies. German courts accept card as authentic," he told her. And quite a day that had been for the Harlequin operatives.

"What happened to that man, Mr. Kostov?"

"He commit suicide." Kostov's answer had the same level of emotion that he might have used to report he was going around the corner to the grocery store. A man had killed himself, but the operation had been a success. It all balanced out in the end.

"Mr. Kostov, did the K.G.B. share its forged-documents expertise with the security agencies of other Communist countries?"

"Yes." He especially liked her legs, but he was put off by her crucifix. They'd told him she was Laszlo's daughter. Had she become religious since learning of her father's crimes?

"Did you share it with the Hungarians?" Ann asked, setting him up for the punchline.

"Yes," he said, flicking a speck of lint off his lapel. "The Hungarians showed great interest in Harlequin."

Ann all but applauded his performance. "No further questions. Your witness," she told Jack.

For a few minutes there was such a commotion in the courtroom that Jack didn't even attempt to respond. Judge Silver pounded once, twice, three times with his gavel, and finally the room quieted. He glared at the spectators' gallery, sending the message that this kind of behavior was *not* tolerated in his courtroom.

Finally Jack stood up, still holding the pen with which

212

he'd been frantically taking notes throughout Kostov's testimony. "In light of this new testimony, Your Honor, may we adjourn until tomorrow morning?" he requested.

Ann smiled graciously. "I have no objection, Your Honor."

Mikey was disappointed. His first day at the trial, and the judge sent everyone home early. At the very least, he'd been hoping to miss a whole day of school. But no such luck. He pleaded and coaxed to go back to Grandpa's house, but Ann was adamant. He could come to lunch with her and Grandpa and Karchy, but afterward—back to class. Karchy would give him a lift. . . . And no playing hooky, she sternly warned the two of them.

For her it was back to work. She walked into the Talbot & Talbot offices, swinging her briefcase, to be greeted by a chorus of secretaries waving handfuls of pink "While You Were Out" slips.

"The *New York Times* called. 'Sixty Minutes' wants to talk to you. George called . . ." The receptionist read from her incoming-calls sheet.

"Judge Silver called," broke in Angela, her personal secretary. "He wants to see you right away."

"What? Now?" Ann's elation immediately abated.

"He said right away," Angela told her.

Ann grabbed the message slips and headed right back out the door, feeling unaccountably anxious. The sooner she found out what was on the judge's mind, the easier she'd breathe.

Jack was already in the judge's chamber and looking far too pleased with himself to suit her. She shrugged off her coat and curtly nodded at him. He barely acknowledged her greeting.

"Sit down, Ms. Talbot," said Judge Silver, gesturing to a couch that was piled high with books and law journals. Ann pushed a few of the magazines out of her way and gingerly made room for herself. Trying to look calm, she waited impatiently for the judge to explain his urgent summons.

"It seems," the judge began, "that the government has uncovered a witness who allegedly served with your client in the gendarmes and can allegedly identify him as a member of the Special Section."

Ann glared daggers at Jack. "You uncover him now? How very handy for you," she said sarcastically, conveniently forgetting that just this morning she'd used the very same tactic.

Judge Silver frowned at her outburst and went on: "He is in Budapest. He is terminally ill and unable to travel. We will hear his testimony in Budapest, at government expense. Your client's expenses will be covered as well, if he decides to come with us."

It took a few seconds for his words to sink in, and then she thought, *Budapest*? They wanted her to go to *Hungary*? The idea was both intriguing and daunting. Her father's bitterness toward the Communist regime, especially after 1956, had deeply colored her feelings about the country—so much so that when she and David spent six weeks in Europe one summer, she'd rejected his suggestion that they visit Mike's birthplace.

The Hungary she knew was more a state of mind than a geographical entity. It was populated by the people she'd grown up with in Berwyn, men who drank beer with Papa after a day at the mill and pinched her cheeks in church on Sundays; plump, motherly women who seemed never to take off their aprons and still clucked over her, even though she was herself a mother. Hungary was deliciously rich dinners at the Rendezvous and dancing 'til you were breathless at the St. Elizabeth's festival; gypsy music, and heated arguments over the failure of the 1956 uprising; travel posters of majestic bridges soaring above the Danube.

Now Judge Silver was asking her—no, *telling* her—to

confront the Hungary that existed outside of Mike Laszlo's memories and beyond the borders of the West Side. Normally, she would have relished the opportunity for an expense-paid trip, even if it was business related. You could usually take the depositions, examine the documents, and still have some free time to explore the interesting museums and poke around the shops. But Hungary was a country you ran away from . . . not a place to go sightseeing like a carefree tourist, who sent home postcards with the message "Wish you were here."

However, she seemed to have no choice in the matter, and at least she spoke the language. As for whether or not Papa would come with her—that was entirely up to him to decide. She broke the news to him later that afternoon over coffee and poppyseed cookies in his kitchen.

"I gotta go Hungary?" He stared at her incredulously, a cookie dangling above his mug, waiting to be dunked. She might as well have been talking about a trip to the moon.

"No. Only if you want to," she quickly reassured him. "*I* have to go."

Mike smacked his fist against the table hard enough that her coffee spilled over the side of the cup. "Lies don't stop," he said fiercely. "We get K.G.B. guy, say card false, they suddenly get witness." He crossed his arms and glared at the far wall, looking more scared than sullen. "I no go. They gonna kill me. It a trap. They put somethin' in food, or accident."

"That's paranoid, Papa," she told him, wondering whether Harry would agree with her.

"*Paranoid?*" he thundered. "They make up all this? *No* paranoia! I no go, Anni. You careful, tubusom. I no can win without you. I know that. Communist know, too," he hinted darkly.

If she were going to preserve her sanity and do the job right, she couldn't let herself be seduced by his fears. She was an American citizen, traveling on government business. You couldn't get much more protected than that. Nobody was going to try and mess with her. "Don't worry, Papa," she said, reaching for another cookie.

But she could see her words did nothing to reassure her father, who shook his head and scowled darkly. You didn't have to be a mind-reader to know what he was thinking: She had better be careful whom she talked to, what streets she wandered down. In Hungary, anything could happen.

Mikey was curled up on Ann's bed watching her pack with the woebegone expression of a little boy who felt as if he were being deserted just when he needed his mother most. "How long are you gonna be gone?" he asked for the third time since she'd told him she had to leave for Hungary the following day.

Ann pulled two wool dresses out of the closet and wrapped them in plastic to keep them from getting wrinkled. "I don't know." She smiled as she repeated what she'd already said the last time he'd asked. "I'll try not to be long." If Mikey ran true to form, he'd miss her desperately until she was out the door and on her way, but he'd do just fine all the while she was gone. For her son, as for herself, anticipation was always the worst part of any difficult situation.

"How come you have to go?" When he stuck out his bottom lip and scowled, he suddenly reminded Ann of his Uncle Karchy.

"It's part of the trial," she explained again, grabbing underwear and a flannel nightgown. Did the hotels have central heating? She threw in a pair of wool socks, in case the room was cold at night. "I have to go there to find out what happened."

Mikey put his fists up in front of his face and angrily punched her pillow. "I don't care what happened!" he stormed. "Who cares? It happened a long time ago."

"It doesn't matter how long ago it happened," she said gently, pushing aside her suitcase and sitting down next to him. She put an arm around him and drew him closer. "It matters *what* happened."

"No, it doesn't!"

"Yes, it does," she quietly insisted, stroking his forehead. Whatever else he took away from this terrible ordeal, he had to understand that some things you couldn't pretend into oblivion.

With surprising strength, he pulled himself out of her embrace. "I know Grandpa didn't do anything anyway. I don't care what they say. What happened—it's *over*!" he flung in her face, trying to articulate his confusion. "How do we know what happened?" he asked, his eyes pleading for an answer he could grasp on to. "*We* didn't see it. People just *say* it. People lie."

"People tell the truth, too," she reminded him.

"I don't want you to go," he whimpered, rolling over to the other side of the bed, as far away from her as he could get.

She reached out and hugged him so tightly she could feel his heartbeat. Her poor innocent baby. "I'll be back as soon as I can," she promised him.

Harry's opinion on the sick witness was that he was possibly legit, more probably not; there was no way of knowing until she got there. And the hell with Mishka going with her, he'd roared before slamming down the phone. Silver had to be out of his mind! He must have passed the word along to David, who called Ann to apologize for having picked a fight with her on Saturday. An old habit, he said sheepishly. Sometimes it was hard to give it up.

To make up for his nastiness, he offered her a lift to the airport in the morning. She told him she'd already arranged a ride with Karchy, but could he keep a close watch on Mikey, so he didn't feel utterly abandoned by his parents? David promised to be the model father while she was away and wished her a safe trip.

At midnight, her passport, visa, and ticket safely stowed in her purse, Ann fell into bed thinking about what it meant to be a "model father." Did Harry qualify for the title? Given the stories she'd heard from David and what she'd seen herself, she thought not. Did Papa? She fell asleep before she could answer her own question.

O'Hare, perennially billed as the world's busiest airport, was living up to its reputation when Karchy and Ann arrived at the departure area. A steady stream of cars pulled in and out, unloading passengers and luggage, while pedestrians dodged the oncoming buses and taxis that careened past along the service road. The airport police kept a sharp eye out for drivers who dared stand for too long at the curb. As for parking—forget about it. A quick farewell kiss, and then it was move along, mister, keep it moving.

Karchý hated tears and mushy good-bye scenes, so he was happy to hurry through the ritual of seeing his sister off. He pulled Ann's overnighter and garment bag out of the car, then tucked a pack of gum in her coat pocket for takeoff and landing.

"Listen, don't worry about nothin', okay?" he told her with a mischievous grin. "I'll take care of Pop. Maybe we'll go down to the bar, slug a few. I already talked to Mikey. We're gonna go downtown, screw around, go to a coupla shows." His face lit up, as if he'd just had an inspiration: "Maybe I'll get him laid or somethin', maybe I'll get Pop laid, too. Hey, maybe I'll even get laid."

Ann gave him a fast peck on the cheek and smiled as she picked up her bags. A thought flashed through her mind: *Come with me, Karchy.* Where did *that* come from? A throwback from when she was a kid and could always depend on big brother Karchy to protect her and fight her battles?

She gave him another kiss—a real one, this time—and turned to go.

"Annie, you got your knife?" he called after her.

"What are you talking about, Karchy?" she asked with a puzzled backward glance.

He grinned broadly and gestured with his hand at his groin, reminding her: *If he needed me, I'd slice some nuts.*

Embarrassed by his crudeness *(You better get real crude, Annie.)*, she blushed and waved at him over her shoulder.

But Karchy had to have the last word. "Hey, Annie!" he yelled. "I love ya!"

She smiled to herself as the automatic doors slid open and she hurried inside the terminal. As usual, it was a madhouse. People rushed frantically to catch their flights, the serpentine ticket lines only seemed to get longer and longer, signs pointed travelers down endless corridors in a perpetual state of renovation. As a native Chicagoan who was used to flying in and out of O'Hare, Ann knew that all you could do was be cool, stay calm, and hope your plane didn't leave when it was supposed to.

Today, however, someone must have been watching over her, because she checked her bags and got her boarding pass in record time. On her way to the gate, she stopped at a newsstand and bought the *Trib* and the *Sun Times*, an armful of magazines, and an English murder mystery, to occupy her during the fourteen- or fifteen-hour flight to Budapest. Thus prepared, she hurried toward the X-ray machine at the end of the hallway.

Someone was there to see her off—George, carrying a large envelope that she apparently intended to give Ann as a bon voyage present. Not breaking her stride, Ann waved her away. She'd had enough of George's manila envelopes and the would-be time bombs ticking inside them.

But George refused to be put off. "Just take it. Read it," she urged, keeping step with her friend.

Ann shook her head and held up her magazines. She had enough to read, thank you very much. Barring some extraordinary evidence from the mystery witness in Budapest, Papa's case was almost closed. George could quit mucking about in his past.

"Annie," George pleaded, "we've known each other a long time. Take it. Read it. Please."

Sure she'd regret it, Ann grabbed the envelope out of George's hand. Okay, was she satisfied? Really, there was such a thing as being *too* conscientious, as George proved now when she persisted in pushing her Tibor Zoldan conspiracy theory. "Tibor Zoldan's sister lives in Budapest," she told Ann. "Go see her."

"What for?" snapped Ann.

George had a look in her eyes that said, This hurts me more than it hurts you. "Read that stuff, Annie. That's what for." Her words tumbled out in a rush as Ann threw her purse and shoulder bag onto the X-ray conveyor belt. "Annie, Mike rented a car the day before Zoldan got hit and run over."

Ann stepped through the barrier and kept right on walking. She had a plane to catch . . . an appointment to keep in Budapest.

CHAPTER
14

The sun was just coming up as Ann's plane began its descent into Ferihegy International Airport. Groggy from having been cooped up for too long, she peered out the window, hoping for her first glimpse of Hungary. To her right, off in the distance, she could just make out the Danube, snaking through the middle of Budapest. Beyond that, a blur of mountains—the Buda Mountain Range, according to the "Welcome to Hungary" brochure she'd found in her seat pocket. Otherwise, the panorama spread out below her in the pale dawn light could have passed for the outskirts of many midwestern cities she'd approached by air. She would have to wait until she was on the ground to get a real view of Budapest.

As she waited in the doorway of the plane for the people ahead of her to leave, she greedily breathed in deep mouthfuls of fresh air. The wind, brisk and refreshing, felt good on her face. According to her watch, still set on Chicago time, it was almost midnight. Here it was close to six o'clock Wednesday morning. No wonder she was feeling stale and cranky.

Trying not to yawn, she carefully negotiated the narrow

stairs and thought about a bath, a nap, hot coffee, a brisk walk. Judge Silver and Jack were coming in on later flights. She'd forgotten to ask whether they were staying at her hotel. Someone would have to be in touch with her to let her know the arrangements. In the meantime, she was on her own and anonymous.

"Ann Talbot?" called a young man in his thirties, who was standing off to the side just at the foot of the ramp.

She glanced around, astonished to have been picked out by a stranger in this crowd of deplaning passengers. "Yes?" she asked warily.

"Come with us, please," said the man, who spoke a clear but accented English. Reaching to take her bag, he introduced himself. "Andras Nagy, from Magyar Turista Agency. We give special services. Welcome to Hungary."

Mindful of her father's dire warnings, she hesitated. Special services? Was that a euphemism for being kidnaped by the Communists? Maybe she was being set up for blackmail, or they were planning to drug her and try to trade her for Papa. *Stop it!* she scolded herself. Talk about paranoia! Next she'd be seeing spies and secret agents lurking around every corner.

Probably this was an intergovernmental thing. The Justice Department must have wired ahead to the appropriate agency, so that her guide would have had a description of her. She couldn't have been hard to spot. How many other well-dressed, midthirtyish women had walked off the plane looking like bewildered tourists?

Trusting her instincts rather than the echo of Mike's ominous admonitions, she smiled tentatively at Andras Nagy and trotted after him, not altogether displeased to have someone to help her past the customs and immigration inspectors. With his help, the entire process, including recovering her luggage, went so smoothly that in less than half an hour she was settled in the back seat of a limo (not as luxurious as Harry's but comfortable nonetheless), on her way to Budapest.

"You in Hungary before?" asked Andras, who was seated up front, next to the driver.

"No." She stared out the window at the passing scenery. The city, just beginning to wake up, struck her as clean, modern, cosmopolitan—nothing at all as she'd imagined.

"Beautiful country," boasted Andras, turning to look at her. He had a sweet smile and the open, friendly face of a man who enjoyed showing off his country for a living. "You like. Have nice big suite at hotel. We check, everything in order," he assured her.

"Do you work for the government?"

He laughed and poked the driver, sharing her joke with him. "No, I tell you—Magyar Turista Agency. Nobody like work for government. No money. Tomorrow, eight o'clock, we drive Fokorhas, hospital," he abruptly changed the subject.

A large, colorful billboard caught her eye: a wall-sized poster advertising the Hungarian National Folkdancers. It was one o'clock in Chicago. What was Papa doing? Was he out buying groceries for dinner? Or maybe he and Mrs. Kish were keeping each other warm.

"You speak Hungarian?" Andras wanted to know.

"Not very well," she answered, shading the truth so that he'd keep on with her in English.

He nodded knowingly. "You get better here."

The Gellert, on the western Buda side of the Danube, turned out to be a beautiful old hotel-cum-health spa that offered medicinal baths fed by naturally heated spring water. As Andras had promised, a large two-room suite had been reserved for her. It was clean and comfortable and elegantly decorated with graceful, turn-of-the-century Art Nouveau furniture.

Best of all, it had a splendid view of the city: Her sitting-room windows overlooked the Danube, spanned by the Liberty Bridge, one of several built in the previous century to connect Buda with its sister, Pest, across the river. Through the windows in her bedroom, she could see to the top of Gellert Hill, crowned by the towering monument erected in honor of the Russian army's efforts to liberate Hungary from the Nazis.

Revived by a hot shower, she turned again to George's file and examined the photograph of Tibor Zoldan, an amiable-looking, clean-shaven fellow who seemed an unlikely suspect in a blackmail scheme. George had written Zoldan's sister's Budapest address in big, black letters that were obviously meant to command Ann's attention. She stared at the note, then dropped it on the table as if it were too hot to hold.

Despite the time difference, she was feeling wide awake now. It would be a shame to waste her few free hours sleeping. Andras had told her to call his office any time she wanted a tour of the city, on foot or by car. Suddenly she felt restless and eager to take a walk, perhaps down to the river, or perhaps she'd stroll north toward Castle Hill.

She was studying a map of the city when she was startled by a knock on the door. Andras, returned to insist she permit him to take her around? It wasn't Andras, however, who greeted her with a warm, engaging smile but a thin, elderly, white-haired man dressed in a suit and tie, carrying a prettily wrapped package.

"Madame Laszlo?" he said, bowing slightly from the waist.

"Yes, I'm Ann Talbot."

"You like choklats, Madame Laszlo?" he asked, giving the word its Hungarian pronunciation. He held out the package for her.

"Thank you," she said, gingerly accepting the gift. Hating herself for being so suspicious, she said, "Are you with the hotel?"

The man smiled. "No, madame. I just a man, Hungarian man. Many here in Budapest—Hungarian men, women—not want your father to be on trial. Innocent man . . . what purpose? Trial bad for Hungarians. Old wounds—Hungarians not like that, not . . . *barbar*. Whole world will see. What purpose? Government here not understand such.''

She looked at him closely, trying to memorize his face. ''What's your name?'' she asked.

''That not important, madame. You taste the choklats, madame. You find . . . very *sweet*,'' he told her, putting a peculiar emphasis on the last word. ''Please, enjoy, Madame.''

He bowed again, the very picture of courtly, Old World charm, and walked away.

''Wait! Who are you?'' she called after him, wanting to know more about these Hungarian men and women who believed her father was innocent. And how had they tracked her down at the Gellert?

But the old man had already disappeared around the corner at the end of the hall.

She stepped back inside her room and quickly tore the wrapping paper off what turned out to be a hinged, copper-colored tin, stamped with the garishly colored image of a gypsy couple holding hands. She opened the box and found two sheets of paper, folded in half, lying on the top. On one of the sheets, someone had written her name: Anna Laszlo. Smoothing them out, she immediately saw that these were photocopies of legal documents.

The sightseeing would have to wait.

Hospital corridors, whether in America or Hungary, all had the same oppressive smell of medicine mixed with illness and death. As she followed Andras through the brightly lit halls of the Fokorhas, Ann thanked God her father was still healthy and resolved to be more vigilant about his diet. The emergency-room doctor had said Mike's blood pressure was high and the trial was putting a strain on his system. As soon as she got home, she was going to insist that he have a complete physical checkup,

225

so that he didn't end up seriously ill in a hospital bed, like Pal Horvath, the new government witness.

It was obviously already past the point where anything could be done to save Horvath, a gaunt-faced man with hollow eyes and a mouth that was marked by pain. He didn't even look up when she walked into his room, where Judge Silver and Jack sat waiting for her, along with an interpreter and a videotape operator.

"Good morning," she said to the judge and exchanged nods with Jack.

"Good morning," Judge Silver replied, motioning her to bring her metal chair closer. "Did you have a good flight?"

"Yes, I did. Thank you."

The formalities taken care of, the judge wanted to begin as soon as possible. Their presence in the room was clearly putting an enormous strain on the witness. "Are we ready?" he said and signaled the technician to begin taping.

Clearing his throat, Judge Silver stated for the record, "The United States of America versus Michael J. Laszlo, case number 260-224. We are at the Fokorhas in Budapest, Hungary, with government witness Pal Horvath. Mr. Burke, are you ready to begin?"

But before Jack could so much as open his mouth, Ann jumped in. "Your Honor, I move to bar this witness's testimony. He is an unreliable witness."

Jack looked incredulous, and Judge Silver peered at her over the tops of his bifocals. "On what basis do you question his reliability?" he demanded, making it crystal clear that her reason had better be irrefutable.

Ann knew she was on safe ground, however, and said, "May I address the witness, Your Honor?"

"Objection, Your Honor," Jack angrily pointed out. "He's *my* witness."

Judge Silver held up a silencing hand. "You may address him as to his reliability, not to the facts of his testimony," he allowed Ann.

Horvath, who didn't understand a word of English, hardly seemed to be following the interplay among his visitors. Now he stared blankly at Ann as she spoke his name and began questioning him in English. "Mr. Horvath, did you, on the fifteenth of April, 1952, in an affidavit given to the Hungarian Security Police, claim that a man named Michael Szanadi was the man known as Mishka who allegedly committed war crimes at the Lanchid Interrogation Center?"

The interpreter translated her question for Horvath, who coughed drily and spoke a few words in Hungarian.

"No, I did not," said the interpreter.

"Mr. Horvath," Ann continued, her face devoid of expression, "did you, on the eighteenth of November, 1973, in another affidavit to the Hungarian Security Police, claim that a man named Michael Bato was the man known as Mishka who allegedly committed war crimes at the Lanchid Interrogation Center?"

Again, they waited tensely for the interpreter to finish. This time, Horvath struggled to sit up, then moaned with pain as he rasped his response.

"I don't know what you're talking about!" the interpreter declared, echoing Horvath's anguished denial.

Ann took pity on the poor man. She'd made her point; no need to press him further. "Your Honor, I have here copies of both of Mr. Horvath's affidavits identifying those two other men as Mishka." She handed the judge the pages she'd found inside the box of chocolates and said, "Can the interpreter translate and read these affidavits for the record, Your Honor?"

"Can *I* see them, Your Honor?" Jack jumped in. He stared grimly at the two documents. The Hungarian words meant nothing to him, but the official-looking seals and stamps looked authentic enough to throw him into despair.

"Mr. Burke?"

Jack returned the papers to the judge and felt his guilty verdict slipping out of his hands.

"Can the interpreter translate and read these affidavits for the record, Your Honor?" Ann moved ahead briskly, anxious to be done with Pal Horvath and on her way.

Judge Silver was as eager as she to put this business behind him and spend some hours touring the city before his return flight to Chicago. He passed the documents to the interpreter and sat back, waiting for him to finish reading them into the videocamera.

As the man's voice droned on, Ann glanced at Horvath, who had closed his eyes and turned his head away, as if he were bored with the proceedings.

". . . I have no doubt in my mind that the man I saw involved in these activities was Michael Bato. Signed, eighteen November, 1973, Pal Horvath," the interpreter concluded.

There was a moment of silence broken only by Horvath's hoarse coughs. Then Judge Silver asked, also for the record, "Mr. Burke, did you have prior knowledge of these affidavits?"

"I did not, Your Honor!" Jack shot back indignantly, stung by the implication that had he known he would have suppressed them.

"How did you find this witness?" said the judge.

"He went to the Hungarian authorities a week ago. The Hungarian authorities notified us. He picked Michael Laszlo out of a photo spread."

Then Ann put into words the very question that was troubling Judge Silver: "If I could find copies of these affidavits, Your Honor, why couldn't the government?"

"We don't have access to Hungarian security files!" Jack flung back at her.

"You mean *I* could get them and *you* couldn't? They're cooperating with you, not with me," she gleefully reminded him. Turning to Judge Silver, she said, "Your

Honor, the Hungarian authorities *must* have known about these previous affidavits. They were in their own files."

And then, remembering the spittle dripping from her father's cheek, she couldn't resist digging the knife deeper into Jack's wound. "They *knew* they were giving you an unreliable witness. They used you."

"That's absurd, Your Honor!" Jack fumed. "The Hungarian authorities didn't investigate this man. He walked in to them. They simply handed him over to us. There's no conspiracy here. Most of the records here aren't even computerized."

His wrath seemed to stir Horvath, who pointed a shaky finger at them and rasped a few words in Hungarian.

"What did he say?" Judge Silver asked the interpreter, who quickly translated: "I have no doubt in my mind that it is Laszlo."

The judge had met such witnesses before—tormented souls who would unequivocally identify multiple alleged perpetrators of the same crime. Forensic psychologists had conjectured about their need to garner attention by testifying publicly against innocent men and women. That their moment in the limelight could result in false convictions seemed not at all to trouble their consciences.

"Your motion to bar Mr. Horvath's testimony is granted," he informed Ann. "As for you, Mr. Burke, you've brought us here on a wild goose chase at great government expense. I cannot approve of your action, either as a judge or as a taxpayer."

"Your Honor, please—"

"Please let me finish, Mr. Burke," Judge Silver admonished him sternly. "I have yet to see enough evidence that Mr. Laszlo committed these heinous crimes."

Jack made a desperate, last-ditch effort: "He lied on his immigration application, Your Honor. He admits it. *That's* what we're charging him with."

"Please. Don't insult everyone's intelligence any further. You know you have to show more than the fact that

229

he lied about his membership in the gendarmes," the judge scoffed disdainfully.

Ann saw her opening and deftly seized the opportunity. "Your Honor," she urged, "I move to dismiss the case against my father."

"Your Honor," Jack protested weakly, "the credibility of this witness doesn't justify the dismissal of these charges."

"*I* will make that determination, Mr. Burke," Judge Silver declared, in a tone that seemed to forbid any further argument. Fast running out of patience for the government prosecutor, he gathered up his coat and nodded at Ann. "I will take the motion under advisement, Ms. Talbot. I hope you have a pleasant flight back."

A moment later he was gone. Ann breathed a quick, silent sigh of relief and stood up to leave. Next to her, Jack was still slumped in his chair, wallowing in his defeat. She could feel him watching her, and as she turned to leave, she allowed herself the barest glimmer of a smile. Then she was out the door and hurrying to put Pal Horvath far behind her.

She was halfway down the corridor when Jack caught up with her. "You'll never be able to look at him the same way again. You know that, don't you?"

The look on her face told him he'd hit a bull's-eye, and he took some solace from that.

"Damn you!" she hissed.

"You'll always think about that girl," he goaded her, "the gun in her mouth, the cigarettes—"

"No!" she shouted, shattering the hospital quiet. A nurse stuck her head out of a room and angrily shushed her.

Jack lowered his voice, but his taunts continued. "Yes, you will. I know you will."

"You'll stop at nothing, will you? You want to persecute him, you want to punish him. *He didn't do any-*

thing!'' she raged, lashing out at him as she'd wanted to do all through the trial.

"You think I care about punishing your old man? I don't. You know what I care about, Ann? I care about remembering. I care about memory. It's too late to change what happened, but it's not too late to remember it. It's not too late to save the memory, so it never happens again."

That idea had kept him going throughout his search for Michael Laszlo. Whenever he'd felt he simply couldn't continue, couldn't read one more page of testimony, couldn't interview one more potential witness, he'd thought about his work as a living monument to Hitler's victims— Mishka's victims.

His impassioned words must have registered with her. He could see by her expression that she was finally listening to him . . . better yet, *hearing* him. "What about your boy?" he asked.

"What does my boy have to do with this?" she retorted, wondering why she was bothering with him.

"Everything! What kind of a country do you want your boy to live in? Do you want him to live in a country that accepts some of the most horrible people in the world just because they don't like our enemies? Do you want him to live a lie? Is that what you want to do to him?"

People passed them in the hall and eyed them curiously. Some took them for lovers and hoped they'd end their lovers' spat. They were obviously very much in love and too handsome a couple to waste their time fighting.

It was hearing him go on about Mikey that finally got to her. Angry with herself for listening to him, she raged, "I *think* you lost your case, and you *know* you lost your case. You're angry and desperate to salvage some pride out of all this. You're so desperate you're even willing to use my boy in your argument. The case is over, Jack. You don't have to argue it anymore."

"You don't think that at all. Are you telling me you don't have any doubts about your old man?"

"Yes, I am," she said without a moment's hesitation.

He couldn't accept that. If she meant it, she was lying to herself. "Just tell me this, Ann," he pressed. "How will you be able to live with him? How will you be able to let your boy live with him?"

He made her think of a rabid dog she'd once seen, wild eyed and foaming at the mouth, driven by some insane impulse to attack at all costs. "I don't have time for this," she said coldly and strode toward the exit sign.

Jack followed, keeping pace as he talked. "This is the old country you've heard about all your life, right? You should feel real at home here."

"I feel at home in Chicago," she said, without looking at him.

"Tell me about it, Ann!" he seethed. "The war was *over*. We were in Germany. The Russians were crossing the Hungarian borders. *It was all over.* And the Hungarians kept killing their Jews, turning their fucking romantic Danube into their own shade of blue."

Why? Why are you doing this? she wanted to ask him. *Why can't you leave me and my father alone?* "Not *all* Hungarians!" she cried. "*Some* Hungarians. Not my dad."

Frustrated by her adamant refusal to credit the damning evidence against Mishka, he grabbed her arm and said softly, "Why don't you go down to the riverbank? Check it out. Look into the water. Maybe you can see your face."

Beyond that, there was nothing more he could tell her.

Andras and the limo were parked in front of the hospital, waiting to whisk madame to wherever was her pleasure. Exhausted by the confrontation with Jack, Ann sank into the back seat and gazed blindly out the window, seeing nothing of the passing cityscape.

"Back to hotel?" Andras asked, as the driver maneuvered the limo through the bottle-necked traffic at the approach to one of the bridges.

"Yes," she said, glancing at the Danube flowing swiftly below them, the bright winter sun glinting off the water. She sighed so heavily that the driver heard her and glanced through the rear-view mirror to make sure madame was all right.

"You like choklat, Madame Laszlo?" the driver asked, pronouncing the word with the same accent as the white-haired man who'd brought her the affidavits. His eyes on the road ahead of him, he reached over his shoulder and handed her a box similar to the one the white-haired man had given her. Their eyes met in the mirror, and the driver smiled.

More long-lost documents? Ann cynically wondered. She pried open the cover and was surprised by the gaily tinkling sound of a Hungarian *csardas*. *A music box.* She stared at the rows of rich-looking bonbons, nestled in gold-foil cups.

"You like choklats, no, Madame Laszlo?" said the driver.

"Yes," she replied, mystified by the meaning of this gift. Pure coincidence? Her logic told her it couldn't be. "What bridge is this?" she asked suddenly.

"Lanchid," Andras told her as the limo rumbled down the ramp and onto the Buda side of the river. "In English, Chain Bridge."

"Can you pull over, please? I'd like to take a walk."

"Of course," said Andras, happy to oblige his client.

She preferred to walk by herself, she told him. So while he and the driver waited in the car, she headed across the field toward the edge of the river, a couple of hundred yards away. The field was covered with a light dusting of snow, beneath which the brown winter grass poked through. Here and there were thin patches of ice, melting in the warm sun and oozing mud that stuck to her shoes.

It was muddier yet when she reached the swampy bank, making her wish she'd thought to wear her boots. Just beyond, the Danube coursed by, on its way from Germany to empty into the Black Sea. She remembered learning in geography class that the Danube was central Europe's most important river—powerful enough to divide the people of Budapest, her teacher had joked.

Several drably painted buildings, one larger than the others, squatted by the side of the river. She squinted at them and tried to imagine one a warehouse . . . an interrogation center. There were children playing nearby and couples strolling in the sunshine.

She watched one little boy, no more than seven, as he ran helter-skelter toward the water, waving his arms and screaming at the gulls overhead. A man and a woman—Ann guessed they were his parents—raced after him, enjoying his enjoyment. He didn't want to be caught, but they scooped him up and hugged him between the two of them. Then he squirmed free and they laughed, all three of them, standing there by the bank of the Danube, in the shadow of the Lanchid.

The child helped her make her decision. Ann turned and walked briskly up the river. She put as much distance as she could between herself and the limousine before she recrossed the field, reaching the street in time to spot a taxi cruising for passengers. With a quick backward glance at the limo, she hailed the cab and jumped in. George had won. She would pay a visit to Tibor Zoldan's sister.

Twenty minutes later, the taxi dropped her off in front of a shabby apartment building, one of many similarly shabby buildings in what appeared to be one of the city's working-class districts. She searched the mailboxes in the dingily lit lobby until she found the name she was looking for—Zoldan. The apartment was three stories up a tiled staircase permeated by food odors that made Ann homesick for Chicago. She almost changed her mind when she got to the second-floor landing, but she forced herself up the last flight. She'd come too far to turn back now.

Her hesitant knock on the door was answered almost immediately by a sweet-faced older woman. "Magda Zoldan?"

"Yes?" the woman answered, in Hungarian.

"I'm from the United States," Ann told her, also in Hungarian. "Do you speak English?"

The woman smiled and smoothed her hand over her skirt. Her clothes were worn but clean, her hair carefully tied at the neck with a ribbon. "Hello. Goo-bye. Okay," she replied, showing off her command of the language.

"Hello," Ann said, shaking the woman's hand. Then she switched to Hungarian. "I was a friend of your brother's in America."

Madga's face lit up with excitement. "Oh! You're a friend of Tibor's! Come in, please, come in."

Her apartment was badly in need of painting, and the fabric covering her couch was frayed and stained. But Ann could see she was a woman who had taste and an appreciation for small, decorative touches—such as the flowered wool shawl she'd thrown over the back of the couch and the hand-painted vase that rested on a lace doily in the middle of her table.

"Sit down, sit down," she insisted hospitably, overjoyed to meet someone who'd known Tibor.

"Thank you. I can't speak Hungarian very well," Ann said apologetically.

"I understand you. Would you like some tea? I'll make you some tea," Magda offered enthusiastically.

Ann shook her head. "No, please." On the way over, she'd thought about what she would tell Magda Zoldan. Now she said, "I just wanted to see you. Tibor spoke so much about you."

"Tibor. He wanted so much to go to America." The woman's voice was full of sadness for her dead brother and his lost dreams. "America must be such a beautiful, wonderful country. He had a friend there. He saw his friend's picture in the newspaper here. He said his friend was rich."

"Who was his friend?" Ann asked, her heart in her mouth. "Maybe I know him."

Magda shrugged. Her brother had kept much to himself. "I don't know."

"Did he have a friend named Mike Laszlo?"

She thought for a moment, then said, "I don't know that name. What's your name?"

"Ann Talbot."

Magda stared at her curiously. An American woman who spoke Hungarian, even though she didn't have a Hungarian name. "He never wrote about you. He never wrote about his other friends either. He did not like to write letters or postcards. I love postcards. I have collected them always."

They exchanged smiles. Magda liked this young woman. She wished she would stay awhile and drink tea and talk about Tibor with her. "What did Tibor do over there . . . in America?"

"Not much." Ann cast about, then decided to put him at the mills with her father. "He—"

But Magda had already moved on. "After he died, they sent me nothing but his cameras and his wallet. His wallet only had a ticket in it."

"What kind of ticket?"

"I'll show you," Magda offered. She went over to her dresser and pulled out Tibor's wallet, which she'd saved along with a few other souvenirs of her past. She gave the ticket to Ann and asked, "What is it?"

"It's a pawn ticket," Ann explained. "He gives them something valuable and borrows money on it."

Magda's eyes lit up. "What did he give them?"

"I don't know." An idea was forming in Ann's head. "Will you let me take this and send you whatever he borrowed money on?"

236

"Yes," Magda eagerly agreed. "I don't have many things to remember him by."

"Okay, I'll send it to you," Ann said, turning the ticket over in her hands.

Magda smiled. "Oh-kay," she mimicked her new American friend. Did Tibor have such nice friends? She'd never even known if he'd been happy in America, or whether his rich friend had given him any money. Probably not, or he wouldn't have had to trade his valuable thing, whatever it was, for the pawn ticket. "Will you send me an American postcard?" she asked Ann wistfully.

Ann felt there was more she should be saying to Magda—some message from America—but she couldn't think what it was. So she smiled and rose to leave. "I'll send you a bunch of American postcards."

Magda stood up slowly, feeling a twinge of arthritis. Probably it would snow again tomorrow. She would put up some soup after the woman left. "Thank you," she said, then regretfully walked her visitor to the door.

Just to the right of the door was a low table decorated with a few framed photographs and another vase of flowers. One picture was of a very pretty, teenaged Magda, holding hands with a man in his twenties. A long, deep scar slashed across the left side of the man's face. Ann stared at the scar and was suddenly transported back to the courtroom.

Magda nodded, as if she understood. "You don't recognize Tibor? He had surgery, three times. Skin grafts. He spent every *forint* he had on it."

Ann tried to keep her voice from trembling as she asked, "What did he do in the war?"

"He was in the army, like everyone else." But she looked away, unable to meet Ann's gaze. Then she recovered herself and said, "You won't forget the postcards?"

It was all beginning to feel too strange and foreign. She'd lost her bearings here in Budapest, in this city divided by the Danube and its memories of the war. No, she wouldn't forget the postcards. She'd send them soon, when she was safely back home in America, where she belonged.

Nevertheless, the next morning there were tears in her eyes as she watched, from the window of her plane, Budapest receding in the distance. She could make out the thick greenish-brown snake that was the Danube, but the bridges were like silver specks, so tiny she might have been imagining them.

"Would you like a *Herald Tribune*?"

Startled, Ann turned and found a stewardess smiling at her. "Would you like a *Herald Tribune*?" the stewardess repeated, holding a stack of the international paper published in Paris.

Ann nodded. She hadn't even looked at a paper in two days. . . .

A huge headline jumped out at her: JUDGE IN LASZLO TRIAL: "NO PROOF OF GUILT."

CHAPTER
15

Logic told her she should put off her visit to the pawnshop until the next day. But Ann couldn't wait. She had to know what Tibor Zoldan had left with the pawnbroker in exchange for probably much less money than the item was worth. She hadn't called ahead from Budapest to tell anyone when she was coming home. So when the plane landed in Chicago, she had nobody waiting for her to whom she'd have to make excuses.

It was five-thirty when she finally extricated herself and her bags from the insanity at international arrivals. Too bad she didn't have an Andras waiting to smooth things over on this end. Having no idea what time pawnshops closed, she took a chance that this one would be open late. Luck was with her, and she didn't have to wait long for a cab. Then it was fingernail-biting time as they hit rush-hour traffic driving to the West Side.

But when the cabbie stopped at the address she'd given, Ann breathed a sigh of relief. The lights were on inside the store, in front of which hung three large metal balls—the medieval symbol of the pawnbroker. For an extra ten bucks, the driver was persuaded to wait for her, and she hurried out of the cab, anxious to solve the mystery.

Walking into the store, she caught a glimpse of herself in the full-length mirror leaning against a wall. Her face was drawn and pale with exhaustion. She looked as if she hadn't slept in days, which wasn't all that far from the truth.

Under other circumstances, she might have been curious about the hidden treasures to be found here among all the clutter and grime. But tonight her curiosity was reserved for whatever it was Zoldan's ticket would redeem.

The proprietor heard her come in and shuffled out to see who was disturbing his supper of a slice of pizza washed down with a shot of whiskey. He didn't bother to hide his surprise. Not too many nice-looking white women frequented his place. This one had some money. He could tell right away from the jewelry she was wearing. But when she handed him the ticket, he looked at it dubiously.

"Jesus Christ, lady, it took you awhile to come back," he growled, scratching his chest.

Ann forced a smile and tried to stifle her impatience as the man disappeared into the back room, for what seemed like forever. When he reappeared, he was shaking his head. "$188.90," he announced with a scowl, as if he were afraid she'd think the price too high.

He plunked down on the counter an ornately carved wooden box. On its cover were two ceramic figures—a man and a woman, both dressed in native Hungarian costumes—poised to dance. The box looked very old and much more valuable than what the pawnbroker had given Zoldan for it.

Ann quickly dug in her wallet for the money and paid the man before he read her mind and decided to up the price. She grabbed the box and was already halfway out the door when the pawnbroker suddenly woke up to the fact that he had a paying customer. "Hey, listen," he called after her, "I got some nice diamond rings."

"Where to next, lady?" the taxi driver wanted to know. She gave him instructions to Wilmette and fretted until he'd pulled onto the Eisenhower Expressway. Finally, she had enough light to get a proper look at Zoldan's box.

On its underside, she discovered a little metal button, which when pushed set free the figurines, who began dancing about the top of the box in time to a gay *csardas*. It was a music box! The dancers continued their *pas de deux* even after she'd opened the lid, to reveal an empty, purple-velvet-lined compartment. So much for her quest for Tibor Zoldan. The trail ended here. She could send the music box back to his sister and never give it another thought.

And then her fingers found another tiny button that set free an artfully concealed shallow drawer. She reached inside and pulled out a photograph, crumbling with age at the edges, but in the darkness, she couldn't make out any of the people in the picture.

"Could you turn the light on?" she called to the driver.

"Aw, lady," he grumbled, "it's hard enough driving—"

But for another ten bucks he was happy to do her the favor.

It took a moment for her eyes to adjust . . . to recognize her father, smiling, dressed in a Special Section uniform. He was holding a rifle in one hand, which he had aimed at another man's head. The other man had his arms around a woman and a small child—and wound around all three of them were several lengths of wire.

There were several more photographs in the drawer, all of them of her father, smiling and pointing his rifle at people in various macabre poses. In the last picture in the series, he had his arm around the shoulder of a terror-crazed young girl. She was naked and staring glassy-eyed into the camera.

The cabbie, who'd been driving for twenty-five years, had seen a lot of strange things go on in the back seat of his car. But he'd never heard anything like the thin, piercing wails coming out of his passenger's mouth. When he checked her out in the rear-view mirror, she was slumped over, her arms wrapped around her chest, rocking back and forth as if she were sick.

"You okay, lady?" he asked, alarmed by the sounds she was making.

And then, thank God, she was home.

She had to see him. Had to hear from his own mouth the answer to the question pounding in her brain: *Why?* Her car keys were in her purse. She didn't even bother to go inside to drop off her suitcase; she just got in the car and drove to Berwyn, not thinking, trying not to feel. When she pulled into her father's driveway, there was only one lone light shining in his bedroom. Ann turned off the motor and tried to summon up the courage to get out of the car.

Suddenly, as if he'd intuited her presence, Mike looked out the window and waved. Then he just as quickly disappeared. The sight of him made her lose her nerve. She wasn't ready to face him . . . not yet. First, she had to sort things out, think about what she was going to do. Trembling with panic and exhaustion, she started the car up and hurriedly backed out of the driveway. She was already halfway down the block by the time Mike opened the door and watched her taillights fade from view.

Her own house was dark and silent, except for the ringing of the phone, which she heard even before she got inside. It shrilled insistently, demanding to be answered, until she picked up the receiver and left it off the hook.

Much, much later, she woke up from her trance and found herself in the living room, sitting in the darkness. She sleepwalked into the kitchen, picked up the phone, and numbly dialed David's number. Her son answered after the first ring.

"Mikey?" She could hardly make her lips form words. "I love you. I just got back. I'll see you tomorrow." That was all she could manage. "I love you," she said again and hung up.

The phone instantly rang again. Ann recoiled as if she'd just heard a rattler's hiss. Papa? She would have to speak to him eventually—in the morning, if not now. And hadn't he always told her not to put off doing the things she didn't want to do?

"Hello?" she said, her voice coming back at her flat and hoarse.

He'd been so worried, he said. He'd called and called and no one answered, and then it was busy for such a long time, and he thought . . .

"It must have fallen off the hook, Papa." She felt like a zombie—devoid of feeling, the living dead.

She didn't sound right. Was she sick? And why had she driven away from his house without coming inside?

She managed to choke out a feeble excuse. "I'm just very tired . . . and I thought you were asleep. No, I didn't see you."

But he was excited. They should celebrate. Had she heard all the way over there in Budapest? Judge Silver . . .

"Yes, I saw it in the paper, Papa," she said. "But I told you, I'm very tired."

Yes, sleep, he told her. She'd earned a good, long sleep. And tomorrow there was a party at Harry's and they could all celebrate together.

"I'll see you there," she mumbled, hardly conscious of what she was saying. "Yes, Papa, I . . . I love you, too."

She fell asleep instantly, curled up against the back of her couch, like a fetus in its mother's womb.

It was past noon when Ann woke up, aching and sore in more muscles than she knew she had. Her body hurt, her eyes hurt, her head hurt—and she was supposed to be at Harry's in an hour. Somehow, she pulled herself together—why did she feel as if she were dressing for a funeral?—and forced herself out of the house. She was

243

going only because Mikey would be there. She wanted to see him and no one else.

A knot of reporters were clustered as close to the mansion as Harry would permit them. Harry and her father stood in their midst, evidently holding forth on their tremendous victory. Watching them, Ann felt sick to her stomach. She hadn't eaten anything since the plane ride, except for a cup of coffee that was burning craters in her stomach.

"Hey! You did it! You fuckin' did it!" shouted Karchy, coming up and surprising her from behind. He threw his arms around her and all but hauled her into the air like a sack of potatoes. "Jesus Christ, Annie, you sliced their nuts off! I love ya! I love ya! Holy shit, do I love ya!"

She pasted on a false smile and asked, "Where's Mikey?"

"Where's Mikey?" he roared with mock indignation. "Is that all you got to say? He's in the house, he'll be right out. C'mon, Pop's been waitin' for you!" He grabbed her hand and started dragging her toward the crowd on the lawn. But she broke away and headed for the house.

"Mikey'll be right out!" Karchy yelled, puzzled by her lack of enthusiasm.

In fact, just as she stepped onto the porch, Mikey came bounding out, screaming, "Mom! Mom!" and he fell right into her hug.

"I missed you. I missed you so much," she said fiercely.

Mikey was bubbling with joy. "Isn't it great about Grandpa? I told you! He didn't do anything—people were just lying! And Mom, guess what?" He abruptly veered off in another direction. "Grandpa Talbot got me a pony! You should see him. C'mon, I'll show him to you!"

She gave him another hug and promised, "I'll be out in a little while."

"Hurry up, Mom," urged Mikey, racing toward the back lawn. "He's so neat!"

Had she ever been so happy as Mikey was today? His grandfather exonerated, *and* a pony, besides. She went over to the window in Harry's office and watched her son jumping up and down between his two grandfathers, who were feeding apples to Mikey's new pet, a beautiful black animal. She couldn't begin to understand about Papa. How the hell would his adoring grandson ever make sense of it? She was his mother—she was supposed to be able to help him through crises. But she felt shamefully ill equipped for this one.

"Anni?" came Mike's voice from the back of the house. "Where are you?" When she didn't respond, he called again, "Anni?"

She couldn't hide from him anymore. "In here, Papa," she called back, feeling—for the first time in her life— scared of him.

She heard his heavy steps outside the room. "Tubush!" He put his arms out to hold her, but then he saw the look on her face and said, "What's the matter, Anni?"

"I know, Papa," she told him, turning her back.

"What you know, Anni?" he demanded, mystified by her behavior. "We win. Trial over. Judge dismiss."

"I know everything, Papa."

Impatient with her theatrics, he pointed out, "Trial over, Anni. What everything? We win. Harry say we gonna sue."

His cold-blooded audacity astonished and frightened her. She turned around and said simply, "Tibor."

"What Tibor?"

"Tibor Zoldan. He was killed," she reminded him. Could he ever forget?

"Ya. Traffic accident. I tell you."

"By a hit-and-run driver." She was summing up her case against him as carefully as any she'd ever tried.

He shrugged his shoulders. "So?"

She ticked off the facts on her fingers. "You rented a

245

car, Papa. The day before he died. In Evanston. Ninety miles away. George got the rental slip.''

"We had meeting, Arpad Circle," Mike defended himself. His voice rose in agitation. "Chevy break down. I get fixed. I rent car, take back when Chevy fix."

But she wasn't buying it—not one word. She'd heard so many lies from him that she wondered how he could still concoct them. "He was blackmailing you," she said.

"*Blackmail?* He friend from camp—"

"I saw the scar, Papa."

"Scar? What scar? He no have scar," Mike protested, genuinely upset.

"Yes, he did. Running down the left side of his face, just like the witness said." She could feel herself shattering into little pieces. What little strength she had left was being sapped by his unrelenting determination to hold up his end of the lie.

Red faced, he clenched his fists. "You think I . . . No, no, no, Anni! You think I—"

"Yes," she whispered. "You killed all of them."

Her face was like a stone as he went to her, pleading, "No, no, Anni! You my girl, Anni, please—"

"Don't touch me!" She shrank back from his hand.

"Anni!" he implored. "You my own—"

"I don't want you to touch me, Papa," she said, her voice like ice. Another minute and she'd be crying. She could feel the tears welling up. Her throat tightened with the effort to stay in control, and she turned again to look out the window. In the back field, Mikey was trying to ride his pony, while Harry stood watch over him.

"How could you have done . . . those things, Papa . . . and raised me the way you raised me?"

He stood motionless and unspeaking, like a stone.

"Answer me, Papa," she implored. "I need you to answer me. Answer me, Papa. Please! Answer me!"

"What happen to you, Anni? What they do to you over

there, Anni? What the Communist do to you, Anni?'' His voice was flooded with sorrow.

She stared at him, nonplussed by what he was saying. Finally, after the silence between them had begun to take on a life of its own, she whispered, "I love you, Papa. But I don't want to see you again. I don't want Mikey to see you."

"No!" he cried, panicked at the thought of losing what was most important to him in the world. "No!"

"You're dead, Papa," she said very quietly.

He saw that she was absolutely serious. Deftly, with the skill of a man who'd had years of experience at duplicity, he began constructing his cover. "You can no do this," he warned her.

"You don't exist." It took everything she had to keep breathing.

"You can no do this to your father!" he growled.

"Good-bye, Papa," she whispered.

"You can no do this! He my grandson! He my boy!" A seething rage was boiling up in him, threatening to spill over, like molten hot lava from a volcano.

"You don't have a grandson," she told him, wanting him to understand exactly how it would be. "You don't have a daughter."

He half raised his hand, as if to strike her, and then he slammed shut the lid of his fury. "You gonna tell Mikey this filth? You gonna poison his mind like they poison you?" he ranted.

"Not unless you force me to," she answered him, sounding far calmer than she felt.

For an instant she thought he might cry, and she hoped not, knowing his tears would undo her. But when he looked up at her, he was smiling—the smile of the young Mishka that she'd seen in the photographs.

"You think I gonna let you say these things to him, Anna? You say these things, you no my daughter no more. You like a stranger, you say these things. You like a

247

stranger tryin' hurt me. I gonna defend myself, Anna. I do everythin' I gotta do, defend myself."

"Are you threatening me, Papa?" she asked, freed of her fear now that she'd seen his weakness.

"No, I no threaten you . . . Anni, my tubush." Mike's face was a heartbreaking collage of pain and anger. "You tell him anything you want. You say anything you want. Mikey not gonna believe you. They gonna say you crazy."

He turned to go, but he had one final thought for her to ponder: "Somethin' happen your mind. You listen your papa, Anna. You tired. You need rest, Anna."

Outside, just below the window where she was standing, Harry was still holding court with the media, who were eating out of his hand like puppies with their master.

"Look, fellas, Mishka's one of the most decent guys I've ever known," he pontificated, sounding as if he were getting ready to run for public office. "Look what they did to him. They put him through a torture test. Let's stop beating a dead Nazi horse. Let's not let a generation of ambitious hotshots persecute innocent men like Mike Laszlo. We're a democracy! We're not the Inquisition. Let's concentrate on the future, not on the past. Let's worry about the grandsons, not the grandfathers."

She *was* worrying about the grandson, who was laughing as he struggled to mount his pony, with a helping hand from his Grandpa Mike. It was a distorted-image picture of a cozy family scene: Karchy, Mikey, Mike—and grouped behind Mike, the collective souls of his dead victims. And watching them from afar was Ann, with tears streaming down her cheeks.

There was some pleasure to be taken in the familiar routines—helping Mikey with his homework, cooking him dinner, tucking him into bed. She wished him "Good night, sleep tight," and hugged him close, then gave him a big kiss on his forehead. Mikey snuggled under the cov-

248

ers, already half asleep. Between his Grandpa's celebration and the pony, he was totally worn out.

But not too tired to pipe up, as she was tiptoeing out the door, "What if we call him Gypsy? My pony," he explained in response to her puzzlement. "What if we call him Gypsy?"

She didn't know how to answer him, except to shake her head, no. He seemed to understand, because he quickly said, "Maybe we should think about it some more."

"I love you," she told him, turning to go.

"Mom!" he called to her with a last burst of energy. "I can go over there and ride him any time I want! Isn't that neat?"

She nodded and stepped into the hallway. But he stopped her a third time and said, "I missed you, Mom," which was what he'd wanted to tell her in the first place.

Halfway down the stairs, she heard a noise coming from his room and turned around to investigate. Through the open doorway, she could see him on the floor, doing push-ups. Her shadow fell across him and he looked up, grinning impishly. "Healthy body makes a healthy spirit. Right, Mom?"

Ann brewed herself a cup of tea and went into her office to write the hardest letter of her life. She sat in front of her typewriter for a long time, wondering how best to tell him. Finally, the words began to flow as naturally and swiftly as the waters of the Danube.

"Dear Jack Burke," she wrote, "I went down to the riverbank. . . .

Jack must have fed the story to the papers as soon as he got her letter. Four days later, the newspaper boy delivered the afternoon edition and Ann found herself staring at front-page headlines about her father. "Michael Laszlo, War Criminal" screamed the top line. Beneath that: "Justice Department Releases Atrocity Photos." The picture of Mike pointing his gun at the family also appeared on the front page; there were more pictures inside, where the story continued.

Mikey was shooting baskets outside when the paper arrived. He seemed to be having a great time; he'd been practicing a lot over the winter, and his aim was improving. Ann finished the article, set her lips, and sighed in preparation for what she had to do.

"Mikey?" she called to him from the back door.

"What, Mom?" he answered, taking a throw from the foul line.

"Come here," she said, and prepared herself to break his heart.

Twelve m[...]
Twelve indo[...]
One UNIFORMLY HOT! miniseries.

Don't miss a story in Harlequin Blaze's
12-book continuity series, featuring irresistible
soldiers from all branches of the armed forces.

Now serving—
those ready and able heroes of the U.S. Navy...

HIGHLY CHARGED!
by Joanne Rock
April 2011

HIGH STAKES SEDUCTION
by Lori Wilde
May 2011

TERMS OF SURRENDER
by Leslie Kelly
June 2011

Uniformly Hot!
The Few. The Proud. The Sexy as Hell.

Available wherever Harlequin books are sold.

Blaze

Dear Reader,

Back in my graduate school days, I studied literature and really enjoyed it. But sometimes the reading was dense and difficult, so I read romance in between the texts on critical theory to mix things up a bit! When it came time to write a Master's thesis, I thought it would be fun if I could combine some of the scholarly needs of the paper with a racy topic that would keep me engaged at the same time. Enter French diarist and erotica writer Anaïs Nin, a brilliant writer and a true character in her own right. I penned a thesis on this intriguing, groundbreaking writer and was sucked right into the drama of her life.

Fast forward a decade and a half and I found myself writing about a literature professor (hmm…). Wouldn't it be fun to have this character inspired by a diarist and erotica author, too? My heroine, Nikki Thornton, is a fun combination of academic and sensualist. Only, what she really needed was to get in touch with her sensual side. Luckily, Brad Riddock, an explosives expert on leave is more than willing to take on the job.

It turned out to be a highly charged tale! Please drop by my website http://joannerock.com this month to enter a contest for a gift card to the bookseller of your choice and a few books to get you inspired!

Happy reading,

Joanne Rock

Joanne Rock

HIGHLY CHARGED!

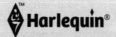

TORONTO NEW YORK LONDON
AMSTERDAM PARIS SYDNEY HAMBURG
STOCKHOLM ATHENS TOKYO MILAN MADRID
PRAGUE WARSAW BUDAPEST AUCKLAND

Recycling programs
for this product may
not exist in your area.

ISBN-13: 978-0-373-79608-3

HIGHLY CHARGED!

www.eHarlequin.com

Printed in U.S.A.

ABOUT THE AUTHOR

Three-time RITA® Award nominee Joanne Rock is the author of more than fifty books for a variety of Harlequin series. She has been an *RT Book Reviews* Career Achievement Nominee and multiple Reviewer's Choice finalist. In addition to her own writing, Joanne teaches writing, film and fiction at Plattsburgh State University in New York. The proud mother of three smart, athletic sons (not that she's biased), she spends a great deal of time on the sidelines or on the bleachers, cheering them on. Learn more about Joanne's life and writing at her website http://joannerock.com or find out what she's working on today by friending her on Facebook!

Books by Joanne Rock

To my sister-in-law, Karen C. Rock,
who made brainstorming this story so much fun.
I appreciate your "year-in, year-out" enthusiasm
that helps me stay excited about whatever I happen
to be working on at the moment. Our visits never
fail to generate ideas and new creative energy.
Thank you for sharing your storytelling wisdom!

Prologue

"CRIMINY!" NIKKI THORNTON punctured her thumb on a thorn from a locust tree branch in her haste to clean up the yard.

A literature professor who was completely out of her element in the landscaping department, Nikki balanced on a stepladder at the edge of her recently inherited property, a home that had belonged to her friend and mentor, Chloe Lissander.

"Of all the luck," Nikki muttered, tugging off her work gloves to assess the damage. She'd been trimming low-hanging branches in a cleanup of the property before the local historical society came in to assess its potential as a historical site. She could not afford to screw up her chance to honor the memory of the only person who'd ever really been there for her.

Chloe Lissander had been a noted author who helped spur the feminist movement with her groundbreaking stories of female sexual empowerment. Nikki had been drawn to the literature's gutsy strength—and more than a little intrigued by the erotic factor. When she'd discovered five years ago that the author lived in close proximity to the university where Nikki was working on her Ph.D., she had wasted no time interviewing her about her writing.

That interview had led to a life-changing friendship with a woman who'd been an inspiration on so many levels. Chloe had become like family to her since Nikki's parents had never been all that interested in the role. Even so, no one had been more blown away than Nikki when Chloe had followed through on her promise to leave her rural Virgina Beach property to Nicole upon Chloe's death six months before.

Chloe's relatives were still in an uproar over it. And as much as Nikki hated to deprive them of the charming farmhouse and surrounding property, she could not ignore Chloe's wishes for the place that had been falling into disrepair for decades. Chloe had entrusted Nikki to live in her childhood home and bring it back to the way it had been in her youth. Nikki had grieved for the loss of her friend for months while Chloe's relatives fought over the will. But now, the probate had been cleared and Nikki had every intention of making Chloe's final wishes for her old home come true.

As soon as she got some antibiotic for the thorn injury.

Setting aside her clippers, Nikki figured the wound was a sign she should quit her work for the day. Tomorrow would come soon enough and she had a to-do list a mile long to get the home ready for the historical society. She was about to climb down her stepladder when a light in a window of the small house next door caught her eye.

Was it dark out already?

She blinked in surprise at how well she could see into the house—the only other home visible from her property. There were no curtains on the windows, just a set of blinds still open. She hadn't gotten a chance to say hello to the neighbor since she knew from Chloe that the lone resident was a military guy who was gone most of the time.

Although…he certainly wasn't away right now. Because there he was in all his buff glory, standing in the window half-naked.

Her mouth went dry at the sight. Her stinging thumb quit hurting.

Taut muscle everywhere. Bronzed skin like a man who'd spent long days in the sun even though it was only April. His hair was dark and slick against his head like he'd just emerged from the shower, a fact underscored by the fact that he had a towel slung low around his hips.

Really low. As in, follow-the-dark-line-of-hair-south-of-his-navel type low. He stalked over to the middle of the sparsely furnished space—a living room, she thought—and retrieved a remote for a big-screen television that he flipped on with a press of his thumb. When he turned to chuck the remote back on a crate that served as a coffee table, Nikki noticed one leg was swathed in gauze up to his knee. An injury of some kind—far worse than the lame hole in her thumb.

Her heart sped at the sight of him. She hadn't meant to spy on him, but she could hardly look away now. A hockey game filled the screen behind him, but the V of his back made for more compelling entertainment than anything carried by a major network.

In a word—*yum*. Despite a formidable command of

the English language she could find nothing else that summed it up so perfectly.

As she stood there, the towel-clad stud turned to face her. Laser-blue eyes flashed on her and for a moment, she was terrified he'd caught her leering at him. Crouching, she tried to hide herself in the overgrown foliage she'd been trimming.

But then he reached for the cord on the wooden blinds at the window and yanked it sideways, slowly disappearing behind the slats. The view went dark, leaving Nikki breathless and buzzing with a physical hum that could only mean one thing.

G.I. Joe had turned her on more in a ten-second peep show than most of the guys she'd gone out with in her spotty dating history. And damn, but that felt much too shallow of her. For a well-educated woman, she sure had gotten carried away by the sight of great abs. A powerful set of shoulders. Then there'd been that intriguing landscape the towel had hidden when he'd turned toward her….

Not that she had any business thinking about *that*. Chastising herself for ogling an unsuspecting stranger, Nikki climbed down the ladder and wondered what Chloe would have said if she could have seen her just now.

Screw the yard work, honey, go knock on his door!

Her friend's voice in her head was so vivid that Nikki had to laugh out loud. Unfortunately, she'd never been as sexually adventurous as Chloe Lissander, whose infamous love life had filled several diaries and inspired her fictionalized erotica. Maybe one day. After she'd gotten the house classified as a historical site, fended off Chloe's relatives and found the two missing diaries so Chloe's publishers could release the full set in their original, uncensored form.

Her fantasies about G.I. Joe would have to wait. Although now that she knew about the view from under the locust tree, Nikki wasn't entirely sure she'd be able to resist the temptation to trim the branches as frequently as possible. Because although she hadn't reached a point in life where she was comfortable being less academic and more sensual, a girl could always dream....

1

Five days later

NAVY LIEUTENANT BRAD RIDDOCK stared at the red
numbers counting down his last seconds on the explosive
device in front of him. Constructed with deceptive sim-
plicity, the bomb had only a handful of wires. A modest
amount of firepower that would take out a building or
two instead of a whole city block.

But looks were deceiving. The wires passed through
a fragile glass casing flecked with white powder on the
inside. Anthrax? Worse? Someone had gotten inventive
to discourage tampering.

Brad knew how to disarm it. But with seconds ticking
by…

Four, three.

He didn't have enough time.

Two…

Sweat rolled down his back as he thought about all
he would lose.

One.

Bang!

Brad jerked upright, gasping. His heart knocked the hell out of his chest; covers tangled around his bare legs like seaweed. The injury on his left calf stung from his sweat.

The soft sounds of a suburban weekend just outside of Virginia Beach greeted his ears. No explosions. No screams from the wounded or dying. Just a few bird calls and the occasional dog bark.

Taking deep breaths to dislodge the cold grip of panic at his throat, Brad wondered why the navy recruiters never warned you that time overseas would make you as jumpy as a cat in a room full of rocking chairs.

Bang!

The second time the crash sounded, he could differentiate the sound from the explosion in his recurring dream. He was home in his own bed, strung out from lack of sleep but still in one piece. And, thankfully, he would remain that way for at least the next two weeks before he shipped out again. Explosions were unlikely in the backyard of a neighborhood so rural it bordered farm country.

"What the hell?" Gladly giving up on sleep after the replay of a nightmare he was already intimately familiar with, Brad reached for a T-shirt at the end of his bed and shrugged it on before grabbing a toothbrush.

Through the crack in his blinds, he could see an obnoxious amount of daylight filtering through as he rinsed and spat. He'd been sleeping so fitfully lately he didn't know if that meant it was past dawn or past noon.

Kicking over a stack of unread newspapers, Brad nearly stepped on a bristly haired stray mutt that had taken up residence with him since he'd been back in town. Scruffing the mutt's head before he pulled on his jeans, Brad strained to hear what was going on outside. A motor thrummed nearby. A road crew at work, maybe?

Bang! Bang!

The thumping was loud and metallic and he ambled onto his lawn to check it out. His yard was quiet—a couple of bent camp chairs pulled up to a fire pit where he'd had a beer with one of his buddies the night before. A bowl he'd bought for the mutt even though he had no business feeding a stray since he wouldn't be around to take care of it next month.

But through the hedges, he could see activity in the neighbor's yard.

He'd heard the woman next door—an eccentric writer who was more wild and crazy at eighty-five than he'd ever been—had died a couple of months ago while he was overseas. Which begged the question, who was the new resident?

Yanking a beer from the cooler that still rested near the fire pit, he took a quick drink—hair of the dog and all that—and then dunked his face in the half-melted ice. *Hoo-yah.*

Skin stinging, he left the beer on a flat rock and strode through the hedge line for a better look at what was going on at the neighbor's place. With two more weeks' mandatory leave, thanks to the navy's resident headshrinkers, Brad had nothing to do but play Good Samaritan anyhow. Dreaming more ways to blow himself up didn't hold much appeal.

And—wow.

The sleek brunette astride a bright red International

Harvester tractor was well worth the trip. Brad leaned
against the trunk of an old dogwood tree to survey the
scene as the woman he didn't recognize steered the old
model-A toward a dilapidated metal storage shed that
appeared to be bent in half as if it was already begging
for mercy. Lowering a plow that had no business playing demolition derby with a garden shed, the brunette
kept her eye on the target as she rammed the big, silver
attachment into the remnants of the structure.

Bang!

The woman knocked it right off its foundation, a grin
of triumph kicking up one side of her lips. On the patio
behind her, a caged blue jay squawked noisily while
a chipmunk behind another set of bars squeaked anxiously. Her idea of pets? Clearly, she was an unusual sort
of woman.

Endlessly long legs showcased by denim cut-offs
made him linger over the view for a moment more. He'd
never seen a plain white tank top worn so well. A sheen
of sweat trickled a path between her breasts, disappearing under the shirt. Olive skin hinted at Mediterranean
or Hispanic ethnicity that didn't quite follow through
in her moss green eyes. A bright turquoise bracelet on
her wrist and yellow flip flops on her feet suggested
she didn't operate heavy equipment often, although that
observation was also supported by the fact that she was
using a farm plow as a wrecking ball.

And—by the way she seemed to be picking up the
dented building—a forklift, as well.

He sauntered closer, determined to find out who she
was and if a call to the cops was in order. But then, as
she loaded the mangled shed into the plow bucket where

it rattled precariously, he thought the better of it. After only a brief battle with the stick shift, she got the tractor into Reverse and stepped on the gas, narrowly missing a grass-munching rabbit. She squealed and braked hard, almost losing her cargo to avoid the furry beast who dove into the cover of trees. Clearly distressed, the woman took a minute to catch her breath before she let off on the brake and sped across the lawn toward an industrial-size Dumpster. She overshot the mark, flying past it with a muttered curse before inching backward, then depositing the twisted gray metal into the bin.

"Take that!" the woman shouted as the shriek of scraping metal echoed on the warm morning breeze. Wiping her hands together with a flourish, she jammed one foot on the clutch and the other on the brake before shutting off the ignition.

And turned surprised green eyes his way.

Her cheeks were flushed from her battle with the shed, but he could have sworn they gained a little more color as she spotted him.

"Can I help you?" Her chin lifted while the caged bird and chipmunk continued to chirp.

Interesting. She headed toward him with a hip-rolling, easy stride that kept his attention a bit longer than was polite.

It had been quite a while since he'd noticed a woman to this degree. Did that mean his enforced downtime was working since he could apparently think about something besides an IED-defusion gone wrong?

"Lieutenant Riddock," his shrink had told him, "you need to relinquish the obsession with one moment in time you can't ever change…"

Or did this sudden interest in a stranger's walk mean he'd really fallen off the deep end since the female to capture his attention took an odd sort of glee in destroying things?

He cleared his throat as he yanked his gaze up from her thighs.

"I live next door." He nodded toward the only other house in a ten-acre radius. "Just thought I'd see who was playing demolition derby on a vacant residence."

"It's not vacant anymore." The yellow flip-flops quit their slap, slap, slap pace as she stopped a few feet away. Forgotten headphones dangled around her neck, the muted tunes classical sounding. "I inherited the house and I'm starting renovations today."

"You call that renovating?" Amused, he peered meaningfully at the exposed shed foundation. "Seems to me you're not going to have anything left by the time you're finished."

"A tacky metal shed circa 1970 was only junking up a turn-of-the-century farmhouse." She folded her arms. "I'm going to strip down some of the add-ons like the detached garage and that old chicken coop in back. I'm trying to have the place declared a historical site and to do that, it needs to be in a form that's closer to its original condition."

His brain was still stuck on the phrase *I'm going to strip down* even though that sentence hadn't taken the direction he had hoped. With an effort, he tried to recall what else she'd said.

"You're one of the relatives?" He recalled old Ms. Lissander had dismissed all her extended family as greedy vultures and wondered where the hot brunette fell in the spectrum. If she was greedy in a hedonistic way he could be totally on board with that. The day was looking up.

Then again, when you awakened to nightmares about blowing up all your friends, that left a lot of room for improvement.

"I'm a student of her writing, actually. I teach literature at Old Dominion University. Nicole Thornton." She extended her right hand, the silver and turquoise bracelet catching the sunlight. "You can call me Nikki."

"Brad Riddock." His palm enveloped her fingers. And no matter that the normal ritual of polite contact was observed according to standard procedure. That garden variety touch blasted his nerve endings faster than the ice cubes he'd dunked his face in. "And I remember Ms. Lissander penned some pretty racy stuff."

Red-hot erotica, in fact, long before the women's movement took hold. The thought of the lady professor studying that kind of thing was intriguing. He was vaguely aware that he hadn't released her hand yet.

Curious, he stroked the juncture between her thumb and her hand. He could have sworn a flicker of awareness darkened her eyes before she snatched her fingers back.

"Chloe Lissander channeled a great deal of passion into everything she did." Nikki nodded toward the white farmhouse behind her. "But by the time she moved back to her childhood home, she didn't have the energy to transform this place the way she wanted. She left it to me in the hope that I'd fulfill her vision."

Nikki stared at the sprawling farmhouse and lop-sided deep porches while Brad considered the way she'd jumped when he touched her. As a man who knew a thing or two about sparks and charges, he guessed his hand wasn't the only one still humming with the aftershock.

This grew more interesting by the minute. He'd never been able to walk away from a situation that could turn explosive at any second. And the gathering heat between him and his new neighbor was a hell of a lot more compelling than the countdown to doomsday he kept seeing in his dreams.

At a time when he needed a distraction more than he needed his next breath, Brad quickly made Nikki Thornton his new number-one priority for the next two weeks until the shrink cleared him for deployment.

"A bit daunting when you look at it from this angle, isn't it?" he remarked, edging a half step closer while her back was turned.

"It's daunting from every angle." Straightening, she smoothed a twitchy hand over her glossy dark hair. "Guess I'd better get to work."

He tracked her movements, wondering how much time they had before this rogue spark combusted. For the first time in his life, he wished he could hasten the explosive process.

"Can I give you a hand?"

SIZING UP HER SUPER STUD neighbor as he sent her surprisingly lustful glances, Nikki could think of numerous uses for his hands, none of which involved hard manual labor. And, judging by the way he'd lingered over their touch, he'd be amenable to a few of them. But she hadn't moved out to the country to moon over a hot guy who only blew through town a couple of times a year between military stints around the world. In all the times Nikki had visited Chloe, she'd never caught a passing glimpse of him until the other night when she'd gotten far more than a peek.

The incident had played and replayed in her dreams ever since.

But even if she'd been in a position to explore her much neglected sensual side, Nikki knew herself well enough to recognize a high risk relationship. She appreciated stability. A sense of home. Community. She'd been shuttled off to strangers as a kid every time her scholarly parents had an opportunity to participate in far-flung archaeological digs or teach at exotic universities, so it was only natural she was drawn to put down her own roots at Chloe's home. Getting involved with a guy who circled the globe for his job would be foolish.

She just hoped her jumpy heartbeat and twitchy skin got the message soon.

Because, no doubt, he was even more incredible looking up close. Tall and lean, he had the easy grace of an athlete when he moved. A tattoo roped one arm, the design thick and intricate with a Celtic feel. The pattern was visible just below the sleeve of his dark blue T-shirt with some kind of navy emblem imprinted on the chest. Sleek muscles beneath the cotton gave the shirt an outline that a store mannequin would have envied, with ridges and rises in all the right places.

But even more than the killer bod, Brad Riddock's face was the sort a woman couldn't look away from. Aquamarine eyes were offset by the slash of straight, dark eyebrows—the menace of the latter preventing the former from being overly beautiful. In the same way, a full, sensuous mouth rested below the sharp blade of his nose, the whole package starkly appealing.

"Not to knock your efforts," he prodded, "but at very least, I could finish up the tractor work without putting any wildlife at risk."

Recalling the incident with the rabbit, she winced.

"I didn't see him at first," she blurted, guilt pinching at the thought of what could have happened if she hadn't stopped in time. "Thank goodness he was so quick to get out of the way or—"

She couldn't finish the thought. Maybe Brad had a point about her not belonging on the heavy equipment.

"I hope the tractor isn't to blame for the rest of the wounded." He pointed toward the two cages on the back patio currently inhabited by a chipmunk and a blue jay.

"Of course not. I pulled the bird from the jaws of a tomcat on the front law and the vet says he needs a few days for his wing to heal before I set him free. And the chipmunk—" But did he really need to know all about the strays she took in, just the way Chloe always had? They had been one great big family of strays. A tradition she enjoyed carrying on in Chloe's absence. "Well, suffice it to say he was injured through no fault of my own."

"I'm on leave from my job with the navy for a couple of weeks. I work in demolitions—explosive ordnance disposal, officially." A shadow crossed his expression before he shrugged and she wondered if his leave had anything to do with the mass of bandages on his left leg. There were less than the first time she'd seen him, but they still covered plenty of his lower limb. "I've been climbing the walls between gigs anyhow. This way I can ensure that my house remains standing through the process and the local rabbits live to tell the tale."

Frowning, she peered into the woods, certain that brown bunny had numerous friends and family. She refused to injure any wildlife in the process of renovating the house.

And she needed to make some progress. If she didn't get the historical society's okay, it left the home all the more vulnerable to Chloe's slew of relatives who didn't care about honoring their famous kin's memory. Once she had that protection of the historical designation, she'd have enough security to turn her attention to Chloe's other request...

"You must ensure the diaries are published in their original form, Nicole." Chloe squeezed her hand from where she lay in a hospital bed, her grip surprisingly vital for a woman that doctors had warned repeatedly would not make it through another night. Seven days after entering the hospital, Chloe seemed to be holding her own, her short nails still painted her favorite shade of fire-engine red.

Nikki admired her so much. It had been a dream come true to meet a literary legend—one who had inspired Nikki on a personal level from the first time she'd read about Chloe's life as a young girl, getting shuffled from house to house the same way Nikki had. They'd both grown up among strangers. Never knowing a real home.

Chloe had gone on to create a sense of home no matter where she lived, circling the globe in search of adventure and taking in strays and strangers wherever she went. Nikki had been pulled into the creative whirlwind of the older woman's world, but she'd never managed to find the source of Chloe's strength. Her belief in herself. Even now, battling kidney failure and the symptoms of early dementia in a sterile white room, Chloe remained a fierce, bright light.

"If they are in the house, Chloe, I promise I will find them." Deep breaths, she reminded herself. She refused to cry in front of someone so strong. "I will make sure the originals are published."

"I hid two of them long ago but I never told anyone where and these days I have such a hard time remembering anything. The vultures don't want those diaries to see the light of day." She frowned, her gray hair sticking up in tufts like a newborn bird's fluffy feathers. A strand of red prayer beads from a Tibetan monk hung from one hand off the side of the bed. The vultures she referred to were family members who visited her twice a day in attempts to coerce her into changing her will or signing over her power of attorney. "They don't even know what I wrote in them to begin with, so don't let their protests stop you. My life is my own to share."

"Of course." Nikki had poured her a glass of water from the plastic pitcher beside the bed, unwilling to think about her life after Chloe's death. She had no idea where to begin looking for diaries that Chloe had forgotten where she'd hidden. "Have a drink and I'll take you for a spin in the corridor. We'll see if the guy in Room 142 is still trying to flash the nurses every chance he gets."

"In a minute." Chloe set the water cup down along with the prayer beads. "I have so much I wanted to share with you, Nicole. You're the daughter I never had, and it has meant a great deal to me that you've been here with me while I prepare for my next big adventure."

She winked a wrinkled eyelid, smiling as if death was a worthy opponent she looked forward to battling. Nikki's breath caught, her chest constricted tight.

"Where else would I be?" she finally managed, thinking Chloe was more pale today than yesterday.

"You should be out in the world, falling in love. Having wild, out of control sex." Edging higher up on the pillow, Chloe nodded toward the wheelchair in the corner. "But since it's too late in the game for me to tell you everything you need to know about that, I'll settle for a ride to Room 142 so we can heckle the old flasher and give the nurses a break."

Nikki shook off the memory that still left her heart in her throat. Maybe she'd get lucky and find those two missing volumes while she worked to methodically clean and organize the property this week.

"I have to warn you, I'm operating on a real budget here," she told Brad finally. She would have hired help in the first place if she could have afforded it. "The inheritance tax cost me my savings, so I really can't pay—"

"All the more reason not to keep a rented tractor sitting idle." He pointed to the equipment parked in the middle of the rolling lawn dotted by overgrown flowerbeds full of heirloom flowers. "You can tell me what's next or if you have plans drawn up for the project, I can look those over instead."

His eyes already roamed the landscape as if assessing the flaws for himself. Any hint of flirtation was gone—although maybe wishful thinking had imagined those hot looks earlier. Right now, he was all business and, amazingly, prepared to offer his services…for what kind of reimbursement?

The thought of being in his debt worried her, but she wasn't in any position to refuse. The property was a gem in the rough, but Chloe's relatives had rented it out for many years while she traveled the globe, and various renters had let it go to seed. Later in life, Chloe had used it as a home base for her work. She'd always had grand plans for it, though, insisting it held special memories of her first real romance. Sadly, the diary that would have chronicled that time period was one of the volumes that remained missing.

"I've got some lists and sketches inside the house if you want to take a look." Pointing the way, she started off in that direction, trying not to dwell on those sexy ultramarine eyes of his. "I really appreciate the help. Chloe's family has been so angry with me that it's nice to find someone who doesn't think this renovation is a terrible idea."

He was quiet for a moment, and she could still feel the hum of awareness from their handshake earlier. She wondered if his eyes were on her now, and peered over her shoulder to check.

But his easy grin didn't betray anything.

"If your property value goes up, mine does too, right?" His gaze went to the roofline of the house where several add-ons through the years had marred the classic lines of the place. And, wow, all those gables and dormers reminded her she sure had a lot of territory to scour for those two missing diaries.

Fine. She hadn't wanted the distraction of an attraction anyhow. Just as well that he didn't seem to have an ulterior agenda by offering her a hand. Or so she told herself. Some perverse part of her mourned the fact that his potent stare wasn't fixed on her anymore.

"I guess you're right."

Now if only she could scrub the memory of what he looked like while stalking around his living room half-naked from her brain.

2

NINE HOURS LATER, BRAD had run out of daylight as he shut off the tractor.

He'd uprooted tree stumps, dug out a couple of old foundations to outbuildings that no longer existed and hacked through an overgrown section of the lawn where a garden would eventually grow. He'd used a jackhammer, an insufficiently powered backhoe and the tractor with a couple of different attachments, all of which could go back to the rental company tomorrow since he'd gone medieval on the workload to make a major dent.

It felt good to work after being idle. It felt even better to impress a woman who'd nabbed a Ph.D. by studying sexy literature. The contrast fascinated him, making him all the more determined to find that sensual side beneath the hardworking professor.

Now the scent of barbecue hung in the air as Nikki lit a few torches around the backyard. She'd been on trash patrol most of the day, arranging for a scrap-metal company to pick up the remains of the shed, some old ladders and the contents of the basement she'd been cleaning. They'd been so busy they'd barely seen each other beyond a few utilitarian conversations to facilitate one another's projects, which was just as well since he'd gotten the distinct impression she would have refused his help if she thought he planned to hit on her.

He knew he hadn't dreamed the leap of attraction between them when they'd shaken hands, but she'd looked about as pleased to realize it as she'd been to find a garter snake hiding in the basement earlier.

He didn't know what that was all about, but he had two weeks left on his "vacation" to figure out a way to bypass it. Nikki was the key to replacing his apocalyptic dreams with something a whole lot more entertaining.

Approaching the old flagstone patio outside her back door, Brad set the tractor keys on a weathered wrought-iron table. At the sound of the metal clinking against the iron, Nikki turned away from the grill, a basting brush in hand.

"I hope you'll stay for dinner." She gestured to the table where he noticed two paper plates and a jug of iced tea. "You worked so hard today, the least I can do is feed you."

She'd changed since he'd chased the snake from the basement. A clean white tank top and khaki cargo shorts hugged her curves. Her damp hair was starting to dry around her face, the glossy brown turning chestnut in the glow from the torchlight.

"I'd accept, but you might faint from the smell." He sniffed the shoulder of his sweat-soaked shirt for confirmation and knew he couldn't share a table with her like this. "Do I have time to shower?"

Her eyes wandered over his chest before she turned back to the grill.

"Sure." She gave a jerky nod that made him wonder what she'd been envisioning. "The chicken will be ready in about ten minutes, but I can turn off the heat and keep it warm for…" she cleared her throat "…whenever you're ready."

Her last words came out a bit garbled, and he noticed she picked up the cup of iced tea she'd poured for herself. She took a long swig and kept her back to him.

Interesting.

"It'll take me ten minutes, tops."

The night air felt cool as he jogged into the darkness, away from the heat of the torches and grill and an even hotter woman. The furry brown mutt he'd been feeding was there at the hedge line, wagging its tail so hard its whole butt shook.

"Hey, Killer." He scratched the dog's head, thinking that taking in strays seemed to be as much a hobby for Nikki as it had been for her predecessor. Chloe Lissander had packed her yard full of bird feeders and bat houses, willing to care for all comers. "I'll pour you some food, but my guess is the grub will be better next door if you want to try your luck."

Inside, he showered in a hurry, eager to take advantage of every minute Nikki was willing to spare for him tonight. She was seriously hot and thinking about her penning lofty critical theories about erotica had kept his imagination steaming along all day.

Ignoring the blinking light on his answering machine, he grabbed some laundry from the dryer, knowing his buddies were calling to check up on him. They'd made noises about having a shindig tomorrow night—a party he should probably attend even though he wasn't much

in the partying mood these days. Making quick work
of feeding the stray, Brad wondered if he could talk his
neighbor into taking in the dog. Hell, if he could talk
her into a kiss he'd be happy. One kiss from her would
be enough to keep his crappy dreams at bay. At least for
one night.

Judging from the resistance he'd sensed in her
initially—because she clearly wouldn't have accepted
help from him if she hadn't been hard-up—she'd only
offered dinner tonight out of gratitude. Somehow, the
sparks that had flown between them when they'd first
touched had put her on guard. She had seemed to shove
aside the obvious attraction and he wasn't sure why. But
he had no intention of letting her ignore the heat simmering whenever they got near each other.

She had no idea how much he needed that kind of
distraction.

As he ducked through the hedgerow he heard an engine rev. The rumble of an old V-8 motor and a vibration
beneath his feet emanated from somewhere near Nikki's
place.

What the hell?

Shoving through the branches, he was just in time to
see the shadowed outline of an old pickup truck spin a
doughnut and burn rubber on the middle of her lawn.

"Hey!" he shouted and took off toward the vehicle,
pain slicing up his injured leg as he ran. He ignored it.

With no headlights on, the truck careened danger-
ously close to the house as it sped toward the road,
spitting chunks of sod. He heard the crash of broken
glass.

Growling, the stray mutt passed Brad, picking up on

his pissed-off vibe at the intruder. Brad was still a good fifteen yards away when the truck hit the main road and gathered speed.

Nikki.

Giving up the chase, he ran toward the front door instead, the burn on his leg still stinging like hell. The dog kept after the truck, barking like a junkyard hound all the way up the deserted county road.

"Nicole!" Brad called, pausing long enough on the porch to assess the damage.

A window was broken on the far right corner. The bastard in the truck must have hurled a brick or a rock before he took off.

"I'm okay." Nikki's voice was surprisingly close. A moment later, her pale face appeared at the broken window pane. "There's a rock on the living room floor."

"Don't touch it." He shoved through the front door; it was swollen in the frame, the wood sticking on all sides. Inside, a glow came from the back of the house, but the front remained dark. "Are there any lights in here?"

He had his phone out to call the cops, still listening for the truck in case it returned.

"Here." She sounded shaken in the second before she clicked on a lamp in the hall.

They were half a step apart and he was in midjog. Her arms went out as a buffer before he collided with her, but all that accomplished was to seal her forearms between their bodies as he pinned her against a wall. The feel of her curves imprinted itself on his body. The scent of earthy, sweaty flesh...

A damn fine opportunity wasted since he needed to find out who was harassing her.

"Sorry." Straightening, he blinked past the retina-blinding lamp as his eyes adjusted.

She still clutched a pair of tongs in one hand from her efforts at the grill. But no matter the circumstances, he was left with an impression of her long, lithe body against his. The memory of silken hair and soft breasts teased the edges of his consciousness as he assessed the damage in the living room.

Shards of glass glittered everywhere on the dusty hardwood floor. Moonlight spilled in the jagged hole, highlighting spiderweb cracks radiating out in every direction on the old-fashioned single pane. While he examined the mess, Nikki phoned the police. She disappeared for a few minutes, her voice growing softer as she gave them the details of the incident. Brad guessed she was storing their dinner in the fridge as she moved around the kitchen, banging doors and cabinets before returning to the living room.

She took a seat on an abandoned piano bench in one corner, the stray dog at her feet, carrying a hunk of boneless chicken with his head held high as if he'd won first prize. The mutt settled close to her, squaring the meat between its front paws before digging in. He wasn't one bit surprised that Nikki had fed the stray without a second thought, never blinking at another animal around the house, although she was careful to keep the dog from the broken glass.

"You don't seem all that surprised about the rock through the window." Brad leaned on the doorframe with one shoulder, studying Nikki's face as she clutched her cell phone in one hand. She was pale and obviously shaken, but there was also a sort of resigned determination. "Is this the first time anything like this has happened here?"

"Actually, it is. But I'd been warned that Chloe's family was not happy to see me inherit the house." She relinquished the phone, setting it on the bench alongside one long, lean thigh.

"I remember Chloe referring to her relatives as a bunch of 'greedy grabbers,' to use her term. Do you think they're the kind of people who would go to criminal lengths to scare you off?"

In the distance, he could hear a police siren and knew she'd only have to re-tell the story when they showed up. But it pissed him off that someone would harass her and he wanted to personally ensure it wouldn't happen again.

"I don't know. There was a lot of grumbling at the reading of the will. The family was mad when her stepfather left it to her in the first place, rather than his biological kids, but the house had been purchased by Chloe's real mother before she abandoned Chloe as a girl." She wrapped her arms around herself as she stared at the broken glass, looking too damn vulnerable in spite of the fact he knew she could operate heavy machinery and bulldoze unsuspecting garden sheds. "The general consensus is that I'm a usurper in the same way Chloe was. They think I don't deserve the house or control of Chloe's literary legacy."

"Did any of these relatives threaten you personally?"

Her dark gaze swung back around to him as the sirens grew louder and a flash of lights circled the room from the cop car pulling in the driveway. The exposed-wood ceiling beams were bathed in the red-and-blue glow.

"No. In fact, several of them helped me move in a couple of weeks ago. But Chloe's oldest stepbrother, Harold, is a local town councilman and he encouraged me to change the locks as soon as possible, implying he couldn't vouch for everyone in the Ralston clan."

Their conversation was cut short by a knock at the door. Nikki rose to admit two uniformed officers while Brad waited on the periphery to give his statement.

He'd started work here today to distract him from his enforced downtime and to take his mind off disturbing dreams. The enticement of a sexy next-door neighbor had been more than enough temptation. But a threat to Nikki's safety?

Today's prankster didn't know who he was dealing with. Because when Brad turned the full focus of his training and determination on the person responsible, the guy would be sorry he ever messed with a woman for whom Brad felt oddly protective. He had two weeks' worth of resentment about an op gone wrong just looking for an outlet.

A little retribution seemed right up his alley.

BY THE TIME THE POLICE had finished, Nikki could smell the scent of barbecue chicken back on the grill.

The thoughtfulness of that simple act speared past the defenses she liked to erect around men who were too handsome for their own good. How could she stay strong against someone who wanted to feed her after a long, tiring day capped off by vandalism?

That would be a feat she couldn't tackle tonight.

Nikki wound her way through the house sorely lacking in furniture but crammed full of clutter, toward the back door. She really needed to start culling Chloe's possessions to make room for her own, but it wouldn't be easy to part with anything. As a kid, Nikki had compensated for her lack of a real home by collecting artifacts from every place she ever visited, in an attempt to surround herself with happy memories if not security. Chloe had been the same way, and their combined hoarding legacy created a staggering amount of material goods. Nikki squeezed past a box of Mexican corn husk dolls she'd made while attending a summer camp as a teen and stepped out onto the back patio.

Brad manned the grill in the moonlight with that cute dog of his at his feet. The torches she'd lit earlier still burned in a ring around the flagstones, illuminating the wrought-iron table and a couple of place settings he'd resurrected from the kitchen counter. A bowl of grapes from the fridge served as a centerpiece next to a half-melted candle he'd stuffed in an empty wine bottle.

His efforts touched her.

"Thank you." She slid into a seat at the table to thwart her sudden urge to fling her arms around him. In one day, this man had accomplished more on Chloe Lissander's neglected property than she'd managed in the last week. He'd relocated the most menacing reptile she'd ever seen, chased off a trespasser and waited with her until the police arrived. Now, he had dinner ready when she was starving and exhausted. No matter that she'd cooked it originally. She could think of boyfriends in her past who wouldn't have bothered to reheat a leftover for her sake.

The buggers.

"Thank *you*. The hard part was already done." He took the chicken off the grill and served it straight to their plates, next to foil packets of veggies and cobs of corn speared with oddball little corn holders shaped like smiling lobsters that had belonged to Chloe. "Plus, I figured the scent of our dinner might chase off the cops once the visit devolved from investigating to blatant flirting."

She was so entranced by the taste of barbecue sauce that it took her a minute to catch his surly tone.

"Flirting? Those two?" She tried to recall one comment that could have been considered remotely personal and failed. "They didn't use my first name once in the entire conversation."

Brad poured tall glasses of tea for both of them while the night music of crickets and whip-poor-wills picked up volume. The scent of his soap mingled with the smell of dinner as he leaned closer.

Memories of the other time she'd seen him after a shower—her semi-accidental voyeurism—shot a flood of heat through her veins. She should have known she'd meet her neighbor face-to-face one day. Should have anticipated this overheated situation. But since he was around the house so rarely, Nikki had just assumed he would ship out before they ever got around to an introduction.

She licked her lips and hoped her heart would quit lapsing into hyperactive mode.

"Are you kidding? All those questions about where you lived before and what you teach at the university were total curiosity on the younger guy's part." He used his fork to tear open the foil veggie packet, releasing a puff of steam into the night. "How much you want to bet he emails you next week and asks to take one of your classes?"

Nikki realized she couldn't recall what either of the officers looked like. How had Brad taken such careful note of what went on, especially since he'd stepped away long before they were finished?

"Too bad I'm not in the market for a man." Better to make that clear straight from the gate—to herself as much as Brad. No matter how much she might find a certain male appealing, she wasn't planning on acting on it.

Brad Riddock would be out of her life faster than a blink, a fact which she couldn't ignore. How many times had she been dumped off on relatives as a kid, only to have her parents promise they'd return by Christmas and then New Year's and then maybe for her birthday in February? She'd fallen for those promises too many times, wanting to believe they'd missed her as much as she'd missed them when they'd left on one exotic adventure after another. But the truth was, they hadn't.

And while she'd sorted through a lot of that hurt during her adult years to become a stronger person, she knew better than to bring that sort of heartache back into her life. Especially when her plate was full with responsibilities to Chloe.

"Why? Is the cop your type?" Brad's blue eyes caught the moonlight, dangerous and alluring.

She swallowed hard at the sudden vision of what it would be like to kiss him. Touch him.

"Actually, no. But he *should* be my type. I'm trying to

stay away from the guys who need saving." She pointed toward the recovering blue jay and chipmunk in their cages on the patio. "I have a problem with trying to solve the world's problems, one broken wing at a time. But I think the police officers were only asking about my past to find out if the trespasser was someone local or if it could have been someone I knew before I moved here."

"It's someone who doesn't want you to stay in this house." His flat assessment sounded so certain.

"Why do you say that?" She agreed one hundred percent, but she had her own reasons.

"The damage done was meant to discourage you from working on the house. The torn-up patch in the yard will cost time and money to fix. The broken window ensures you don't feel safe in addition to the expense to replace it. I'd say it's an attack on the property as much as you."

Her last bite of chicken leg turned dry in her throat at the thought of someone escalating a campaign to chase her out. Damn it, she'd never had a real home before. She wouldn't let anyone scare her away from this one. She'd stayed up late on this very patio with Chloe on summer nights, sharing stories from their past and dreams for the future. That time had been magical for her and no amount of vandalism could steal that warmth in her heart when she walked through this place.

"Chloe hinted there were people in her life who wouldn't want her missing diaries to be published."

"Why?" Brad shook his head. "Do you know what's in them?"

"Chloe said those years had been too special for her

to share with the world yet, but that one day her story would finally be revealed." Nikki had been over and over her final conversations with the older woman before her death, never making full sense of the bits and pieces she'd heard since the hints at a young romance had been at odds with the later diaries' depiction of a wild and sexually adventurous decade from her mid-twenties to late thirties. "She was in and out of consciousness the last few days of her life. I sat with her whenever I wasn't on campus because she did so much for me through the years—cheered on my writing, gave me exclusive interviews to nail down a doctorate that was a shoo-in for publication. So I wanted to do whatever I could for her at the end since her family was less than supportive."

Nikki liked to think she and Chloe had been family to each other. Her chest tightened to think about how fortunate she was to have had Chloe in her life—someone who cared when her dissertation committee gave her a hard time or her short-lived relationship with a history professor burned out. Nikki's own parents were in the mountains of Peru the last time they'd contacted her—four months ago to email condolences on Chloe's death.

"She didn't have any kids, did she?" Brad glanced toward the bushes at the edge of the property where lightning bugs blinked on and off.

Clearing her throat, she dragged her eyes away from him and focused on the lightning bugs.

"No kids. At least, she doesn't acknowledge any. A rumor persists that she had children living overseas since she spent many years in Europe after World War II. But I don't believe it for a second. She was far too loving a person to distance herself from any blood relative. The gossip is just another bit of the drama from a life lived unconventionally. Her books were part of the fuel for the women's movement with the way they embraced a more sexually free lifestyle."

She couldn't begin to explain all the convoluted drama of Chloe's life. Chloe's sensual memoirs accounted for her popularity as much as her novels. She'd chronicled many passionate encounters using carefully hidden identities to protect the people those relationships were based on. The edited diaries—at least five of the seven—had already been published with names changed to protect the innocent. But Chloe had promised her fans that after her death, all seven of the diaries—in their original forms—would be available to her readers.

"So when you say her family wasn't supportive, who are we talking about? Siblings?"

She sensed a methodical mind at work as Brad formulated a picture of Chloe's family. Better to focus on his brain than the appealing lure of his physique. Beneath the table, their feet vied for rights to the same real estate, occasionally bumping or brushing against each other. She felt edgy from those small touches, twitchy from the desire to lay her hand in the center of that broad, hard chest. With an effort, she recalled his question.

"Two stepbrothers—Harold and Norman Ralston. She didn't know her real father, and her mother married her stepfather when Chloe was three years old." Nikki had cringed at the stories Chloe had told about her early life—stories that would have landed her in child protective services today. "Then the mother abandoned the family when Chloe was eight, leaving her to be raised by the stepfather's revolving girlfriends in a household with no blood relatives."

In addition to all the material help Chloe Lissander had given Nikki, her life had been an inspiration to help Nikki forgive her parents for emotional scars that couldn't compare to what her mentor had endured.

"Yet she inherited the house over her step-brothers?"

"Apparently Chloe's mother paid for the house. Giving it to her daughter after the stepfather's death was his way to make amends, perhaps." Nikki shrugged, never having been able to wade through the family politics effectively. The Ralston family was well known in this part of Virginia, with Harold the patriarch a longtime councilman and active member of every local club and volunteer organization. He was staid and somber to Chloe's wild and unconventional. The two had never seen eye to eye.

"And you think these stepbrothers could have reasons for not wanting you here beyond the obvious land grab?" He cleaned his plate and shoved it aside, giving her his undivided attention.

The effect of those eyes probing hers was unnerving. Or, if she was honest with herself, exciting. Swallowing hard, she reached for her iced tea before she answered.

"I think they fear the unexpurgated version of her diaries for some reason." Them and half the county. "I've been waiting to read them all as a set once I find the two that are missing. But supposition says they'll be as racy as the fictional erotica."

His eyes glowed a warmer shade of blue at the mention of the sexual content.

"Unexpurgated?"

"Unabridged. You know, the original version before the author and the publisher scrub out parts that could be libelous. It's common knowledge that Chloe gave her permission for all the original, unedited diaries to be published after her death."

"And how would vandalizing the house prevent that? Are you in charge of those diaries?" The methodical mind was at work again, she could hear it in his tone.

She should be relieved he wasn't thinking about the heat that lurked between them, but she missed the warmth of that knowing gaze of his. She was playing with fire to have him here, close enough to touch, all the while knowing she shouldn't get involved.

"Some of them. But even I don't know the location of the two that went missing long ago. Chloe hid them at some point, then apparently forgot their location as dementia set in." She gestured toward the dilapidated house with a sweeping arm. "She asked me to do everything possible to be sure all the diaries are found and released as she promised her fans. I mean to do everything in my power to make sure that happens."

A cool breeze chilled her skin as the torches died down.

"So maybe your vandal doesn't want you to find those diaries." He reached across the table and laid a warm hand on her arm. "Are you cold?"

From anyone else, the gesture would have been harmless enough. But she'd been attracted from the first moment she'd seen him half-naked. The tug of sensual interest had been confirmed in no uncertain terms this morning when he'd introduced himself. And any defense against the attraction had been sandblasted away by his help and thoughtfulness throughout this draining day.

She wanted Lieutenant Brad Riddock. Badly.

"I'm okay," she managed, her voice cracking on a dry note while his palm made her heartbeat flutter like a sixteen-year-old girl's.

She would have eased out from under that touch if she could have, but her body scoffed at the very idea. Besides, he would move his hand of his own accord any second now. Right?

But the moment drew out. They sat motionless, touching without speaking, until it became a grown-up game of chicken. Who would draw away first?

"I want you to feel safe here," he said finally, sliding his palm down her forearm toward her hand.

Stroking her? Or taking the scenic route away from her body?

She tracked his progress with hyperawareness, unsure how to draw a boundary and not quite recalling why she should.

"I'll be fine," she assured him, though it was probably easier to feel invincible with those strong fingers resting on her skin.

"I'd like to make sure of that." Beneath the table, his knee brushed hers briefly, distracting her. "How about I sleep downstairs tonight to keep an eye on things?"

Everything inside her stilled.

"You want to stay *here?*" In the same house as her?

Her pulse raced even though she knew that was a bad, bad idea. And—curse him—his thumb rested on a place

along her wrist where he'd probably feel the manic rush
of blood through her veins.

"I could pitch a tent out front if you'd rather." Relin-
quishing her arm, his easy reform of the original suggestion made her feel like a heel for not agreeing in the
first place. "That would send a message that someone's
looking out for you if anyone decides to come back
tonight."

The warmth inside her chilled at the thought. Did she
really want to be here alone while someone bold enough
to tear up the lawn and break her windows still lurked
free?

"I hadn't thought about that," she admitted, looking at Brad's prominent muscles with new eyes. They
weren't just for show. Who would dare to mess with him?
Besides, she had the animals to think about. She'd feel
better with help to watch over the place. "Actually, the
house has plenty of rooms to spare if you really don't
mind—"

"Honestly, I'll sleep better knowing I'm already on
site if anything happens." Standing, he blocked one of
the torches from view, his big, imposing body backlit
like an action-movie poster. "If I go home tonight, I'd
only be lying there with one eye open anyhow."

"That's really kind of you." She couldn't imagine
why he'd gone to so much trouble on her account today.
"Thank you."

"Not a problem." With a nod, he turned on his heel.
"I'll just go grab a few things."

In no time, he was jogging across the lawn toward his
house, his little brown dog wagging its tail but not fol-

lowing, almost as if the scruffy furball knew his owner would be right back.

Nikki forced herself to pick up the plates instead of staring after him like his adoring mutt. What was she thinking to have a man she hardly knew stay in the house with her tonight?

A man she'd drooled over when he'd thought no one was looking.

If he'd flirted with her more, she might have been more guarded about letting him stay. But how could she argue with a man who'd done nothing but help her out today? Besides, she was genuinely worried about the troublemakers returning.

While Nikki would make sure Chloe's wishes were honored, Chloe wouldn't want her to sacrifice her personal safety to fulfill that promise.

Brad Riddock would keep her safe. He was a one-man protective detail.

She trusted *that* completely. She just hoped she could trust herself around those sexy stares of his that came out of nowhere and lit up her insides like a Christmas tree. Between the postvandalism adrenaline, the physical exhaustion from all the work of the last week and the memories of what she'd seen of Brad through the branches of her locust tree five nights ago, Nikki didn't know how she'd begin to scavenge any distance from a man who'd slid past her barriers faster than anyone she'd ever known.

3

AN HOUR LATER, FIST RAPPING on Nikki's back door, Brad reminded himself that his reasons for sleeping over had been semi-altruistic. He genuinely wanted to keep her safe because he hated the idea of some redneck yahoo four-wheeling through her yard and destroying the property she'd been working so hard to restore. Someone obviously hoped to scare her, and Brad had a real problem with intimidation tactics deployed on single women in old, secluded houses.

So, damn it, *that's* why he was here tonight and not because his mouth watered at the sound of her bare feet padding along the hardwood to answer the door. Not because being with her overloaded his senses so much he wouldn't have room to replay worn-out nightmares.

The bolt slid free on the other side of the door and she opened it wide to admit him.

"Come on in." She still wore the low-slung cotton shorts and white tank top she'd had on during dinner.

Of course. Duh. Could he help it if male fantasies had her answering the door in a lace negligee and high-heeled slippers? Or maybe dark stockings on her long legs and nothing else?

He really needed to get a grip.

"Thanks." He edged past her into the kitchen where the only illumination came from a glass-front china cabinet with a lamp inside. "I would have been over sooner, but I had a few calls to return. My buddies are trying to talk me into a big beach shindig tomorrow night."

But he'd already ear-marked that time for Nikki. He'd be here for as long—and as much—as she wanted him over the next two weeks.

Setting his bag on the floor near the cabinet, he noticed the books displayed inside. *Bedroom Lessons. Secret Games. Lies from the Backseat.* The covers were suggestive without being lewd. He'd read a couple of Chloe's novels shortly after he'd met his neighbor, just out of curiosity.

The rest of the house wasn't as well packaged as the books, though. The old farmhouse didn't have much furniture, and the pieces that were sitting in corners were covered with books and papers, boxes and piles of correspondence. But underneath the clutter, a fine structure lurked. The paneled wainscoting and polished, exposed ceiling beams were carefully crafted, still beautiful a hundred years after someone had taken the time to carve them.

"It's generous of you to do this in the first place. I'm sure you have other ways you'd rather be spending your downtime." Nikki closed the door behind him, sealing them in the dark house. From a few rooms away, he could hear soft music playing—something with a jazz blues vibe. A shelf full of Russian nesting dolls hovered precariously over old road signs proclaiming Farm Fresh Eggs and U-Pick. The sound of the dishwasher hummed nearby and Killer's nails clicked along the worn hardwood as the dog approached to greet him.

Had she even noticed she'd been dog-sitting all the time he'd been gone? The animal seemed right at home circling Nikki's feet and she'd already laid out bowls of food and water for him. She seemed to like taking care of people and creatures alike. Damn but he hoped she wasn't just being nice to him because he looked about as desperate as Killer had when the dog showed up on his doorstep last week.

"Not really. I'm supposed to be in physical therapy for my leg a few times a week, but mostly I'm just counting down the days until I can go back to work."

Days he'd rather fill getting to know the sexy professor...who wanted to keep her distance. He bent to scratch the dog's ears while she waved him forward into a dim hallway.

"I put some sheets on a futon in the den." She paused outside an archway across from the living room. Her eyes dipped south of the belt, and for a moment, he enjoyed a rush of pure male pride. Until her gaze kept going lower. Lower. "I noticed the bandages earlier. What exactly happened to your leg?"

So much for male pride.

The remembered sound of an explosion echoed between his ears. Light flashed behind his eyelids as he blinked away crap memories.

"Occupational hazard."

Eyes wide, she reached forward as if to touch him and then pulled back fast.

"Didn't you say you work with explosives?" She kept her hand—the one that had been bold enough to reach for him—in a tight grip.

Had there been a lockdown on touching that he didn't know about? And didn't it suck that the only time she'd been tempted to reach out was when she saw him as another wounded cause? Frustration gnawed the back of his neck until he had to roll his shoulders to shove it aside.

"Not a big deal." His injuries didn't compare to the rest of the damage done that day. Skin would grow back. "But I'm not at liberty to discuss the details."

That wasn't one hundred percent accurate, but it gave him the ability to opt out of the discussion. He strode past her toward the room she'd pointed out.

A sturdy armoire stood sentinel in one corner, surrounded by stacks of old travelogues and picture books of Italy. An antique roll-top desk was likewise hidden by paperwork piled on the floor. It was tough to weed through the belongings to tell what was Nikki's and what would have been Chloe's. He kept an eye out for clues to the lady professor's personality, curious about what made her tick.

"It sounds like a dangerous line of work." She remained in the archway, keeping her distance. "Is that why I haven't seen you around before now? Were you deployed?"

"I'm on the second leg of back-to-back tours in Iraq. I've got four months left once I return." He dropped into a chair near the armoire—a straight-back that looked as if it came from a dining room set. Two others that matched it were strewn around the room amid the books and a hodgepodge of furnishings. "A buddy of mine—Joe Staley—checks on my house every couple of weeks, but other than that, you wouldn't see anyone around. How long have you been here?"

"Back when Chloe was alive, I visited during the summers and at the holidays. Since her death, I received keys to the property from the probate court six weeks ago, but between selling my condo and moving in stages, I've only been here for the last two."

"That's how long I've been home." He stood up again to pull one of the other chairs closer. They were the only seating options in the room besides the futon that was made up like a bed. "Have a seat. You must be exhausted after everything you did today."

She looked from him to the chair. He'd seen people eyeball IEDs with less trepidation. How could a woman who dismantled buildings with such zest turn so damn cautious when it came to him?

"Maybe for a minute." She strode into the den, taking the route that would keep her farthest from the makeshift bed as she made her way toward the sturdy ladder-back with its blue velvet cushion. "I don't want to keep you from sleeping."

"I don't need much sack time." Strike that. He would gladly submit to an abundance of sack time if it involved sharing his bed. It was *sleep* he didn't need. But he felt pretty sure she would only get flustered by the distinction. "I'm a night owl by nature."

"Me, too. Even tonight when I'm tired, I'll stay up and think about all I have to do tomorrow." She settled into the chair across from him and he wished he'd placed it closer to his.

He had no idea when or how he'd make his first move with her, but now that he sat near her in this big, echoing house he realized more than ever that he wanted her. The scent of her shampoo teased his nose, clean and floral.

"The curse of ambition."

"More like obsession." She seemed to relax a little now that they were seated across from one another. Her shoulders sagged against the heavy ladder-back. "I'm determined to restore the house to honor Chloe's memory. She really helped inspire women, writing openly and honestly about her passions, not omitting any of the messy parts. It's difficult for writers to be so personally vulnerable. Her fans love her for the risks she took, both with the erotica and with her journals."

"So she inspired you, too. Are you writing a memoir?" He refrained from mentioning how amenable he'd be to helping her write erotica. He had at least twenty scene ideas in mind. Most involved rolling around with her on that futon so close he could practically touch it. But any scenario that put her naked and under him would be worth commemorating in print.

"No. At least, not yet. I just want to pay her back for the help she gave me as a struggling graduate student. I would have never published my dissertation or even finished the degree program if it wasn't for Chloe's help. I was really floundering when I found her. I owe her my whole teaching career."

He waited for a moment, in case she decided to add in a confidential whisper that she was working on an erotica project when she wasn't busy overhauling the old house.

No such admission seemed forthcoming.

"So you've spent the last couple of weeks making plans for renovating the house and turning it into something that her fans will enjoy," he said finally.

"Yes." She folded her arms, the action drawing his attention to high, round breasts that deserved a whole chapter, if and when they got around to penning a joint sexy memoir that chronicled their soon-to-be affair. "I've been working on the house plans and starting on the grounds—"

Her mouth snapped shut suddenly. Strangely. As if she'd said too much and wanted to stop herself. Of course, that was ridiculous since they'd been in the middle of an innocuous conversation about how she'd spent the last couple of weeks working around the property.

"So what else have you been doing in the yard?" It wasn't just small talk. He wanted to know. Big changes were in order here, and he was curious about the end results.

More than that, he was curious about her. He'd never talk her into that affair if he didn't get to know her better.

"Um." She straightened, the veneer of relaxation gone. "Just pulling up some weeds and mowing down the brush." She jumped up out of her chair. "Can I get you a drink?"

"No, thank you." He rose as well, wondering why she'd turned edgy all of the sudden. Had he allowed his explicit thoughts about her to show in his expression? "Is everything okay?"

"Sure—yes," she blurted awkwardly. "Fine. Perhaps I'll get a drink for me."

He steadied her shoulders, just to keep her in place a moment longer.

"Does it make you nervous, having me here?" he asked. His heart thudded low and hard at the feel of her against his fingertips.

He meant to release her—and he would in a moment—but he had the distinct impression she'd bolt the second he let go.

It seemed an odd reaction when they'd already been together most of the day. She hadn't been this jumpy when they'd sat across the dinner table from each other.

"Not at all." She seemed to realize how ridiculous that sounded when she was poised for flight, because she took a deep breath and quit edging toward the kitchen. "Okay, maybe a little nervous."

His hands fell away. Maybe it would be tougher than he'd bargained to work his way into her favor anytime soon.

"I must have really read this wrong." He took a step back, not wanting to intimidate her. "Because even though I only offered to come here tonight to keep you safe, I have to admit I thought there was a connection between us earlier today."

Speechless, she shook her head, dark hair dusting her shoulders. Was she mute with horror at the prospect? Or simply denying she'd felt any such thing? This was going downhill in a hurry.

"When we shook hands this morning," he continued, hating that he had to explain it to her when it had been plain as day to him, "I could have sworn there was a moment—"

"I know." She backed up a step, as well, and he felt like crap for making her feel that was necessary. "I felt it, too."

Her words eased some of the sting, at least.

"So you know what I'm talking about?"

"Yes. But that's what makes me nervous. I'm not in a position to indulge those feelings right now. And if anything, I felt it all the more this morning because—technically—it wasn't the first time I'd seen you."

She held herself very still, yet Brad could have sworn she shook. Rattled, really. Her whole body seemed to vibrate with a kind of nervous energy as she held herself rigidly away from him. He went from worried to angry. He hadn't done anything inappropriate. Had given her no reason to appear so damn anxious.

"What do you mean?"

"I have something to confess, and I'm not proud of it."

When he said nothing, she cleared her throat.

"I was clipping the hedges between our houses earlier this week and I saw you then."

"That's not much of a confession." He was missing something here.

Two bright spots of color burned on her cheeks.

"I saw you mostly naked."

MAYBE SHE SHOULDN'T HAVE admitted it.

The temperature in the room rose from chilly to tropical in about a second and a half. It was as if someone had suddenly cranked the thermostat. The atmosphere between them crackled with awareness.

It was lucky he was trained to deal with explosives

since she felt like the tension was going to detonate inside her any moment.

"Brad?" She sounded uncertain to her own ears.

"Where did you see me *mostly* naked?" His voice was throaty and low. Dangerous.

Sexual?

She wasn't sure. Her heart fluttered nervously in her chest. Being with him alone had been a bad idea. He was too much of a test of her restraint. And after a long, trying year of being at Chloe's side to the end, then fighting the relatives to ensure Chloe's wishes were honored, she just didn't have the emotional resources to hold strong in the face of such blatant temptation.

She'd always wanted to test out her wild and impulsive side—a side buried so damn deep she wouldn't think she even had one except that she'd been drawn to the beautiful erotica she'd written her dissertation on even before she'd met Chloe and formed a friendship with her. But once she and Chloe had grown close, Chloe liked to tease her that she just hadn't found the right guy to explore her erotic side with… And why did those conversations come roaring back to her right now when she needed to address Brad's question?

"I saw you in your house." An uncomfortable heat crawled up her back and lingered on her neck. "It was an accident. You didn't have the blinds closed and I happened to be trimming the honeysuckle vines under the locust tree when all of a sudden—there you were."

An ill-timed smile got away from her.

But damn it, that moment was a happy memory and it had been a total accident. Maybe now wasn't the time to admit she'd purposely left the locust untrimmed to space it out over the days that followed, quite possibly coinciding with his shower time.

He seemed to have enough to process right now. And she didn't have as much bad-girl chutzpah as Chloe Lissander had.

"You *spied* on me. That feels like an invasion of privacy." His face was inscrutable and she wondered if anger lurked beneath the surface. "An invasion of space."

She cringed. Guilt nipped.

"I hadn't really thought about it that way, but yes, I guess so."

"I think I'm going to return the favor."

Before she could reason out what *that* meant, he stepped forward, nudging one knee between her thighs.

With a yelp of surprise, she grabbed his upper arms, steadying herself while she reshuffled her feet.

"I don't know that—"

"I do."

They were the last words he spoke before he lowered his mouth to hers.

4

NIKKI HAD WRITTEN A DOCTORAL dissertation on Chloe Lissander's erotica. In seventy-five pages, she'd catalogued the emotional nuances underlying well-known pieces of explicit literature, highlighting sex as a multi-layered metaphor for different kinds of intimacies.

But a year's worth of research and twelve pages of footnotes hadn't prepared her for the blatant eroticism of Brad Riddock's kiss.

As they stood together in the darkened den, his body engulfed hers. The steel bands of his arms locked her against the heat of his chest. Their hips aligned. Legs interwove. Somehow, her arms had wrapped around his neck, utterly compliant before her brain even had time to process what was happening.

His body touched hers in so many places, she couldn't begin to absorb it all. The raw heat of him singed her senses. The clean scent of his skin ignited a rush of longing so strong she could scarcely stand, her knees as liquid and pliable as the rest of her.

But most of all, she noticed his kiss.

His tongue stroked a path along her lower lip as if he had all the time in the world. Slow. Seductive.

Nikki swayed on her feet, caught off guard. She had dreamed about this man before she knew him, pictured him doing sweetly wicked things to her body as a pleasurable diversion before she fell asleep at night. But no amount of imagination could have anticipated the way her blood simmered in her veins at his touch, every nerve ending jumping to life.

He smoothed his palms down her spine, pressing her closer one vertebra at a time until her stomach met the rigid length of his arousal. Her heart pounded so hard she could feel the pulse leap at the base of her throat. Her body molded to his as her desire increased, higher and higher still in a wave of heat that had her breasts swelling between them.

An appreciative growl rumbled in his chest, vibrating against her sensitive breasts then deeper, right through her. The sound revved her in all the right places, firing a sharp ache between her thighs…

"Wait." She pulled away. Breathless.

Brad loomed over her, all taut power and male strength. His eyes focused on her mouth, as if he was waiting for a signal to go in for the kill. To ravish her thoroughly and leave her begging for more.

Which was exactly what would happen if she didn't pull herself together.

"What are we doing?" she whispered to herself as much as him, untwining her arms from around his neck.

He blinked, as if he'd only just realized she'd pulled back. But then, leisurely, he released her.

He skimmed his hands slowly, slowly away, leaving a trail of tingling skin in his wake.

"I believe—" he lifted a finger to her lower lip and brushed one last touch along the soft fullness "—we were teaching you a lesson about invasion of privacy. Or invasion of space, maybe."

"*That* was my lesson?" Tough to sound indignant while panting with lust, but she made a credible effort. "What happened to 'two wrongs don't make a right'?"

She resisted the urge to take one more step back. Not because she was so anxious to escape his touch, but because she didn't trust herself around such tangible temptation.

He sank down to the futon mattress, lowering his muscular bulk so that he was eye level with her navel. And what vivid imaginings that position conjured for her. Now, she didn't just *step* back from him. This time, she all but scurried to return to the antique chair.

"Don't even try to tell me that was wrong." He leaned his elbows onto his knees.

While the posture was relaxed, the words were anything but.

She suspected he would kiss her all over again if she didn't agree the connection had been very, very right.

"Maybe not in a literal sense." She didn't think trotting out any of her dissertation theories on sexual chemistry as metaphor would be appreciated at this particular moment. Even though she could make a great case for his kiss as domination—the emotional equivalent of a demand for attention.

Affection?

No. She couldn't afford to apply literary thinking to

her personal life. That would only confuse a situation that should remain perfectly clear. Hands off the military man who was just passing through her life.

"Not in any sense." He rose to his feet and her heartbeat quickened automatically. But he didn't come closer. Instead, he disappeared into the darkened hall and returned holding one of Chloe's books.

Secret Games.

Before she could ask what he was up to, he cracked open the copy that must have come from the display cabinet in the kitchen. She realized she was rubbing a finger over her just-kissed lips and quickly knotted her hands in her lap.

"You said you were a student of Chloe's work, right?" He kept flipping through pages as he spoke, sauntering closer until he stood a few feet from her chair.

Good thing she'd threaded her fingers together so she couldn't reach out and touch at will.

"Yes. I didn't realize you were, too." She couldn't imagine what he searched for in the book that some critics had panned as "pornography for the high-brow," and others lauded as "Kama Sutra for a new era."

"Here." He pointed at the text, as if to mark his place. "'Why should we plead propriety like a defense when we both want to tear off our clothes? Is it not enough proof of compatibility that just one stroke of the tongue—a thoroughly French kiss—has the power to—'"

"Point made." She leapt from her seat to cut him off, recalling exactly where the passage went from there.

"There are just a few more lines." He studied her from over the top of the book, clearly amused.

"I'm quite familiar with them." While she was no

prude by any stretch, she wasn't sure her overheated libido could handle hearing Brad read about a tongue stroke inspiring imagined, phantom licks along a throbbing sex. Just the thought of it made her feel light-headed. "And any discussion of phantom licks is more than I can handle on a first date. Er—not that this is a date."

Flustered, she clamped her mouth shut.

Brad closed the book. If he was tempted to grin at her discomfort, he did a good job of hiding it.

"I would like to have a date with you." He stared at her with serious eyes, his expression thoughtful.

The hot rush of hormones made it difficult for her to process his words.

"I—" As a woman who made her living teaching the written word, she found it surprising to feel speechless. Taking a deep breath, she tried again. "We shouldn't date based on physical attraction. No matter what the book says."

Down that path lay heartache, especially with a man dedicated to a job on the other side of the world.

"So you wrote a dissertation on Ms. Lissander's work and you don't buy in to it?" He laid the book on the mantelpiece beside her collection of commemorative shot glasses from each state in the U.S. She'd been shuffled through all fifty before her sixteenth birthday. Sometimes her parents had driven her great distances to find the next friend or relative willing to take her in for a month or two.

Brad's assertion hurt for reasons he couldn't possibly understand. Chloe Lissander had survived a childhood far darker than anything Nikki had endured. Yet she'd emerged from it a bold and full-blown character with a big heart to match. She'd lit up rooms when she entered. She'd sized up people quickly and shrewdly, recognizing their foibles but always seeing room for beauty.

And Chloe had loved so deeply and fully. Fearlessly. Nikki admired her so much.

"In theory, yes, I buy in to her ideas. In personal practice? Chloe's approach to life is a lot to live up to." She didn't know what else to say, feeling unaccountably prickly and possibly a little disappointed in herself. "I guess I'm just not there yet."

When he didn't respond right away, she forged back into the silence to smooth over the awkward moment.

"I'm surprised you're so familiar with her work."

He shrugged, straightening a glass in the elevated back row so the words *Rhode Island* could be seen more easily.

"She gave me one of her books one day after I helped her trim some branches on that hickory tree in back." He gestured, but she knew the one he meant. "She told me to 'read and learn' so I could improve my love life."

Nikki smiled, picturing Chloe's audacious claim. "She wanted to be sure everyone experienced the world as vividly—as passionately—as she did."

"I was too busy to pick it up for a few months, but when I did—holy cow." He rubbed his chest as if the message of the book had just socked him there. "I was floored at the story and damn intrigued to think an elderly woman could write about anonymous sex as a life-changing experience. It was just so damn unexpected from the sweet little old lady next door, even if she did flirt with me all the time."

Nikki watched as Brad reordered the glasses on

the mantelpiece in east-to-west order. So methodical. No wonder the Navy liked his skills in explosive situations.

"Her diaries are just as sexy as the fiction." Although maybe once she recovered all of the original diaries, they would have a different tone than the edited material. Nikki knew names had been changed and some events downplayed or omitted in the diaries that had been published in Chloe's lifetime. She'd been very protective of her family and friends. Was that why her family resented their lack of control over the eccentric author's estate? Maybe they didn't want to be eviscerated in print for all eternity.

"But you'd rather not discuss them in a personal sense." He repeated her protest from earlier, as if seeking clarification on the topic now that she wasn't as hot and bothered.

Which made her review her thoughts on their kiss and his request for a date. She still felt like getting involved would be hazardous to her heart. But now guilt tweaked her conscience since she knew Chloe would have called her a coward for not embracing life.

Passion.

"Maybe, for tonight at least, it would be safer to get some rest instead." The room seemed cooler now that the heat of their kiss had died down, the mild spring breeze drifting gently through from an open window. Or maybe she just felt a chill because she'd been reminded what a muddle her life was in on a personal level. She'd achieved so much professionally, but hadn't bothered to figure out who she was in her private life. She had problems with commitment thanks to her family situation, but she'd always assumed she would explore that secret sensual side one day. Her interest in erotica had clued her in to that sexy streak, but her personal fears had kept her from exploring it in real life.

On paper, of course, had been another matter. Her dissertation had raised more than a few eyebrows around campus.

"It was a damn long day," he agreed, putting one hand on his hip and twisting his shoulder backward as if to work out a kink.

The move put a vast array of muscles on display, rippling under the fabric of his T-shirt. Reminding her she'd stifled her sensual side for far too long.

"Thank you for staying here tonight." She would sleep better knowing a trained military man was looking out for her.

As long as she didn't let erotic dreams of Brad keep her awake.

"No problem. But I've got to be honest. My ulterior motive is that date. And definitely another kiss."

He edged past her toward the futon before stripping off his T-shirt and tossing it on the mattress.

Her eyes widened at the sight of so much bronzed bare skin. The V of the muscles in his back tapering down to narrow hips. Time to leave before she weakened.

Her mouth was too dry to say goodnight as she slipped from the room to find her own bed. Alone. One thing was certain though. Her hope of a good night's sleep was busted.

BRAD LISTENED TO NIKKI's speedy retreating footsteps, knowing he'd probably pushed too hard, too fast. But with only two weeks left before he went back overseas, he couldn't afford to let things take their natural course with her. If he didn't pursue her now, she could be dating some other guy by the time he returned four months later. Stripping down to his boxers, he thought about sliding between the sheets and taking a shot at sleep. His muscles were tight from hard work so different from what he'd been doing. And his head was full of Nikki instead of bombs and regrets. Both those things should help him get some real rest that wasn't interrupted by crap dreams.

But Nikki might be a little *too* much on his mind. He'd intended to make her admit an attraction when he pulled out that Chloe Lissander book. But there had been a noticeable effect on him, too. He couldn't just dole out comments about throbbing sex around her and expect to walk away relaxed.

Far from it.

He scanned the room for a distraction and his gaze landed on the collection of matching book spines with Chloe's name. Her diaries.

Not the erotica that had helped ramp up the night in the first place. But the published and edited tales of her real sex life that apparently only told half the story. Snagging one of them from the shelf, he figured he might as well learn more about the woman who'd inspired Nikki to tackle the project of renovating the aging house.

Besides, what if the writing contained a clue about who was harassing her? He should know the major players in Chloe's life. He felt protective of Nikki. Responsible for her. Maybe it was just an inflated reaction after what had happened in Iraq—the need to save somebody to ease memories of the ones he hadn't been able to protect.

Tension tightened his shoulders as he forced his eyes down the page in front of him—the date established the writing from the spring of 1943. Maybe this would help him take his mind off Nikki enough to rest. Retreating when he had had been wise, because the sooner Nikki felt safe, the sooner she'd be able to relax with him. Trust him.

He knew she must be interested if she'd spied on him. The thought of her watching him like that turned him inside out. Now he needed her to focus all that pent-up sexy professor energy his way so they could start turning fantasies into reality.

Los Angeles
1943

> *Dear Eduardo,*
> *You have been gone only four weeks and already I am beside myself. I know I should think of your sacrifice for your country and the honor in your service. And truly, I am so very proud of you. But I am weak and think more often about how much I miss you. Maybe if I was a wise and unselfish woman of the world, I would spend my days knitting you scarves and writing diverting letters that would cheer you. But I am still piqued at you for the way we parted. You left me in an unpardonable state of longing.*
> *Your forsaken love,*
> *Chloe*

U.S.S. Zeilin
1943

>*My Dearest Malcontent,*
>*Excuse my penmanship if it is a bit shaky. I have caught cold, you see, and all my comrades agree it is because I'm the only man in the company without a scarf from home. But since your knitting talents are not your best asset and you have so many extraordinary others, perhaps you would strive to be a bit more diverting in your letters to keep me amused. Although I am not really ill, I am honestly cold at heart and could use all the warmth you can spare. Don't hesitate to be graphic. Hearing about your state of longing in detail would do wonders to raise my temperature. If you are diverting enough, I promise to hurry home all the faster to divest you of that inconvenient virginity I insisted you maintain before I left.*
>*Frozen Until I Hear From You,*
>*Eduardo*

BRAD TURNED THE PAGE in the diary, but the next entry from Chloe was not a letter. Instead, she discussed the weather in California when they'd made a trip to see her stepbrother Harold before he left for his next assignment. No mention of Eduardo.

Out of sight, out of mind? Brad didn't want to think that had been the case. He knew his naval history enough to know the *Zeilin* would have a rough time of it that year. If Eduardo was cold, he could have easily been part of the transport's Attu landing—a hairy operation in the Aleutian Islands during a foggy, frigid spring. And damn it, how had he gone from thinking about Nikki to another crap mission?

He supposed the idea of Chloe forgetting about Eduardo while the guy was freezing his ass off in Alaska struck too close to home. But more often than not, those relationships couldn't survive time and distance. Maybe Eduardo had been right to concentrate on the physical in their letters.

Live for the here and now. When you risked everything day in and day out to perform a job you believed in, sometimes the best approach was to scrape together whatever happiness you could before it vanished. Or—in his case—exploded.

5

THE SHOUT IN THE MIDDLE of the night brought Nikki upright in bed.

Had the vandals returned to do more damage? Before she was fully awake, she was on her feet and running across her bedroom to the window overlooking the garden. Her gaze swept the landscape, the dark shape of the tractor taking form on the side of the yard. The overgrown rock garden tumbling down toward a small pond that needed to be cleaned and filled. But there were no people that she could see. All was quiet. Dark.

Her heart still pounding hard, she stood motionless. Alert to any hint of sound.

"Get them out of here!" Brad's voice cut through the silence like a sonic boom.

She jerked away from the window—startled. Scared for him. Who else was in the house?

"Brad," she shouted, running barefoot through the dark house. Thank God for the moonlight filtering in bare windows she hadn't bothered to cover yet. "Brad, what's going on? Whoever is down there, I have a gun and I'm not afraid to use it!"

Heart in her throat, she plucked the cordless phone off an upstairs table. She pounded down the stairs double time and skidded down the hall into the den. At first, she didn't see anyone. On the verge of calling the police for the second time in a handful of hours, she stilled as she heard Brad's voice. He bit off a ripe curse. Trying to quiet the rush of blood in her ears, she strained to listen to see where the sound came from. Then, a dark shape moved in the far corner of the room.

Brad's blanket. Brad.

He was here. Alone. Dreaming.

Though relieved the vandals hadn't returned, Nikki had a whole new batch of different things to worry about now. First and foremost, should she wake him? She could hear his breath coming fast, a whispered litany of words muttered into the pillow and punctuated by curses. Clearly, he was distressed. But wasn't it a mistake to awaken someone in the midst of a nightmare for fear they'd remember it all the more vividly?

"Get down!" he shouted, spiking up off the futon and scaring her so badly she stumbled back a step.

His eyes were vague and distant, the way her old roommate in college had looked when she sleepwalked. The dream had him in a powerful grip. She couldn't let him battle it out any longer.

"Brad." She approached the bed, reaching out to touch the bare expanse of his chest. "Wake up."

His skin burned even though the house remained cool after the sun went down. Fever?

His hand locked around her wrist, eyes open but unseeing as he turned toward her. His hold was tight and unrelenting, her arm captured at an awkward angle until she lowered herself to the bed beside him. Her crisp cotton nightgown rode up her thigh and she shifted awkwardly to stay covered. She hadn't given a thought to what she was wearing when she'd leapt out of bed, the lightweight cotton and Battenberg lace providing little coverage.

"They shouldn't be here," he told her, his voice softer but no less urgent.

"You're sleeping," she assured him, flexing her fingers against his chest to increase the pressure—to get through that foggy barrier where dreams seemed so real. "You're at my house. Nikki's."

The sound of her name finally had a noticeable effect. The ragged breathing slowed. His eyes cleared by degrees, revealing a tortured shade of blue.

"Are you okay?" She kept her hand on his chest, thinking she might be all that anchored him to the here and now. "Bad dream?"

He shook his head. But she didn't take that to mean "no" so much as that he had no intention of speaking about whatever had just happened.

"But maybe if you talked about it—"

"I can't." The words were harsh, but there was such starkness behind them that she couldn't possibly take offense.

"Is there anything I can do?" She didn't know how to help when she didn't know what was wrong. But the tension and raw emotion hung in the air even if he didn't have one word to say about them.

His gaze narrowed as he finally gave her his full attention. Somehow, he'd shaken off the dream for at least that moment. His nostrils flared. His lips parted.

She thought he would speak, but instead he loosened his grip on her wrist, his thumb soothing the place where his fingers had been the moment before.

"Nikki," he said finally. "Kiss me."

Her heart did a kind of stop, drop and roll in her chest. He was obviously upset. And it was clear he didn't want to talk about it. He needed something else from her right now.

The intimacy of being on this futon with him, the sheets tangled around his legs so badly that it was very evident he wore a pair of boxers and no more, suddenly seemed very unwise. Hadn't she run from this moment just a couple of hours ago?

But she was right back here, inches away from a guy who'd dominated her fantasies for over a week. And he needed her.

Whether or not he could articulate it in so many words, she understood that much.

"It's not a date," Brad whispered, so close that his jaw brushed her cheek while he spoke into her ear. "Just a kiss."

The open windows ushered in the scent of honeysuckle, the fragrance that reminded her of those nights when she'd peered in through his window at this very chest. Those nights, when he'd been wrapped in a haphazard towel, and she'd seen the vee of dark hair pointing a path down his abs.

Now, hypnotized by a man far more complicated than she'd imagined, stuck in this moment that felt more like a dream, Nikki couldn't imagine why a sane woman would say no to a kiss. It wasn't a date. It wasn't a relationship.

He needed her kiss and she wanted to give him one he'd never, ever forget.

"Okay. But you gave me the last one. I'm in charge this time."

His touch skimmed up her arm to the loose sleeve of her nightgown, reminding her she wore precious little in the way of clothes, too. Her breasts pebbled at his touch.

"I want your mouth on me any way I can have it." His questing fingers dipped beneath the fabric to cup her shoulder, his palm within deliciously easy striking distance of one tight, aching nipple.

Still, she wouldn't waste her one opportunity to kiss him by falling on him with more hunger than finesse. She cupped his face in one hand, the bristles of late-night stubble scratching pleasurably along her palm. And, once she was certain he no longer lingered in a dream, she guided him closer. Closer.

Her eyelids fell shut at the last moment and still her mouth landed precisely where she'd wanted it, brushing his with featherweight pressure. Her breasts knew no such restraint, however, shamelessly pressing against the solid wall of muscle of his chest.

He groaned, and she thought she echoed it, the vibration of pleasure a mutual music that made all her nerve endings tingle. His hands speared deeper under her nightdress until they spanned her bare back and pressed her tight to him. He felt so very good. Even better than in her fevered dreams about him. The temptation to strip off her nightclothes and climb into the sheets with him was strong, but she'd only signed on for the kiss. And by God, it was going to be a good one.

With a dart of her tongue, she massaged his lower lip. She remembered the words of the book he'd quoted about the phantom licks along a throbbing sex and wondered if he'd been equally plagued by the notion. Ah, but it was different for a man, wasn't it?

Parting his lips with hers, she captured his tongue and drew on it lightly. His grip on her lower back tightened, his own back arching in response.

No question, he'd felt a few phantom strokes right where she'd wanted.

Giving herself over to the pure pleasure of the moment, she reveled in the sensuality of that hot connection. All around her, a cool spring breeze blew against her skin wherever Brad didn't touch her. By contrast, she burned everywhere his body grazed.

More.

When she pushed closer, he lifted her onto his lap.

Her thigh met the impressive resistance of his erection. She gasped at the feel of it, as rigid and well proportioned as everything else on him. "Come here," he urged, tugging her down to the open futon with him as he fell back onto the pillows.

Not that she required urging. She didn't think she could stop until she knew what it felt like to have his hand palm her breast. Everything about Brad's kiss excited her, made her want more and more.

She normally felt clumsy in bed, her experience limited because of her focus on her career and her reservations about romance in general. But here in this awkward futon with Brad, Nikki felt like a goddess of pleasure. Her senses roared to life. Her sex clenched with readiness until her thighs turned damp.

And still the kiss went on and on. Languid. Delicious. She wanted more and couldn't wait any longer, then remembered he'd promised a kiss only.

Gladly, she ended any moral dilemma he might have had about that promise by transplanting his palm to the aching weight of her breast.

Freed to touch her, Brad squeezed gently, circling the tight crest with his finger until she whimpered impatiently. Only then did he leave her mouth to trail kisses down her throat to the swell of cleavage above the neck of her nightgown. It required only the smallest effort to sweep aside lace to expose her nipple. He feasted on her there, treating each breast with thorough reverence.

And still there was no moment when she wanted to stop, no natural breaking-away point when she feared what came next might be a disappointment. No, she knew now that this highly charged current between them would only get hotter and more powerful the longer they lay together. Even now, her body wept for the completion he could offer. She had to squeeze her thighs tight against it, and that only made it worse.

"Nik?" Brad's whisper in her ear sent sweet ribbons of pleasure chasing down her neck.

"Mmm?" She smoothed her palm across the plane of his chest and down to a tight six-pack.

"I need to stop here if we're not going to finish this tonight."

She struggled to make sense of that, her skin burning for more of anything he wanted to give her, not sure how she could peel herself away from him. He was addictive. She didn't think she could get enough of him, let alone walk away. But that's what he was warning her about, wasn't it? She'd made it clear they couldn't go any further and yet she was writhing around in his bed as if she hadn't known the man all of one day.

"Oh, my goodness." She gazed at him in the moonlight, his aquamarine eyes promising fulfillment such as she'd never experienced. She'd been the one to set the ground rules, hadn't she? Yet he'd been the one who had to remind her of them. "I'm so sorry."

Tugging her nightdress back into place, she covered her breasts.

"Don't be sorry on my account." He lay very still, not touching her, his breathing shallow. "I've been dreaming about what you would feel like all day."

Embarrassed, she sat up, pulling her hem down as far as it would go and not coming close to her knees. His reference to dreaming made her remember the nightmare he'd had and how haunted he'd looked afterward. Why had he needed the distraction of a kiss so badly?

"But if you hadn't stopped me, I would have—" She shook her head, knowing she must have looked like a tease when she put his hand on her breast. How quickly she'd forgotten all about the nightmare and how upset he'd been. "I don't know what came over me. I've never—"

"You can't imagine how happy it makes me to think I could affect you like that." He stroked her hair, the barest brush of his fingers through tangled locks, and she felt all mushy inside. "But I know you have reservations. I can promise you I won't take advantage of this thing between us until I'm sure all of you is on board with taking it further."

Her eyes burned at the realization that he would hold

back like that for her, even though she hadn't been able to restrain herself. Brad Riddock had needed her for comfort and it had turned into something combustible.

"Thank you." But she *wouldn't* get carried away like that again. "And I promise I will be far better behaved in the future. Between being exhausted from working so hard and then waking up to your shout, I think I was in a kind of dream state myself." Would he talk about what was bothering him now that he was more relaxed? "Do you know what you were dreaming about earlier? I was really worried about you."

"Nothing." He yanked the covers back up, establishing a barrier between them as tangible as his suddenly cool tone. "It was nothing. We'd better get some sleep if we want to get any work done tomorrow."

"Sure." Nikki rose, feeling dismissed and unsteady, the floor cold under her feet. She felt hypersensitive to everything around her, her body still abuzz with unfulfilled hunger. She'd been moments away from giving him everything, so it hurt to be shut out now. Still, she couldn't resist calling back to him when she reached the door. "Sleep well."

His grunt of assent could have meant anything. Leaving her to wonder if his growled response was a sign he was more annoyed by having to cut things short than he let on.

Or was he frustrated with her for asking about his nightmare? Tomorrow, she would find out.

HE WAS SCREWED IN THE HEAD.

Brad lay in the dark long after Nikki walked away,

trying to come up with any other answer beside the obvious to explain the persistence of his nightmares.

He was sleeping in the home of a gorgeous woman who wanted him as much as he wanted her. She'd felt like an angel in his hands, her body so smooth and perfect. Her touch had been sweet and gentle when she'd awoken him from his private hell. And when things turned carnal, she'd been right there with him. Her brain might not have approved the plan yet, but her body had spoken volumes—enough to assure him they'd be finding mutual bliss together soon. He'd kissed her before bed. He'd worked his way into her good graces.

By all accounts, he should have gone to bed one happy freaking dude. Still, he'd woken up screaming like a pansy and replaying the scene in his mind before that bomb had exploded and sent his world to shit.

Brad had been wearing protective gear that afternoon when he'd dismantled the IED. The local kid who'd secretly followed him into the field hadn't been so lucky. The kid's father—a subsistence farmer with more offspring than resources—had pulled the kid back, shielding him at the last second. Saving the boy. Losing an arm.

How the hell would he farm now? Brad had the benefit of the U.S. government to swoop in and provide top-notch medical care for the burns and shrapnel wounds in his leg. What did the Middle Eastern farmer have for support? While military hospitals patched up any number of civilian casualties, the guy had refused assistance from a military doc for fear of retaliation from insurgents in his town.

And Brad blamed himself. Not for detonating the

bomb. That was his job. He was guilty for befriending the kid in the first place, working around the language barrier to form a bond with a local boy in need of a role model. Some freaking hero he was.

He didn't know what to do with all his anger. And it only pissed him off more that he was stuck here—motionless and useless in Virginia.

At this rate, he'd be lucky to receive his Get Out of Jail Free card from the base shrink. He pounded his head against the pillows that smelled like Nikki's shampoo. Obviously, he'd lie through his teeth when they asked him if he was still having nightmares. But what if the flashbacks interfered with his ability to do his job?

That, he could not even consider.

Nikki had no idea how much he needed her. How much he wanted to be here, away from the four walls at home that he'd been starting to climb. At least here, she'd awakened him before the worst of the dream came, when he started to re-order all the sequence of events to try and come up with a scenario that wouldn't have resulted in a bomb going off and almost killing that kid.

Tonight, she'd ended up in his bed afterward. And he didn't mind waiting for her to be ready for more. He wanted to be around her in the hope all the work and the sex thoughts would chase away the bad crap clogging up his brain.

Burying his head in the pillow, he inhaled her scent. Focused on the memory of her soft skin and the sound of her sweet sighs every time he'd touched her. He wished he could indulge in those thoughts just for the pure pleasure of it.

But he had the feeling they were the only way he'd

keep from losing his mind tonight. At least, she'd made it clear she didn't want a relationship, so he didn't have to feel guilty about the fact that he didn't have jack shit inside himself to offer a woman emotionally.

6

"SO WHO IS EDUARDO?"

Brad's question surprised her the next afternoon as Nikki picked up a broken beer bottle from an overgrown garden. They'd settled into a work routine early, perhaps hoping mutual avoidance would solve some of the issues between them. Apparently he wasn't any more ready to talk about what had happened the night before than she was. She was so mixed up and confused, part of her longing to tug him back into the house to finish what they'd started. Another part insisted she keep her distance from a guy who just might be battling demons even darker than her own.

The memory of his eyes when he'd awakened from the nightmare flitted through her consciousness, reminding her how much he'd needed her touch. How much the distraction of it had worked—for a while, at least.

They'd both gotten up just after sunrise and she'd wondered more than once if he'd had as much trouble as her sleeping the night before. He'd returned the tractor and the other tools to the rental company and had come back with a new socket set and some wrenches he'd purchased for a housewarming present. He'd promised she'd be repairing her own plumbing in no time.

But other than that, they'd spoken very little until now...

"Eduardo?"

She blinked up at him in the bright sun. He was chucking rocks into the back of a trailer from a low garden wall that had fallen into disrepair.

"From Chloe's diary," he clarified, pausing to brush the dirt from his hands as he leaned on the metal rails of the trailer hooked up to his pickup truck. "I did some reading last night to help me get a handle on all the players in Chloe's life. One of the early published diaries—1943—had correspondence with some Eduardo guy overseas."

"Right." She watched a bead of sweat trickle down the column of his throat, ending at the neck of his T-shirt, and wished she'd tasted him right there when she'd had the chance. "His identity is disputed by the handful of people who've studied the diaries. Some say Eduardo is a disguised version of Harry Benton, a naval captain she befriended. Others say Eduardo is the real name of a seaman she met who later died in the war effort."

"Isn't it as simple as looking at the ship's roster? He served on a naval transport ship."

She'd forgotten that detail, recalling he was in the service but not which branch. A chill danced over Nikki's skin. While she wasn't normally the superstitious sort, she found it interesting that her life continued to parallel Chloe's even now. Chloe had identified with her from the start because they'd both come from homes where they were shuffled around to reluctant relatives and mostly ignored. They'd shared an interest in life writing. Erotica. Now, it seemed, they shared a wild attraction to a hot navy guy.

Had Eduardo been as closed off about his work as Brad was with her? She thought again about how quickly he'd dismissed her offer to talk with him the night before. He hadn't even considered confiding in her.

"There's no Eduardo on record, so that's one of many names Chloe used to hide someone's identity. The missing diaries are for mid-1943 to 1945, so when we find those volumes, we'll know who Eduardo really was." There was so much scholarship that needed to be done on Chloe's life and work. Nikki wanted to be sure her friend's accomplishments and contributions to literature were well-documented.

"Aren't you tempted to start searching?" He looked ready to take apart the house himself.

If he was this dedicated to his work in the service, he must be a highly prized officer.

"Very tempted. But I need to get the house in shape for that historical society visit next week. I think the chances are good the Ralston family will try to find a reason to contest the will and take the house. But if I can have the property declared a historical site, that will at least give Chloe's home some protection from them. Once I get that security, I'll start looking for those diaries in earnest." Right now, making improvements to the house felt like the best way to keep Chloe's legacy intact.

Before Brad could reply, the stray dog who followed him around—Killer, he'd christened him—began to bark. Nikki turned to see what had caught the animal's attention at the same time a middle-aged, wintry blonde stepped around the corner of the house. She wore plaid shorts with a pink polo shirt and carried a casserole dish in one hand.

"Hello?"

"Get ready," Nikki muttered under her breath, leaning close to Brad and inhaling the scent of clean sweat. "You wanted to meet the people in Chloe's life? Now's your chance."

Nikki turned to the visitor and waved. "Hi, Angelica."

As they waited for the woman to pick her way down the slope of the lawn in her pristine kelly green tennis shoes, Nikki got in a last minute aside to Brad. "She's Harold Ralston's granddaughter."

She also happened to be one of the people the World War II veteran had warned Nikki about. Angelica had had her eye on Chloe's house from the time she was a little girl, apparently. Her grandfather had told her that it would not be passed down through their family, but as the product of an entitled upbringing, Angelica had never gotten the message.

Still, she was the first to try and disguise her animosity toward Nikki, sending over her teenagers to help Nikki move in two weeks ago.

"I come bearing casserole," Angelica announced, shoving the silver foil container toward her. "My father called to tell me about your little *incident* last night. I thought I'd bring some baked ziti for comfort food. Am I the first to arrive?"

Peering around the yard, Angelica lifted her big sunglasses, propping them on her forehead before she gave Brad the once-over. Nikki noticed the ziti had come from a local Italian restaurant, the gesture probably a store-bought excuse to poke around the property.

"Angelica, this is Brad." Nikki wasn't surprised the family had been curious about the vandalism the night before. The Ralstons were usually in the know on everything that happened in town. Harold Ralston was the area's favorite son, a WWII veteran who'd been decorated for his heroism during the war in the Pacific. Someone from the police or the local paper had probably called him last night to let him know there'd been trouble at Chloe's old house. "He lives next door and has been kind enough to help me clean up around here. Brad, Angelica lives in town and her grandfather grew up with Chloe."

"We can't choose our family, though," Angelica joked, "so don't hold that against me! But seriously, Nicole, how are you holding up? I heard they threw a rock in the window?"

She squinted toward the house, shielding her eyes. Knowing she'd want the grand tour of the damage—wasn't that always what nosy neighbors wanted?—Nikki turned to lead the way up to the back porch, balancing the ziti.

Brad didn't follow, though. His gruff tone surprised her as he remained behind them.

"Angelica, do you think someone in Chloe's family is behind this?" Arms folded, his eyes bored into the other woman's as if he could ferret out the truth if he looked deep enough.

Angelica laughed, albeit a bit nervously. "With this family, you never can tell."

She made to follow Nikki, but Brad didn't relent.

"I'm serious. This is more than just disgruntled gossip. Someone threw a rock in the window that could have seriously injured her." He appeared more than a little pissed about it, in fact. A shiver danced over Nikki's skin at the realization he would protect her—not just from thieves in the night, but from a wolf in sheep's clothing like Angelica of the plaid golf shorts. "Do you think anyone in the family means to harm Nikki?"

WHEN IT TOOK ANGELICA more than a few seconds to answer, Brad sensed some sort of confession was forthcoming. A name maybe? It seemed the only plausible reason that Angelica would stall for so long. Was she genuinely worried or merely trying to think up a good cover story to throw blame in another direction? But before she could utter any helpful insider information, a man's voice shouted down to them from the side of the house closest to the driveway.

"Hey, girlie! Help an old man down." A tall, thin older man leaned on a cane, waving impatiently with his other hand. He wore a sweater-vest over a long-sleeved shirt despite the warm spring weather. A dark green baseball cap with the insignia for army infantry caught Brad's eye.

Nikki's grip tightened on his arm. "It's Chloe's oldest stepbrother—Harold. He's the local city councilman and he's been running this town behind the scenes for almost a decade, I hear. He's the one who told me I should change my locks."

"Coming, Grampy!" shouted Angelica, bolting away on her green Keds as if she'd been caught selling secrets of international consequence.

While Angelica helped her grandfather down a path near a patch of foxgloves on one side of the house, Brad lingered by Nikki, inhaling deeply. She smelled so good. The scent of her, the feel of her body so close to his, brought him right back to the night before when he'd had her on top of him, pulling his hand to where she wanted his touch.

And damn, but those memories provided some serious sexual firepower to distract him when he should be watching the byplay among the relatives. Angelica peered into the windows of Chloe's house more often than she watched the path in front of her grandfather.

"Do you want me to escort them from the property?" He spoke softly into Nikki's ear. He would have been resentful to have his time with her interrupted by anyone. But add in the fact that these people had apparently all been opposed to her taking possession of her mentor's home in the first place, and he had little patience for their questionable offers of empathy.

"I was trying to maintain peaceable relations with them." Nikki glanced up at him through thick, dark lashes. He'd avoided looking at her for too long today, plagued by how much he wanted her in his bed—and not just because he hoped to chase away his nightmares. He hated thinking about showing her that weakness.

He ground his teeth together and tried to focus on the issue at hand.

"Why? It's your place now and you've got work to do."

"They are still Chloe's family. They didn't do much for her, but I don't think she'd want me to make the house off-limits to them either." She chewed her lip, though, a sure sign she wasn't completely confident of that fact. "I don't know. Maybe I'm just so romanced by the idea of a big family that I don't want to see their bad side. No one ever brought me a casserole until I moved here."

He couldn't imagine putting up with resentful relatives for the sake of baked ziti, but he heard what was unsaid. "You don't have much family?"

"None that care to stick around for more than a once-a-year visit." She stared at the grandfather and granddaughter who were exchanging heated whispers while the blue jay with the recovering wing squawked from the patio. "Which, I guess, is not that unusual for a grown family that lives far apart. But even as a kid, I never saw my folks much."

Brad thought about that, seeing her need to take in the wounded in a new light. She saved the abandoned. Gave a family to those in need. Even tolerated Chloe's step-clan because she'd befriended the writer.

The relatives would pay dearly if they were hurling rocks through her window when she'd rolled out the welcome mat for them. Brad would find a way to speak to Angelica Ralston soon and see what she knew.

"Sometimes the key to being a functional relative is to know when to put up a few boundaries."

She nodded her agreement but went over to greet the Ralston patriarch.

"Hello, Harold." She introduced the guy to Brad, and after some small talk about his deployment and temporary leave, Brad felt himself relaxing a bit.

"I hear you had some trouble last night?" The older man's craggy face was etched with concern.

While Nikki pointed out the tire marks on the lawn,

Angelica continued to poke around the lawn, peering into crevices in an old rock wall and surreptitiously searching the foundation of the farmhouse for cracks and holes. Seeking a spot where the missing diaries could be hiding?

"The police have been alerted," Nikki was saying to the elderly town councilman. "I should have changed the locks when you told me to since there was an attempt to break in to one of the metal sheds."

Harold studied his granddaughter with narrowed gray eyes. "I don't suppose you've asked this one for an alibi?" He jerked a thumb in Angelica's direction.

"I can't imagine—" Nikki began.

"Her husband's landscaping business is in trouble. I wouldn't be surprised if she's hoping for a new source of income. She always said this place would made a great bed-and-breakfast." He straightened his cap with a weathered hand as he looked up at the house where he'd grown up.

"I'll change the locks right away," Nikki assured him, subtly guiding him back toward the driveway, and his old model Cadillac.

"Thanks for coming," Brad offered, seeing that Nikki was handling the drawing of boundaries pretty well on her own. "I set up an appointment with a security company first thing this morning to wire the place with alarms, so we'll be able to catch whoever has been harassing her."

Angelica's head shot up at that comment, her cell phone glued to one ear as she gave up searching the house foundation. She appeared more than a little interested in the new security measures.

"Good idea, son." Harold patted Brad on the shoulder. "I'm glad to see Nikki has a military man looking out for her."

After goodbyes all around and another thank-you from Nikki for the ziti, Angelica and her grandfather were settled into their respective vehicles and retreating from the secluded property.

"Brilliant comment about the security company," Nikki remarked, grinning as she sidled up next to him. "Now they'll think twice before trespassing. And if I know the Ralston clan, word will spread quickly among them that the place will be wired with alarms."

Brad planned to follow through on that lie as soon as possible; he made a mental note to call a security company for her.

"That's assuming any of them are guilty." Brad kept an eye on Harold's car as it slowly backed out of the driveway. "But word will spread. I'll put up a few signs from one of the security companies tomorrow even if they can't make it out here that fast. For now, however, I have another proposition."

A flush of color washed over her cheeks, making him wonder what kind of proposition she was visualizing. He'd bet it was a whole lot more interesting than what he actually had in mind.

"Proposition?" Her voice pitched unnaturally high.

"It's not what you're thinking." He plucked the stick from her hand and laid it on the shelf next to the gas grill. "I told you I'd take things slow. I just thought I'd see if you wanted to ditch this place for a couple of hours for a party my friends are having on the beach."

He hadn't planned on going, but the vulnerable look

in her eyes when she'd been touched by a store-bought baked ziti had gotten to him. She deserved to surround herself with good people.

Her expression now was difficult to read as she tilted her head to one side, studying him.

"Do you think it's wise to leave the place unattended when the vandals might come back?" She peered over her shoulder at the white clapboard farmhouse as the sun dipped lower on the horizon.

"We can move the animals' cages over to my house just until we come back. It's better for us to be at a party than to be sitting inside this place if any more rocks are thrown through the window anyway." The thought ticked him off anew. He'd find out who was messing with her before he returned to Iraq.

She stared at him for a long moment. What kind of reservations could she have?

"Besides," he continued, "I don't know about you, but I didn't get much sleep last night. Maybe a party would—"

"A party is a great idea," she agreed quickly, apparently spurred by the reminder that they'd been too close for comfort the night before. Well, too close for her comfort, maybe.

He'd be very glad for a whole lot more of that tonight.

"I'll just run upstairs and change—" She pulled her cell phone from her jeans pocket and he realized it was buzzing. "Just a sec."

She pressed a button and reviewed the screen—a text message as opposed to a call. He thought about going back to his place to grab clean clothes, also, but her gasp halted him.

She stood rigid, staring down at the phone.

"What?" Instantly alert, he moved closer, his hands hovering close to her waist without really touching. "Everything okay?"

Face pale, she flipped the view screen toward him so he could see what caught her attention.

Your security won't prevent me from getting what I want.

The number it came from was blocked.

"Those ballsy SOBs." He took out his own phone. "I'm calling the cops. That message should be easy to trace and it was probably one of the brain trust that just pulled out of the yard."

"Okay." She nodded, her brow furrowed with worry. Or was it betrayal? No doubt it felt that way given the warm reception she'd just given two members of the Ralston family. And who else could have spread the word about the upcoming security measures?

He gripped her hand, hating that someone was trying to scare her. And doing a damn good job.

"I'll stay here while you go upstairs and get changed."

"Changed?"

"For the beach party." The grim determination in his voice probably didn't inspire visions of limboing on the sand. "Why should we change a good plan just because of some disgruntled half-wit who didn't get his share of the silverware? You deserve some fun. You've worked really hard the last two days."

She hesitated a moment longer, but as the color came back into her face, she nodded.

"You're right." She squeezed his hand in return, a surprising—and welcome—touch. "It'll be fun to get away for a few hours."

Brad watched her walk away, hoping he wasn't making a mistake to leaving the property tonight. He didn't think Angelica or Harold were guilty as it would be ridiculously dumb to text message a threat two minutes after pulling out of Nikki's driveway. But his bogus claim about installing security must have traveled at the speed of sound around Virginia Beach. Or at least to one very guilty individual…

He couldn't help a quick glance over his shoulder, but there was no one around. He'd hand the matter over to the police and treat Nikki to a night out. A chance to meet genuine people. He didn't care to think too deeply about why he was introducing her to the people he thought of as his family. Mostly, he just wanted to show her a good time and feel normal for a few hours.

It didn't have a damn thing to do with wanting a replay of the night before. But if she ended up in his arms again, he had every intention of keeping her there until the sun rose.

7

NIKKI COULDN'T REMEMBER the last time she'd taken a day for herself at the shore.

Wind whipped through her hair as Brad's mud-splattered Jeep bypassed the resort area of Virginia Beach for the quieter sand dunes farther south. The scent of the nearby ocean helped her to put aside the problems that awaited her back home with the threats and harassment. Tonight would be *fun*. She couldn't help but think Chloe would approve of her taking time off. For all that Nikki wanted to celebrate her friend's life and share the eccentric writer's work with the world, she knew she lost sight of Chloe's "seize the day" mentality all too often.

Ocean spray cooled the breeze as the houses became more secluded. Brad pointed out a place just a few moments before a volleyball net and a bonfire came into view. His friend had access to the house for the weekend and had invited his whole unit, apparently. About twenty cars with tailgates pulled down filled an empty field next to picnic blankets and lawn chairs. Southern rock music from another era blasted over one truck's speakers. A few grills congregated to the side of a party already well underway.

Brad had barely jerked to a gravel-spitting halt before a preschool-age boy lurched out of a young woman's arms to run toward the vehicle. Nikki worked on unloading her beach bag while Brad motioned that he would keep an eye on the boy. The young woman nodded and went to sit with a few young mothers in the shade on a blanket with some snoozing infants.

"Lieutenant Brad!" The little boy who'd targeted Brad came barreling closer.

Brad dropped the cooler and swung the child high enough to make him squeal then effortlessly held him at eye level.

"You're almost too big for this. Must've grown a foot since the last time," Brad teased as he pretended to stagger. He swung the boy around once more for good measure. Seagulls took flight, shrilling in agitation at the commotion before Brad set the boy down.

A few guys jogged up from the beach to grab chairs and a tabletop grill off the back of the Jeep. Raucous laughter and shrieks of "In your face," "Score!" and "Take that, loser!" floated up from the shoreline and the volleyball game in progress. Nikki's stomach rumbled at the savory smell of roasting hot dogs and hamburgers as she took in the sudden barrage of people and sound.

"Who's this, your *girlfriend?*" The blond-haired boy pointed at Nikki as he ambled beside them, rolling his eyes and nudging Brad meaningfully.

Good question, thought Nikki, guessing the child was about five or six years old. She got busy digging in her beach bag to avoid overt eavesdropping. Good thing she'd packed the sunscreen. The late-afternoon sun sizzled along her bare shoulders, and reflected off the beach's pristine white sand. The humid, salt-filled air began curling her long hair.

So much for pricey salon products.

"Nikki, meet Nate—although she'll probably wish later she hadn't." Brad hauled Nate up to her. A sand-encrusted hand thrust forward to meet hers.

Good thing she'd remembered hand wipes, too. She grasped Nate's sticky grip. "Nice to meet you."

He shook quickly and then reached for her new beach bag. "May I help you, ma'am?"

Nate looked to Brad who nodded approvingly.

"Just bring it down to the rest of the unit," Brad ordered. "We'll be there in a sec." He turned back to the Jeep, lifting the hem of his olive green tank to mop his brow. His powerful back muscles rippled tantalizingly into view, leaving Nikki in a heated state that had little to do with the 90 degree day.

"Roger that," shouted Nate as he leapt over a split-rail fence and raced away, beach bag contents spewing in his wake.

"He's a character," said Brad as he tugged a cooler on wheels and gestured to the woman who'd been watching Nate that the child was headed her way again.

Walking down to the beach, Nikki picked up sunscreen, hair clips and a cheap pair of shades from where they'd fallen into the tall sea grass. Her flip-flops sank into the powdery sand, the warm, soft grains caressing her ankles. The sparkling navy and white-capped ocean lay just yards ahead. Oblivious to the surrounding beauty, the fierce volleyball competition raged. The thudding ball, cheers, jeers and groans drowned out the sound of the music and brown-blue swells steadily rolling ashore.

"How do you know him?" It dawned on Nikki that she'd never asked Brad if he'd been married. Could the boy have been his son? He'd clearly behaved like a father.

Uncertainty gripped her. Was coming here an invitation to further their ambiguous relationship? What did they really know about each other?

Brad's relaxed expression tightened. "His father and I served in the same unit. Lieutenant Frank Peterson. Best IED defuser we had. His wife was eight months pregnant with Nate when an advance team of mine sweepers and metal detectors missed a more unconventional weapon before Frank's team—our team—went in. Frank was right there, warning everyone it wasn't safe—"

When he broke off, Nikki impulsively stroked the back of his rigid neck.

"How awful." She couldn't imagine how hard that had been for Frank's wife, not to mention Brad's team. And poor Nate, missing out on the chance to know his dad. "I'm sorry."

The words were a lame offering, not coming close to easing the grief in the air.

"Yeah. Me, too," Brad bit out. He shook off her hand like a pestering fly.

Hurt, Nikki wasn't sure what to say. He didn't want her comfort. She was already in over her head and their afternoon together had barely gotten underway. Pausing by the break in the split-rail fence that acted as the last barrier between them and the party, she needed to clear the air before they went any farther.

"Look, maybe this wasn't such a good idea." Her sunglasses protested her tight grip with a small cracking sound. She eased her clenched fist, unsure of her role here.

Maybe Brad was better at giving help than he was at accepting what someone else had to offer.

He whirled to face her, kicking up sand he stopped so quick.

"It's a great idea." Even he must have heard how ludicrous that sounded when spoken through gritted teeth because he seemed to take a deep breath. "I'm just not good at talking about that stuff with people who—"

She lifted an eyebrow, curious how he'd finish that sentence.

"With anyone," he finished. "It's been a while since I've been with someone so I haven't had any reason to share things like that."

"It's been a while for me, too." Her last boyfriend had gotten fed up with how much time she spent on her dissertation and that had been—too many years ago.

Most guys were at least mildly intrigued at the idea of a woman writing her doctoral project on erotica. Jake had mostly been bugged she couldn't make it to more Washington Nationals games with him on his weekends off. But that was the last thing she wanted to discuss.

"Umm, aren't we a little late for this shindig of yours?"

Brad exhaled with a grin. "I like my hot dogs burnt."

Nikki started forward. "Funny. I feel the same way about marshmallows."

"One burnt marshmallow coming up. But first—" he scooped up the cooler and sprinted toward a dozen men and women dressed in khaki or athletic gear "—volleyball."

Nikki gave him time to collect assorted high fives and shoulder punches, following more slowly. When she arrived, she tried to keep up as Brad's military family introduced themselves. Like him, they served in an explosive ordnance disposal mobile unit. Some were on leave, while others had returned home after completing tours of duty. They insisted she join their game, their athletic builds promising certain humiliation for her limited skills. Was a sudden urge to read *Wuthering Heights* a plausible excuse?

"Come on, Nikki, it'll be fun," grunted a six-feet-seven-inch behemoth with a pulsing forehead. How exactly was she getting out of dodging speeding missiles for the next hour or two?

"None of us are pros," a majorly toned woman assured her as she spiked a perfect serve to the opposite corner. "We just play for fun."

The other players' anxious glances at Nikki's delicate frame belied this white lie. They were warriors who would fight like their lives depended on every point. Nikki would just get caught in the cross fire.

Her rescue came from an unexpected source as the blond-haired child appeared at her leg, his sitter a few steps behind.

"Wanna build sand castles?"

Nikki would have kissed Nate if she wasn't sure she'd

stick to him. Digging in wet, gritty sand never sounded so good. She assured his sitter she would take good care of him before she strolled down to the rolling surf. A few younger couples had laid out beach blankets here and one dad with a whistle around his neck and a lawn chair in the surf seemed to have appointed himself the unofficial lifeguard for the handful of kids in attendance. Rather than get her sundress dirty, she pulled it overhead, revealing a white bikini she should have replaced after inadvertently shrinking it. Under the bright, dipping sun and pink-veined sky, she felt far more exposed than when she'd tried it on in her shadowed bedroom. Fortunately, her companion was mostly interested in her ability to fashion model turrets.

She knelt down and began scooping sand. The cool sea surged beneath her, complementing the balmy air. Nate's chatter was as steady as the cawing seagulls.

"Lieutenant Brad and me go to the county fair every year. Do you like chickens? One time, we saw one with two heads, but Lieutenant Brad said it was made of rubber and not worth our nickel, even though it cost fifty cents to see it. I didn't say nothing, seeing as he's got medals and all, but he doesn't know his numbers. I can count to a hundred, and backward, too. Want to hear? one hundred, ninety-nine, ninety-eight, ninety-seven…"

The soft, salty air, the child's babble and the mindless task of pushing sand lulled her into a relaxed state she hadn't experienced in weeks. This was just what she'd needed after the vandalism at Chloe's place. She smiled skyward with the sheer pleasure of being here, in this peaceful moment. She glanced over at the maniacal battle raging on the court.

Twenty yards away a shirtless Brad stretched up at the net, spiking the ball. Every glistening, sweat-coated muscle sparkled in sharp relief. His sculpted biceps, lats and pecs would have made Michelangelo weep. Nikki's breath caught in her throat. So much for a peaceful moment. Brad turned to receive his teammates' high fives for the game-winning point. But his hand froze in mid-air when he caught Nikki's stare. She dropped her gaze and began plopping more sand on their blob of a castle. Could she have been any more obvious? Her mouth had probably watered like a damn spigot.

"Don't feel bad," a soft voice beside her drawled. "All the ladies react that way to Brad." Nikki looked up to see a lovely blonde wearing a blue Staples polo shirt and beige khaki pants.

"Mama!" screamed Nate, flinging himself heart, soul and sand-encrusted body into her arms. "You're done work?"

"For today," she said wearily. She began plucking Nate's tentaclelike limbs from her. She gave up and smiled at Nikki, extending a hand.

"Ashley."

Nikki uselessly swiped her gritty hands on her equally filthy thighs then gave up and shook hands. "Nikki."

"And you're here with Brad, I'm assuming." Her full-throated chuckle was infectious, making it impossible for Nikki to feel embarrassed. "You could have swallowed him whole with those eyes."

"That obvious?" Nikki laughed.

"Definitely. I was lucky enough to find it twice in my

life." She looked back up toward the volleyball court as the game disbanded and crowds started circling the grills.

Brad detached himself from the rest along with a tall, dark-haired man in red Hawaiian surfer shorts who looked like he hadn't shaved in two weeks. The guy wore aviator shades that he flipped up onto his head as he spied Ashley and Nate. He smiled and jogged down toward them, wrapping an arm around Ashley.

"This is Joe Staley, my fiancé." Ashley took care of the introductions as Brad joined them.

He winked at Nikki before planting a hard kiss on her mouth to leave her breathless. Then, never missing a beat, he half-tackled Nate, spinning the boy into an airplane position so they could race up and down the beach, Nate's arms extended wide. Dog tags swung wildly from his small neck, the reflective metal flashing in the setting sun.

Still trying to gather her bearings after a kiss that made her heart beat faster, Nikki watched Brad crash-land them both into the surf before diving him into another rushing wave. She could believe that for the right man, risking your heart would absolutely be worth it. But seeing so many couples off and young families playing at the beach would make anyone feel a little sentimental toward romance.

"Congratulations to you both," Nikki offered before Joe joined Brad and Nate in the water. A lot of the volleyball players had jogged down to the water for a quick dip before dinner.

"Thank you." Ashley gathered up a few shovels and pails that Nate had used, putting everything in a grocery sack. "I feel really fortunate to have found Joe. It was a hard few years after I lost Frank. I went home for a couple of years because it hurt to be around all this." She gestured toward the heart of the party, apparently referring to the tight-knit group around them. "But I brought Nate last year to see where his dad had worked and Joe and I—well. I was lucky."

"Nate seems really at home here," Nikki observed, understanding the appeal of an extended family, even if you weren't related by blood. She would have appreciated having this kind of network when she was a kid.

"He loves Virginia. And he took to all of the guys in the unit right away, especially Brad." Ashley stepped back as a Frisbee headed their way, followed by a squealing girl in a local college T-shirt. "I really hope it works out for the two of you."

Nikki shook her head as she watched a young man from Brad's unit tug the girl into the bushes for a kiss. "It's not like that between us. He's just been helping me renovate before he ships out in a couple of weeks."

Ashley's unique, full-throated chuckle erupted. "With the way you two were eyeing each other? Highly unlikely. And don't waste your time denying it. One thing I've learned is that every moment is precious and there are no guarantees you'll get them back."

Ashley's words struck Nikki's heart like a gong, echoing everything Chloe had ever preached about life. The message had a serendipitous feel as she watched Brad and Nate arrive with a spray of sand. Ashley's fiancé lumbered up a few steps behind.

"Mommy, were you watching? Brad flew me real

high and he's gonna take me to the fair before he goes back."

Ashley extricated Nate. "I'm sure he will, honey. Now, it's time we get going. Almost bedtime." She turned to Nikki. "It was nice meeting you. Brad's never let us meet anyone before, but I can see he was holding out for someone special."

Brad's eyes flowed like blue quicksilver to Nikki's. She only tore her gaze away to watch the young couple depart with Nate. Ashley stopped to thank one of the servicewomen for watching the boy, giving her a quick hug. Nikki looked back at Brad, his piercing eyes still locked on her.

"You're really good with him." She admired the way he extended warmth to a child not his own. Other than Chloe, she'd never experienced that kind of loyalty. In her world, relationships were undependable at best, absent at worst. Brad was obviously a man to be counted on—as much as his dangerous occupation allowed.

He shrugged. "Unit 12 takes care of its own. It's what Frank would have done for any of us."

Understanding now that this was tricky terrain for him, she left it at that, grateful just to be with him and very ready to live in the moment. She didn't protest when he led her toward the grills for some dinner with his friends. Snatching her sundress on the way, she pulled on the cover-up and enjoyed every minute of the next two hours until the sun started to set and her glances at Brad turned as long and lingering as his were toward her.

She wanted more. Today had showed her that in no uncertain terms.

After one particularly scorching look, it was all she could do not to lift her barely touched beer bottle to her forehead and let the chilly drink cool her down.

Peering around at the crowd thinning out, she set down her drink.

"I think I might need a swim," she croaked, her skin on fire as his gaze drifted down to her sand-dusted cleavage where her sundress was only half-buttoned. She raced for the water, diving in for a quick rinse, not caring about the dress. She had a towel somewhere.

She stumbled as a fierce undertow nearly swept her off her feet.

Brad reached her in a flash, steadying her with his electric touch. His hand traced a stream of water that made her dress cling to her spine. His head lowered to meet hers until hooting and hollering erupted from the committed party crowd still hanging around the bonfire.

Nikki grabbed his hand. No privacy here.

"Want to take a walk?"

He nodded mutely, tugging her toward shore just long enough to grab a couple of towels and her bag. She wrung out her clothes on the sand and then took his hand as they set off down the beach.

Every moment was precious. And since she'd never get this night back again, she planned to make sure she had no regrets about how she spent the rest of it.

BRAD COULDN'T PINPOINT what had happened to change Nikki's mind about taking thing further between them, but there could be no mistaking the vibe she'd been sending his way tonight.

And he could not believe his luck. Two days ago, he'd been alone, replaying the IED nightmare like a skipping CD. Now, a smart, sexy professor meandered down the Virginia seashore beside him, her arm brushing his often enough to keep him very aware of her soft skin and tantalizing body. Red streaked the horizon, the sun barely holding itself above the waterline. In moments it would slip from view, leaving him alone with Nikki on the darkening coastline.

The sounds and signs of civilization disappeared as they strolled toward rockier, ungroomed beaches thick with tall grasses and sea oats. No one from the party would wander out this far. Although Brad made sure to choose a cove that tucked behind a boulder the size of Montana.

The only sounds now were their slapping feet against the cooling sand, squawking gulls and the waves rhythmically pounding the shore. He'd always been drawn to the water, making his navy career a natural fit.

Maybe a better man would ask himself why, after hitting the brakes on sex last night, Nikki was now driving him to distraction with come-hither looks. But hell. If she was offering, he was taking. And from the flirtatious smiles flashing his way, he'd say all systems were go.

He swung her around, reeling in his stunning catch. Her green eyes glowed in the twilight. Shadows gathered in the deep valley of her breasts. He fantasized about removing the bikini top she wore, speculating he could have it off in one deft finger flick.

But discipline kicked in. He knew better than to tackle a woman as soon as he got her alone. Although it had been touch and go there for a while when they'd been sitting next to each other at the bonfire.

"So did you enjoy the party?"

"Definitely." She sidestepped a tortoise and Brad counted his blessings the thing hadn't been limping or he probably would have been tasked with finding a cage for an impromptu rescue mission.

"That was great of you to hang out with Nate, especially after I shut you down when we were talking about Frank."

Nikki let go of his hands and sat down beside a shimmering tide pool. She was silent for a few minutes then reached behind to pull him down beside her.

"It's hard to find the right words sometimes. I'm sure you're feeling the loss of your friend all the more with whatever you're going through now." She glanced meaningfully at his leg and the patch job still obvious on his calf.

And damn, but these academic types were way too observant.

"Sounds like you've gone through a lot yourself." Brad wasn't ready to talk about the IED that had blasted him along with that farmer. "What did you mean when you said your folks weren't around much?"

"They're professors, like me. To continue studying, they traveled. A lot. Something that's not exactly easy to do dragging a kid around."

"So let me guess, they dragged you to your relatives' houses instead?" Brad's blood pressure increased just imagining Nikki abandoned like that as a kid.

"Relatives, friends, colleagues." Nikki shrugged,

her throat constricting. "Basically anyone with a free bed."

"And this went on for how long?" Brad demanded, frustration at her parents roughening his voice.

"Still is. I last saw my mom and dad four years ago."

"Wow. That has to suck." Brad ran his hands up and down her arms. No wonder she was gun-shy of getting involved with a traveling bomb detonator.

How her parents could have abandoned her he'd never understand. When he had kids, he'd be there for them one hundred percent. He wished he could have been there for Nikki growing up. Hell. He wished he could be there for her now.

"Yeah, especially when I was younger. But reading about Chloe's childhood helped me to see my own differently."

Nikki stroked his biceps, setting the hairs at the nape of his neck on end.

"I mean, waiting for life to hand you a guarantee before you let yourself enjoy it is a waste of time." Her stroking extended up to his shoulder. "All my life, I waited for my parents to show up and love me. And when they finally did, all I could think about was when they would leave again. I don't want to wait around to be happy anymore."

She paused, letting that newsflash sink in. When it did, he began to understand her change of heart.

"Life doesn't hand you any guarantees. You told me that on our way into the party and your friend Ashley kind of said the same thing another way. It's funny how the universe has a way of sending you the messages you need to hear, and I've been beaten over the head with that one."

She grinned and he couldn't help but think he didn't want to hear the messages the universe had been broadcasting for him every night when he closed his eyes. He'd never be effective at doing his job again if he allowed one crap outcome to rattle his nerve.

But he didn't want to consider that now, not when Nikki had come around to his way of thinking.

"I hope I can be a part of helping you find some happiness today." Brad reached for her face, tracing its curves. He tugged her gently toward him, pressing his lips against hers.

No sooner had he brushed a kiss over her lips than she pulled back.

"Wait a second," Nikki whispered, rising to her feet.

Brad groaned inwardly. "Make it a nanosecond, and we've got a deal."

Nikki reached behind her back and undid the string of her bikini top. A light breeze lifted the material's edges, giving him an enticing peek at the full underside of her breasts.

"A gust of wind would be good right now," Brad drawled, eying the half-undone swimsuit.

Twirling the loose strings on either side, Nikki grinned. "Why? Are you getting hot?"

"Whoa." He got to his feet, his blood surging south and making him damn lightheaded. "Didn't anyone ever tell you not to tease a red-blooded sailor on leave? You're playing with fire."

"Hey, I wrote a whole dissertation on erotica. I need some practical applications for my theories."

"Well, you can be damn sure that your education isn't going to waste." Her enticing words, actions and smoking body were a huge turn-on. Clearly, she intended to seduce him.

And even though he wanted her right here and right now, he didn't mind waiting to see what she had in store for him. He made no move, watching her curves silhouetted against the rising moon. A strong wave crashed against her knees, soaking her bikini.

She lifted her long, wet curls and undid the neck string, forcing the breath from his lungs.

The top slid, but then was neatly caught at the last minute. She held the material at chest level with one arm. Fortunately, enough flesh spilled out to keep him from howling in frustration.

"You want to see more?"

Nikki's voice was a siren call to his senses.

She dropped her arm, giving Brad a brief glimpse of her full breasts and creamy skin before she whirled around and faced the sea. She looked over her shoulder and smiled coyly.

"Hope you like the bottom half as much as the top."

Brad's eyes drank in the pert, rounded cheeks barely covered by the scrap of white cloth.

"I'd like it better if it wore as little as the top."

Nikki plucked the strings on either side of her waist, letting the bikini bottom drop to the ocean floor. She dropped to her knees to retrieve it, arching her back to reach the escaping piece. He sucked in his breath, too damn mesmerized by the show to help.

She rolled over in the rushing surf and stood, every inch the mermaid of a sailor's dreams. Her perfect breasts jiggled tantalizingly as she swayed toward him. She halted just out of hand's reach, tossing her bikini on the sand. Her slender hips and nipped-in waist rose above a dark triangle he hungered to explore.

"Come in with me." She turned and splashed back into the pounding surf, her heart-shaped backside bouncing seductively.

Game over.

Brad leapt after her, predator to prey. He caught her two long strides from the shore, hauling her against him. Her cool, wet skin didn't even come close to stanching the inferno within.

Her hands trailed along his waistband, making his abdominal muscles tense and contract. With a quick snap, she'd unbuttoned his shorts, stroking the tip of his cock. She rubbed the moist surface.

"Looks like someone's already getting wet," Nikki whispered, dragging the shorts down and off before he flung them onto the shore.

"I bet I'm not the only one," he choked out, stroking up her bare leg and down to the vee of her thighs. Dampness flooded his impatient fingers. Hot flesh welcomed him as she snaked one long limb around his waist, giving him even deeper access. He cupped her sex, lingering over its wet warmth.

He swelled with satisfaction as she moaned and he wanted nothing so much as to be inside her. But like any military man, his mission always came first. Unleashing

Nikki's wild nature was his number one objective. Her sighs deepened as he found the tight nub that would bring her the most pleasure. He circled it with his thumb until her head lolled back, her spine arching.

His hand faltered as he took in the bounty inches from his salivating mouth. He intensified his strokes while licking the ocean salt from each taut nipple, tugging and nipping. Her leg tightened around him, pulling him closer. She shuddered beneath his insistent hand, her back arching, hips thrusting forward, pressing hard against his engorged staff. His enjoyment at her reaching satisfaction was almost as intense as if he'd achieved it himself.

While the waves continued to roll over their feet, her ragged breath slowed. Her leg dropped. Brad tightened his grip around her waist, propping her up in the pulsing tide. She'd turned as limp as a ragdoll.

Mission accomplished.

Several seconds passed as she rested her burning cheek against his rigid shoulder. He wanted to give her a minute to recover but he was hanging by a thread. He counted backward; a trick he used on high-pressure missions. He'd reached ninety-two when he felt her delicate fingers lowering to his waist. His erection.

Her cool fingers wrapped around him, gently skimming up and down the length. If she kept that up, he'd lose it in no time. What number had he left off at?

She sank to her knees, her beautiful body backlit by the glowing moon, sea foam rushing around her. He descended with her, pulling her onto his lap to shield her from the rolling waves. Her thighs straddled him as she rocked back and forth against his near-bursting hardness.

He cupped her bottom, kneading the firm flesh. He used the leverage to press her core against him, making her gasp once more.

"Don't move," he commanded, leaning close enough to the shoreline to retrieve his shorts half-floating in the surf. His wallet was soaked, but thanks to the wonders of foil packaging, the condom he had in there would be fine. He could replace the money. But this moment—never.

He couldn't get enough of her. Her body was a marvel he wanted to explore at leisure, if only he had the patience. As it was, he was barely able to contain himself once they'd rolled the condom in place. He traced the delicate flare of her hips, the inward turn of her waist and the slender rib cage—stopping at the soft underside of her breasts. He palmed them, groaning at their satisfying weight, delighting in the way they spilled from his hands. He lifted one to his mouth, eliciting another cry from Nikki. Her pleasure was his greatest turn-on.

And he couldn't hold back another minute.

In one swift move, he twisted her beneath him and entered her in a smooth, long stroke.

His hips thrust powerfully, feeling her tighten around him with every stroke. Her hips arched up to meet each possessive push, her hands gripping his taut backside, pulling him in deeper. The urgent noises she made set his male instincts into overdrive.

He tried to slow down, to make the pleasure last for both of them. But he hadn't been kidding when he said she'd been playing with fire. It had been a long time for him and he needed this. Needed her.

Their synchronized motion increased to a frenzied, heart-stopping tempo. Her breath came in fast pants which intensified to soft cries that were music to his ears. Her tight spasms and the surf pounding the beach in unison with his thrusts were too much. His release exploded in a tidal wave that left him drained and utterly sated.

He held her for a long moment. Then he rolled over and stared at the twinkling stars overhead. His pulse still pounded hard as he turned to look at her delicate profile. She was more adventurous than he'd imagined with her impromptu striptease and rollicking around in the surf. Hell, she'd been more than a match for him.

A star shot across the sky. Nikki gasped, his first indication she'd regained her wits.

"Quick, wish on it!" she urged. Her hand snaked out and caught his as they tracked the blazing trail against the midnight sky.

The sighting had been fast and vivid. He would have missed it if he'd blinked. But it had been there, brightening the sky until it burned into nothing. Would his relationship with Nikki be the same? A flash of hot color and joy in his life for two short weeks before he had to return to the reality of his job overseas? He hated to think about it like that. But with Nikki quietly contemplating the darkness alongside him, Brad guessed they might be thinking the very same thing.

Tightening his hold on her in the water, he pressed a kiss to her forehead. He'd drag them to the shore in a minute. But if this was all the time they had together, he planned to drink in every second and make the most of this affair while it still burned hot and bright.

8

NIKKI SLOWLY SWAM TO consciousness, anchored in Brad's arms. A rough military blanket enveloped them, keeping the damp, morning sea air out and their fiery body heat in.

He'd retrieved the blanket from the roll that contained his beach towel after they'd returned to dry land farther up the beach late last night. He'd built a fire out of driftwood using little more than a Bic lighter and ingenuity, providing them with a bonfire of their own until just a couple of hours ago. Apparently Brad had come more prepared for their walk last night than she had, although she congratulated herself on the bottle of water in her purse.

Nestled against Brad's steely contours, Nikki couldn't help but replay last night's sensational sex. She squirmed backward, fitting her bottom snugly into the curve of his muscular flanks. Rock-hard arms tightened around her reflexively.

Returning to sleep was definitely out of the question.

She blushed, recollecting her uninhibited behavior

last night. What had come over her? A few weeks in Chloe's house and she'd become a wanton woman.

Chloe would approve. Did she?

A long, low ship horn reverberated across the sea. Nikki cracked open her eyes, hoping the day hadn't yet dawned. She wasn't ready to face last night's impulsive actions.

She took a fortifying breath of the briny ocean air and peered about. The world was gray and shadowed. Darn. Sunrise, and reality, were only moments away.

She thought about waking Brad, wanting to share their first sunrise together, then stopped. She was getting way ahead of herself. They had less than two weeks together.

How foolish to imagine a future with him full of "firsts."

The deep rumbling of Brad's wide chest vibrated against her back. She hated to wake him from such a peaceful sleep. After his nightmarish evening the other night, he deserved the rest.

Hopefully, he'd keep sleeping so she could sort out her feelings. She inhaled his musky, masculine scent. The longer she lingered, the less clearly she could think.

She carefully eased out of his arms. A lonely rush of chilled air buffeted her as she emerged. Quickly, she tightened the blanket around him. He stirred slightly, his arms reaching out into her now-empty space. He sighed deeply, but didn't wake.

A short stroll brought her to the ocean's edge. Her beach dress billowed behind her in the brisk, morning breeze. She inhaled the scent of salt, fish and seaweed. Overhead, fishing birds floated like feathered kites.

Two brown pelicans squabbled over a catch, their long bills clicking and snapping.

Someone always wanted what someone else had. Like her situation with Chloe's family. They'd inherited most of Chloe's estate. Why was there so much animosity over her ramshackle house and personal diaries? It just didn't add up.

As if on cue, her cell phone trilled. She rushed to her beach bag and flipped it open. A text message icon popped up.

In eleven days, you'll be alone again, unprotected. We'll be waiting.

Anger surged. Did they think she was a frightened child to be scared by poisonous texts and a broken window? She could take care of herself.

Besides, Brad was more than her protector; he was now her lover—for nearly two glorious weeks. Nikki smiled, recalling the way his insistent hands had lit her on fire. She'd never felt so uninhibited, a thought that thrilled and frightened her.

What if her heart opened up to him as easily as her body? Her feet burrowed in the wet sand as she crossed her arms against a chilly ocean gust.

She glanced back at Brad, the hard planes of his face relaxed into an impossibly handsome visage.

Was a highly charged, two-week affair possible without putting her heart on the line?

The text message got it right in one sense. When Brad's leave ended, she would be unprotected. But it wasn't her physical safety she worried about. If she got too attached, she'd be devastated when he left. She was all too familiar with that feeling.

Nikki's stomach churned with uncertainty as she turned back to the rough sea. For now, she needed to keep her guard up.

Feet padded behind her. Nikki's back stiffened as she was engulfed in Brad's powerful embrace. He rested his head atop hers, pulling her close.

"Morning, beautiful," he murmured huskily in her ear. Heavy black clouds gathered on the horizon.

Nikki's traitorous heart drummed, nearly drowning out the rising waves.

"Looks like rain," she replied. Lightning forked in the distance. An ominous rumble confirmed her prediction.

"'Red sky at night, sailors' delight, red sky in the morning, sailors take warning.'" He tossed out the old adage as he trailed a molten flow of kisses down her neck, wreaking havoc with her senses and her willpower.

It would be so difficult to keep things light between them.

"Then we should both be warned," Nikki managed, breathless from his touch. "We'd better get going before the downpour arrives."

Brad's eyebrows slashed downward, his inscrutable eyes narrowing. But the whole concept of "no guarantees" was his rule. So why did he appear more frustrated than relieved?

"Sure thing" came the clipped reply. He shook out the blanket and slid on his shorts before she'd even picked up her beach bag.

He strode up the beach, away from the shore and their night together.

Nikki jogged to keep up. What was his deal? Good thing she'd kept her distance after all. Her bare toes tangled in something, slowing her down. She prepared to pull seaweed from her foot and discovered she'd tripped on a half-buried metal chain. She squatted for a closer look. Lt. Frank Peterson's dog tags. Nate must have lost them in the roughhousing yesterday.

Her fingers traced the embossed letters for a moment before she tucked them into her dress pocket. The tags felt so small compared to the hero they represented. How could an entire life be reduced to a piece of metal and a loyal woman's memories?

What would it be like to be that woman?

The first raindrops fell as she reached Brad scrambling to gather the rest of their belongings by the volleyball net—their strained silence as charged as the electrified air.

They raced up the path to the open field that had served as a parking lot yesterday, trees swaying wildly overhead. The wind howled, whipping the leafy canopy into a frenzy. Just as the downpour hit, they clambered into the Jeep.

Nikki sighed. That was close.

Strangely, the deluge had kept things from getting too heavy. She'd survived one morning after without falling hopelessly in love with Brad Riddock. Only eleven more to go.

AT NIKKI'S HOUSE, BRAD HANDED over her beach bag after walking her to the door. He didn't know what to make of the cool distance she'd opted for this morning, but a gentleman walked a woman to the door and he'd damn well honor the code even if she didn't seem to want him there.

Nikki pushed back her dark hair, the curls soft and abundant after she'd fallen asleep with it wet the night before. "I didn't mean to be standoffish this morning, Brad. But I thought maybe we needed a break after how intense things were last night."

Okay. Way to address the issue head-on. He appreciated that. Nodding, he wished his chest weren't so damn tight. Wasn't this what he'd wanted?

"I figured as much." But that didn't take away how much it sucked to be shot down when he'd already been planning how to get her naked again.

"I'd still be grateful if you'd like to sleep here tonight," she continued, setting her beach bag on the patio table. "I just need some time to think before then."

Relief flooded through him. She hadn't shut him out.

Killer barked from the porch, interrupting their one-sided conversation.

"Come here, boy," Brad called. Killer looked from Brad to Nikki, whined, but refused to leave the porch. "You like her better now, huh?" He reached up and rubbed the dog's belly through the peeling porch spindles. "Can't say I blame you."

The blue jay squawked and the chipmunk squealed as Nikki ascended the steps. She gave them a quick once-over, then turned to pet Killer, as well.

"Brad, you're okay with that, right?" Her green eyes peered down at him anxiously. "I'm sure you don't want to complicate things either."

Brad took the porch steps in one bound and backed

her up against a newel post. He kissed her long and hard. Palming her ass, he hauled her up against him. When he released her, she grabbed hold of the post and gasped for breath.

Ego appeased, he grinned.

"Darlin'," Brad said as he backed down the steps, "this can be as simple as we want to make it."

He hopped in his Jeep and roared out of her driveway. If she needed time to mull things over, let her think about that.

He drove to the VA facility with the windows down. The air had lost its oppressive humidity and blew in the smell of freshly cut grass. The lighter weather matched his optimistic mood. He'd gone all night without playing host to the recurring dream. That meant he was straightening out, right? He couldn't wait to tell the shrink as much, except—oh, yeah, he'd only copped to a couple of nightmares in the first place.

But first came rehab. He rode the exercise bike then went through his prescribed routine of leg pumps, curls and extensions. The large, airy space was filled with dozens of bikes, elliptical machines, weight benches and other work-out equipment. Grunts accompanied the clanging of metal on metal. The stench of sweat and iron made Brad's nose curl. Not that he should talk. He reeked as bad as the other ten servicemen in the gym, but figured he'd hold off on a shower until after he'd worked out. One, Brad noticed, had lost an arm.

"Hey." The guy lifted his chin at him as he hand-curled forty pounds.

"Impressive." Brad gestured to the oversize dumbbell while he worked on a military press with the barbell.

The soldier grinned and finished another set of ten before lightly placing the weight in its slot and grabbing the fifty pounder.

"James," grunted the wounded warrior. He worked through another impossible set.

"Brad." He mopped his brow, amazed the guy had barely broken a sweat. It felt like a hundred degrees.

"Navy?" James asked, finishing his last set at the same time Brad ended a round of squats.

"Unit 12—Norfolk."

"Unit 4."

An assault unit. That explained the guy's Hulk-like strength.

"You with the explosive division?" James asked, flipping a towel over one shoulder as they headed toward the locker room.

"Yeah." Brad thought about that missing arm, wary about where the conversation could land.

"IED specialist?"

"That would be me."

"Bad-ass, dude." James grinned then expertly disrobed and disappeared into the steaming showers. Brad followed suit two stalls down, and when he emerged, he found James twirling his locker combination one-handed, a towel securely tucked around his waist. The exposed amputation must have been healing for a while, the rounded, puckered flesh no longer red.

"You never seen one?" James asked, catching his stare.

"I've seen them." He grimaced, his mind flashing to the Iraqi farmer's grisly wound. "But they're usually fresh."

James's locker clicked open and he efficiently donned his clothes, even buttoning his shirt with ease. Seeing how well he'd adapted made Brad wonder if the Iraqi farmer could recover some degree of normalcy after his injury.

"Can I ask you something?"

"Depends."

"You get that from a bomb or gun?"

"IED." He shrugged casually, shouldering his gym bag. "But what's the difference? Life's gonna bite you in the ass whenever it wants. It's not like we got any say about it, right?"

"I hear that," Brad echoed, knowing it with one hundred percent freaking certainty.

He dressed quickly and headed to a private psych facility a few blocks away; the base counselor had had too many patients to take him on. Just as well since it sort of sucked running into guys you knew while traipsing in and out of the shrink's office. Not that there was a stigma attached to the whole ordeal…far from it. If you did combat time, chances were good you'd be in there for one thing or another eventually. But the anonymity here, away from the base, was just fine with him.

The assistant at the front desk waved him in and he put on his game face.

"Come in, Lieutenant," boomed his doctor, Sean Leonard. He came out from behind his desk to gesture toward the informal seating nearby. "Have a seat."

"Thank you." Brad dropped into a straight-backed solid-oak chair that must have predated WWII. He glanced at the clock. The large white hand ticked. Only fifty-nine more minutes to go.

Dr. Leonard took out a file, flipped it open and rapidly perused its contents. He glanced up, his eyes keen. He had the clean-cut appearance of someone who'd taken care of himself his whole life—from the fit runner's physique to the brown eyes that broadcast simple sincerity. Under any other circumstances, Brad would have probably liked him.

"The last time we spoke you said your most recent nightmare was the one witnessed by Lieutenant Staley a week ago."

"That's correct." Ashley's fiancé had borrowed his car and walked in on the nightly horror show. Brad didn't know who'd been more freaked out—him to know someone else had witnessed his demons, or Joe who sure as hell hadn't wanted a backstage pass to another guy's private hell.

"Any more since then?"

"No, sir," he lied.

The doc made a note in the chart.

"How often do you think of the incident in Mosul?"

"How often?" Brad stalled, unsure what the normal response would be.

"How frequently do you picture the events that precipitated your leave?" the doctor asked again patiently.

Brad went with the truth because, damn it, you'd have to be born without a freaking conscience not to think about it sometimes.

"At least once or twice daily, sir."

The pen flashed again. A lengthy scrawl of sentences followed. Brad looked around the wood-paneled room, noting the doc's educational certificates and citation awards. A yellowed picture of a much younger Leonard, his redheaded wife and their three freckled children hung on the wall beside his oversize desk.

"Would you describe your feelings and thoughts when you think of the incident?"

Sweat popped along his brow and he wished he'd thought to tell the shrink right off that he'd been working out first. Because, damn it, that's why a bead had rolled down his back just now and not because of some knee-jerk reaction at the thought of talking about his freaking *feelings*. No way was he getting into all that.

"Regret." Brad resisted the urge to mop his forehead and ended up looking at the clock instead.

Damn.

"And what is it that you regret, Lieutenant?" the doctor queried, still scribbling.

The guy's cool detachment bugged him. How could he sit across from him, dry as a freaking Right Guard commercial, while Brad sweated it out trying to find the correct answers to impossible questions that would allow him to go back out and do his job?

"How about regret that a civilian lost his arm? Regret that befriending the civilian's son led to his father's injury. Mix in some regret that the same kid had to see the horror with his own eyes and then top it all off with a crapload of regret that getting close to anyone ends up being dangerous as hell in my experience!"

The quiet in the room seemed intense after an outburst that had ended with a little more volume than he'd intended. Taking a deep breath, he swallowed back any urge to say more.

The doctor finally looked up; his brown eyes assessing Brad carefully.

"Regret is a normal emotion," the shrink began. "But thinking that personal closeness is dangerous is not."

Brad kept his face impassive. Never show doubt or fear.

"Would you describe the relationships you are currently in?" asked the doc. Brad was not falling for that game again.

"I have a dog." The mutt had adopted him before he'd found Nikki, after all. Surely that counted as a relationship. "He's a scrawny thing—maybe some daschund in the mix—so I called him Killer—you know, help the little guy's self-image."

Leonard didn't seem inclined to discuss the psychology of small canines.

"How long have you had the dog?"

Brad swallowed. "One week."

"I see. Your parents?"

"Passed away ten years ago, sir."

"I'm sorry to hear that. And my apologies, Lieutenant. I see there's a note in your file about the plane crash." The oak chair squeaked as he squirmed under the doc's penetrating stare. "Any other relationships?"

Since he didn't want to get into his need to help out Frank's widow and her son, he found himself saying, "A girl, Nikki."

The pen clicked again, poised over the folder.

"And what is the status of your relationship?"

Good question. If only he knew the answer.

"Physical, I think."

"So no emotional attachment?"

Brad hesitated. He couldn't bring himself to deny the feelings she aroused in him. For that matter, something about Leonard's tone made him think that a lack of emotional attachment equated with a one-way pass to Crazy Town.

"I wouldn't go that far, sir. It's just hard to say where things will lead when we only met three days ago."

The pen started scribbling furiously and Brad wondered why his relationships were so important. Wasn't emotional detachment critical to his job?

"Brad, our time is nearly up," began Doc Leonard. Brad looked up at the clock, shocked the minutes went so quickly this time. "But I want to see you back next week and hear how things are going with Nikki and—" he looked down at his notes "—Killer."

Brad stood quickly, ready to jet out of there.

The doc raised a thick, gnarled finger, holding him. "This week explore what you've begun with Nikki, beyond the physical. Try to remember that not every personal relationship is harmful. That's not to say either one of you won't get hurt in the process, but the point is, you have to be open, and willing to try." His yellowed teeth flashed in a kindly smile. Brad suddenly realized that the doc was older than he thought and had probably worked beyond his retirement.

"Yes, sir." Brad nodded his thanks before hightailing it out of there with an appointment card in hand. The session might have moved faster today, but he still couldn't wait to leave.

And, hot damn, had he just received a prescription

for hanging out more with Nikki? For the first time in the history of his crappy injury, he decided he would be a very compliant patient.

9

MIDAFTERNOON SUN ROASTING the back of her neck, Nikki was grateful for an excuse to shut off the power sander when her cell phone rang in the middle of the afternoon. Still, she approached the device like a rattlesnake, knowing chances were high it would be another creepy text message. She really needed to create a separate ring tone for her texts.

"Hello?" She didn't recognize the number, but at least it was a real call and not a text.

"I'm looking for the hot professor that all the kids at school have been talking about—"

"Hi, Brad." She peeled off the gloves she'd been wearing and leaned back on the porch spindles she'd tackled today. "I'm glad you called. I forgot to tell you I found Nate's dog tags on the beach this morning. You'll probably want to contact his mom to let her know you have them."

"I'll do that. I have to call Ashley anyway to set up a time to take Nate to the fair this week." He sounded as if he was in the Jeep, the drone of an engine combining with the whip of wind in the background. "How's it going at the house? No trouble with harassers?"

"It's been quiet except for the power sander." She brushed some paint chips from her T-shirt.

"Any time to search for the diaries?"

"No. But I'll step up my efforts on that score now that we've made some serious progress on the house. If the Ralston family succeeds in taking the house from me, I'll want to know that I searched the property as much as possible first. Having all the original diaries published together was really important to Chloe." And from a scholarly perspective, Nikki couldn't wait to read them to see what they contained that was so important to her friend. What secrets might they reveal?

"I think the harassment is going to stop once the diaries are made public. My gut says whoever is behind the threats is trying to suppress their release. So the sooner we find them and hand them over to a publisher, the safer you'll be." His voice took on that growly tone that sent a ridiculous thrill through her.

"You might be right." She clutched the phone tighter, enjoying the completely unfamiliar feeling of having someone look after her. She could become way too used to this. "What have you been doing today?"

"Miss me already?"

"Possibly." She hugged herself like a teenager on the phone with her first boyfriend. Damn it, how old was she? "But don't evade the question."

"I went for a workout and a round of therapy for my leg." The way he said it—stilted, somehow—reminded her that he'd never told her the circumstances surrounding the wound.

She sensed it all tied in with the nightmare.

"You can tell me all about it when we're searching for the diaries tonight." Maybe this time *she'd* distract *him* with readings from Chloe's work.

"Is there a striptease involved?"

Her breath caught as her heartbeat sped up. "If that's what it takes…"

"I've got one more stop to make and then I'll be over there."

She was wound up now, eager to see what would happen if she let her guard down again. He'd made her feel so incredible on the beach. And she'd had enough time to corral her emotions since the morning. She could handle this.

"You're sure it can't wait?" she asked, as breathless as if he'd just touched her.

"I'm stopping by Angelica's house to see what she's not telling about family members who might have it in for you. She knows something." He lowered his voice. "If it was anything else, I'd blow it off and see you now."

A smile warmed her insides. She liked that he had priorities.

"Are you sure you don't want to let the police talk to her?" She agreed that Angelica had appeared as though she had something to share before they'd been interrupted when she'd brought the casserole. "They know we're suspicious of the Ralston family."

"But with the grandfather a city councilman and the father a prominent businessperson, I'm not sure how willing the police will be to rock that boat without more evidence."

"You may have a point." She sighed at the thought

of waiting longer to see him. "Then I guess we'll have to let the anticipation build."

Heat washed over her skin as she imagined how hot things might get between them tonight.

Maybe she'd do a little prep on the erotica front by doing some reading before he arrived.

"I'll be there soon," he promised.

And even though a lot of people in her life had let her down on that score, she absolutely believed Brad when he said he'd show.

"I'll look forward to it," she purred through the phone, done with the sanding for the day.

SEXUAL URGES SURGED THROUGH him like adrenaline as he downshifted to exit the highway. He wanted to be with Nikki now. And he would damn well quiz her about that erotica dissertation to find out all the details. He'd learn what appealed to her most and then incorporate it into his personal repertoire posthaste.

He tried to shut down those thoughts as he arrived at Angelica's house—her address as easy to secure as looking in the phone book. He drove up her circular driveway, parking in front of an imposing white Tudor home with two-story columns and shiny black shutters. The overpowering aroma of her rose-lined circular driveway, complete with a burbling stone fountain, reminded him of a funeral parlor. Even though it wasn't his cup of tea, it was obvious this woman didn't need Chloe Lissander's house for any financial reasons.

The heavy brass knocker thudded loudly against a mammoth front door with glass side panels.

Within moments, a blonde teenage girl opened the

door. She wore a red-and-white cheerleader outfit emblazoned with the word *Chiefs*. She looked him up and down.

"Can I help you?" she asked, smiling flirtatiously.

"Let's start with you acting your age and end with you getting your mother."

The teenager's lower lip pouted. She strode down a gleaming marble hall screaming, "Ma!" He stood in the open doorway.

Angelica's Ked sneakers, red this time, flashed down a curved mahogany staircase. She, too, was dressed in red and white. Her warm-up suit had *Chiefs* stretched across its front, as well.

"Lieutenant Riddock, so nice to see you." She batted her lashes like a woman who'd had lots of practice. Like mother like daughter. "Won't you come in?"

She led him across the two-story foyer into a bright room with floor-to-ceiling windows and yellow, floral-patterned couches. The scent of lemony furniture polish suggested a recent cleaning.

"I'm sorry that we can't visit longer, but Emily and I have cheer practice." Angelica lifted her chin. "I'm the coach."

"This will just take a moment." Brad would have his answers.

"I appreciate that. The competition to lead a five-time National Division–winning cheer team is fierce, but we…"

Brad stared at her until she brushed imaginary lint from her pristine track suit.

She babbled on. "You can't imagine the dirty doings going on behind the smiling hurdler jumps and basket throws. I mean we don't use dagger hands for nothing."

"The dirty doings going on with Nikki are the reason I'm here," said Brad.

"I'm not sure what you mean." Angelica straightened.

"Mean-girl tricks might work in cheerleading, but they are not going to continue with Nikki," he began forcefully.

"You don't mean to suggest I threw that rock in her window?" Angelica held up her scarlet-tipped nails. "Do you really think I would jeopardize a hundred-dollar manicure?"

"No. But I think you have an idea who did. Scaring Nikki is going to stop. I expect you to tell me everything you know."

Angelica's eyebrows lifted as much as Botox allowed. "The fact that Chloe left her home to some random university professor is crazy. The house and its contents should stay in the family."

Brad looked around Angelica's far more lavish home.

"Your father is the most successful contractor in town, and your grandfather is a city councilman. Nikki said Chloe left your family her money, not that you need it. So why the opposition?"

"I'm sorry, I really need to go—"

"You need to tell me who is threatening Nikki." He brought out the military don't-eff-with-me stare. "This isn't some adolescent game."

Angelica's eyes locked with his, her expression too

frozen to read. The room was silent save for the whirring ceiling fan. Finally, she exhaled, shoulders slumped.

"Look. All I know is something I overheard between Grampy and Dad."

"And that was…?" Brad urged, thinking a woman who took as much pride in her ruthlessness and competitive drive as Angelica did would throw her family under the bus in a heartbeat. But he still couldn't imagine why she'd give a rat's ass about an eccentric author's ramshackle property.

"Something about some missing diaries and something that happened back in WWII."

"Why would they care about that?"

"All I know is that Grampy served in the war, so I think it's related somehow." She pointed to a framed black-and-white photo of a young army sergeant above her mantel.

Brad's mind buzzed. They wanted the diaries back because they revealed something that happened during the war? Something no one knew even now.

It had to be bad to warrant this level of interest. Had it been the kind of personal transgression that could break up a family? An unethical act that could taint a councilman's political career?

"Did Harold serve in Alaska—on the Aleutian Islands?"

Angelica's eyes widened. "Army Infantry. He was on Attu when American forces recaptured it. How did you know?"

Just a hunch. One that proved Eduardo and the councilman—one retired Sergeant Harold Ralston—

had crossed paths on an infamous mission during WWII. Coincidence?

Probably not, unless of course, Angelica excelled at deflecting blame. In which case, she'd be sending him on one heck of a wild goose chase.

"Thanks," he muttered to Angelica, showing himself to the door.

Brad threw himself in the Jeep and chewed up a couple of bushes in his haste to return to the house. Angelica might not be targeting Nikki to find those diaries, but someone in her family sure as hell wanted them. And without knowing what the stakes were for that person, Brad had no way of telling how far they would go to get what they wanted.

SHE WAS ALL ALONE.

Nikki felt almost guilty stealing outdoors in the late afternoon with the book of erotica in hand. What naughty intentions she had. But it was all Brad's fault.

The man had a potent physical affect on her. She felt like a different person around him. Her senses had never been more alive. The sun warmed her skin in a full body caress. The scent of cut grass hung in the air with a sweetness that made her breathe deep.

A chittering from the chipmunk's cage caught her attention, distracting her from her private destination point. She squatted for a closer look. The animal's torn ear had healthy pink edges without sign of infection or inflammation.

"Guess it's time for you to go, buddy." Nikki hoisted the metal confine and carried it down to the wooded area behind the house. Beneath a wild cherry tree, she opened the cage and backed away.

The chipmunk hesitated, cowering in the back of his cage, but before long, the call of another chipmunk tempted him outside. Soon, he scampered about with two other friends, seeming to find his place in the world.

Leaving the cage behind, Nikki ventured deeper into the woods with her book. Once, Chloe had mentioned a private wildflower meadow that held special memories for her and she hadn't made time yet to hunt it down since she'd inherited the home. She'd called it her secret garden.

Dense underbrush tickled Nikki bare legs as she hiked. Overhead, a woodpecker tapped a rotted tree, the hollow sound echoing through the woods. Gradually, the filtered light dappling her arms and face grew more intense. She burst into an open, fragrant space. Purple coneflowers, Queen Anne's lace and black-eyed Susans rippled in a delicate dance with the breeze. Monarch butterflies flitted from bloom to bloom, their beauty as colorful as their targets. Nikki inhaled the floral-scented air and wished she could bottle the heady fragrance.

In the center lay a large limestone rock in varying shades of gray and brown. Perfect for sun-bathing.

She picked her way across the meadow and stretched out on the warm stone. Cloud puffs sailed across a cerulean sky as she cracked open the book and began to read. Erotica was so much more fun when it wasn't the subject of scholarly dissection. Now, she could just imagine her and Brad in the place of the frolicking couple in her book. Her eyes drifted closed, lulled to sleep by the humming bees, warbling larks and rustling trees…

A soft caress against her cheek woke her. Brad's lustrous blue eyes gazed down at her, his dimples creasing in an incredibly hot smile. Nikki brought his head down, kissing him long and deep. She groaned as his lips possessed hers, their stroking tongues tangling.

Grabbing his wide shoulders, she pulled him on top of her. The feel of his muscular torso, powerful legs and hardening erection made her moan. She slid his hands over her sensitive breasts, desperate for his touch. When she could no longer take the mounting tension, she guided his hand lower. She spread her legs, feeling the pulsing heat of the bright afternoon sun between her hips. He stroked her slippery softness with increasing speed until she screamed, the fierceness of her release waking her.

She bolted upright and shook her head. Brad was nowhere in sight.

An erotic dream. Her first.

Yet the dampness between her thighs suggested parts of her reverie had been very real. Her cheeks flushed at the memory even as she smiled. If she and Brad ever did work on something more long-term, she could at least envision how she might get through the deployments without him. The dream had been like having him right there beside her.

Not that she was imagining some rosy future, damn it. The thought was just that—a thought.

The tall grass flattened as she jumped down. She strode from the private paradise, eager to return home and start the search for Chloe's missing diaries. After this and last night's tantalizing experiences, Nikki understood better why Chloe had exhorted her to express her sensual nature.

Chloe had been a visionary—a woman before her time who'd embraced her passion rather than suppress it. Generations later, why did Nikki struggle to do the same?

She needed to learn what made Chloe so fearless. Understanding the source of her strength might empower Nikki to take an emotional risk with Brad.

In minutes she'd reached the porch, given the nearly healed blue jay food and water, and let Killer inside. She gave him a cold drink and bowl of kibble before taking the stairs two at a time. After a quick shower and change of clothes, she grabbed one of Chloe's earliest diaries from a mahogany bookcase in the bedroom.

This one was an original, but Nikki wasn't certain how many people knew it since Chloe had sewn the binding of a dry, nineteenth-century political treatise onto the journal. She hadn't given Nikki the original diaries for her dissertation, but had assured her she'd have access to them after her death. And she'd been true to her word. Nikki has hoped to gather all the books before she sat down to read them as a set. But since she hadn't found the others yet, maybe there would be a clue as to where the missing journals were located here.

The lowering sun glowed through her eyelet lace curtains in the master bedroom. No way was she reading this indoors when spring beckoned outside. She grabbed a pillow and blanket before climbing through the gable window. It was a slippery scramble across the slate roof to a flat widow's walk encircled by an intricate, black iron fence.

Inside the enclosure, she leaned against the downy
pillow and began leafing through the journal. Much of
it was the same as the published, edited diaries she was
already so familiar with. There were no references to
Eduardo, the mystery lover, in this diary since it traced
events prior to 1943. However, as Nicky leafed through
the pages, a yellowed scrap of paper fluttered loose from
the book. At first, she thought she'd found an old letter.
But as she opened it, she realized she'd found a misplaced diary entry from one of the volumes they were
missing.

The entry was dated April, 1943.

Dear Diary,
Eduardo's last letter filled me with longing. He
asked for letters to keep him warm, despite having
left me too innocent to write such heated words. I
have yet to reply, afraid my inexperienced scrib-
bling will be all wrong.

Today, I stumbled upon the means to ending
that ignorance in the most unexpected and plea-
surable way. As usual, I finished my afternoon
stroll at the secret garden meadow, picking a
wildflower bouquet. I rested on the rock, the si-
lent witness to our final tryst. The copper veins
running through the gray stone reminded me of
Eduardo's bronzed skin. How it glistened in the
sun when he'd doffed his uniform shirt!

He'd begged me to stop as I traced the firm
squares of his stomach with a white daisy. I
wanted to make him break his pledge to keep me
pure until our wedding—a secret event I dare only

share with you, Diary. How I wished to be that flower, especially when it dipped beneath his belt buckle. The effect was immediate. He sat up as if stung, breathing hard. How could a simple flower evoke such a powerful response?

Impulsively, I decided to recreate that moment, hoping to alleviate my yearning. I stepped out of my dress, unrolled my stockings and lay on the rock, twirling a wild red rose—the rest of my bouquet scattered around me.

My stomach quivered at the soft touch of the flower petals against my bare skin. No wonder Eduardo had gasped when I'd done the same to him. My pulse quickened. I traced the bloom up my rib cage and stopped, wondering if I dared go farther. I unhooked my bra, imagining Eduardo's strong hands on my back. My breasts sprang free, as if seeking his touch. I blushed hot at the thought of him fondling them, cupping their heavy fullness.

I brushed the rose against each quivering nipple, pretending his fingers brought me this intense pleasure. A tightening began in my lower abdomen, tempting me to bring the flower lower where I wanted it most. As I rested it on my sensitive inner thighs, a loud groan tore the quiet country air. I was amazed the crude sound was mine! I inched the rose higher, eliciting another wail in the back of my throat. What a relief that Eduardo hadn't witnessed me in such a state. Yet perhaps this is what he wants to hear in my letters after all.

When the silken petals brushed my most

intimate place, it forced the breath from my lungs. Never had such fierce delight overtaken me. A deep, desperate craving for more instantly followed. I widened my legs and began tracing the flower along damp, tender flesh. Quickening pants erupted with every silken stroke. Eventually, the rose broke under the passionate pressure. Unable to stop, my hand took over. I imagined Eduardo's touch instead of mine.

Within moments, exquisite release swept over me, shaking me to my very core. I shrieked in mindless bliss as tremors of ecstasy rippled through my womb. When the spasms ceased, I lay upon the rock as limp as a dishrag hung out to dry.

This, then, was how I'd made Eduardo feel on our last day together. What torture he'd endured! If I knew the frantic need such innocent actions created, I would have insisted we reach this fiery fulfillment together. I will not miss such an opportunity with him again.

I hunger for his return, ready to share these delights. Our time apart reminds me of the frenzied moments before today's ecstatic release—full of pleasure, longing, need and desperation. Such tortuous feelings heighten the thrill of fulfillment. Separation will be the spice that sweetens our time together.

I must go and write Eduardo. My letter will be hot enough to melt glaciers! Let's hope he keeps it safe from you-know-who. If my parents found out about Eduardo, they'd lock me in a convent—and

*undoubtedly ban me from the forest. Both would
be terrible fates—for I have many fantasies to play
out in the meadow until my love returns.
Good night, dearest Diary.*

A secret wedding? Nikki wondered if it had ever
taken place. Not once had Chloe mentioned Eduardo or
any engagement. Had she hidden such a thing the whole
time Nikki had known her? She took a deep breath and
shuddered. Once more her life had strangely paralleled
Chloe's.

If rocks could talk…

She peered through the bars of the widow's walk,
seeking signs of Brad. He would want to know about
the diary entry. But instead of the rumble of a Jeep's
engine, she heard only a weak meow whispered down
from above. Nikki squinted through the dense white oak
towering over her. Finally, she spotted it, nearly a good
fifty feet from the ground. On a branch narrower than
her wrist clung a tiny ginger kitten.

A wind gust buffeted the limb. The kitten held on,
swaying perilously.

Nikki's hand rose to her mouth, panicked at the
kitty's dangerous predicament. She had no idea if she
was strong enough to climb that high. And if she did
reach it, would her weight send them both tumbling?

Nikki stepped over the low wrought-iron railing. A
slate shingle slid beneath her foot and dropped over the
edge. She flinched as it shattered into pieces three stories
below.

Another desperate meow sounded. Nikki inhaled
deeply, grabbed hold of the nearest ranch, and peered

up. The kitten seemed so far away. He must be hungry to scale those heights in search of food.

"Don't worry," she called with more confidence than she felt. "I'm coming." As if understanding, the kitten meowed even louder.

Where was a hero when she needed one?

As if on cue, Brad's Jeep swerved into view.

10

BRAD'S TIRES CRUNCHED over fragmented stone as he screeched to a halt. This mess of gray rock hadn't been here this morning. Had Nikki been working on another project? Or had someone been here causing more damage?

He took the porch steps in one bound and slammed through the screen door.

Why had she left it unlocked when someone was out to cause trouble for her?

"Nikki!" he shouted from the living room. Book piles littered the floor, unchanged to his trained eye. The plywood-covered front window was still intact—but that didn't mean an intruder hadn't strolled right through the front door.

Brad ran his hands through his closely cropped hair, tugging the short strands in frustration. Did she not grasp the danger she faced? Maybe hearing Angelica's news would make her take things more seriously. Either way, dead bolts were going on the doors tomorrow.

He raced to the kitchen. Killer wagged his scruffy tail, but barely lifted his head from a bowl of dog food, his ears flopping on the sides to drag on the floor. Nikki's keys, cell phone and beach bag lay on the table. She had to be home, so why couldn't she hear him?

His protective instincts shifted into overdrive. He flipped open her cell, scanning for clues—like more threatening texts.

He swore when he read this morning's message.

Those bastards. As if he would leave Nikki alone and unprotected. Brad vowed her crisis would be resolved before he left. And when he finished with the responsible parties, *they'd* wish they'd had more protection.

But why hadn't Nikki shared it with him?

Upstairs, he checked her bedroom. A yellow terry-cloth robe sprawled across the bottom of her white, four-poster bed. Open drawers spilling tops and shorts suggested she'd dressed quickly.

Had she heard an intruder? Gotten an unexpected visitor?

As he turned to go downstairs, he heard more stone shatter in the still, early evening air. Instinctively, he ducked, then sprang to the window.

At the edge of an unstable slate roof perched Nikki, her fingers wrapped around an overhead branch barely within reach. In attempting to keep her balance, she must have sent the tile flying. That at least explained the mess in her driveway.

His breath caught at the precariousness of her position. Given the degree she leaned out from the rooftop, she had nowhere to go but down.

"Nikki," he called softly. "Don't turn and don't let go. I'm coming for you."

She nodded but otherwise remained silent. Probably

frozen in fear. Why would she do something so crazy? Had someone threatened her, forced her out here?

He slipped out the window. His sneakers slid slightly on the tiled surface. Another part of the old house that needed work. One wrong move and he might send them both flying.

He reached her in three heart-pounding steps.

"On the count of three, you'll feel my arms around you. Then, and only then, will you let go, pushing backward with your feet at the same time. Got it?" he directed.

"I can't," she whispered.

"Yes, you can." He'd used the same tone with edgy insurgents. Calm, authoritative. "I won't let you fall. You're a hundred percent safe."

A stiff breeze picked up, rustling the oak canopy.

Brad swore inwardly as Nikki swayed with the branch, one of her feet momentarily losing contact with the roof.

"Actually, I'm not trying to get back to the roof." Her dark curls bounced as she nodded upward. "I was on my way out to get the kitten."

For the first time, Brad heard a soft meow from above. Was she risking her life for an animal? He pictured the blue jay and chipmunk. She was serious.

Time to change strategies.

He peered through the tree limbs to find the kitten's location. It wasn't too far above her head. And he could hardly argue with her obstinate compulsion to help those in danger. They had more in common than great sex.

He'd take care of this crisis himself—as soon as he'd secured Nikki.

"I see it." He took off his shoes as he prepared to go out on a limb. "And if you let go when I grab you, I promise to go after it. Okay?"

"Thanks, Brad."

"Ready?"

She nodded.

"One. Two. Three." He grabbed her by the waist as she let go. Their combined backward momentum sent them sprawling against the hard roof. For a few heart-stopping moments they lay against the cold stone roof, Nikki flung over his chest.

Reminding him why he'd rushed over here like a bat out of hell. Not just to tell her what he'd found out at Angelica's. But to strip all her clothes off and bury himself deep inside her.

She squirmed to his side then sat up, clearly thinking about cat rescue more than sex right now. As another frantic *meow* floated down, he knew he needed to get moving.

He half walked, half slid to the roof edge, grabbed the nearby branch and vaulted up.

"Be careful," she called.

He didn't respond. This operation required focus and daring. Being careful would only keep him on the ground.

NO MAN SHE'D EVER KNOWN would have done this for her. Nikki hadn't dated widely, but she hadn't been a nun either. And thinking back over the guys who'd been in her life, she was certain none of them would have res-cued a cat fifty feet up on a swaying oak limb. None of them had understood how important it was to her to take in a stray that might otherwise be forgotten. Alone.

She'd already dashed into the pantry for some pet food and milk for the poor little thing, laying the bowls at the foot of the bed for when Brad saved the animal.

"Hey, kitty," Brad called. He stretched, full out, along a limb above her that didn't look any thicker than his arm. It dipped with his weight but seemed to be holding, for the moment. Just out of reach huddled the miniature beige-and-white-striped feline.

She saw him extend his hand, his fingertips just brushing the kitten's branch.

"Wouldn't you like to come with me? We have warm milk inside," he coaxed.

The kitten's ears pitched forward, listening.

"Come here, kitty. Come on."

Another breeze sent Brad and the kitten gliding through the air. Nikki covered her mouth to keep in a cry of dismay, waiting for one or both to tumble to the ground. Miraculously, they held on. When the wind stilled, the kitten inched closer, sniffing Brad's finger. He held up his hand and the kitten butted its head against it. Instantly, Brad snatched the young animal, holding it gently by the scruff of the neck.

Her relief suddenly turned to concern. It dawned on Nikki that Brad's one-handed descent would be far more dangerous than his climb. Fearlessly, he swung and dropped from limb to limb with agility even an Olympic gymnast would envy. Within moments, he reached the roof.

The ungrateful animal clawed its way free and leapt through the open window to safety in her bedroom.

Straight to the bowls she'd laid out. The ginger kitten dug in, winding its tiny tail around its body to devour the meal. She'd just adopted a new pet.

"You're a hero." Nikki flung herself in Brad's arms, eager to give him a proper thank-you. Relief and gratitude mingled with all the other things she felt for Brad—warmth, attraction, admiration…it was starting to form one heck of a powerful package of emotions.

She rubbed the bunching back muscles beneath his snug, army-issue tank. How could a woman express herself in the face of his completely unselfish act? "Thank you." She wanted to make sure he understood how much she appreciated what he'd done.

"You're welcome." He breathed the words over her mouth before brushing another kiss along her lips. "I locked the door downstairs if you're ready to shower me with gratitude."

"Mmm." She pressed herself to him fully, loving the feel of his toned, hard body.

"Come on." He tugged her back into the house as the twilight shadows deepened.

Nikki let herself be led, more than ready for him after allowing the anticipation to build all afternoon. She toppled him to the bed as she dropped inside the window, landing on the four poster with more eagerness than finesse.

"I had a dream about you today," she confided, her skin tingling with hunger and memories.

"Please say this dream ended with us naked," he murmured, already nibbling her sensitive earlobe. Electricity sizzled along her neck.

"At the start, I was in a secret meadow, thinking about

us," she began, trying to shrug out of her tank top to provide him greater access.

"You're starting at the beginning of the dream? You have a habit of making me wait." Brad's tongue traveled a serpentine path to her jaw and throat.

She almost tore her own shirt off. "I pulled you on top of me."

"Like this?" Brad stretched out over her in a single, fluid motion.

She rolled her hips against his and arched her spine. He'd hardly arrived and she was already so keyed up she couldn't think.

His hands tangled in her hair. His teeth found the neckline of her tank top and yanked down enough to expose the swell of her breast.

Suddenly the sun slipped away, leaving them in near darkness.

Not that Nikki needed to see Brad's raw masculine appeal to enjoy it. The feel of his shifting shoulder muscles made her shiver with pleasure. His lean, six-pack stomach pressed firmly against hers. Solidly muscular thighs settled with a satisfying heaviness between her thighs.

Erotic dreams and the touch of flower petals had nothing on this. Right now, she wanted to feel the strength and power of him, to revel in the all the hard planes of his body.

He lifted his mouth from her breast long enough to peel her shirt off. She helped him by opening the front clasp of her bra, feeling the cool night air rush against her exposed breasts from the open window. Her fingers tangled in Brad's hair as she guided him toward them, feeling deep satisfaction as he suckled each one long and hard.

She licked a path along his shoulder, savoring the taste of him. The clean scent of soap mingled with the musky hint of male. She nipped him with her teeth and then shivered as he returned the favor on the underside of her breast. Slick heat built between her thighs. Her hips gyrated against the exhilarating stiffness of his lengthy manhood, eliciting a ragged sigh from Brad.

"You feel good," Brad whispered against her chest. He mapped the deep valley between her breasts with his hands before traveling lower to the edge of her jean shorts. He unsnapped and pulled them to her ankles in one hard tug.

Vaguely, she thought she ought to halt him since he deserved all the sensual attention tonight. But then his teeth locked on the lace of her panties and she couldn't have moved if she'd tried. His breath caressed her hip bone. He pulled the lace down, down. She wriggled to help him inch the fabric off, needing to be naked for him.

More than ready for what came next.

He shouldered his way between her thighs, making a place for himself there. She twisted helplessly against the pillow, a willing prisoner of his hands on her hips and his…mouth.

His kiss came hard and unrelenting, a deep stroke of his tongue into the heart of her. She came instantly, shattering so fast he had to hold her to keep her together. Or at least she felt like he did. Her whole body convulsed and swayed, bucking against him as he worked every last spasm from her.

She was pretty sure she didn't remember her own name by the time he was done. The aftershocks went on and on, shivering up her nerve endings in a slow, sensuous dance each time.

By the time he lifted himself off her and ditched his shorts, she was drowning in endorphins and driven by the need to give him every bit as much pleasure as he'd given her.

Reaching across the bed, she retrieved a condom from her nightstand drawer and opened the packet with shaky hands still trembling from the overdose of feel-good action in her neurons.

Straddling him, she rolled the sheath slowly down his straining erection. Then, positioning him right where she wanted him, she guided him inside—only slightly. She suspended herself for a moment, letting anticipation build.

She leaned over and licked a flat nipple. His pectoral muscles tightened beneath her mouth. And as much as she wanted to slide down the length of him to take him deep inside her, she knew it was important to savor rather than rush. Gently, she swayed her hips, letting the heat crank up all over again.

His gasps mingled with her sighs. She felt a trail of sweat on Brad's chest and she knew the effort to hold back cost him, as well.

On instinct, she lowered herself swiftly, burying him within her. He guided her upward then pulled her down, the friction impossibly good.

She undulated her hips, prolonging their enjoyment. But then Brad's hand cupped a breast while the other stroked her mound and she knew she didn't have much time left. Exquisite pleasure sizzled through her. She bucked wildly against him with abandon. His powerful hips thrust upward to meet her, driving him impossibly deeper each time.

She didn't know how long they were locked together that way, but soon, an uncontrollable, shuddering contraction racked her. In the next instant, Brad stiffened and found his release, his shout of satisfaction driving her higher.

When she'd wrung every ounce of pleasure she could from them both, Nikki collapsed against him, nearly unconscious. It was several minutes before she realized he spoke.

A deep sigh of satisfaction escaped her as she nestled against the strong, muscular planes of his chest. Exhaustion overtook her. She struggled to keep her eyes open. There was something she needed to say.

"Thank you," she whispered.

His sexy baritone filled her ear.

"You are incredible." Brad's arms tightened around her.

She knew there were things they both needed to say. Important things. But right now, the moment was too perfect to do anything besides hold each other. And Brad seemed to agree; he pulled a corner of the quilt over her shoulder and held her while she drifted toward sleep. It was the most beautiful evening she could remember.

Until the sound of gunfire split the night.

11

IT WASN'T THE FIRST TIME Brad had awakened to gun-shots.

He knifed out of bed and yanked on shorts. Nikki stared at him with wide, frightened eyes, the whites so saucer-round he could see them in the moonlit bed-room.

"Call the police," he spoke softly, still listening to whatever was happening outside. The view from outside the upstairs window didn't reveal any activity, just the dark sweep of leaves blowing in a soft spring breeze. "I'm going to check downstairs. Stay up here and lock the door."

She nodded jerkily, already pushing buttons on her cell phone.

Another shot rang out and he identified an odd sort of pistol. An antique weapon maybe? As he pounded down the stairs and through the living room, he wished he could remember the training he'd had on gun acoustics better. He'd learned to differentiate an M-4 shot from an M-16, but he couldn't tell much about the quick blast that had sounded somewhere close to Nikki's house.

He burst outside, desperate to get some kind of visual or to at least gauge where the shots had been fired from. He didn't even know if they were aiming toward the house or if some wing nut could be attempting target practice in the dark. But his gut told him Nikki was at risk.

He stood still on the patio for a moment, listening. The screen door banged behind him, echoing through the night. Perhaps it was that sound that startled the unwanted visitor because a moment later, a truck engine fired to life.

Brad's feet churned up the ground as he tore off to the east, toward the fading rumble. He couldn't even discern the outline of the truck, but the dull gleam of the dark paint job and a glint of chrome gave him the impression of a newer model vehicle. Midsize. The license plates had been removed, leaving a blank void where they ought to be.

The bright white Chiefs bumper sticker remained intact, however. Giving Brad a damn good clue where to look next.

AN HOUR LATER, AFTER the police pulled out of the driveway, Nikki had to drag Brad back into the old farmhouse to keep him from driving over to Angelica's house for a little frontier justice.

Or, at the very least, to see what kinds of cars lurked in her garages.

"Did you see the way those cops shut down at the mention of the Ralston name?" he fumed, glaring through the sagging screen door in the direction the law enforcement officers had driven. "They're not going to take on the town's big dogs."

Brad had asked the officers to look into the where-abouts of Angelica's family that night, citing the Chiefs bumper sticker and his conversation with the woman earlier in which he'd pressed for more information about who in the family might be out to get Chloe. Privately, Brad had told Nikki that Angelica had admitted her grandfather had served on a mission in the northern Pacific, probably at the same time as Chloe's mysterious Eduardo. But their exchange had been cut short by the investigators and she still wasn't sure what to make of that information.

Nikki called to Killer before she locked up for the night. The dog raced through the screen door as she held it open, his nails skidding on the hardwood before he slowed his pace.

"Maybe they were just being diplomatic. They can't appear to take sides, right? And a city councilman in a small town can be very influential, so it's not surprising they'd be cautious where he's concerned." She rubbed a hand on her arm to ward off a chill. She'd thrown on a hoodie with a pair of pajama pants for the pow-wow on the lawn after the shooter had driven away, but they hadn't been enough to prevent the evening from giving her goosebumps.

The chill had more to do with someone wanting her out of the house badly enough to fire shots at the place than any reaction to the spring temperature.

"Right." There could be no mistaking the strong taint of sarcasm in his response. He punched the butcher-block countertop in the kitchen while she shut off the lights. "I'm telling you, the only way we're going to get to the bottom of this is to find the diaries and see what secret Chloe sat on her whole life. I can't believe if it was that damn important, her family wouldn't have harassed her more while she was alive. Not that I wish they'd done that, but why the big press to find the books now?"

Nikki warmed inside at the fierceness of his tone, far too swayed by his he-man protectiveness. In fact, she was pretty sure her heart fluttered a little. Truly.

Fluttered.

"I don't know. Maybe her family thought the diaries would be lost forever once they heard she'd been diagnosed with dementia. Perhaps they assumed she would forget where they were hidden and the books would never see the light of day. Which is sort of what happened, except they hadn't counted on me inheriting the house and having access to search for them." She twined her fingers through his and urged him toward the stairs. "But I discovered today that I didn't know Chloe as well as I thought I did. I started reading one of the original diaries and a misplaced entry from the missing 1943 volume fell out of the pages."

"You have some of the original diaries here?" He stopped on the third step near a painting of the Seine that Chloe had purchased from a street artist on a long-ago trip to Paris. "And you've never read them?"

"Chloe showed them to me ages ago. But I never read them because they were personal. She didn't publish them unedited when she was alive because of the private nature of the contents."

"Maybe the big mystery is hidden in the diaries you

already have." He started up the steps again. "Are they up in your bedroom?"

"Yes, but—" She hurried to follow him as he passed her. Quickly, she explained the revelation about a secret engagement to Eduardo. "So I'm beginning to think the edited diaries might vary quite a bit from the versions she first penned."

They hurried down the hall, past an old mannequin wearing a negligee that would have been suggestive in its time.

"No doubt." Brad dropped onto the bed where they'd made love just a few hours ago, now occupied by the sleeping ginger kitten he'd rescued from the oak tree. "Do you think her family even knows now about an engagement to this Eduardo guy? Could there be any reason they'd want to lock that down?"

He cracked open the journal that Nikki had already read while she rounded up four others that had been hidden behind the covers of various books Chloe kept on her shelves.

"This isn't the forties. What taboos could there be about a marriage that would bother anyone in this day and age?" She stacked up the other diaries on the bed and sat down next to Brad to read. "I don't think that's it."

Nikki wished she'd quizzed Chloe about the journals a little more, but the older woman had been so distracted at the end and Nikki hadn't wanted to press.

An hour of side by side reading passed before Brad's cell phone rang, startling them both and sending the recently rescued ginger kitten diving under a pillow.

"Riddock," he barked into the phone. A long silence

followed as he listened. "Of course we're pressing charges," he shot back finally. "If anything, the kid is probably guilty of a whole slew more of—"

His jaw went rigid as the party on the other line— a police officer, obviously—cut him off. Nikki stared down at the passage in Chloe's journal that he'd been reading before the call came—the scene of self-discovery in the meadow that she'd read earlier. He said little else before disconnecting the call.

"They found the person who fired the shots?"

She didn't realize she felt cold all over again until Brad pulled her hip next to his, wrapping her in one arm.

"They're saying it was Angelica's daughter and her boyfriend."

"Emily? The cheerleader?" Nikki found it hard to believe. "I'm being harassed by a high school junior?"

"Apparently the boyfriend is a track star who 'borrowed' the starting pistol from the school to make the sound of gunfire. But since it's a closed barrel weapon, there was no possibility of injury and the police encouraged us to let them off with a warning. At most, they could receive a misdemeanor for violating local noise ordinances."

"They weren't interested in asking the kids about the threatening text messages or the brick through the window?" As much as she'd like to think she'd been a victim of teenage mischief gone too far, it seemed rooted deeper than that.

"The boyfriend drives a brand-spanking-new Ford F-150, so it definitely wasn't the old pickup that tore up the yard."

Nikki stared unseeing down at Chloe's journal in her lap as she thought about the dismissive attitude of the police. Even if the kids hadn't been the ones to tear up the lawn, they were joyriding, shooting off things that could be mistaken for gunshots—what if some poor scared homeowner shot back? Wasn't there a zero tolerance policy for underage kids with things that clearly looked like guns? Rules should be rules no matter how rich your daddy was.

"My head's too foggy for this," she announced, slamming the book closed in her frustration. "We've been puzzling over this for too long and it should be simpler. If Chloe didn't reveal what happened to those original diaries in the first place, she must have felt some sort of security that I'd find them without her help, right?"

Brad shrugged. "You knew her a lot better than me."

Nikki nodded. "I don't want to waste my time left with you by talking about ancient history. I feel like I've shared my whole life with you these last few days and I hardly know anything about you besides the fact that you're a kick-butt volleyball player and you can climb tree branches like Tarzan."

Shuffling aside the stacks of leather-bound volumes, she lay down on the rumpled white chenille bedspread, plucking the kitten from its resting place to resettle the animal under her chin.

Brad switched off the bedside Tiffany lamp so that only the moonlight and the glowing numbers from a bedside clock lit the room. Her heartbeat jumped and skipped at the sensation of having him here, in her bed, all to herself. Last night had been fueled by a need to take a risk and indulge her pleasures for the sake of feeling fully alive and uninhibited. Earlier today she'd been overwhelmed by gratitude at what he'd done for her in rescuing the kitten. But right now, there was no urgency. No rush to prove anything to herself.

Just a room ripe with the possibility for intimacy.

"Don't forget my mad skills with a tractor," he prompted, reaching toward the bedside table to retrieve something.

A daisy from the wildflower bouquet she'd collected on her walk this afternoon.

He held it over her, allowing a droplet of water from the stem to fall on the skin bared above the zipper teeth of her hoodie. The bead rolled down into the hollow at the base of her throat.

"Brad?" Did he know he was dripping flower water on her? By the way he held the stem, poised and steady above her, she'd say yes.

"Hmm?" He scooped up the kitten with his other hand and tucked it onto a pillow on the floor.

"What are you doing?" She noticed the flower stem never wavered even with all his maneuvering.

"I'm helping you get to know me better."

Drip.

"How so?" The droplets warmed against her skin, then rolled down the side of her neck, pooling somewhere along the base of her scalp.

"I'm making sure that the next time you list the things you know about me, you include something like 'Sexual Dynamo.'" He said it with a perfectly straight face.

As if he really felt his bedroom prowess was on par in importance with his military training or his strong sense of honor. Maybe she knew more about him than she gave herself credit for.

"And covering me with flower water will help your cause?" She decided to feign ignorance of what he had in mind. It served him right when she had the strong suspicion he'd led the conversation away from himself very purposely.

Dropping the stem to the zipper on her sweatshirt, he used it to lower the teeth inch by inch. Slowly, he revealed the lace-and-silk bra she'd wriggled into after the gunfire sounded. Then, popping the zipper free at the base, he skimmed the flower petals along the tops of her breasts.

He brushed the petals down onto the navy blue lace of her bra, circling the nipple so lightly she began to fully appreciate his intent. He meant to recreate the scene in the diary. The sensual encounter in the secret garden meadow.

She would have smiled if she hadn't been frozen in place by the erotic tease of such a delicate touch when the heavy heat of Brad's hands waited so close by— restrained by his need to build anticipation.

Instead, a gasp caught in her throat, a soft inhalation that whispered against her lips. Her eyes slid closed, her body focused on the trail of the silky soft petals along her skin.

Being distracted had never been such a pleasure.

BRAD PROMISED HIMSELF he'd talk to Nikki more later. That way, he didn't have to feel like he was being purposely evasive.

Right now, he just wanted to stock up on memories

with her to take with him when he left in ten days. After reading the scene in the meadow that Chloe had written—and knowing that Nikki had dreamed about him in that very same spot today—he wanted to implant himself in that moment somehow. He couldn't be there with her earlier, but he could give her the sensual thrills for real that she'd only imagined. When they were half a world apart, he wanted to know he'd imprinted himself in her memory in every way possible.

"I think you need to be more naked for the full impact," he observed as she strained against the clothing he'd left on her.

Setting aside the flower, he tugged down the straps of her bra before he unhooked it. He was careful not to touch her too much because his restraint couldn't be trusted. If he started, he might not be able to stop.

The lace cups fell away from her breasts and his mouth went dry. He'd never get tired of seeing her.

"Just keep in mind that turnabout is fair play." She undid the ties on her pajama pants for him, the sound of silk sliding through her fingers like a sigh.

"I'm very aware." He allowed himself one kiss just below her navel, his tongue darting across her skin for a taste while he shoved the filmy fabric down her legs. He straightened to find her panties—

Absent?

He swallowed his tongue. Her body was utterly perfect in the moonlight, her breasts puckering for his kiss. Her legs parted just enough to give him room there.

"You went commando," he finally managed, the word pushed from a dry throat as he fought the urge to cover her.

"I dressed in a hurry," she reminded him, smoothing her palm down her hip and halting just above the cradle of her thighs.

He watched, mesmerized, as her fingers played over her skin. Then, recalling her threat about turning the tables, he put the daisy stem in her hand.

"Why don't you show me where you want me first?" He'd have to work up to teasing her with the flower when he wasn't plagued with this fierceness to have her. As it was, his pulse slammed through his veins harder than if he was facing down a booby-trapped bomb.

She surprised him by skimming the petals higher. Higher. Finally landing on her lips to circle her mouth.

"Oh, yeah, I want that, too." Leaning over her, he claimed her mouth in a hungry, possessive kiss. He stroked her tongue with long, sinuous licks, savoring her like the last of an ice cream cone.

She followed his movements with her own, her fingers clamping around his neck to keep him close. He inhaled her. Devoured her. And she writhed under him impatiently, arching her back to graze her breasts against him.

With superhuman effort, he forced himself back, inserting some space between them on the bed.

"Where else, Nikki?" He gazed down into her dark, slumberous eyes glittering in the moon glow. "Where else should I touch you?"

The daisy had grown a little bedraggled, crushed between them during the kiss. But she splayed the petals against her neck and rubbed them along her throat, lingering at the soft depression at the base.

He leaned forward, eager to follow through. Dying for another taste of her. But she placed her palm on his chest and held him back with gentle force. Confused, he saw her continue the flower's journey. Lower. Lower.

His head swam.

He had a vague impression of her circling back up to the rosy pink crests of her breasts, but by then, he was already on her. He slid his thigh between hers, bracketing her hips with his hands to keep her steady. He kissed her neck, taking a straight line to the deep cleavage between her breasts. She smelled like flowers and meadows, soap and sex. He'd only known her a short time, but he'd recognize the scent of her anywhere.

He couldn't kiss her enough and shed his clothes, too, but he made a hell of an effort at both. She helped him, her hands shoving away his shirt and hauling down his shorts whenever his attention lingered too long on her. He throbbed to be inside her, his erection straining to painful lengths. She helped him there, too, pulling a whole strand of condoms off the nightstand until she managed to tear off one and roll it over him.

"I can't wait," she pleaded in his ear, her words a strange manifestation of what he'd just been thinking himself.

Palming her thigh, he shifted her where he wanted her, his thumb grazing the damp, pulsing heart of her sex. She rolled her hips toward him in blatant invitation and he plunged deep. Hard.

Their shout of satisfaction mingled into one sound and he stayed there, buried inside her, for a long, hot moment. He cupped her face in his hand, needing to connect with her in every way possible. The commune that went on there was wordless but profound. He could have lost himself in her dark gaze. Breaking the moment with a blink, he slowly withdrew from her, only to return harder. Deeper.

They danced together that way for endless moments, as if time stopped to give them the gift of the night. He wrapped her in his arms and rolled her on top of him, wanting to see her, poised above him with her dark hair tousled in a wild, silken tangle, her lips full and red from his kisses, a slight sheen on her skin.

She was more than beautiful. She was The One.

The realization startled him almost as much as her sudden arch against him, her body racking in spasms so hard he could feel them squeeze his release from him in turn. His breath left his body in a whoosh and he wasn't sure if it was ever coming back. But the grand finale she'd wrung from him was so amazing he couldn't find it in himself to care.

For long minutes they lay beside each other in the half light, breathing in the cool spring air blowing in the open window. He wasn't sure what to say next. The moment seemed so fragile and so ripe for shared declarations neither of them were ready to make yet.

If anything, the connection he'd felt to her scared the hell out of him when he didn't have his head screwed on straight and didn't know what the future held for him— professionally or personally. Too late, he understood Doc Leonard had been right and that Brad should have been focusing on getting to know her better—and not just in the physical sense.

Funny that he'd initiated sex because he hadn't been ready to share anything more about himself when she'd wanted to talk. Yet what they'd just shared had somehow tied them together more deeply than he could even begin to comprehend.

And as scared as he was of screwing up with her and sending her running, he realized he couldn't avoid the inevitable any longer. Not with a woman who'd given herself to him the way Nikki just had.

Come hell or high water, he'd at least give her what she'd asked for.

"I couldn't defuse a bomb fast enough." He hated trotting out his baggage for a woman he really didn't want to send running. "That's what happened to my leg."

The trees outside the window creaked and moaned in the gathering wind, the overgrown branches scraping the window screen like fingernails on chalkboard. Or maybe it was just because the truth raked him raw that the sound went right through him like that.

"Is that why you had a nightmare on the futon?" She lay very still beside him, staring up at the ceiling as the cool breeze blew through the room. "Because of that bomb?"

"Pretty much. The explosive in the dream is a little different. The circumstances more muted. But I know what it means. It started coming to me right after that accident."

"You've had it more than once?" She sounded concerned, and she hadn't even heard about the Iraqi farmer or his kid yet.

His chest hurt and he had to tell himself not to be such a candy ass. His leg would heal. He had to keep in perspective how lucky he'd been.

"I've had it a lot," he admitted, able to tell her the

truth since she wasn't the one who had to sign off on the papers that would clear him to go back to work. "But last night, I didn't have it when I was with you. I've been seeing a shrink—that is, a psychiatrist—and he seems to want to know I've gotten over those dreams before I return to Iraq."

If she thought seeing the doc made him a head case, she hid it well. She turned toward him, settling her head on his biceps in a way that felt…nice.

"You must have been very fortunate not to have been hurt worse. As the guy defusing the explosive, you're obviously the closest person to it, right?"

He closed his eyes; seeing that day vividly behind his eyelids, he wrenched them back open again.

"Yes. But we have protective gear. I'd suited up to check out the bomb. It wouldn't have been a big deal except—" His throat caught on a dry note. "There were civilians nearby."

"Oh, God." Her hand flew to her mouth. "There were other casualties?"

"No deaths." He tried to remind himself of that, but sometimes the farmer's fate had felt worse than a death if he hadn't received good medical treatment. Or if he couldn't figure out how to adapt with only one arm. But since meeting James, he had at least a little ray of optimism for how some people made that work. "But there was a kid nearby, a boy I'd befriended other times when I was off the base. I tried to tell him to go, but with the language barrier and everything splitting my attention, his father had to come out to the field to haul him away. The kid was fine, but his father lost his arm."

She covered her eyes as if she couldn't bear the vision

that created for her. And yeah, he totally understood how that felt. He was sweating even though he wasn't hot, the ceiling fan clicking overhead not doing him a damn bit of good. If he wasn't careful, the shakes would kick in soon.

"How awful for all of you." Her hand slid away and her eyes glistened with unshed tears when she met his gaze. "For you. For the boy. For the dad." She shook her head in mute sympathy. "But thank God that boy was okay and the father saved him in time."

It hadn't occurred to him to thank God for any part of that hellish day. His muscles eased a fraction even though he still felt nauseous.

"The kid had to see the whole thing." He couldn't get past that part. That and the fact that the boy had been there because of Brad in the first place. "He was in that field to see me. Because we were pals after I'd seen him around town a few times."

"You're so good with kids." She brushed her fingers along his chest and then laid her hand there, over his heart. "And I'm sure you can imagine exactly how that farmer felt seeing his boy in danger. He was ready to sacrifice his life for his son, as any good parent would be. But he'll walk away from that injury and have more days to be with his boy. If you ask him, I'll bet he's thankful at how it turned out."

Brad wasn't so sure he agreed. He hadn't even brought up the fact that the guy might not have had good medical care afterward. He just didn't know. But Nikki had shown him a different perspective on the day. If a bomb threatened Nate, hell yes, Brad would gladly throw himself between the kid and danger. It felt different to be the hero though, than the guy who'd failed to defuse the bomb in time.

He closed his eyes, weary of the dream and the past that he could never set right. A moment he'd never be able to change.

"I hear what you're saying," he told her finally, glad to at least have shared it with her. He hadn't told anybody else but the shrink and that had only been because he'd had no choice. "But I'm not quite there yet as far as dealing with it goes."

She reached over him to plant a kiss on his cheek.

"You're an amazing man. And you do a job that would scare most people out of their shoes. Thank you." She eased back down to tuck into the cradle of his arm, her dark hair blanketing him in silky curls. "I hope tomorrow you'll tell me all about the explosives you disarmed successfully. I'll bet there are lots more of those."

There were. He just hadn't thought about those in quite a while.

As Nikki's breathing turned into a slow, even rhythm, his chest slowly eased. She hadn't been horror stricken or run screaming when he told her. She even behaved as if he still had something to offer.

Maybe he really could kick the nightmares and get on top of the memories before he returned. Trouble was, between the incredible sex and the warmth in his chest that he felt after talking to her just now, he had a whole new fear churning around in his gut.

He was falling for the last woman on the planet who would want to be with a military man for more than a heated affair. And wasn't that just a bomb of another kind altogether?

12

NIKKI AWOKE WITH A START, heart beating fast.

Ears straining in the darkness just before dawn, she wondered what had disturbed her. Another gunshot? Brad saying something in his sleep? But no, the world was quiet all around her. Her gorgeous hunk of a military man slept soundly by her side, a sight that touched her heart all the more knowing that he had trouble sleeping peacefully because of the awful dreams.

Not wanting to wake him, she tucked the quilt higher on his shoulder and remained still. His adopted dog—soon to be her adopted dog, no doubt—snoozed in a ball between their feet at the end of the bed. The ginger kitten was tucked up against Killer's belly, chin on her paws.

Lying back on her pillow, Nikki stared up at the exposed-beam ceiling and struggled to recall what had brought her awake so suddenly. A dream, she recalled.

She'd been dreaming about the wildflower meadow…

That's it!

She gasped, excitement surging through her veins at

the realization that had just blasted through her brainwaves.

He rolled over toward her automatically, apparently having heard her sharp intake of breath. His arm wrapped around her waist to draw her closer. Her skin tingled in response before she remembered she couldn't indulge herself right now.

"I'm sorry to disturb you." She wriggled back a little before she got caught up in the feel of him. "Go back to sleep."

"What is it?" He sat up, instantly alert, and she cursed herself for bothering him. "I'm awake."

When it become obvious he wasn't falling back to sleep, she figured there was no harm in sharing the news.

"I just realized I know where the missing diaries are."

"You found them in the middle of the night?" He peered around as if expecting to see the volumes.

Killer yawned and stretched before sighing and dropping his head back down to the bed, uninterested.

"No, but I was having a dream and realized where they must be."

"Well?" Brad lifted a dark eyebrow, appearing skeptical.

"Where would you hide your most secret things?" She could see it perfectly now, understanding what Chloe had done.

"Safe-deposit box?"

"Secret things go in a secret place. Like Chloe's secret garden meadow."

"The place you went today?"

"Yes!" She nodded, thinking they'd be able to see well enough if they left now. The sun was going to be over the horizon any moment. "Chloe never mentions it in the original diaries, yet she specifically showed it to me once. And she always referred to it as her secret place. Where else would you hide a secret but a secret place?"

"You knew her better than me." Brad shrugged, still appearing unconvinced. "If you think she'd do something like that, we can go take a look."

She practically bolted out of bed. The cat and dog both jerked upright. "The only trouble is, I'm pretty sure they're hidden under the biggest rock you can imagine."

THE GOOD NEWS WAS, HE KNEW exactly where to rent a metal detector.

When Brad had returned the tractor to the local equipment-rental place, he happened to notice they had a few metal detectors available. And after seeing the behemoth that Nikki wanted him to move, he figured that was their best bet. Nothing short of an earthquake would dislodge that sucker, so he felt pretty sure Chloe Lissander hadn't managed the job to hide the journals under it in the first place.

"So you think the journals are in a box that will set off the metal detector," Nikki mused as she walked another slow circle around the huge rock in the middle of the wildflower meadow. Her long, dark curls swayed in the breeze. She wore a bright pink sweatsuit with the name of her university stitched on the sleeve of the hoodie—Old Dominion.

"Absolutely. She wouldn't bury it without protection from the elements. She probably just tucked it near here, but I hate to dig up the whole perimeter of the rock when we can find it faster with the metal detector. That way, if it's not by the big-ass boulder, we can expand the search easily."

She nodded, but she was biting her lip in thought.

He could tell she was disappointed he hadn't offered to start shoveling now, but he didn't want to undertake backbreaking labor without a plan.

"What makes you think this place is such a secret anymore? If Chloe grew up in that house, her whole family must know about the meadow and how she liked it out here." He could see why it was a special spot. Different from the surrounding woods, the sudden pop of color up here was unexpected.

And the thought of Nikki lying half-naked on that rock just yesterday, stretched out like some kind of pagan sacrifice and dreaming about him...

He'd be lucky to leave the meadow without begging for a reenactment so he could see that for himself.

"Chloe's family didn't own this part of the property when she was younger. She bought it about ten years ago when the former owner died." She paused her circling by a thatch of some purplish flowers and knelt down to examine the ground there. "When she was growing up here, she said the boys rode their bikes into town to hang out with their friends. She was the one who roamed the countryside on her own."

He supposed she could have bought up the land to ensure her secrets were safe there. And who knew how long ago she actually "lost" the diaries? She could have hidden them there at any point over the years.

"See anything?" He moved closer, wondering what caught her eye.

"Chloe loved Virginia bluebells." Pointing to the spiky blooms, she grinned. "I'm betting this is the spot."

They walked back through the woods together, crossing a dead log over a rushing creek and climbing down a tall hill. In the few years he'd owned the house right next door to Nikki's, he'd never known any of this existed. His first glimpse of her place from this angle was a revelation, as well. The old farmhouse with its oddly fanciful widow's walk truly was a neat property.

"The house is going to be really cool one day," he told her, knowing Nikki would make sure it came together just the way it should. She'd worked so hard already. "Is it the first place you've owned?"

She nodded. "My first real home."

No wonder it meant the world to her; she'd never had a place to call home in the tumultuous race from house to house that had constituted her childhood. Understanding that made him all the more determined to get as much done as he could before he left in nine days. By the time he came back, they'd probably be ready to put on some finishing touches if the contractors she hired didn't—

Shit.

Had he really thought about a future with her?

He'd tried not to think about his realization of the night before, hoping maybe he'd been wrong about what he felt for her. Didn't he know better than to start something with a woman so intent on putting down roots and staying in one place? Things his job just didn't make possible?

No doubt about it, he should be putting on the brakes before someone got hurt. Tough to do when he had nothing else to do for the next nine days but climb the walls and return to his nightmares. Not to mention, he wanted to keep her safe from whoever was trying to oust her.

Speaking of which.

"Uh-oh," Nikki muttered at the same moment he saw a sporty Mercedes convertible in the driveway. Bright red.

He'd recognize the car of a wealthy cheerleader mom from a mile away.

"We can see about a restraining order," he suggested, though Nikki was already shaking her head and picking up her pace to greet the visitors.

"I'm not going to cut them all off because one or two of them are making trouble." Still, she threaded her arm through his and he liked that she reached his way for back-up.

Yeah, he was liking that a whole lot. The protective charge that gave him made him want to give the sporty Mercedes a good he-man shove right out of the driveway and the Ralstons out of Nikki's life.

"Trouble is, we don't know who to trust." He could see Angelica now. And she'd brought her precocious teen with her. Their bright red track jackets contrasted with the house's faded red screen door.

"Hi there," Nikki called, waving at them with her free arm.

Brad tucked the other arm even tighter to his side,

wondering what Nikki would think if he installed eight-foot fencing and a security gate.

"Hello." Angelica shoved her daughter forward as Brad and Nikki closed the distance between them. "Emily has something to say to you."

The teenage flirt who Brad had met at the door yesterday now had puffy red eyes and a far more contrite demeanor. She looked as if she'd been up all night and—considering the late-night trouble she'd caused—she probably had.

"I'm sorry!" she blurted, staring at the ground while Angelica stepped back a few feet to give her space. "My boyfriend was the one with the idea to fire the shot because he said he heard Granddaddy saying we should chase you back to Tennessee or wherever it is you come from." Emily glanced up, shrugging helplessly as if she couldn't be responsible for what her grandfather said.

Brad had a feeling where this was leading, directly to a request for Nikki not to press charges, and it was all he could do not to order both of them off the property. But that wasn't his call and it wasn't his land. And, oh, man, this possessive thing was going to be tough to fight. He had Nikki clamped to his side as if the cheerleader might drag her off any second. He carefully loosened his grip to a more appropriate reassuring squeeze.

"So you came out here in the middle of the night to scare me because it was your boyfriend's idea?" Nikki did not sound like a woman swayed by teenage tears and he had a vision of her as a kick-butt mom some day. He'd bet she'd seen plenty of adolescent-drama teaching college courses.

"I—we—that is, I'd been drinking a little." She

lowered her voice over this part and peered back at her mother as if scared to confess it.

And to be fair, Angelica looked like she might take the girl's head off, but she simply kept her arms tightly crossed, her Botox no match for her frown. Brad could almost feel sorry for her.

Emily turned her attention back to Nikki. "But I'm breaking up with him today. He's a bad influence and I'm really sorry. I guess he thought that prank we pulled would impress my granddad enough to give him a job on his crew, but—" she rolled her eyes in a move perfected by girls of that demographic everywhere "—guess that's not gonna happen now, is it?"

Nikki pursed her lips.

Emily cleared her throat. "Anyway, I'm sorry for what I did and I came to offer my help in fixing up the house if you want. I can rake or mow or—" she peered around the property "—something. I understand if you want to press charges, and either way the offer stands because Ralstons fix their mistakes."

After this last bit, and Brad admitted it was a good ploy, the girl dared a hopeful glance back at her mother, who continued to glare at her.

Nikki gave a nod.

"I appreciate the offer and I will take it into consideration after I speak to the police this afternoon. Thank you for coming."

Angelica returned the nod, and then marched her daughter back to the sports car, depositing her in the front seat before the two of them roared away.

"How much you want to bet there are no slots on the

cheer team for kids with police charges pending?" Brad observed.

"For a Ralston? In this town? There'll be a slot even if she's serving hard time. That offer to work off the bad behavior is all Angelica's doing. I know you don't think much of her, but I'm telling you, she's not half-bad."

"So when are we going to talk to the granddad who put the target on your back?"

Nikki spun in his arm, smiling. "We don't have to, because we're going to find the diaries today and have all our answers straight from Chloe herself."

She pressed against him in a way that made him think he could have her all to himself in that bed upstairs with just a little effort. And he wanted that. Badly.

But she was looking forward to digging up around the rock and he needed to be careful of falling any deeper into dangerous terrain with her. He settled for pulling his keys out of his pocket instead.

"How about we go rent a metal detector?"

"Deal." She headed toward the Jeep. "But if we find those diaries under the purple flowers, just like I said? I'm going to seduce you on that rock and use one of those blooms to torment you just like you did to me last night."

His mouth watered on cue.

As they tore out of the driveway and up the street toward the heart of the town, Brad knew he should say something to Nikki about the things he was feeling for her—to give her a chance to cool things off if she wanted. Who'd have thought a brief no-strings affair could have tied his heart in knots within days? But when a woman went Terminator on your nightmares and warmed your bed in the most amazing way possible, any guy would be in trouble.

His efforts to help Nikki find her inner vixen had worked a little too well. She seemed to be thriving on the sensual combustion while Brad had taken a direct hit.

Doc Leonard had tried to tell him not to focus so much on the physical, but he'd figured being with Nikki was the best thing that had happened to him in a hell of a long time, so what could go wrong?

Yeah, that's why Leonard had the psych degree and Brad was the one sitting for the head exam.

NIKKI THOUGHT SHE NOTICED a distance in Brad that afternoon as they worked with the metal detector around the rock in the garden meadow. She wasn't quite sure when it had taken root, but it sat between them like a palpable thing despite the gorgeous day and an activity that was a heck of a lot easier than tearing down the chicken coop or reshingling the porch roof, or any of the other hundreds of tasks she needed to tackle at the house.

Now, digging in the third spot the metal detector had chimed, she took a break with her shovel while he continued to spear down into the earth with his. Muscles strained and flexed in the warm spring sun, his arms moving in easy harmony with the demands he made of his body. Dirt lifted and relocated according to his dictate, worms and roots tangling together as he pulled up weeds and stones. She debated asking him if anything was wrong, but part of her hated to wade into that territory with him. He'd demonstrated a clear discomfort with talking about his feelings—shutting her out more times than he'd let her in. Or maybe he was simply re-inforcing the boundaries between them, making sure things didn't become too entangled before he returned to his life overseas without her.

"Did you see something?" Brad had paused in the digging, his gaze shifting between the gaping hole in the meadow floor and the pile of displaced earth beside it.

Wrenching her attention back to the present, she brought her shovel over to the mound of dirt and began sifting through it.

"Not really." Certainly nothing the size of two miss-ing diaries. Then her shovel tip scraped along something metallic. "Oh, wait."

He yanked the hem of his T-shirt up to wipe at the sheen of sweat on his forehead, providing her with a tantalizing glimpse of six-pack abs and a narrow waist. The band of his boxers peeked just over the low-riding cargo shorts.

The temptation to drag her knuckle along that bare patch of skin bit her hard. Not only because she wanted him. Also because there was no confusion about where they stood with each other on a physical plane. While they were getting naked, they understood each other perfectly.

"You see something?" He peered down into the raked-through earth beside her, his shoulder brushing hers.

Shovel slipping under the edge of her find, she held it up for him to look at.

"Can you tell what it is?" Not a book by any stretch.

They'd dug up a coin and a wad of aluminum foil the first two times the detector had beeped.

He removed the object from the blade and shook it off. "Congratulations, you're the proud owner of an old brass candlestick."

Disheartened, she eyed the purple flowers again.

He must have caught the direction of her gaze because he tossed aside the candlestick and circled the patch of Virginia bluebells by the rock.

"You're convinced it's under here?" He knelt to examine the base of the dense green leaves dotted with buds and a few early blooms. "Even though the metal detector didn't go off?"

"Didn't they say the device wasn't all that reliable below twelve inches? Maybe the journals are just buried deeper than that." She couldn't explain why she had such a good feeling about that spot.

"Can't hurt to try." He forked the shovel down into the earth again, stepping on the heel of the blade to drive it deeper.

Nikki's heartbeat quickened as he dug around the flowers and pried them out, preserving the roots in a wad of earth and laying them aside to replant. She joined in the effort and they tunneled farther and farther down, widening the gouge in the earth until they stood in a shallow hole about a foot deep and six feet wide. He'd burrowed out more than twice as much as she had so far and her still arms were shaky from the strain.

"Maybe this wasn't such a good idea." Defeated, she set aside the shovel, wondering if she'd been a nutcase to come out here because of a dream. "I didn't really have any concrete proof the journals were in the meadow anyway. I probably should have waited—"

"Can you hand me the metal detector?" He pointed to the device where he'd last laid it down, close to her feet.

"Sure." She hefted it up, even that much weight feeling like a chore after all those shovelfuls of dirt to unearth a bunch of nothing. "But I don't see—"

As he fired up the detector again, she finally understood his intent. Now that he'd excavated down another foot, he would be able to use the equipment to test what lay beneath this area for the next twelve inches. He double-checked the discriminator dial to be sure it was set to pick up anything, then began slow, methodical sweeps of the new terrain.

The strong, steady beep began about a foot away from the rock. Their eyes met. Held.

She brought him his shovel at the same time she carried over her own. In wordless agreement, they each began to dig. And as intrigued and excited as she was about the potential find, Nikki couldn't help but spare a thought that maybe she and Brad understood each other out of bed after all. They'd worked effectively together on the big dig today and they'd also been one heck of a team the day they'd tackled the hard chores at Nikki's house, ending with a dinner she'd cooked but that he warmed up and served.

Those were small things, maybe. But she liked the idea of working beside him, understanding what he wanted before he asked half the time.

Her heart ached with the knowledge that it wouldn't last—

Clink.

His shovel hit something with a metallic thud.

Nikki's pulse spiked again, her hopes elevated even though she told herself it was probably nothing. A fork, maybe. Or some old toy that had been lost and forgotten for decades...

"I feel a definite straight edge." Brad set the shovel down and worked with his hands, brushing, digging and tugging.

He withdrew a rectangular tin box about six by eight inches that had probably been painted at one time. Now, crusty and warped, and dented from the shovel, the container protested his efforts to pry it open. Nikki watched, holding her breath, as he gripped the box under one arm and tugged hard against the lid until it finally popped free. A leather pouch tumbled onto the ground, the string that tied it closed slipping partially open. The corner of a binding—a book binding—peeked through the slit.

"Oh!" She reached for it, lifting the heavy packet out of the dirt. Opening it the rest of the way, she found two books inside and a stack of letters tied with bale twine.

"Jane Eyre?" Brad read one of the titles over her shoulder. *"The House of the Seven Gables?"*

"She liked to hide the journals inside the covers of books her stepbrothers wouldn't pick up." All her tiredness from shoveling was gone. New energy poured through her, her veins tingling with the electric pulse of discovery. "Which apparently wasn't hard since they hated to read."

"These are really what we've been looking for?" He took one of the books from her hand and opened the cover.

Chloe's handwriting was immediately recognizable.

"Mine says 1944," Nikki pointed out, showing him the frontispiece for her book. "Yours says summer 1943. We've got them."

"What now?" He wiped his palms on his cargo shorts. "Once you hand these over to Chloe's publisher, you're home free, right? The Ralstons have no reason to threaten and make trouble anymore after the publication is a done deal. Whatever bad news is in here about them, the whole world will know it soon enough."

She sensed an eagerness to be done with the whole sordid mess. To be done with her?

She wished the idea hadn't come to mind so readily. What if he'd only stuck to her side to protect her? He'd go back to sleeping at his house. Maybe he'd go back to being just a next-door neighbor.

"If we're right about the Ralstons being the guilty party, yes." She flipped a couple of pages, mindful of the soil on her hands. "But I'd like to have a quick preview of what's in here before we do anything."

She needed to know how things turned out between Chloe and Eduardo. Had she sent her fiancé off to war and never seen him again? She wanted some reason to hope that relationships could work even in the face of insurmountable odds. But Chloe and Eduardo hadn't worked out since Chloe was a single woman until the day she died. Nikki had to know what happened between them, even knowing the inevitable heartache ahead. Kind of like her own life…

Nikki's eyes cut to Brad as a lump rose in her throat. When he said nothing, frowning his disagreement, she swallowed the lump down so she could speak again.

"As the caretaker of Chloe's literary legacy, I really need to know what's in here first. If I could just go home and have a day or two to read—"

"We can make copies so the publisher has them simultaneously. That would end the threat." Brad's methodical brain worked as quickly as his hands, which were already shoveling in the hole he'd dug. "Then you'd have time to read them and you'd still be safe."

How…practical.

"Aren't you a little curious to find out what happened to Chloe and Eduardo? Maybe these books will tell us Eduardo's real identity since we know that's not his true name." She wanted to cut the bale twine on the stack of letters and see if they were signed "Eduardo," as well. But even more, she wanted Brad to care about this romance as much as she did.

No, she wanted him to care about *their* romance as much as she did. But she could practically see him thinking through what it would mean to have the threat of danger gone. He'd be free to return to his house, free to do whatever it was he'd been doing before they'd met.

She listened to the wind flit through the trees while she waited for his answer.

"I'm more interested in finding out what incriminating things these books have to say about the Ralstons." His jaw flexed as he worked, frustration evident. "What past sins were so important to hide that they had to threaten you?"

So that's what it had been about for him. Protecting her. Having a cause even when he was taking a leave from the military. Honor and a sense of justice were innate facets of his personality.

"So we can take today to read?" she prodded, hurt and trying not to show it.

The triumph of their find had been tainted by the realization that Brad wanted—needed—to back off their relationship.

He nodded. "One more day."

It sounded like more than the end of the Ralstons' reign of harassment. It sounded like the end of her time with Brad.

13

BRAD HAD NEW RESPECT for the rigors of scholarship after four hours of closely reading the diaries for any signs of what the Ralston family was so desperate to suppress. He'd assumed he and Nikki would open a journal, find a dark secret and be done with the mysterious threats. The Ralstons would have to face up to whatever bad family karma they had going, and that would be that.

But he'd mostly read a lot of steamy letters between Eduardo and Chloe—a tough gig sitting across the patio from Nikki, who looked even hotter in her nerdy professor glasses that she used for reading than she had in a string bikini. And he still had no further clue of Eduardo's real identity, what happened to the couple after the war or why the Ralstons felt the need to hide any of it. The guy Chloe referred to as "Eduardo" even signed his letters that way, making them wonder if it was a nickname or family name he went by—like calling John "Jack" or Margaret "Molly."

Nikki had been thrilled that there were letters from Chloe in the pile in addition to the letters from Eduardo.

She seemed to think that meant the guy had survived the war, envisioning Eduardo returning home to add the letters he'd received to the one he'd sent. Brad hadn't told her his own theory—that the letters might have been returned to her as a courtesy by one of Eduardo's friends afterward.

Brad identified a little too well with the guy.

Now, poring over the find in Nikki's sunny backyard, a pitcher of sweet tea between them, Brad tried to maintain focus. Chloe was missing her man overseas. She'd had to make up excuses to her family regarding why she didn't want to date other men, but as far as he could tell, she never revealed that she had a sweetheart in the war. Why keep so many secrets?

"You sure we can't flip to the back and read the last pages first?" He'd asked her that one before—about both the stack of letters and the diaries. "What if we're wading through these page by page and nothing happens until the very end?"

Although, truth be told, he'd sneaked a peek at the final page of the journal on his lap a few hours ago, and it had looked fairly benign. There'd been a mention of a New Year's Eve party and some discussion of what to wear, a lengthy debate he couldn't relate to since guys tended to sniff out whatever was clean and go with that. Chloe's ending wasn't exactly earth-shattering stuff.

"It's not fiction," she informed him, peering over her black eyeglass frames like a megahot librarian. "Chloe didn't write her diaries in a way that built tension and plot into some kind of explosive moment at the end. She just wrote down what happened to her on a day-to-day basis. Some days were more exciting than others and we'll miss important information if we don't read each entry carefully."

"Well, I can tell you one thing." He set aside the journal and turned his attention back to the letters, still convinced that Chloe's fiancé was the real key to the mystery. "This Eduardo guy is having one hell of a rough time."

U.S.S. Zeilin
1943

My Dearest Spitfire,
Our ship is frozen in ice and every churn of the ocean beneath the hull slaps frosty chunks in a teeth-grinding wail against our sides. Absurdly, it is foggy here even in the frozen temperatures, so the world is endlessly white.

On another note, I am abashed to admit that some of your letters have attracted the attention of military censors. While I have been warned that your warming words may be inappropriately stirring, I believe two were confiscated specifically so they could heat censors in need of a bit of feminine warmth. Your support of the war effort is commendable.

Because of this interest in our correspondence, I will refrain from saying any more about your relative. I will see him soon enough when we reach our destination. I have heard he takes more pleasure than most in the harshness of his mission.

I propose a worldwide tour when I am done with this war so you may experience all the places

*you dream of. You will live in peace from those
who upset you, free to write every day in your
inimitable way, and I will have you all to myself.
Be thinking of where you'd like to go first. I shall
come to spirit you away when you least expect
it.*

Yours,

Eduardo

"Brad?" Nikki peered his way across the patio table,
a curious expression on her face as she covered his hand
with hers. "Have you found anything?"

He wondered how she knew. He was going to miss
this connection with her.

"I'm not sure." He stared at the yellowed page written half a century ago, the words deliberately vague
because of military censors. "I wouldn't have looked
at it twice if I didn't know someone wanted to suppress
these things."

Turning the crinkled paper her way, he watched
Nikki's reactions as she smiled over the bit about Chloe's
war efforts. The corners of her lips flattened and turned
downward as she read about the stepbrother. When she
was done, she glanced up at him, but he could see her
thoughts were still swirling around in that quick mind
of hers.

"They planned to travel the world together." Nikki's
expression was distant, full of hope for dreams that
weren't even her own.

No surprise that she craved happy endings. Brad
couldn't make that happen for her any more than Eduardo had done for Chloe.

"Maybe she decided to follow through on their plan even when he didn't—that is, even though he might not have come home." Brad knew she didn't like the idea of Eduardo not returning from the war.

Her gaze cleared. Focused on him.

"What if he *did* come home and she never told anyone she spent the time abroad with him?" She flipped through the diary pages now, breaking her own rule about looking ahead. "We know she went on to visit every corner of the globe. What if she was still hiding their relationship even long afterward?"

"Why?" That made no sense to Brad and she had keyed in on a completely different point in the letter than the one he'd tried to show her. "Chloe Lissander was an icon of the sexual revolution for her forthright accounts of sex. That doesn't sound like the kind of woman who would try to hide her lover."

"Maybe they were threatened by her family somehow. They must not have wanted her to be with him if she went to so much trouble to hide his identity."

Brad took the letter back and glanced over the words again.

"You see this part?" He pointed to the paragraph about the "relative" that had to be Harold Ralston. "He talks about Chloe's stepbrother taking 'pleasure' in the harshness of the mission."

She nodded. "Harold isn't exactly the warm and fuzzy type. Maybe he liked ordering people around and being the boss. He had a squad underneath him, I hear."

"Or else he liked to play God with a weapon in his hand."

Nikki frowned. "What do you mean?"

He hated pointing out stuff like this since he took a lot of pride in his service. Dishonorable behavior in the military was rare. That didn't mean it didn't happen.

"It's probably a stretch, but I'd be on the lookout in the rest of the letters for anything that hints at bloodlust in Harold. Possibly war crimes. We have a lot of watch systems in place today for guys who can't handle the stress, but back in that time—"

"You think Harold could be guilty of something… like that?" Nikki's jaw fell open, her voice lowering as if someone was watching from the bushes.

He shrugged. "I have no idea. But there's a dark secret in here the Ralston family wants to hide. I'm just pointing out possibilities."

"Eduardo did make a point of telling Chloe he couldn't speak plainly." She pondered a moment then rose to her feet. "It would make sense if he hid something with vague words after a comment like that. Almost like he was warning her that he was understating, right? I'm going to retrieve the rest of the diaries."

Standing, he followed her toward the screen door leading to the kitchen.

"Maybe we should grab a bag so we can carry it all down to a copy center."

He almost slammed into her back, not realizing she'd come to a dead halt in front of him.

She spun to face him, her pretty mouth parted in an "oh" of surprise.

"I thought we agreed this was going to be a reading day?" There was an edge to her tone he couldn't quite interpret.

"It has been." Where had she been for the last four

hours? His eyes ached from studying all those pages. "But if we don't make copies of everything today, we won't have anything to overnight to the publisher in the morning."

Her lips pursed, then flattened in a thin line.

"And then I'll be safe," she monotoned, not sounding nearly as relieved about that as she should.

"Exactly. Then things can get back to normal—"

"That will make it easier for you when you go, won't it?" She gripped the stone wall ringing two sides of the patio, her fingers clenched in a crevice where a rock had fallen out of place. "It's good to have no loose ends."

He understood the tension between them now.

Damn it. This wasn't how he wanted to spend his time before shipping out—arguing and drawing boundaries. "I thought we agreed not to let this get too complicated."

"And it hasn't." She bit the words out with crisp articulation, but he guessed there was real hurt behind them. "You're making sure to remind me every day how simple this needs to be. But it doesn't feel all that simple to me. And if you're already looking for the exit four days after we met, maybe that's a sign you ought to just leave now."

He blinked. She wanted him gone?

"How did this go from a discussion of making some copies to you trying to show me the door?" His chest tightened and he felt like he couldn't get quite as much air as he wanted.

"You can't deny a certain coolness descended over things today, can you?" Nikki propped a hand on her hip, her tank top riding high above her green and purple floral shorts. "I offered to play sex games with a flower and you know what your response was?"

He remembered her saying something about that. And he recalled himself salivating before he tried to rein himself in.

But had he ever replied?

"Nothing," she informed him. "Absolute silence. You can't pretend that you're not pulling away. And I'm okay with that if this is too much too soon, but I wish you wouldn't pretend like things are the same between us when I can see your thoughts are already a few thousand miles away from me."

"Nikki—" The word stuck in his throat a little and he had to clear it. "You don't understand."

He'd hardly had time to wrap his head around what he was feeling. This week had been like a pressure cooker, their days together all the more intense for him because of the bad dreams and lack of sleep. What could he say to her that wouldn't send her running even faster?

"Actually, I think I do." Her voice softened and he thought she blinked away some moisture in the corners of her eyes. "I understand too well. Why don't I go get the diaries and we'll make the copies tonight?"

He took a breath again, grateful she'd decided to be reasonable.

"We still have time to make an announcement to the local press," she continued, outlining the plan. "We'll spread the word about the journals being in the mail and you'll be free to sleep in your own bed tonight." She leaned closer to give him a kiss on the cheek.

The brush of her lips on his skin was so quick he hardly had time to enjoy it. But then again, as his brain processed her words, he realized he wouldn't have enjoyed it anyhow.

Nikki hadn't come to some equitable compromise.

She'd just kissed him goodbye.

IT WASN'T LIKE SHE WAS MAD as she pounded her way upstairs to the bedroom, taking the steps two at a time. It was more like she was wounded. Deeply.

She flung herself into the bedroom and onto the bed, taking refuge in the chenille that had covered them just the night before. She'd get up in another minute. For now, she needed to catch her breath before the big bubble of emotions swelling in her chest threatened to burst like a raincloud and pour tears down her cheeks as if she was five years old again.

Crap. She would not, could not let this happen to her. How could she have given a man so much power over her heart in such a short space of time? Dragging in deep breaths, she released the blanket and forced herself upright. The wide-eyed ginger kitten that Brad had rescued snuggled on a pillow near the headboard. He stared at her with the same eerie animal empathy that had sucked Nikki in the first time one of her distant cousin's dogs had licked her tears away after her parents had dumped her off on their relative's doorstep.

That dog had been her best friend and her security blanket rolled in one for the next six months. And she'd been okay then. She would be okay again now, too. Even after Brad left. Which made her wonder—if she was so freaking strong, why couldn't she have at least tried a relationship with him?

Maybe after all the time she'd spent fending for

herself, she was actually really well equipped to deal with Brad's deployments. What if she'd been seriously underestimating herself, only looking at safe relationships that didn't begin to fulfill her emotionally?

The ginger kitten mewed at her and marched closer, lifting little paws high on the squishy bed, perhaps trying to keep her claws from getting stuck in the chenille. Nikki scooped her up, remembering how Brad had gone out on that limb for her.

Yet, when the opportunity had arrived, she hadn't done the same for him. She'd confronted him out of fear, suggesting they break things off the minute she sensed he was pulling away. Not exactly healthy to strike first to avoid being hit yourself. In fact, that sounded juvenile and not at all like the woman she wanted to be.

Would Chloe have ever behaved that way?

Cuddling the kitten closer, Nikki rose from the bed. Leaving the diaries on the bookshelves, she went downstairs, her heart picking up speed along with her feet. She didn't quite know what to say to Brad, but she'd think of that once she saw him. Once she assured herself he hadn't already left.

Hurrying into the kitchen, she was about to head for the screen door when a big, bulky object on the kitchen counter caught her attention. Had it been there when she came in and she hadn't seen it?

For a moment, she wondered if it was a package from a delivery service that Brad had brought inside for her. It looked like a box from the back. But as she rounded the butcher block counter top island and saw the front, she froze.

The face of the object revealed a wire contraption

with simple circuitry attached to fat sticks covered in brown paper. A digital timer with bright green numbers ticked away softly in the quiet kitchen.

1:45, 1:44, 1:43...

She could actually count along with it and know how many seconds it took her to find her voice. Honest to God, nothing came out at first when she tried to scream.

Squeezing the kitten tight in her arms, she bolted for the screen door just as a shriek finally rose from her throat.

_14_

"BOMB!" NIKKI'S SCREAM was a nightmare come to life.

Brad sprinted toward the house as she bolted through the screen door onto the patio. Face drained of color, she shouted as she ran toward him with the kitten in a stranglehold.

"Where?" He halted her and held her steady long enough to get the answers he needed. "Where is it exactly?"

"Kitchen counter." She breathed hard. Possibly the start of hyperventilation. "It's counting down. Only a minute and a half left."

"Take the animals to my house. Get in the basement. Call 911." He spent a precious extra half second waiting to see if she understood, waiting to be sure she would do this.

At her nod, he took off running toward the house. Someone must have entered her home while they'd been out digging or at the rental place.

He leaped a patio chair like a hurdle, never slowing

down. The screen door damn near came off the frame as he wrenched it open and skidded into the kitchen.

He saw it immediately. Bulky, homemade construction. Simple wiring. The kind of thing they might have made back in the Second World War...

Timer ticking down.

1:15, 1:14, 1:13...

Not enough time to transport it elsewhere for safer defusion. Not enough time to call in a team of specialists.

Sufficient dynamite to level Nikki's house to rubble.

Worse, there was a good chance this much firepower could take out his house next door. Where he'd sent her for safety. While he trusted she would be more protected in the basement, that didn't mean she would escape without injury. Flying debris, falling beams, sudden fires...

He couldn't let anything happen to her, not to mention anyone who might be driving by their properties.

Sweat beaded on his brow. His nightmare was playing out just as he'd seen it in his dreams so many times over the last weeks. He was face-to-face with a bomb. Lives were in his hands. The life of someone he cared about.

He had to defuse it.

Wiping his hands on a kitchen towel, he dried the sweat so nothing slipped. Precision was everything. Sinking to eye level with the bomb, he tracked the wires to see how they went together.

1:01, 1:00, :59...

Three months ago, he would have done this in the blink of an eye. But since the premature detonation in a barren field in Iraq? He quaked inside like the San Andreas fault even though his hands remained rock steady.

He cursed every foul oath he knew in a slow, purposeful stream. Sort of like the release valve on a pressure cooker. Then, he retrieved a pair of butcher's scissors from the block on the counter and hoped they were sharp.

They were his wire cutters.

:40, :39, :38...

Why hurry now? He had time to think about whether or not he was doing the right thing. He could still sprint back to join Nikki in the basement next door. But then, he'd be writing off this house that was the only home she'd ever known.

A home he'd even—briefly—pictured himself in one day. With her.

It didn't matter that Nikki had given him his walking papers. He would sleep better knowing she was here, in this house she loved, safe.

Because so help him, he would defuse this freaking bomb and deliver it to the local cop shop with a red ribbon tied around it to bring down whoever had placed it here. That was the best reason of all to defuse it.

The possibility of fingerprints.

:10, :09, :08...

Brad slid the lower blade of the kitchen scissors under a faded red wire. You had to respect these homemade bombs cobbled together by people who didn't know what they were doing.

Taking a deep breath, he closed the scissors.

Snip...

HAD A MILLION YEARS PASSED or did it just feel that way?

Nikki checked her cell phone in the dim light of Brad's basement. The digital clock display said it had been a minute since she'd called 911, so surely if the bomb was going to go off it would have already happened by now?

The thought made her ill. She should have stopped Brad from going into the house. She should have insisted they both run like hell down the street. Good God, how did he make such quick life-and-death decisions for a living? She would be a basketcase by lunch the first day on the job.

No wonder he had nightmares.

Beside her feet, the blue jay squawked in his cage, thoroughly furious at being dragged across the lawn and shoved into a dark basement. The kitten had leaped from her arms to explore a shelf of paint cans and Killer stood on the washing machine to stare out a high window with her, his nails clicking impatiently on the metal as he danced in place and waited for something to happen.

And waited.

When another minute ticked by on the clock in her phone, she knew the bomb must not have gone off. Brad had defused it, thank God. So where was he?

Whistling to Killer, she turned away from the washing machine while the dog jumped down. In the distance, she could hear sirens wailing, a speedy answer to her call for help. What could have happened to Brad?

Fear clogged her throat. She'd only just started breathing again after the shock of finding a bomb in the kitchen. Now this? She hurried up the steps and through Brad's living room to the front door. Pushing out into the bright afternoon, she rushed toward Chloe's farmhouse. Her house now.

The home Brad had saved.

Killer raced at her feet as the sound of the sirens grew louder. The dog jockeyed to stay ahead of her and nearly tripped her as they leaped up onto the patio of the farmhouse and practically fell through the screen door.

Inside the house, she couldn't think through what she was seeing. Harold Ralston—Chloe's stepbrother, the prominent city councilman—held a knife in his hand. For a split second, she'd glimpsed a view of the weapon pointed in Brad's direction, but with the distraction of her arrival, Brad gripped the old man's arm in a vise and snapped his wrist backward.

The butcher knife clattered to the floor.

Nikki screamed as the men continued to grapple. Behind her, cop cars flooded the driveway. Uniformed officers shouted to one another as they hurried toward the house and shoved past her.

In no time, the police had Harold and Brad surrounded, although even then they appeared hesitant about cuffing a local war hero. Nikki couldn't point to the knife and the explosives fast enough, encouraging the officers to check the old man's truck for tire prints that matched her torn-up yard.

While she vented about being terrorized by Chloe's stepbrother, she noticed Brad explaining quietly to one of the senior officers that the IED and the knife would both be covered with Harold's fingerprints.

Finally, the officers removed Harold Ralston from the farmhouse while the older man cursed them, Nikki and his "slut" of a stepsister the whole way. Clearly, there'd been no love lost between Harold and Chloe.

Indignant on her friend's behalf, she followed the cop and his captive out the door.

"What did you hope to accomplish by blowing up the house?" Nikki guessed the answers must be in the diaries, but she wanted to know now.

Harold strained at the cuffs, surprisingly strong for his age and more than a little pissed off.

"I wasn't going to blow up the house. I knew your boyfriend could defuse a bomb. I just wanted to scare you off so you didn't find Chloe's diaries." His face contorted into a look of rage. "I told Chloe's fiancé I'd kill him if he ever showed his face around my sister again. Who'd have thought the little prick would get his revenge after he died?" Harold snarled at her, a line of spittle hanging from one corner of his lip as on a rabid dog. The councilman's comb-over stood high in the spring breeze.

An officer nearby scribbled notes on the exchange.

Nikki felt Brad's presence behind her, listening, and longed to lean back against him and feel his solid warmth. She was just thankful he was alive. Brad had won the day, his smarts and quick reactions overriding any crap from his past after what happened in Iraq. He'd proven to himself he was healed. He would be cleared to return to duty, free to do the job he loved.

As much as she would miss him—miss *them*—she was glad for him.

"The pen is mightier than the sword," she reminded no one in particular, understanding Eduardo's revenge must somehow be part of those missing diaries.

But Harold wasn't done. And the cop who held him seemed as interested in what he had to say as her, his feet glued to the flagstone path while the old man talked.

"Soon the whole world will know Chloe's fiancé was the hero and not me," Harold groused. "Did you know, back then, they didn't give out as many medals to the mixed-breeds who fought in the war? So I made a lot more out of old Ekualo's act of bravery than he would have if he'd tried to claim he saved all those half-drowned men. The infantry guys he pulled on the ship were too frozen and confused to know who saved them."

Nikki tried to take in what he was saying.

"Ekualo?"

"Eduardo," Harold clarified, rolling his eyes. "She called him that all the time, but her fiancé was just an ordinary Hawaiian-Philipino she met when she saw me off in California. We thought the guy looked like a Jap anyhow—"

"Enough." Nikki shook her head, not wanting to hear even one more syllable of a racist rant about Chloe's beloved Eduardo. Ekualo. No wonder the name hadn't been on the ship's registry. She hadn't been looking for the Hawaiian version of Eduardo. Chloe's fiancé had been the war hero all along and Harold Ralston had stolen the tale of his bravery, while he'd kept his sister far away with a man the family didn't approve of. "You're lucky you soaked up someone else's glory for as long as you did."

The police officer who held Harold's arm nudged him forward as the councilman kept muttering.

"Never did understand why he didn't take the credit

for what he did that day," he told the young officer. "Who the hell jumps into ten-foot swells to drag a whole infantry unit to safety and never tells anyone?"

Ekualo had, Nikki thought. He hadn't needed glory or recognition for his heroism because he had Chloe to come home to. She'd bet anything there wasn't one word about his heroic deeds in Chloe's diaries—that's why she and Brad hadn't found anything in those hours of reading. Some men did their duty with honor, and the reward of a job well done—a life saved—was enough. Chloe hadn't hidden the diaries because she was worried Harold would try to defend the proof he wasn't a hero. Nikki suspected she'd hidden them because they revealed the truth about her relationship with Eduardo that her own family still didn't know to this day.

She couldn't wait to read the rest of the recovered journals to find out if her hunch could be right or if she was just weaving a romantic ending for a couple who were never able to be together.

But right now, more than anything, she wanted to thank Brad. To throw her arms around his neck, to listen to the steady beat of his heart and reassure herself he was still in one piece.

But the man she wanted to be with was already shaking off police questions and sauntering across the lawn toward his own house. Away from her.

"Brad, wait." She called to him, assuring a police officer still in her yard that she would be available for questions after they'd "secured the scene." Whatever that meant.

Slowing, Brad turned to face her midway between their houses where a few white birch trees grew in a semicircle around an old rock garden she hoped to re-store. Killer scampered between them, still not knowing where he belonged. She could *really* relate.

"I'll send your animals back," he assured her, even though she hadn't been about to ask about the blue jay or the cat. "I'm glad you're all safe."

"Thanks to you." She slowed her jog when she'd al-most reached him, not sure how to read his body lan-guage but fairly certain he wasn't ready for her to fling her arms around him and cover him with kisses and gratitude. Not just because of their fight earlier, but be-cause of what he'd been through with disarming the explosive. "I was so scared when you were in there."

"That makes two of us," he admitted, his gaze going back to the farmhouse as one car pulled away with Har-old inside. Two other officers were posting crime-scene tape, cordoning off the screen door.

"Thank you for saving the house. And saving me." She didn't want to play it safe right now. She needed to tell him she wanted to be with him even if he wasn't ready for more. At least she'd know she'd said the words. "Brad, I'm sorry for what I said before—about wanting you to leave. I was hurt and confused but I knew as soon as I walked in the house to get the diaries that it had been really stupid to push you away when I wanted to pull you closer."

Her heart pounded so fast. She had the sense that if she didn't say it all now, in a rush, didn't put it all on the table, she might never get it out. He was leaving soon and each day was incredibly precious, something she realized now more than ever. She—they—didn't have the luxury of time.

He stared at her. Waiting for a chance to tell her she was crazy? Cringing that she was making it all the more difficult for them to end this civilly? She didn't know. But she knew she had to take this chance or she would always regret it. Chloe would want her to take this chance.

"I probably should have just been honest with you before—" he began.

A stabbing pain kicked through her and she didn't want him to say anything yet. She covered his lips with her fingers, not caring if anyone else saw or if the officers next door had to wait five more minutes to speak to them. Heaven knew, they'd tried to talk to the police often enough when they hadn't wanted to hear from them.

"Wait. Just—wait. I know this has been a crazy few days, but I'll take however many of those days I can have with you. If a one-day-at-a-time approach works better for you after all you've been through, I'm willing to try that. If that means it ends tomorrow or next week or next year—well, I won't like it, but I'd prefer any of that to ending it today."

"You're serious?" He stared at her with a steady gaze, his face inscrutable.

The moment rivaled finding the bomb in the kitchen for its level of scariness. She swallowed. Jumped in.

"Very serious."

A fresh-faced officer lumbered across the yard toward them, a pen in hand.

"Folks, we're ready to take your statements anytime," he called from a few yards away.

Killer barked at him.

"Nikki's been through a lot." Brad nodded toward her and put a protective arm around her waist. "Can you give us a few minutes?"

Nikki resisted the urge to simply close her eyes and curl into the warmth of Brad's chest. She wasn't sure how much of the display of affection was for show to ward off the questions.

The cop nodded. "No problem. But the sooner we can talk to you, the sooner we'll be out of your hair tonight."

"Understood." Brad steered them a few steps farther away from the scene, closer to his house.

He hadn't let go of her yet. Could she take that as a good sign?

"Nikki, the whole reason I pulled back today was more for your benefit than mine." He turned her to face him, lifting his hands to her shoulders.

The sun dipped behind them, the trees on fire with the burnished golden light. What a long, long day it had been.

"Why would that help me?"

"Because after the kind of childhood you had, I knew you wouldn't want any part of my lifestyle. I'm all over the globe, all the time."

Her heart stuttered a little. Did that mean he'd been thinking about a future, if only for a moment?

"It's true I've been looking forward to having a real home." She stared at Chloe's house, crawling with police investigators and crime-scene photographers. "But I think it's possible to have a home base and still travel. What's important is that you're with the one you care about when you can be. Chloe lived overseas for almost

twenty years and still kept this house for when she returned home."

Almost twenty years that the groundbreaking sensual novelist had chronicled in those diaries. Nearly two
decades of passionate affairs, the inspiration for erotica
that had made a whole generation hot and bothered. Had
she really been inspired by lovers all over the globe? Or
was it possible one special man—a man whose identity
she'd taken great pains to protect—had simply appeared
in her diaries under a whole host of exotic names?

It was exactly the kind of game Chloe would have
loved.

"You would consider that?" He leaned closer. His
grip on her shoulders tightened ever so subtly.

She thought about those same hands dismantling a
bomb in her kitchen and tears sprang to her eyes. She
was so lucky to have a man like this in her life. For
however long she could.

"Definitely." She had no reservations. "I still want to
get the house in order. But after that—if necessary—
I could pack my bags and teach my classes online
anywhere."

He was quiet so long she felt a wave of panic swell
inside her. She guessed that methodical mind was at
work putting the pieces in order, seeing if it could all
add up.

He hauled her to him with a fierceness that stunned
her. He pressed her hard against his body, his face buried
in her neck.

"I knew it. I knew last night. You're the one for me,
Nicole Thornton." He whispered the words into her ear,

his cheek rubbing against her hair and sending shivery sensations down her spine.

She angled back, wanting to see his face since she hadn't been expecting such an emphatic declaration from the guy who'd pushed her away with both hands earlier. That didn't stop her heart from skipping a beat or ten.

"Really?" She cupped the hard line of his jaw, her thumb tracing the rough cheek he hadn't been able to shave today after she'd awoken him at dawn. Her strong warrior. "You thought that just last night and yet you scared the living daylights out of me today, letting me think it was over?"

"I didn't want to put too much pressure on you. Or me. Or—hell, I just didn't want to jinx the whole thing. But I am so on board with this—you can't imagine." He wrapped her tight again, his hot, hard body communicating a desire to possess her right then and there.

She loved that.

And she was going to love him. She knew it deep in her soul. But she didn't want to jinx it either. He'd find out soon enough.

"We're going to write hot letters to each other while you're away," she insisted. "Just like Chloe and Eduardo, only better because there are no military censors to worry about now."

"But unlike Eduardo, I have no intention of keeping you pure before I leave." The look he gave her was so thoroughly wicked she felt a little breathless.

"I certainly hope not." She peered back toward the farmhouse at the police tape outlining the patio. "Looks like I'm going to have to bunk at your place tonight anyhow, so you can get started robbing me of my purity as soon as possible."

His feet started moving toward his house and then stalled.

"Too bad we have to talk to the cops first." He lifted his head to look back toward Nikki's place.

"Think of it as an opportunity to build anticipation," she reminded him, trailing teasing fingers down his chest. "We're going to be doing that a lot."

His predatory growl rumbled through his chest and excited her to her toes.

"We're going to talk fast." He sifted his fingers through her hair and cradled the back of her head in his hands. "I'm having you in my bed in an hour, no excuses. And to give you something to think about until then…"

He plucked a fat purple iris bloom from a nearby stalk and tucked the flower behind her ear. One silken petal stroked over her temple in a touch as sensual as his whisper.

"…this will help remind you what I'm going to do to you later."

The heat that smoked through her body was only a precursor to what was building in her heart. If it was this good now, what would it be like in a year? Ten?

Her toes curled inside her tennis shoes.

"It's a date."

Epilogue
<u></u>

Four months later

"Do you want more?"

Nikki hovered over him, her mostly naked body never quite close enough after being away from her for so long.

"Yes, ma'am. Much more." He reached for her, but she danced backward with the frying pan full of chicken cacciatore in hand.

"I meant more chicken." Laughing, she put the cast-iron skillet on the stove in the renovated farmhouse. "Finish your dinner first, then we'll see about the rest."

"Food can wait. I've only been home four days. If it was up to me, we'd still be horizontal." He should have thought to hire a caterer for the first week since they'd never have to get out of bed then. "Your letters nearly killed me, woman."

This time when he reached for her, she wrapped her arms around his neck and slid into his lap at the dinner table. He forked the last few bites into his mouth with her all over him and that was just how he liked it.

"I was only trying to build anticipation." She grinned shamelessly, nipping his neck with her teeth. "I didn't know I'd created a firestorm in such a short time."

She'd sworn the time had passed quickly enough and that she'd looked forward to him coming home more than she'd worried about him. Maybe after waiting for a year at a time to see her absentee parents, eighteen weeks wasn't a big deal to her.

"Short?" He, on the other hand, had missed her every minute. "It felt like forever to me. I'm thinking it won't be long until I take that training position they've been mentioning. That way, I'd be here all the time."

He ran his hands over her bare thigh, her pink negligee keeping her covered while effectively driving him crazy to see the rest of her. Touch the rest of her. Taste the rest of her.

"I'm with you either way," she promised, tracing the outline of muscles in his biceps.

He knew they turned her on so he flexed big-time in the hope of getting her back into bed sooner rather than later. In fact, he knew a lot about Nikki Thornton after corresponding with her for the last four months. Oh, sure, they'd emailed and set up video chats so they could see each other. But his lady professor was big on old-fashioned letters, and he had to admit he felt like he knew her inside and out now.

And while he knew more than her turn-ons, he had to admit they'd come in really handy since he'd returned home from Mosul for good. He'd stay on base for a while and then they'd decide where to ship him next.

"I can't believe all you accomplished in the house."

Looking around the big, old-fashioned country kitchen, he would have never guessed it was the same place he'd found books stuffed in the wine rack.

Now, the refinished hardwood floors gleamed in the candlelight from their late-night meal. A cast-iron candelabra hung over a repurposed butcher block counter that now served as the dining table. All over the property, windows closed properly, rooms were painted, flowers bloomed. The blue jay was gone, but there was a ferret to take its place. It hadn't been injured, but according to Nikki it needed a home.

"Really?" She looked around the room. "You can thank Emily Ralston for a lot of it. She worked hard once I forgave her for scaring me with the gunshot. She has a much better boyfriend now. Oh, and did I tell you she took that kitten you rescued?"

"Yeah, you did." He kissed her temple and decided they'd been out of bed long enough. The pink slip she was wearing was more than he could handle. "It sounds like you've been a good influence on her."

Nikki was helping the girl with her college search, encouraging her to go out of state to expand her horizons outside the sphere of influence of her family. Angelica hadn't fought the idea, perhaps recognizing the slippery ethics of some of her relatives wasn't helping her daughter.

"I'm glad that she's happy. It hasn't been easy for the family since the truth came out about Harold." She held on to him tighter as they turned sideways to pass through the door to the bedroom.

Unlike Emily, Harold Ralston hadn't fared well while

Brad had been overseas. He was in jail and had been forced to come clean about a few indiscretions over the years with city money in his position as city councilman. The town wasn't quite as enamored with the Ralston name anymore.

"Harold's loss is Ekualo's gain." Brad took care settling her on the bed they'd left rumpled and unmade. Her skin looked golden and warm against the crisp white sheets, her dark hair spilling over the pillow.

Too soon, she sat up, her eyes bright. "It sounds like Ekualo did pretty well for himself even without any medals."

That caught his interest, as he'd identified with the guy right from the start.

"How so?" He watched as Nikki tugged a sheaf of papers out from under a book on the nightstand.

She handed it to him, pointing to the top sheet.

"A marriage certificate." It was a photocopy from an Italian courthouse. Barely legible. Dated 1945. "Eduardo and Chloe were married? All that time she was writing about her wild affairs—"

"All of them were actually with Ekualo. She just used other men's names to act out different kinds of scenarios and to tantalize her husband. It's a good thing we didn't print the diaries right away, because I actually found a foreword for the unexpurgated version that Chloe penned herself." She pointed toward the next piece of paper, also a photocopy, of a letter in Chloe's hand. "She apologizes to readers for the deception and explains how the diaries sprang from the sexy letters. The two of them continued to write about steamy encounters after they were married and then they acted them out."

"The erotic diaries were…a lie?" He wondered what the revelation would do to her fan base as he flipped through the other papers, one of which showed Eduardo's death certificate from 1963—car accident. He'd died young, yes. But he'd had almost twenty years with the woman he loved. Twenty amazing years chronicled in literature that would live on long after all of them. "Her books helped spur the sexual revolution. How will readers feel about that when they find out?"

Nikki frowned. "I don't think anyone is going to be disappointed with the idea that fantastic sex is possible with your husband."

Brad grinned, his imagination lighting with a few ideas of his own he wouldn't mind playing out—as long as each one was with Nikki. "I guess not."

"You want to see if it's possible after five times in a day?" Nikki lifted an eyebrow and hiked the hem of her slip suggestively.

"Are you kidding me?" He set the papers aside on the nightstand, leaving Eduardo and Chloe to the past and ready to take on a future with the most amazing woman imaginable. "How about we see if it's possible after ten?"

"Shouldn't we go for quality over quantity?" she teased.

"Woman, you've built enough anticipation for a few hundred times at least." He pinned her arms over her head, liking the look of her all stretched out and at his disposal.

"Really?" She rubbed her thigh against his and his blood practically simmered on cue. "I guess you'd better get to work, Lieutenant. Consider yourself on special duty…"

* * * * *

Harlequin® *Blaze*™

COMING NEXT MONTH

Available April 26, 2011

HBCNM0411

REQUEST YOUR FREE BOOKS!
2 FREE NOVELS PLUS 2 FREE GIFTS!

Harlequin® *Blaze*™

red-hot reads!

*With an evil force hell-bent on destruction,
two enemies must unite to find a truth that turns
all-too-personal when passions collide.*

*Enjoy a sneak peek in Jenna Kernan's next installment
in her original* TRACKER *series,* GHOST STALKER,
available in May, only from Harlequin Nocturne.

"**W**ho are you?" he snarled.

Jessie lifted her chin. "Your better."

His smile was cold. "Such arrogance could only come from a Niyanoka."

She nodded. "Why are you here?"

"I don't know." He glanced about her room. "I asked the birds to take me to a healer."

"And they have done so. Is that *all* you asked?"

"No. To lead them away from my friends." His eyes fluttered and she saw them roll over white.

Jessie straightened, preparing to flee, but he roused himself and mastered the momentary weakness. His eyes snapped open, locking on her.

Her heart hammered as she inched back.

"Lead who away?" she whispered, suddenly afraid of the answer.

"The ghosts. Nagi sent them to attack me so I would bring them to her."

The wolf must be deranged because Nagi did not send ghosts to attack living creatures. He captured the evil ones after their death if they refused to walk the Way of Souls, forcing them to face judgment.

"Her? The healer you seek is also female?"

"Michaela. She's Niyanoka, like you. The last Seer of Souls and Nagi wants her dead."

Jessie fell back to her seat on the carpet as the possibility of this ricocheted in her brain. Could it be true?

"Why should I believe you?" But she knew why. His black aura, the part that said he had been touched by death. Only a ghost could do that. But it made no sense.

Why would Nagi hunt one of her people and why would a Skinwalker want to protect her? She had been trained from birth to hate the Skinwalkers, to consider them a threat.

His intent blue eyes pinned her. Jessie felt her mouth go dry as she considered the impossible. Could the trickster be speaking the truth? Great Mystery, what evil was this?

She stared in astonishment. There was only one way to find her answers. But she had never even met a Skinwalker before and so did not even know if they dreamed.

But if he dreamed, she would have her chance to learn the truth.

Look for GHOST STALKER by Jenna Kernan,
available May only from Harlequin Nocturne,
wherever books and ebooks are sold.